Phenomenal Praise for
Vicki Lewis Thompson's Novels

THE NERD WHO LOVED ME

"A winner...Thompson has written a laugh-out-loud, sexy romp that will capture readers from page one."
—*The Best Reviews*

"This extremely sexy and humorous book is over-the-top . . . her characters are so visual with the sparkling dialogue . . . another bright, shining star for Vicki Lewis Thompson."

—*Rendezvous*

"Smart, spunky and delightfully over the top, Thompson's newest Nerd romance possesses all the sparkle and vibrancy of a Vegas show, and it's just as sexy."

—*Publishers Weekly*

NERD IN SHINING ARMOR

"Ms. Thompson continues to set the romance world on fire and keep it burning."
—*WritersUnlimited.com*

"The heart of this story is the endearing development of a relationship between Gen and Jack...will likely rescue you from reading doldrums."

—*Romantic Times*

MORE...

St. Martin's Paperbacks Titles
by Vicki Lewis Thompson

The Nerd Who Loved Me

Nerd Gone Wild

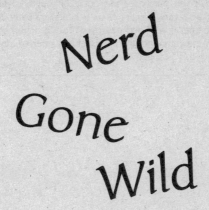

Nerd Gone Wild

Vicki Lewis Thompson

St. Martin's Paperbacks

NERD GONE WILD

Copyright © 2005 by Vicki Lewis Thompson.

ISBN: 0-312-99866-X
EAN: 80312-99866-0

Printed in the United States of America

St. Martin's Paperbacks edition / February 2005

St. Martin's Paperbacks are published by St. Martin's Press, 175 Fifth Avenue, New York, NY 10010.

10 9 8 7 6 5 4 3 2 1

To Jayne Ann Krentz,
a most generous and savvy friend.
Thank you.

Acknowledgments

Without the help of friends and family, this book would never have been written. Special thanks to Carrie Alexander, my cold weather guru, Roz Denny Fox for research info, Patricia Knoll and Alison Hentges for unwavering support, my husband Larry for dealing with the details of life while I was otherwise occupied, my daughter, personal assistant, and webmistress Audrey Sharpe for handling my promo and Web site while I was glued to the keyboard, and my son Nathan Thompson and his wife Lauri for understanding I had a tight schedule and couldn't visit until the book was done! As always, I owe much gratitude to my terrific agent Maureen Walters, my amazing editor Jennifer Enderlin, and a crackerjack marketing team at St. Martin's Press.

Chapter One

"Here in Porcupine, some folks have sex just to keep warm." Betsy Baylor, sole proprietor of the Loose Moose Lodge, leaned her sizable forearms on the walnut registration desk, obviously trolling for a response.

Ally Jarrett, sole guest at the Loose Moose, had intended to pass through the lobby with a smile and a wave. But Betsy's observation wasn't easily ignored.

Knowing she'd probably regret it, Ally paused. "Well, it is pretty cold out there."

"Cold enough to freeze your nose hairs, sweetheart. But it was hot times in this hotel." Betsy gazed around the small lobby filled with antiques and memorabilia from the Gold Rush days. "If only I had a time machine. I'd give anything to see this place when it was a whorehouse."

"It must have been something, all right." Ally inched toward the front door. She already knew some of the history because Betsy had talked her arm off during breakfast.

After coming in late last night, Ally had been so pumped about finally being in Alaska that she'd stayed awake for hours. Consequently she'd slept until early afternoon, but Betsy had been kind enough to feed her breakfast, anyway, so she hated to blow the woman off.

Still, she was antsy to get outside. Her digital camera was tucked into her backpack and she'd bundled up in boots, parka, gloves, and knit cap. If she stood around too long discussing prostitution with Betsy, she'd start to sweat under all those layers.

"Of course, the ladies of the night wouldn't have been out here. They would have lounged around in the parlor. That's my room now, but I've tried to keep it authentic. Want to see?"

"Well, actually, I was on my way out to—"

"It'll only take a minute."

"Sure." Pulling off her gloves, she unzipped her parka so she wouldn't roast. No point in alienating her landlady on the first day.

She felt sure Betsy had been lying in wait for her, dreaming of more human interaction. Oh, well. Betsy couldn't possibly be as bad as Mitchell J. Carruthers, Jr. Thank God she'd left that dweeb back in California.

Not that she wasn't grateful for the competent way he'd handled the details of Grammy's estate. He'd been a blessing in the first couple of months, when Ally had been too busy grieving to give a damn about paperwork. But lately Mitchell had begun to hover, just like Grammy used to. Ally was through being hovered over.

"You will not believe your eyes when you see what

I've done with the room." Betsy reached under the desk and pulled out a dome-shaped silver bell, the kind that rang when you slapped a hand down on it. "I'll leave this here in case my other guest shows up while I'm giving you the tour. I don't like to keep folks waiting, especially when they've been traveling and might need to pee."

"Someone else is coming in today?" Ally was glad to hear it. That would take some of the pressure off her to be social. In the short time she'd been here, she'd already had several prolonged conversations with Betsy.

"Yessiree." Betsy led the way toward a door that opened off the lobby. "And I'm glad for the business. Winter's always slow. In the summertime I run my ass off." She laughed. "Not so's you'd notice, unfortunately. My family's known for big ears and big behinds."

"There are worse things to be known for." But Ally had to admit Betsy was carrying on the family tradition. Underneath her black stretch pants her buns bobbled and curtsied to each other, as Grammy used to say.

"Men tell me there's more of me to love. Besides that, I'm well insulated, which is a bonus in Alaska." Betsy opened the door. "You might want to fatten up a little if you're planning on staying on a while, like you said."

"Thanks. I'll take that under advisement." She followed Betsy through the door.

"Ta-da!" Betsy swept a hand around the room.

Ally blinked. "Wow." She'd never seen anything like it except in really cheesy movies. Everything was red—red flocked wallpaper, red velvet drapes, and more red velvet covering both Victorian settees. It was like standing inside a giant model of a blood vessel, which she'd done once during a field trip in fourth grade.

What wasn't red was gold, including the player piano taking up one corner of the room and a large armoire in another corner. All the picture frames were gold and all the pictures inside the frames were nudes. Some Ally recognized as prints by famous artists, and some looked as if they'd come straight out of *Playboy*.

Betsy beamed with obvious pride. "Like it?"

"It's amazing." Ally didn't know if *like* was the word she would have used. But the room certainly was drenched in sex. "So this is how it would have looked in the early nineteen hundreds?" *Minus the centerfolds.*

"That's what my research tells me. I've had to make a couple of modifications for my own personal comfort." She pointed toward a door in the far wall. "Had to add on a bathroom, so I could use this as my suite."

"You sleep in here?" Ally couldn't picture Betsy curling up on one of the settees, and surely all that red would give a person terminal insomnia.

"Sure do." Betsy reached up, grabbed a handle set in the wall, and lowered a Murphy bed. The sheets were red satin and the white comforter was covered with hearts. "Look over your head."

Ally gazed up at a mirrored image of Betsy and the Murphy bed. Ye Gods. Hugh Hefner City. "Huh."

"Men love this room," Betsy said. "That's how I landed all seven of my husbands, by showing them this room." She winked at Ally. "And of course the Murphy bed and the mirror didn't hurt my cause, either."

Ally gulped and tried to erase the image of Betsy and some guy getting it on in reflected glory. "I suppose they wouldn't." Seven husbands. Betsy didn't seem to take any pains with her appearance. She wore zero makeup and it looked as if she cut her gray hair herself.

Both last night and today she'd worn her black stretch pants paired with an old plaid flannel shirt. Ally would never guess the woman had any dates, let alone enough exes to make up a basketball team plus subs. Maybe it was pheromones.

"Me and Liz," Betsy said. "Two peas in a pod, except she's Taylor and I'm Baylor. That's my maiden name, y'know. Never did see the sense in changing it when I got hitched, which is a good thing, considering how many times I've done the deed."

Ally wanted to ask what happened to those seven guys, but she didn't know how to ask without sounding like she was afraid there were seven bodies under the floorboards. Which she was.

"Good food and steady sex," Betsy said. "That's how to get a man. Trouble is, I eventually find out they have some habit or other that I can't abide, and I have to kick 'em out."

"Oh." Ally was extremely relieved to hear they'd been thrown out and not dispatched with a kitchen knife.

Betsy laughed. "You should see your face! You thought I'd done away with all of them, didn't you?"

"No, of course not." Ally chuckled merrily, hoping to demonstrate that that had been the furthest thing from her mind.

"Yes you did. It's untamed up here, but not quite that untamed."

"I knew that."

"I have to say, though, that sometimes I felt like it.

The nights are long and a man can get on your nerves, y'know?"

"I do know." Ally thought of Mitchell. But Mitchell was almost three thousand miles away. Far, far out of hovering distance.

"I probably could get away with it, though," Betsy said. "Porcupinians watch out for their own, and I make the best moose-meat pie north of Sitka. I don't think anybody would've turned me in."

"Are you . . . thinking of getting married again?" Maybe the second guest was a guy, and he'd be dazzled by the red room and the mirror on the ceiling and Betsy's powerful pheromones. Then Ally could go about her business without fear of conversational ambush.

"Well, certainly I'm thinking of getting married! I can't be seen living with somebody. I have a reputation to protect. So if I want to have regular sex, I need to find husband number eight."

"Absolutely."

"But you see, the pool of candidates is small in Porcupine."

"I understand."

"But maybe someone will show up."

"That would be nice." Ally would live in hope. The Loose Moose was perfect for her needs, but she'd hate to spend the next few months dodging Betsy.

"Of course there's always Clyde Hammacher. He would love to get into my—" A sharp *bing* from the lobby kept Betsy from elaborating on what Clyde would love to get into. "That must be my other guest!"

Please let him be male, single, and susceptible to nudes

and red walls. "Great. Then I'll just be on my way. I want to get some shots before the light fades."

Ally left Betsy's suite and, out of curiosity, glanced over to see if fate had provided Betsy with a candidate for husband number eight. Then she stopped dead in her tracks and stared.

Consequently Betsy bumped into her from behind, nearly sending her sprawling. "Sorry," Betsy murmured. "Didn't know you were about to put on the brakes."

Ally tried to say something, but words failed her. It couldn't be. But it was. Her worst nightmare. Mitchell J. Carruthers, Jr., was in the Loose Moose lobby.

A tall guy to begin with, Mitchell presently looked like a giant Popsicle in his neon orange parka, complete with a bright orange knit cap. The yellow pom-pom on top added another inch to his already considerable height. Then there were the fuzzy orange earmuffs.

A person would have to work hard to look that dorky, although Mitchell seemed to take to it naturally. His glasses were fogged and he was busy cleaning them with his handkerchief. Otherwise he might have noticed her gawking at him.

Betsy scooted around her and walked behind the registration desk. "You must be Mr. Carruthers," she said in a cheerful, "I like men" tone.

As much as Ally sympathized with Betsy's situation, Betsy could not have Mitchell as her next dearly beloved, because Mitchell was taking the next plane out of here. That would be absolutely necessary to keep Ally from murdering him. She didn't know any special dishes with moose meat or any other ingredient, and therefore had no way of endearing herself to the Porcupinians so they wouldn't turn her over to the cops. Mitchell had to go.

She cleared her throat. "Excuse me, but what are you doing here?"

He glanced in her direction. "Oh, hi, Ally."

Betsy glanced in Ally's direction, too, her mouth open. "You two know each other? My, now *that*'s a coincidence."

"Isn't it?" Adrenaline made Ally light-headed. "Did you follow me up here, Mitchell?"

He tucked his handkerchief into his coat pocket. "Yes, as a matter of fact, I did."

She clenched her fists so that she wouldn't run over and start punching him. It wouldn't do much good, anyway. With all that orange padding he wouldn't feel a thing. "Why did you follow me up here?"

"Well, because there are still several loose ends concerning your grandmother's estate, and they need your personal attention."

She wanted to slap a hand over his mouth. Her heiress status was *not* supposed to be common knowledge up here. She wanted to make it on her own, to be accepted for herself and not the millions she was worth.

Giving him a look that she hoped would freeze his tongue to the roof of his mouth, she tried to repair the damage. "How silly. You'd think I was some kind of heiress. What a laugh."

"You are—"

"Grammy would spin in her grave if she knew you were wasting her money like this."

He gazed at her steadily. "It's necessary, Ally."

"All right." She didn't believe it, so she decided to call his bluff. "What is it? Papers to sign?"

"Well, yes, and—"

"Get 'em out. I'll sign them right this minute, while Betsy's checking on flights back to L.A. I wouldn't want you to waste any more time than necessary. I know you're eager to get back to warm, sunny California." After all, he'd lectured her about the inadvisability of traveling to Alaska in February, so he couldn't be happy about stepping into this deep freeze.

Betsy gasped. "You're not expecting him to go home already?" She looked crestfallen.

"The sooner the better," Ally said. "I'm sorry you felt the trip was necessary, Mitchell, but since you're here, let's take care of everything with the expediency you so cherish so you can be on your way."

He gazed at her. "I'm afraid that won't be possible."

She tried not to panic. "What do you mean?"

"I came in right ahead of a blizzard. I was on the last plane they allowed to land at the Fairbanks airport. The man who brought me here—"

"That would be Rudy, our shuttle driver," Betsy said.

"Right." Mitchell nodded. "Rudy. Has a Ford Bronco."

"By the name of Slewfoot Sue," Betsy said. "And he also keeps chickens. Can you picture a big ol' guy like Rudy raising chickens? He does, though. Keeps them in his kitchen during the winter, so they won't—"

"Excuse me a minute, Betsy." Ally needed more information, and she needed it now, before delving any deeper into the life and times of Rudy the chicken farmer. "I want to get something clarified with Mitchell. If a blizzard has shut down the Fairbanks airport, why don't we have a blizzard here? We're not all that far away."

"Rudy outran it," Mitchell said. "We had quite a wild ride getting here because he didn't want to get caught out there in bad weather. I'm sure the storm will hit any minute."

As if on cue, the wind began to howl through a crack in the front door. Ally wanted to howl right along with it.

"I think the storm's here," Betsy said, looking delighted. "There was mention of a blizzard coming in. This time of year, they can last for days." She smiled at Mitchell and rubbed her hands together. "Well! I guess we'd better get you checked in!"

Days. Ally stood rooted to the spot, still unable to comprehend that this could happen. Right now she could think of only one solution. "Is there a bar in town?"

Betsy managed to tear her attention away from Mitchell, who was calmly filling out a registration form. "Two doors down on your right," she said. "It's called the Top Hat. Clyde Hammacher runs it, and he calls it that because he used to dance on Broadway. Only he's not gay. A lot of those dancers are, but Clyde—"

"Yes, I believe you mentioned Clyde." He'd been the one who would love to get into something of Betsy's. "Thank you," she said, zipping her parka and putting on her gloves. "See you two later."

"If you'll wait a minute, I'll come with you," Mitchell said.

Ally closed her eyes. She was in hell. "Thanks, but I'm really thirsty, so I'm going over now. Besides, I think you should get Betsy to give you the parlor tour before you do one single other thing in Porcupine."

Mitchell looked puzzled. "Parlor tour?"

"I was just showing Ally," Betsy said. "It's worth seeing, if I do say so myself. Did you know this used to be the most famous whorehouse in Alaska?"

Ally headed for the door, abandoning the field to Betsy. If Ally couldn't get Mitchell to leave, then maybe she could get him to fixate on Betsy. Sure, he was a good fifteen years younger than their landlady, but when he got a look at that Murphy bed with the mirror in the ceiling, he might go wild. You never knew with nerds.

"I hadn't heard that it was a whorehouse," Mitchell said.

"Oh, yes. Just picture this place swarming with eager men, men who had been out in the gold fields with no female companionship for weeks. You can imagine how much they wanted—"

Ally opened the front door and a gust of wind and snow hit her in the face, nearly knocking her down. Betsy was right. Bulking up was important in this country.

"Be careful out there!" Betsy called. "Don't get blown away!"

"I won't!" Lowering her head, Ally shoved herself outside and somehow managed to haul the door closed again. Swirling snow cut her visibility to almost nothing. It was so cold that breathing made her chest ache.

She hoped to hell this blizzard wouldn't go on for days. She had things to do and people to see. Trying to photograph wildlife in a blizzard didn't make much sense, even to someone as inexperienced as she was.

Then there was Uncle Kurt, who was planning to drive up from Anchorage to see her. He'd found a wildlife photographer to be her mentor, although he was keeping the identity of the photographer a secret, which was so like Uncle Kurt, a man who loved surprises and spontaneity. She didn't want Mitchell hanging around until then. Instinctively she knew they wouldn't get along.

By shielding her eyes, she could just barely make out the red neon outline of a top hat on a sign jutting out from a building on her right. She wondered if a bar in Porcupine, Alaska, served Irish coffee. If not, she'd drink whatever they had that would dull the impact of Mitchell showing up here.

He'd already leaked information about the inheritance, although maybe Ally had stuck her thumb in that particular dike for now. Still, his presence here would make it seem that she was worth more than she'd let on. Even worse than that, he was ruining her precious freedom.

Maybe by now Betsy had lured him into her parlor. But Ally stopped short of imagining what might happen after that. Some things were way too disturbing to contemplate.

Even if Mitchell allowed himself to fall under Betsy's spell, he would be on the next plane out of Fairbanks if Ally had anything to say about it. As Grammy's sole heir, she should have the power to send his royal nerdness right back where he came from. All she needed was clear skies.

Chapter Two

Mitch figured out pretty fast that Betsy was eager to get chummy with any guy with a pulse. He hoped he wouldn't have to be too direct in his refusal and alienate her, because she probably knew everyone in town. A person like that could come in very handy.

"So, would you like to see my parlor, Mitchell?" She eyed him coyly. "I guarantee you've never experienced anything so unique."

"That sounds great, but I'd like to go up to my room first." He pulled off his knit cap and reached for the room key she'd laid on the counter.

"Well, of course you would." She beat him to the room key, snatching it from under his nose. "You've had a long trip, and those tiny airplane bathrooms must be cramped for a tall man like yourself." She batted her eyelashes. "Come with me. I'll show you the way."

Just what he'd been afraid of. "If you'll point me in

the direction of room twenty-one, I'm sure I can find it.
I hate to put you to any extra trouble."

"It's no trouble." She came out from behind the registration desk, obviously ready to rumble. "Are you hungry? Technically I only serve breakfast, but considering
you've come all the way from L.A., I'd be happy to
make you something warm. A man needs good, hearty
food, and the airlines aren't serving meals the way they
used to."

In point of fact, Mitch was starving. But he had a
feeling that allowing Betsy to cook him a meal would
constitute foreplay in her mind. "Thanks, but I had
something to eat during my layover in Seattle." Still, his
mouth watered at the idea of home-cooked food.

"I could warm up some moose-meat pie in nothing
flat."

Then again, maybe he'd survive on the hamburger
he'd grabbed in the airport. He'd seen pictures of moose,
and they didn't look at all like the kind of creature he'd
want to dine on. "Thanks, but I'm stuffed."

"If you change your mind, let me know. I enjoy cooking for a man." She started up the wooden stairs to the
second floor.

Mitch hefted his suitcase and followed. So far this
trip was about as nightmarish as he'd envisioned.

Betsy mounted those stairs without breaking a sweat
or breathing hard. Mitch had to hand it to her. For a
plus-sized woman she was in remarkable shape.

"Down this hallway," she said, not even puffing from
the climb.

Mitch didn't puff, either, because he'd worked out
every night in the Jarrett mansion's fully equipped weight

room. He'd had to pick times when Ally was occupied elsewhere, because keeping in shape wouldn't fit very well with the image of him he wanted her to have. Better that she think of him as a weakling.

"Here we are." Betsy opened the door with the metal key.

"Uh, if you don't mind my asking, which room is Ally using?"

She gazed at him for a moment before answering. "I wondered if it was like that. You made it sound like business, but there's more to it, isn't there?"

"What do you mean?" Betsy couldn't have seen through his nerd persona that fast. Ally hadn't, and she'd been around him for months.

"A man like you doesn't jump on a plane and fly three thousand miles for a few signatures on a piece of paper."

Mitch lapsed into nerd-speak. "Of course I do. It's my job. If everything isn't accomplished in a timely manner, then—"

"You have a thing for her, don't you?"

Mitch spotted a way to head off Betsy's potential advances and grabbed it. "Okay, you caught me. I adore that woman. But please don't tell her."

"Oh, I think she already knows, or if not, she'll soon figure it out. She's a smart girl, and it doesn't take a genius to see that when a man chases a woman all the way to Alaska, he has a serious case of the hots for her." Betsy sighed. "Which is too bad, because I'm definitely in the market."

"I'm honored to know that you'd be interested in me. If I didn't have something going with Ally, you'd be at the top of my list." God, if that didn't sound stuffy and boring, but it was exactly the tone he was after.

Her cheeks turned pink. "I'll take that as a real compliment, considering our age difference. But I want you to think about this—older women tend to be far more grateful for the attention of a man."

Mitch managed to keep a straight face. "I'm sure that's true, and that means I'm missing out, which is my misfortune."

"And if you don't mind my saying so, you have an uphill road with Ally. She didn't look especially glad to see you."

Now there was an understatement. "We've, uh, had some areas of disagreement." Ally considered him a meddling geek, which is what he wanted her to think. If she ever found out that her late grandmother had hired him as her bodyguard, she'd have a fit. He'd never met a more independent spirit.

"Well, remember, if things don't work out, I'll be handy, for a shoulder to cry on or something more . . . comforting." She winked at him and walked into his room. "So this is it. If you need anything, you'll have to come down and ask for it personally. I have phone jacks, but I ended up taking the phones out. Too much trouble with people making long-distance calls."

One less thing for him to plant a bug in. "That's okay. I have my cell." Following her into the room, he left the door wide open, just in case Betsy decided to lunge, after all.

"You'd be better off using the phone at the desk. Cell phone reception is terrible here in Porcupine."

"I don't suppose there's a local Internet number?"

Probably a dumb question. He took in the furnishings at a glance—old wooden dresser, double bed supported by an iron bedstead, lace curtains at a window covered in frost. The light had already started to fade. Night came early up here.

Betsy shook her head. "Nope. Not many Porcupinians bother with the Internet. Long-distance charges would eat us alive." She leaned closer. "Besides, all that's just an unnecessary distraction, don't you think? Shouldn't you be concentrating on what you came here for, instead of worrying about business?"

"Good point." He couldn't very well let her know that what he came here for could be better accomplished if he had good phone connections and easy Internet access.

"Here are the facilities." Betsy walked over to a door and opened it. "There's only one bathroom for every two rooms, so you share with the person on the other side. That would be Ally."

He blinked in surprise. The arrangement suited him perfectly, but he'd bet Ally would have a few things to say about it. "Are you sure that will be okay with her?"

"She knew when she made the reservation that all the rooms share a bath with another room. Here at the lodge, that's what folks have to do. This is the Loose Moose, not the Hyatt Regency."

"I understand that, but if we're the only two people here, it seems like she could have her own bathroom." And he could picture her demanding it the minute she realized he was on the other side of her bathroom door. Might as well settle it now and avoid a scene.

"She could, but that would mean me cleaning two

bathrooms and turning up the heat for two bathrooms. Heat is expensive, and cleaning is my job in the winter. I don't bring in a cleaning woman, on account of business being slow. I would appreciate it if you two would be willing to share."

"I'm more than willing to share. It's just—"

"Mitchell, for pity's sake. Do you realize that you're trying to change what is going to be to your advantage?"

From a surveillance standpoint, she was absolutely right, but he decided to play dumb. "How's that?"

She blew out a breath. "I see you might need some coaching if you intend to get anywhere with Ally. Maybe that's why she's so put out with you. You may be a smart man when it comes to office matters, but when it comes to women, I'm afraid you're not up to snuff."

"Could be. You'd better draw me a picture."

She nodded. "Only too happy to help. Even if I'm not getting any, that doesn't mean I begrudge others their fun. See, sharing a bathroom will be cozy, almost like you're in the same suite." She wiggled her eyebrows. "Think of the opportunities. Her in there naked. Or you in there naked."

"I . . . ah . . . see what you mean." And he didn't want to go down that road, ever.

The day he'd met Ally ten months ago she'd just climbed out of the swimming pool at the Jarrett mansion in Bel Air. He'd noted immediately that she was gorgeous.

What wasn't to like about silky black hair slicked back from a cameo face lit with intelligent green eyes? And that wasn't taking into consideration a figure that was an outstanding endorsement for Speedo. But he'd

killed his tug of sexual interest then, and he would continue to kill it.

Lusting after Ally violated the spirit of the assignment he'd been given by Ally's grandmother. Because
of the respect he had for Madeline Jarrett, he wouldn't
let her down, even though she'd never know.

When Madeline was dying of cancer, she'd hired him
to pose as her personal assistant. Four months ago she'd
passed on, leaving a will that officially commissioned him
to handle the estate. Unofficially he was to safeguard Ally.
Orphaned at a young age, Ally had become the focus of
her grandmother's life and the ultimate recipient of the
Jarrett fortune, making her a very wealthy young woman
in need of protection.

Enter Mitch, who covered his PI and bodyguard status
by disguising himself as a nerd. He wished the pretense
hadn't been so easy to maintain. In no time the routine
had come back to him. Once again he felt like the skinny
eighth-grader he used to be, the one with bad eyes, good
report cards, and a fondness for detail. In high school
he'd bulked up, bought contacts, and let his grades slip.
Goodbye, geek, hello, cool dude.

Now he'd reversed the process, and it had been dis-
couragingly simple to do. Apparently you could take the
boy out of Nerdville, but you couldn't take Nerdville out
of the boy. After all his efforts to turn himself into
James Bond, he'd slipped into the role of Bill Gates in
no time. Fortunately, Ally wasn't attracted to nerds.

"So all you have to do," Betsy said, "is let Ally know
that she'll be helping me out by saving the cost of heat-
ing and the work of cleaning. She's a nice person. She
won't want to make extra work or waste resources."

"Okay, I'll try that." He even thought it might work. Ally *was* a nice person. She'd put her own life on hold for some time because her sick grandmother had craved having her near.

Mitch wasn't surprised that Ally wanted to escape now that the need for hanging around the mansion was gone. He just wished she hadn't decided to escape up here. It could be a coincidence that Kurt Jarrett lived in Alaska, but Mitch didn't think so. He guessed that Ally had been in contact with her stepuncle, who had to be stewing because he'd been cut out of the will.

"Then I'll go on downstairs," Betsy said. "Holler if you need anything." She patted his arm on her way out the door.

Mitch waited until he heard her footsteps on the stairs before he closed and locked his bedroom door. After throwing his ugly orange parka on the bed, he went into the bathroom and tried the door into Ally's room. It was open.

The security in this place sucked. No one should be required to share a bathroom with a stranger, and apparently that happened at the Loose Moose on a regular basis. The wrong kind of bathroom-mate could steal you blind.

But for him, this setup was ideal. He could bug at will. Her bedroom was similar to his, only with a slightly different type of wooden dresser against the wall, an iron bedstead with more curvy scrollwork, and another color and pattern for the comforter. Without warning, he had a sudden, potent image of Ally naked on that bed, fingers wrapped around those curved iron pieces while he . . . *Wow, where had that come from?*

Wherever it had come from, he was sending it right back, plus the erection that had come along for the ride. His job was to protect Ally from gold diggers, not turn into one. It would look like the fox guarding the henhouse, and if she didn't immediately see it, someone would inevitably point it out to her.

Mitch looked in the closet and noticed two decent-sized suitcases on the floor. She had a couple of light-weight jackets hanging in the closet, along with several long-sleeved cotton shirts. The dresser was stuffed with sweaters in various colors of the rainbow, sweats, and jeans.

And underwear. He didn't spend much time looking at the underwear. Dangerous territory, considering that little flash of sexual urgency that had taken him by sur-prise. Maybe Betsy had created a monster with her sug-gestive comments.

In any case, Ally had enough clothes to last her a while, especially if Porcupine had a Laundromat. She hadn't brought a single skirt, or anything to dress up in, for that matter. That figured. She was here to tramp around in the snowy woods and take pictures of what-ever showed up.

Returning to the bathroom, Mitch found her tooth-brush and toothpaste on the counter beside the sink, along with a hairbrush, some lotion, and a tube of lip-stick. Unless she'd taken all her makeup with her in her backpack, which didn't seem likely, she hadn't brought anything on this trip except lipstick.

That fit with his image of Ally. She was the type to travel light, unwilling to let anything, or anyone, slow her down. That was why she resented him so much. She saw him as an anchor. And he was more of an anchor than she guessed.

The bathroom had no tub, only a shower stall. He pulled back the plastic curtain decorated with moose and canoes. Her shampoo and conditioner sat on a ledge in there, along with a razor. He would have taken her for a girl who got herself waxed. Then again, waxing might not be an option in Porcupine. Maybe she'd thought ahead.

When a picture of Ally in the shower shaving her legs wandered into his misbehaving brain, he got rid of it faster than he had the naked-on-the-bed scene. If he kept disciplining his mind this way, soon he'd think of her in a strictly platonic way. Or at least, that was the idea.

He needed to get over to the Top Hat bar, though. From the way she'd skedaddled out of the lodge, she'd been eager to tip back a few, and he didn't want to deal with her when she was sloshed—sloshed because she was ticked off about his arrival, to be more precise about it.

Moving faster now, he returned to his room and unzipped his suitcase. For now, he'd install one listening device under her bed. That way he'd be alerted to her movements. He was back in her room attaching the bug to the leg of the bed under a decorative skirt when a paralyzing thought came to him. What if she liked to masturbate?

Oh, hell, she probably didn't do that, and he had a one-track mind to even be thinking such a thing. Or if she did do that normally, she'd be too tired from all her adventures in the snow and trying to take pictures of wild animals to think about sex. But she had Betsy for a landlady, and Betsy lived and breathed the subject.

All righty then, if she masturbated, so be it. He'd deal with that when it happened. Surveillance meant sometimes hearing things that made you uncomfortable, even things that made you feel horny. On the PI side of his business, he'd come across plenty of sexual situations—a man with more than one woman, a woman with more than one guy, men with men, women with women, and even men and/or women with animals.

He was tough. He could handle a simple masturbation scene if the need should arise. Bad choice of words. If the need came up. That was no better. Shit. He'd just do it. No problem. Part of the job.

One bug was enough for now. He had a nifty little gizmo to plant in her backpack when he got the chance, a personal sort of LoJack that would allow him to trace her anywhere she went. He'd tried to plant it before she'd left for Alaska, but he hadn't been able to without taking a big risk that she'd suspect him of being up to something.

Her grandmother had been worried about fortune hunters in general, but she'd been specifically worried about Kurt Jarrett. With Madeline dead, Ally was the only person standing between Kurt and the Jarrett fortune. If anything happened to Ally, Kurt, the only remaining relative, would get it all. That meant Mitch had to be very alert and very cautious. Extremely cautious.

At last he was ready to head to the bar. Putting on the orange parka, the orange knit hat with the pom-pom, and the earmuffs was a humiliating experience. He'd searched the discount stores until he'd found this hideous ensemble and whenever he had it on he tried to avoid seeing any reflection of himself anywhere.

Leaving on the lamp sitting on top of the dresser, he left the room, locked up and pocketed the key. He wasn't surprised upon descending the stairs to find Betsy ensconced behind the registration counter once again.

"Just take a minute to see the parlor," she said.

"I really should get over there and find out what Ally's up to."

"It'll only take a minute. Maybe it'll inspire you."

Mitch took off his earmuffs and unzipped his jacket. "If we make it quick."

Ten minutes later, Mitch emerged from the parlor biting the inside of his mouth to keep from laughing. Entertainment in Alaska must be severely limited if Betsy had snared seven men with that over-the-top setting.

"Unbelievable, isn't it?" Betsy said, following him out.

"Mm." Mitch nodded energetically, not trusting himself to speak.

"Good luck with Ally. I'll probably be over there in a little while, myself. Most everyone in Porcupine usually ends up at the Top Hat before the night is through."

Mitch cleared his throat. "Then I'll see you later, Betsy." Bracing himself, he opened the door. The wind cut right through him and it felt as if icicles were piercing his eyeballs. The temperature had dropped at least another twenty degrees since he was out here last.

With great effort he closed the door behind him, located the Top Hat by the jaunty neon sign, and started toward it. He hated cold weather, hated snow, hated sleet, ice, cold wind—all that winter nonsense. That's why he'd moved from Chicago to L.A. eight years ago.

Then he'd struggled to build his investigative and personal protection business in sunny Southern California because he simply could not tolerate the idea of going back to cold weather. Now look at him. Freezing his ass off in Alaska, for God's sake.

The job wasn't supposed to be like this. When Madeline had hired him, he'd pictured keeping an eye on Ally in Southern California. Where it was warm. He hadn't known about this Kurt Jarrett/Alaska angle.

Grumbling to himself, Mitch took off his glasses because they were crusted with ice. The clear-lens glasses were only for show, anyway, part of his nerd disguise. He wore contacts. He couldn't afford to go with prescription glasses because if they happened to come off in a tight situation he'd be nearly blind.

The door to the Top Hat opened out, and he had to give it a mighty pull to conquer the wind wanting to keep it closed. When he jumped inside, the door slammed behind him with a loud whack.

Nobody noticed. Everyone was too busy clapping and cheering for the woman dancing on top of the bar. The woman was Ally.

Chapter Three

After three Irish coffees, Ally had decided it was the best drink in the world. What other combo could hype you up and drown your inhibitions, all in one fell swoop? And as for the jukebox in the corner of the Top Hat, it had the most brilliant selections she'd ever heard. When "Louie Louie" had come on, what was a girl supposed to do? She'd started to shake her booty.

Then Rudy, the red-haired, substantially bearded guy who raised chickens and transported people to and from the Fairbanks airport in a truck called Slewfoot Sue, had lifted her up on the bar so everyone could see what a great dancer she was. After three Irish coffees, she was one amazing dancer. She tossed her hair around and gave them the old bump-and-grind like a pro.

Apparently they loved it, because the clapping and cheering drowned out "Louie Louie." That was okay, because she'd found her own personal rhythm. She was smokin'.

Or at least she was smokin' until her heart began racing a little too fast and she found herself short of breath. So she wound up for a big finish that included a few breast shimmies and nearly made her fall off the bar. But she regained her balance and swept both arms out in a low bow. The whistles and stomping were extremely gratifying.

Feeling a wee bit dizzy, she looked out over the audience, which was comprised of maybe six or eight lumberjack types like Rudy. What a terrific bunch of guys. She blew them all kisses and did her Elvis impersonation. "Thankyou. Thankyouverymuch."

Then her gaze drifted from the smiling faces of her fans as she sensed another presence in the room. Her attention was drawn like a moth to the flame of a giant orange parka positioned right by the door. Oh, crap. Mitchell J. Carruthers, Jr., the Terminator of All Things Joyful, had arrived.

She glanced down at Clyde, bartender, owner of the Top Hat, and the man who would love to get into something or other belonging to Betsy. Betsy would make two of him, so the pairing would be like Jack Sprat and his wife.

But it was not her place to judge. It was her place to drink, especially now that an orange Popsicle man was standing by the door. " 'Nother Irish coffee, Clyde, if you please."

"Comin' up, Ally. Nice dancing for an amateur."

"Thanks. I'm sure you can do better. You wanna be next?"

"Nah, at least not until Dave shows up to help out. Somebody has to mix drinks, or the boys will turn ugly."

Her tongue felt a little thicker than usual. "Those boys could never turn ugly. They're sweetie pies."

"Deny them their booze and they'll go from sweetie pies to shitheads in no time."

"No!" She couldn't believe it.

"Yep." Clyde put whipped cream on her drink with a whoosh from a pressurized can. "You drinking this standing up or sitting down?"

Ally glanced over at the orange Popsicle man. He was on the move. She decided sitting down was a prudent idea. "Sitting." She just wasn't sure how to accomplish that, being so wobbly and all.

Suddenly the orange Popsicle man was standing right by the bar. He even spoke. "Let me give you a hand."

She gazed down at Mitchell. "Does a Popsicle man have hands?" Then she giggled at her own joke.

"Come on, Ally. I don't want you to fall off."

She frowned, thoroughly insulted. "You're doing it. Hovering."

Rudy appeared next to Mitchell. "Need some help down, Ally?"

"Thank you, kind sir." She put her hand in Rudy's, gave a haughty glance in Mitchell's direction, and allowed Rudy to grab her around the waist and swing her effortlessly to the ground.

She couldn't be sure because her vision was a little blurry, but she thought that Mitchell looked annoyed. Good. He'd come to Alaska uninvited and he dressed funny. He deserved to be annoyed. She was annoyed, too, dammit. And more than slightly dizzy.

Grabbing the nearest chair, she plopped into it. To her dismay, Mitchell sat in a chair at the same table and proceeded to take off his orange hat and orange coat. Worse yet, when Clyde brought her drink over, he stopped to ask Mitchell what he was having and Mitchell ordered a draft.

If she'd felt up to it, Ally would have changed tables. But then Rudy pulled up a chair, too, and grabbed his beer from another table, reaching out one long arm to snag it. So he sloshed some on the floor. So what? Ally was still impressed by his manly actions, and even more by his red beard, which hung down to the fourth button on his flannel shirt.

Ignoring Mitchell, Ally leaned toward Rudy. "Awesome beard you have there."

Rudy smiled, which also made for an interesting sight. Rudy hadn't managed to keep very many of his teeth. "Glad you like it, Ally."

"What happened to your teeth?" Dimly she realized that might not be a polite question to ask, but she had sipped her way right past polite and was now in the neighborhood of total honesty.

"Bar fights, mostly," Rudy said.

"Outstanding." That made him even more of a manly man, in Ally's estimation. She'd bet Mitchell had never been in a bar fight. This might be his first visit to a bar, for all she knew. He might be a bar virgin. The thought made her giggle again.

Speaking of Mitchell, he seemed to be trying to get her attention by clearing his throat and saying her name. She continued to ignore him and picked up her Irish coffee to lick the whipped cream off the top. Yummy.

"Ally," Rudy said, "your friend Mitchell wants to say somethin' to you."

Ally licked a hole in the whipped cream and took a drink of her Irish coffee. "He's not my friend."

"Well, maybe not, but he did come all the way up here from L.A. just to see you. I know that, on account of I'm the one who drove him here from the Fairbanks airport."

"Ally." Mitchell sounded determined. "We do have something to discuss. It's about the Loose Moose Lodge."

Ally sighed and turned to him. Maybe if she found out what was on his mind, he'd go away. "What about it?" She took note of Mitchell's outfit—an out-of-date tan sport coat and a brown and orange tie. Then she remembered that she'd been hoping Betsy would seduce him. Mitchell did not look seduced, though. His ugly tie was still in place.

She peered at him. "Did Betsy take you into her parlor?"

"Yes, but I—"

Rudy started to laugh. "That parlor's something, ain't it? All them naked women, and the red walls and the mirror in the ceiling. Looks like there should be one of them orgies going on in there."

Ally studied Mitchell to see if he'd start to blush, which might mean something had happened in the parlor. "What did you think of it, Mitchell?"

He gazed at her. "Interesting."

She had to admit that Mitchell had a sensuous mouth, a point she hadn't noticed about him before. He had a decent chin, too, with a Dudley Do-Right cleft. A chin like that would be tricky to shave unless you were careful, but Mitchell was the kind of man who would be careful.

She watched his mouth move while he said the word *interesting* and imagined those lips doing lovely things to a woman, providing the guy working the equipment knew how to use it. Mitchell probably didn't.

"Did the bed and mirror turn you on?" She hoped so. She hoped he planned to go back and spend the whole night with Betsy. Maybe Betsy could teach him how to employ his lips to best advantage.

"No. But I wanted to let you know that—"

"Well, shoot. I was hoping it would. Betsy needs company, you know."

"She's always needing company," Rudy said. "She tried to get me in that parlor once, but Betsy's not my type. My type's more like you, Ally."

She beamed at him. "Why, thank you, Rudy. I like you, too." She thought she heard Mitchell groan, and out of common decency she turned to him. Besides, if he was sick, they'd have to get him out of here to a hospital far, far away. "Mitchell, do you hurt somewhere?"

"I'm fine," he said. "Just ducky." Then his beer arrived.

To Ally's surprise, he took a good long swallow of it. She watched him in amazement. He ended up with a little droplet of beer on his top lip, and he licked it off. A funny little jolt hit her. A sexual jolt. Now that was ridiculous. She must be really drunk.

"Wow, Mitchell," she said. "I guess you were thirsty."

"Yeah." He set his beer down and looked her in the eye.

She knew he had brown eyes, but she couldn't see

them very well at the moment because one of the neon
signs behind the bar reflected in his glasses. Wearing the
knit cap had tousled his hair, which partly disguised an
essentially boring haircut. His hair was thick, though,
and a nice shade of brown. *Queer Eye for the Straight
Guy* could do wonders for Mitchell.

"We need to talk about something," he said. "You
know how at the Loose Moose there's a connecting bathroom between two bedrooms?"

"Um, yes, I guess." She tried to think why he'd be
telling her this. Then it hit her. "No! Don't you dare say
we're sharing!"

"At Betsy's request. She—"

"You asked her, didn't you? So you could hover!"

He sighed. "No, I didn't ask. She set it up that way
because she doesn't want to heat and clean two bathrooms. She said you'd understand."

She glared at him, wishing she could call him a liar.
But what he'd said didn't sound like a lie. It sounded exactly like the sort of thing Betsy would do, for the sake
of efficiency.

Ally could demand her own bathroom, of course, but
she wasn't the sort of person to do that. She *especially*
didn't want to do that now that Mitchell had partially let
the cat out of the bag about her inheritance. Demanding
her own bathroom would make her look spoiled, the
kind of woman who was used to luxury. She didn't want
anyone here to know that.

She might be stuck with this bathroom situation. Taking another fortifying swig of her Irish coffee, she turned
to Mitchell. "How soon do you expect to be leaving?"

"I guess that depends a lot on the weather."

Ally appealed to Rudy. "You've lived here a long time, right?"

"Since I was just a little guy."

Ally didn't think Rudy had ever been little. "So what about this blizzard? Could it let up by tomorrow?"

Rudy shrugged his massive shoulders. "It's possible. Then again, it could blow clear into next week. My chickens might be able to tell me."

Mitchell put down his almost-empty beer glass. "Your *chickens*?"

Ally nodded, smiling fondly at her new best friend Rudy. "Rudy is tuned in to his chickens. And chickens are tuned in to the universe. Right, Rudy?"

"Chickens lay nature's perfect food, the egg."

"Exactly." Ally shot Mitchell a triumphant look. "You see?"

"I don't see what eggs have to do with weather."

"I was gettin' to that," Rudy said. "Go ahead and laugh, but I live with chickens, and chickens know what's goin' on. When I got up, they were all restless, hoppin' around on the kitchen counter, wouldn't settle down under the table, where they usually nest, so I knew that blizzard was headed our way." He sighed. "I love those chickens."

"They really live in your kitchen?" Mitchell eyed Rudy over the rim of his beer glass. "I thought Betsy was exaggerating."

"In the winter they live there, on account of the cold. Which is the reason Lurleen gave for takin' off right after Christmas, but I don't think that was the reason at all. I think it's because she found a guy who gave her multis."

"Multis?" Ally wondered if that was some rare Alaskan gemstone.

"Multiple orgasms." Rudy gulped his beer and wiped his mouth with the back of his hand. "She was always goin' on about how that's what she wanted, and I wasn't providin' them."

"Well, now, that's sad," Ally said, "because she's the one in charge of her orgasms, not you." She could have sworn Mitchell made a choking sound, but when she looked over at him, he was drinking the last of his beer like nothing was wrong.

"How do you mean?" Rudy asked. "I thought it was my fault whether she had just one or more than one."

Ally tapped her head. "It's all up here."

"Gee, I thought it was all down there." Rudy pointed toward his crotch.

"The most important sexual organ is the brain." Feeling very wise, indeed, Ally took a sip of her Irish coffee. Not only was she an excellent dancer tonight, but suddenly she realized how much she intuitively knew about sex, even though she hadn't had a whole lot of it in her life. Two brief affairs wasn't much to brag about. But she'd read *Cosmo* for like, forever.

"In that case, I'm in trouble," Rudy said. "I'm not that smart."

"No, no, we're talking about *her* brain. Oh, I'm not saying that it doesn't help if a guy can last more than twenty seconds, and if he's good at foreplay, but basically, the woman has to put herself in the right frame of mind."

She glanced at Mitchell, who probably didn't have a clue what she was talking about. "Isn't that true,

Mitchell?" Yeah, like he'd really know. If he made love the way he dressed, she pitied his girlfriend.

"Absolutely," Mitchell said, with an air of authority.

She challenged him with a long, hard stare. But eventually her stare slipped down to that excellent mouth of his. Besides having very erotic contours, his mouth looked exceptional when he smiled, like now.

With a tiny shiver of appreciation, she glanced away. Those lips might be nice to look at, but they were attached to Mitchell, the man who seemed determined to clip her wings before she'd even had a chance to take a test flight. And he'd be hovering around making her life miserable until the blizzard ended. Bummer.

Mitch wanted another beer. Or six. Ally Jarrett had been overprotected all her life, and now he was the poor schmuck who had to handle her first taste of freedom. Oh, joy. She'd seemed relatively easy to deal with back in L.A. Obviously she'd been waiting until she was in the middle of nowhere to cut loose.

Dancing on the bar, drinking like a fish, and making cow eyes at the natives—he didn't know how in hell he'd rein her in without causing her to explode in fury. She already hated every interfering move he made.

Meanwhile he had to pretend to be unaffected by her actions. He had to ignore the wave of lust that had swamped him when he'd witnessed her shimmy-and-shake routine on top of the bar. And she kept looking at his mouth with this dreamy expression. Women who did that generally wanted to be kissed.

He would control the urge to grant her unspoken wish,

but if she felt like kissing somebody, she might settle for Rudy, instead. Now there was a prospect that really would have Madeline spinning in her grave—her precious granddaughter and sole heir to the Jarrett fortune making out with a backwoods lumberjack who was missing several teeth and allowed chickens to live in his house.

Fortunately Rudy seemed like an unassuming type. So far he hadn't shown any inclination to take advantage of Ally. Mitch wouldn't bet that all the other men in the room had Rudy's temperament, though, and if Ally had decided to turn into a barfly, she'd get into trouble sooner or later.

As Mitch calculated his next move, Ally continued to educate Rudy on the mysteries of female sexuality. Mitch had checked into her background months ago and knew that her sexual experience was as limited as every other area of her life. There'd been one serious boyfriend in college and another semi-serious one since then.

Both guys were now married to other women. Recently, Ally hadn't dated at all. Her grandmother's illness and then grief over her death had seemed to absorb the bulk of Ally's attention.

Which meant she was ripe for attaching herself to a guy, any guy. Still, he had a hard time imagining her choosing Rudy once she sobered up. Even so, there would be others hanging around the new girl in town, and Mitch had been charged with keeping her from making a terrible mistake. Until now he hadn't realized how impossible that might be.

Ally drained the last of her drink and pushed herself unsteadily to her feet. "If you'll excuse me, I need to visit the ladies' room."

Mitch stood automatically. "Do you need any—"

"No, Mitchell." She drew herself up, as if trying to look taller and more in control of the situation. She was still a foot shorter than he was, and still smashed. "I can handle a potty break on my own, thank you very much."

He sincerely hoped so. He'd hate to be forced to go in there after her.

"It's right down that hall, first door to your left. Can't miss it. Says *Women* right on the door." Rudy pointed toward the back of the bar. He'd also stood, and was gazing at her as if he wanted to walk her there.

Ally flicked a glance over both of them and gave them a lopsided grin. "I can deal with this. You may both be seated."

"Okay." Rudy dropped back into his chair with a thud that made the wood creak. "Don't be long." He gazed after her with obvious adoration.

As Mitch also sat down, he recognized a golden opportunity to institute his latest strategy. "Rudy, I need some help."

Rudy turned his head. "Sure thing. Here in Porcupine we help one another."

"It's about Ally."

"Isn't she wonderful?" Rudy smiled, displaying the gaps between his teeth.

"I'm crazy about her." Mitch put on his most sincere expression. "I'm hoping we can work things out between us."

Rudy looked doubtful. "I don't think she's crazy about you, Mitchell. Sorry to have to tell you that, but she told me you were *driving* her crazy. But that's not the same thing. In fact, it's the opposite."

"I know. She's upset with me. But underneath, I think she likes me a lot."

"You do? Then why did she tell me a while ago that she thought you were a dickhead?"

Mitch winced. "Love and hate can be two sides of the same coin."

"Or sometimes hate is just hate. Like that guy who took Lurleen away. I can tell you that I sincerely hate him. There's no love on the other side of that coin."

"So where is she?"

Rudy shrugged. "Don't know. I wish she'd come back, though. Now that Ally's told me all about women's orgasms and such, I can work with Lurleen on them multis."

"Maybe I could help you find Lurleen." It might cost him some Internet long distance, but at least he might be able to get Rudy focused on a different woman. "What's her last name?"

"Engledorfer."

"That should make it a lot easier."

"If you could really find Lurleen for me, that would be great, 'specially if you have dibs on Ally."

"Well, she doesn't exactly know my intentions." Now there was a true statement.

"You mean she doesn't know you're crazy about her? Don't you think you oughta tell her?"

"Not yet. The timing needs to be right. So I'd appreciate if you wouldn't say anything to her about our conversation."

Rudy nodded. "If you're sure. Personally, I think you should say somethin'."

"I will. When the time's right."

Rudy leaned toward him and lowered his voice. "But let's make us a deal. If you tell her, and she doesn't want to have nothin' to do with you, and you find Lurleen, but she doesn't want to have nothin' to do with me, *then* can I go for Ally?"

Mitch figured with all those contingencies he was safe. "Yeah," he said. "I guess that would be okay."

Chapter Four

Ally couldn't remember the last time she'd had such an excellent buzz going. Dirty dancing on the bar and flirting with a rough-and-ready guy like Rudy were the kinds of thing she'd always wanted to try, but as Madeline Jarrett's granddaughter she hadn't dared. Grammy would have been so embarrassed by that kind of behavior.

Grammy's embarrassment wasn't a factor anymore, though, and Ally had enjoyed the hell out of busting loose. To think she owed it all to Mitchell. When he'd appeared, reminding her of all the restrictions she'd had back in L.A., something had snapped inside. Yes, it had taken three Irish coffees to get up her nerve, but she'd finally found her inner wild girl.

As she washed her hands and looked at herself in the dingy mirror over the bathroom sink, she decided to give that wild girl a rest. Her hair was tangled and her face flushed and puffy. Besides, Mitchell was liable to gain some advantage over her if she didn't stay sharp.

A little food and she'd be fine. From what Rudy had told her, the Top Hat was also Porcupine's best restaurant. Actually it was Porcupine's only restaurant, but at least she was in the right place. She wasn't up to plowing through snowdrifts looking for a bite to eat.

Judging from the noise filtering through the bathroom door, the Top Hat was swinging into high gear. Apparently Porcupinians knew how to party. When she stepped into the hall, whistles and rhythmic clapping nearly drowned out the jukebox. And through it all, she could hear the staccato beat of tap shoes.

At the entrance to the hallway she paused and glanced at the table where Mitchell and Rudy were sitting. Betsy was ensconced at the table with them. While Clyde tap-danced on the bar to "Luck Be a Lady Tonight," Betsy used both hands to beat a rhythm on the table while she wiggled in time to the music. Rudy was a half-beat off with his clapping, but to compensate he'd add an eardrum-piercing whistle every so often.

Mitchell wasn't clapping or whistling. He looked over and spotted her, then turned away, as if he didn't want her to know he'd been keeping watch. Instead he acted as if Clyde's performance and the bowl of unshelled peanuts that had appeared on the table required all his attention. He didn't go so far as to clap, though.

Seeing the peanuts made Ally's stomach rumble. Betsy and Rudy were tossing their shells on the floor, but Mitchell had a neat little pile in front of him. Ally shook her head. Poor Mitchell was so out of his element here. She wondered again why he'd come.

His explanation was full of holes. Mitchell was efficiency personified, which meant he tied up loose ends like nobody's business. In the four months since Grammy's death, he'd quietly taken care of everything, barely needing Ally's input. Yet when she'd announced her trip to Alaska, he'd suddenly come up with a bunch of issues demanding her attention—bogus things like whether she intended to take Grammy's seat on the board of the Historic Lampposts Preservation League.

He'd tried every conceivable argument to convince her to stay, from terrible weather reports to dire warnings about grizzlies hiding behind every tree. She'd told him the part about the grizzlies made her more eager to go, although bears were hibernating now. In the end, she'd left, because Mitchell had no power to stop her.

But he'd followed her up here, and right away, too, as if his presence were absolutely required. She couldn't figure it out, unless . . . he had a secret crush on her. She hated to think that was true, because she didn't want to be forced to deal with it. But a secret crush was the only thing that made any sense.

She was still just schnockered enough to ask him. Walking straight to the table, she quickly sat down before either Mitchell or Rudy could leap up and hold her chair.

"Welcome back!" Rudy said with a huge grin. "Have some peanuts."

"Thanks." She grabbed a handful. "Hi, Betsy."

Betsy smiled as she kept drumming on the table. "Hi, yourself."

"Enjoying Clyde's performance, I see."

"Not so much. He's a terrible show-off, don't you think?"

"I think he's pretty good. A lot better than I was a little while ago." Ally checked on Mitchell from the corner of her eye, looking for telltale signs of infatuation. She wondered how infatuation would manifest itself in a guy like Mitchell. Buying an open-ended ticket to Alaska was darned incriminating, she had to say.

"Well, I suppose he has a sense of rhythm," Betsy said grudgingly. "But I don't know why he has to put on a demonstration all the time."

Probably because he wants to get into something belonging to you, Betsy. He thinks demonstrating his sense of rhythm will get you hot. "I think good rhythm is important," Ally said, hoping to help Clyde's cause.

"I suppose. Too bad he's so full of himself." Betsy continued to drum on the table and wiggle.

Ally thought Betsy was a lot more interested in Clyde's sense of rhythm than she wanted anyone to know. And as Ally listened to Rudy's off-tempo clapping, she had new insight into why he might have lost his lady love. Bad rhythm could be extremely distracting. She couldn't tell whether Mitchell had a sense of rhythm or not, because he was just sitting there.

Or was he? Looking closer, she noticed that his forefinger was tapping, ever so gently, on the table. In perfect time. Well, now. Chalk one up for the giant Popsicle. And speaking of Popsicles, she admitted to mild curiosity about what size Mitchell was packing under those geeky pants he wore.

That's where four Irish coffees could land a girl, speculating about equipment she had no intention of using. But she did need to find out Mitchell's intentions while she still had some Dutch courage left.

After fortifying herself with more peanuts and deliberately throwing the shells on the floor, she turned to
him. "Mitchell, lean over here a minute." No point in humiliating the man in public. Between Clyde's metal taps
crick-cracking on the bar and the blare of the jukebox,
no one would hear her if she kept the conversation low.

"What?" Mitchell looked wary as he came closer.

"Don't worry. I'm not going to sock you in the jaw."

"That's nice to know." A glint of humor flashed in his
brown eyes.

He looked good with that glint of humor. It went well
with the sensual shape of his mouth and his Dudley Do-
Right chin. She cleared her throat and lowered her voice.
"Mitchell, do you have a thing for me?"

He frowned and leaned closer. "A what?"

"A thing," she said, raising her voice a fraction.

"What kind of thing?"

She rolled her eyes. Mr. Smooth Operator he was not.
She'd have to be more blunt. And louder. Nobody was
listening, anyway. "Do you have the hots for me?" Too
late she realized the music had stopped and her words
had neatly filled that little dead space between the end
of the performance and the start of the applause. That
very explicit question of hers seemed to echo through
the room as everyone turned to stare.

Mitchell looked as if he'd been run over by Rudy's
Bronco, Slewfoot Sue. He swallowed. "Um . . ."

Ally wanted to crawl under the table. If she hadn't had
so much booze, she might have done it. Poor Mitchell. He
was a pain in the ass, but he didn't deserve this.

"Go on, 'fess up, Mitchell," Betsy said, loudly enough
for everyone to hear. "I told you she'd guess."

Rudy touched Ally's arm. "He's crazy about you. Told me so when you went to the bathroom."

Ally glanced at Betsy and Rudy, astonished by this new piece of information. "He told you guys?"

They both nodded.

Oh, God. Mitchell must really have it bad if he'd confided in the first two people he'd met in Porcupine. How unbelievably awkward. She couldn't be furious with a guy who'd impetuously followed his heart. She just wished his heart hadn't led him to her.

Mitchell cleared his throat. "Ally, I think—"

"We have to talk. Alone."

He nodded. "Yep."

And yet she had more pressing matters than public humiliation to think about. If they both went back to the Loose Moose to talk without getting any food first, she would be in terrible shape. "The thing is, I'm starving. I need to eat something, especially after four Irish coffees."

"Four?" His eyes widened.

"Yes, four, and there's enough mellow mood left over to get me through this unfortunate episode. I would suggest, however, that you have several more glasses of beer. You'll be amazed at how that helps neutralize the shock."

He shook his head. "I just need to eat."

Betsy punched him on the arm. "Shame on you, Mitchell! You told me you didn't want anything! I was ready to feed you leftover moose-meat pie and you turned it down!"

Rudy groaned. "He turned it down? Can I have whatever you were plannin' to give him?"

"No, you cannot." Betsy stood and pulled on her coat. "Mitchell, Ally, come with me right this minute.

I'm going to warm up a hearty portion of my famous moose-meat pie."

Mitchell exchanged a look of dismay with Ally, and for the first time in their relationship, she felt a common bond. Neither of them was ready to face Betsy's famous moose-meat pie. But they didn't have a lot of choice, now that they'd both admitted they were hungry. If they turned down a chance to eat one of Porcupine's greatest delicacies, they'd be outcasts.

Mitchell might not care, but Ally did. She wanted to be accepted here, because this was where she intended to launch her career as a wildlife photographer. When she was an internationally famous photog, she planned to refer fondly to the tiny town of Porcupine, whose residents had taken her into their hearts. She didn't want anything to screw with that.

"Sounds wonderful, Betsy." She stood and put on her jacket, knit cap, and gloves.

Rudy stood, too. "How much pie you got, Betsy?"

"Never you mind, Rudy. You're not going over there with us. I can be discreet and retire to my private quarters, but you'd end up hanging around and ruining their private moment."

"No I wouldn't. I'd just eat and leave. I haven't had some of your moose-meat pie since before Lurleen left. And don't forget, I'm the one who brought you the moose meat in the first place."

"Only because you were in the right place at the right time!" called out one of the other men. "Lucky son of a bitch, to come along right after that logging truck hit it."

Ally winced and snuck a peek at Mitchell.

He stopped zipping his parka. "You mean this moose

was . . . roadkill?" He looked somewhat green around the gills.

"Very *fresh* roadkill," Rudy said. "The truck didn't even run over it. Just knocked it to the side of the road, neat as you please. Dented up the truck grille some, but the loggers are used to that."

"Doesn't matter about the details." Betsy pulled up the hood on her stoplight-red coat and tied the string under her chin. "Once I get my hands on moose meat, it becomes food for the gods. Now let's move, people. I'm getting a hot flash."

Clyde hurried over. "You're not really leaving, are you?"

Ally heard the plea in his question. He'd hoped Betsy would hang around.

Betsy glared down at him. "Why, yes, we are, Clyde. I wasn't aware I was supposed to ask your permission."

"But . . . but you're taking away two new paying customers. And I heard you say you're going to *feed* them. I suppose you'll stay over there and eat, too! So how'm I supposed to make a living if you do that, Betsy?"

"Clyde, these two have recently experienced a humiliating moment, and they need some privacy. Can you be a little sensitive to that?"

"Me?" Clyde got red in the face and drew himself to his full height of at least five-four. "You're calling me insensitive? I put aside an excellent caribou steak for your dinner! And now you're leaving!"

"Did I ask you to do that?"

"Yes, you most certainly did. This morning when I saw you over at Heavenly Provisions."

"Did not."

"Did, too."

"Did not. Clyde, I'm leaving now. Ally and Mitchell, let's go."

"Did, too!" Clyde called after them. "Standing right by the smoked salmon on special!"

Ignoring him, Betsy led the way out of the Top Hat. Ally had the presence of mind to grab her backpack from the corner where she'd stashed it before she followed Betsy out the door. At first Betsy blocked some of the wind, but once she moved away from the door, the arctic blast belting Ally in the face made her gasp.

Ducking her head, she leaned into the wind.

"Jesus!" Behind her, Mitchell came out the door and it slammed behind him with a heavy clunk. "How does anybody stand this?"

Ally wondered the same thing. The wind brought tears that froze to her cheeks. But she'd never admit to anyone, especially Mitchell, that she found the weather intimidating. This was her first full day. She'd get used to it. By next winter, she'd spit in the face of a wind like this.

But not tonight. And not literally. Anybody who spit into this wind would get stabbed in the eye when that spit came back as an icicle. She'd never been so cold in her life.

She'd be willing to eat roadkill moose-meat pie for the privilege of getting warm again. Even more significant, she'd be willing to end up in a kitchen alone with Mitchell if she were guaranteed a toasty place with zero wind.

Ah, Mitchell. What a dork. She hated the idea of hurting the tender feelings of any human being, but Mitchell had to face facts. Despite his delectable-looking mouth and his sense of rhythm, despite the glint of humor that had made him seem semi-sexy for a split second, he was still Mitchell the Nerd. And she would never, ever, in a million, trillion years, be his main squeeze.

Mitch wondered what he'd done to deserve this—plowing his way through nut-numbing wind and snow so that he could dine on roadkill. He'd tried to live a decent life, pay taxes, contribute to charity, and support the Dodgers, win or lose. He recycled. He'd thought his reward for all that had been Madeline Jarrett hiring him. It appeared that, instead, he was being punished for some unforgivable transgression.

He should be working on whatever story he planned to tell Ally once they were alone, but his brain was frozen solid. Madeline had made it very clear that he was not to reveal that he'd been hired to guard Ally unless her life was in immediate danger. A woman like Ally, Madeline had said, would hate the idea of a bodyguard and would sabotage his efforts if she knew about them.

This damn weather was enough sabotage to deal with. If he had to live in a place like this—which would never happen, but say he was forced at gunpoint by aliens with superhuman strength—then he'd construct a series of heated tunnels between buildings so that he never had to go outside in the winter.

He trudged along behind Ally, who seemed to be using Betsy as a windbreak. Mitch didn't blame her. As the tallest member of the three blind mice, he caught the gale full in the face, or what used to be his face. He couldn't feel his lips anymore. When he finally got inside, they might crack and fall off.

After what seemed like about a hundred years, Betsy opened the front door of the Loose Moose and they all funneled inside, stomping their boots on the mat in front of the door. Stomping was good, Mitch decided. If he stomped hard enough, he might get some circulation back in his toes.

"Hang your coats on that rack by the door and stick your boots underneath the bench." Betsy unzipped her coat and flipped back her hood. "With you two being the only ones in the lodge, you might as well use that spot for your stuff, instead of letting it drip all the way up the stairs. I'll go on back to the kitchen and turn on the oven."

Ally's teeth chattered as she took off her coat and draped it over a brass hook by the door. "I wonder if I c-could c-crawl in the oven with the moose-meat pie."

Mitch itched to tell her *I told you so,* but he didn't. He needed her to like him a little bit so she wouldn't dig in her heels at every suggestion he made. "Does Betsy have a dog?" He hung up his coat beside hers. God, it was orange. It hurt his eyes every time he looked at it.

"I haven't seen a dog since I've been here." Ally sat down on the bench and tugged off her boots. The extreme cold seemed to have sobered her right up. "Why?"

He lowered his voice. "We need a way to make the moose-meat pie disappear."

"I'm thinking the garbage disposal. But then what will we eat? I really am hungry."

"Yeah, me, too. Maybe we can find some bread and peanut butter in her cupboards." He was a little sorry to watch tipsy Ally being replaced by in-control Ally. She might be more of a problem for him under the influence, but she sure was funny.

She thought he'd been paralyzed by humiliation back at the Top Hat, when in fact he'd been clenching his jaw to keep from laughing. When she'd sent her loaded question sailing right into that moment of dead silence, he'd nearly lost it. Talk about hilarious.

Now that he was thawing out, he could appreciate it all over again, except he had to be careful not to start smiling for no apparent reason. People tended to get nervous around that kind of behavior. He sat down next to Ally and began taking off his boots, too.

"Whatever you do, don't let on that you're not looking forward to eating her special dish," she said.

He was offended that she'd even feel the need to warn him. "You think I'm that much of a social klutz?" Then he realized that she probably did think so. And he had made that remark about roadkill, which had popped out of his mouth before he could stop it.

"I just want to make sure we don't insult Betsy's cooking," Ally said.

"Don't worry. I won't insult her cooking." An aroma that wasn't half bad drifted into the hotel lobby. "Who knows? Maybe we'll like it."

Ally shuddered. "I've never eaten anything that was hit by a logging truck."

"I know what you mean. Personally, I'd rather stick with the stuff that was hit by a Toyota."

She looked at him, her eyes wide. Then she broke into a slow grin. "I'll be damned. You just made a joke."

"Is there a law against that in Alaska?"

"I didn't think you had a sense of humor." Then she clapped her hand over her mouth. "Geez, that sounded awful. I meant to say that I'd never seen that side of you. You're always so serious."

"I've been dealing with serious business."

"True." She gripped the edge of the bench and swung her feet, which were covered with thick white socks. When she looked at him, her gaze was assessing, as if she'd never really observed him closely.

He fell back on nerdspeak. "Under the circumstances, it wouldn't have been particularly appropriate for me to walk around the mansion cracking jokes."

She nodded. "Although I probably could have used a few. Still, I see your point. When someone is handling an estate that size, he probably has to be careful about being funny."

"I figured that." He realized they'd never sat this close to each other, or spent this much time gazing into each other's eyes. He should interrupt the moment before it got too cozy. But he didn't.

"I don't know if I've ever said this, but I'm grateful for the way you took care of all the details after Grammy died. I couldn't have. I was a real basket case. Your calm attitude helped to keep me steady."

Maybe that was why he'd continued to sit here, because he'd wanted that validation from her. Sure, he got paid well, but he liked knowing that he'd been of help. "I think she anticipated you would be very upset, which is why she brought me in."

The longer they sat there, the more he found himself staring at her soft cheeks, tinged pink by the wind, and her full mouth, which had been rubbed free of all lipstick. Her eyes looked very green. It occurred to him that he was within kissing distance. The fact that he even thought of that showed how much trouble he was in.

Ally nodded. "She was always watching out for me. And a good part of the time I resented that."

"You were all she had." Unable to stop himself, he drifted closer to her.

"I know. And I did understand, but . . ."

"You felt smothered." Not much distance remained between his mouth and hers.

"Yeah." She didn't move away. For some reason, she was acting as if she wouldn't mind being kissed.

"Moose-meat pie is ready! Come and get it!" Betsy's command galloped out from the kitchen, stampeding the possibilities starting to gather around the bench.

Ally smiled and stood. "Moose-meat's on. We wouldn't want to let it get cold."

"Nope." Mitch looked into her eyes and wondered if she felt the tiniest bit frustrated, too. "God knows I need something hot right now."

"Yeah." Her gaze simmered. "Me, too." She turned and sashayed into the kitchen.

Mitch had to take a moment to control his reaction before he could stand up and follow her. Wow. So much for platonic.

Chapter Five

Kurt Jarrett stood naked in his bedroom in Anchorage, listening to the TV weather report and muttering to himself.

"Come on, Kurt, baby." Vivian walked in front of him in full dominatrix gear, her boobs sticking out of their leather harness, her long legs encased in thigh-high boots with a four-inch heel. She wore a studded belt, but her crotch and ass were conveniently bare.

He wasn't interested. "I don't wanna."

"But you will." She jingled a bit and bridle. "Time to give mama a ride."

"I don't feel like it, Viv. This blizzard's ruining everything."

"Not ruining, Kurt. Delaying. Now quit whining and get on the floor."

"What if Ally loses interest? I want to call her up at that lodge. Why can't I call her?"

"We've been through all that." Vivian tossed her long blond hair over her shoulder. "We don't know how this will shake out, whether we go with Plan A or Plan B. If it turns out to be Plan B, we don't want a bunch of phone logs showing up someday, now do we?"

"Yeah, yeah, I guess you're right. But if I can't call her, then I need to drive up to Porcupine right away, while she's still in the mood to let me help her with this photography thing."

"Let's talk about my mood." Vivian flicked the tip of the reins sharply across his butt.

"Ouch!"

"I'm in the mood for a ride." She snapped the tip of the rein, catching him again, but harder this time.

"That hurts, Viv!"

She laughed. "That's the idea. You know you want it."

"No I don't." But he did, and nobody knew that better than Vivian. "I can't lose out on this money. She's vulnerable right now. I can probably talk her into anything. But I need to strike while the iron is hot."

"What a concept." Vivian whipped both reins across his stinging butt. "On your knees, now!"

"I want it to stop snowing." He slowly lowered himself to all fours. "My knees hurt. I'm too old for this."

"Shut up and arch your back." She stepped astride and settled herself. Then she forced the bit into his mouth and adjusted the bridle around his head.

He tried to act like none of that affected him, but the taste of metal made him hard. She was everything he wanted in a woman—tough, unshockable, insatiable . . . and refined. No matter what things she did to him, she never talked dirty. Kurt hated a foul-mouthed woman almost as much as he hated his dear departed step-mother, Madeline Jarrett.

Vivian pulled back sharply on the reins, stretching his mouth. Then she brought the reins down hard on his butt. "Buck, you wild stallion! And make it good or no treat for you!"

As she continued to whip him, he took her around the bedroom, bucking and arching his back while she rocked back and forth, whooping and hollering, getting her jollies until his backbone was slippery from all the fun she was having up there. The harder she whipped him, the more he felt like coming.

But after two years of playing these games with him, she knew right when to stop. Although she could come all she wanted, he wasn't allowed until she told him he could. Sometimes she'd forbid him to come at all. Then he had to masturbate in secret and hope she didn't find out. Once she'd caught him at it and he'd had to spend two days with his hands cuffed behind his back.

This time he thought she'd let him come, if only to cheer him up on account of the blizzard. Standing, she took off her studded belt and wrapped it around his neck with the studs pressing against his throat. Then she pulled the bit roughly from his mouth and tossed the bridle aside while she kept a firm grip on the belt around his neck.

Sitting on a leather ottoman, she spread her legs and used the belt to jerk his head into position. Her voice was harsh. "Do me!"

Her juices made the cuts on his mouth sting, but he knew better than to complain. If he did this part well, she might give him a treat. He set to work.

She tightened the belt around his neck. "Faster!"

He could barely breathe, but he licked faster, and she started to holler. He thought she might choke him to death, but finally she loosened her hold on the belt.

With a sigh, she stood. "We're done. Get dressed."

"Done? Vivian, please!"

"Why should I? You're not rich yet."

"I will be!" He lifted his face, looking up that long, tight body. Only she understood him. He needed her more than air and water. "Please, Viv. Oh, please."

She glanced down, her gaze haughty. "It's extra trouble."

"I know, I know, but I need it, Viv. Don't stop now. Please don't."

"You're such a baby."

"Please!"

"Crawl over and bring it back in your teeth."

Desperate, he crawled to the chair where she'd left the dildo hanging carelessly by its strap. He had to open his mouth wide and bite down hard, but he managed to get a good hold on it. He crawled back to her, the strap dragging against the carpet.

"Good doggie." She ran her fingers through his hair before tightening her grip and yanking his head up. "You want that?"

He nodded frantically.

"You'd better pray you'll be rich soon, buster." With a weary sigh, she released her grip on his hair and strapped on the dildo. She made him stand up, lean over and brace his hands against the dresser, so she wouldn't have to work too hard.

But at least she was willing to pick up the bridle again and whip him good first. She even oiled the dildo. He was practically weeping with gratitude by the time his orgasm arrived. He would do anything for this woman. Anything.

As Ally took a seat at Betsy's kitchen table, she wondered how she'd come so close to kissing Mitchell. Kissing Mitchell would be a very bad idea, and yet if Betsy hadn't called them to supper, Ally might be in a liplock with him right this very minute. She still had the urge.

Betsy put a steaming plate in front of each of them. Then she set down two bottles of beer with a clunk. "Enjoy. And if you're hungry after you finish this, feel free to have anything you can find. There's some leftover blackberry pie in the refrigerator. I'm going back to the Top Hat."

Ally couldn't imagine anyone going back out into that deep freeze except for an emergency. Besides, a chaperone might be a good idea. "You don't have to leave, Betsy."

"Yes I do. I have to go back and set that Clyde Hammacher straight. I don't know what he's talking about, raving on about that caribou steak. If I don't go over there and convince him that as usual he's mistaken, he'll continue to insist that I'm the one with the poor memory. I can't let some scrawny little pipsqueak get the better of me."

Ally smiled to herself. Betsy was definitely intrigued by the scrawny little pipsqueak.

"We'll clean up the kitchen when we're finished," Mitchell said.

"Yes, definitely," Ally added.

"No problem." Betsy picked up her red coat from the back of a chair and shoved her arms into it. "In bear season, we can't leave any dirty plates in the sink or the grizzlies might smell the food and break into the kitchen to get it. They make a helluva mess, too."

Mitchell's eyes widened. "Bears are right here in town?"

Ally put a hand on his arm. "It's okay, Mitchell. The bears have gone nighty-night until spring."

"Yeah, but still . . . bears in the kitchen?"

"It's happened," Betsy said. "See, the Loose Moose straddles two worlds." She shoved her feet into her boots and leaned over with a grunt to snap the metal fastenings. "The front part of the lodge is in town, and the back is on the outskirts." She straightened up and grappled with the bottom pieces of her coat's zipper. "My back porch butts right up against the forest. I've had all manner of critters peering in my kitchen window."

"Is that right?" Mitchell glanced nervously at the window, but between the frost coating the outside and the steam fogging the inside, the glass was in no shape for viewing from either side.

"You betcha." Betsy zipped her coat. "We used to have a regular around here we called 'the Peeping Caribou.' If God had given that animal the gift of speech, he'd have told some X-rated stories, guaranteed."

"And that," Ally said, "is why I chose Porcupine as my headquarters, Mitchell."

"X-rated stories?"

"Ha, ha. No, because it's Critter City. I talked to Betsy on the phone and knew this would be the perfect place."

"And I thought it was real gutsy of you to come up in the winter," Betsy said.

Ally glanced at Mitchell. "Some people thought it was pretty stupid."

Looking testy, he gestured toward the window. "Okay, now tell me, do you see a Peeking Caribou out there?"

"Doesn't matter," Betsy said. "There's still stuff to take pictures of. Wolves in the snow would make a dandy picture. Once the storm's over, you'll find plenty to do."

"Wolves are on the top of my list."

"Not mine," Mitchell muttered under his breath.

She couldn't blame him for feeling grouchy. He hadn't had the best of circumstances so far on this trip. First the blizzard, and then she'd embarrassed him in public, and now his only hot meal was something that smelled okay but probably tasted disgusting. On top of that, Mitchell had more disappointment coming in the form of rejection, once Betsy left the kitchen.

Betsy pulled up her hood. "I'm off, then. Don't do anything I wouldn't do." She laughed. "And that means your options are wide open. Don't wait up for me, either. When Clyde and me get to fighting, it can go on a long time. He's one stubborn idiot." Betsy started out of the kitchen, her boots landing heavily on the wooden floorboards.

Mitchell leaned toward Ally. "Listen, before this charade goes any further, I want you to know that this business about me being interested in you has been—"

"I forgot something!" Betsy clomped back into the kitchen. "If you should need 'em, I keep condoms in my bathroom medicine cabinet."

Ally's jaw dropped. She didn't dare look at Mitchell, who was making a choking sound, as if he'd just swallowed his tongue. From the corner of her eye she saw him reach for his beer.

With her hood up, Betsy was probably oblivious to their reaction. "My bathroom's through there." She pointed to a door beside the stove. "It's open, so help yourselves. I have plenty. Now I'm *really* leaving."

Ally held her breath until she heard the front door open and close. Then she let it out in a rush. "Whew." She sneaked a glance at Mitchell. "You okay?"

"Um, sure." He cleared his throat and shifted in his chair. He was gripping his fork so tightly that his knuckles were white. "Ally, things are getting way out of control, here. I want you to know—"

"No, let me go first." She looked into his eyes. "I'm afraid you've wasted your trip. I'm so sorry that you came all the way up here. I wish you'd mentioned this before I left, and we could have cleared it up then."

"Ally, let me say something. I—"

"Don't say it, Mitchell. It will make no difference. Although I appreciate everything you've done for Grammy and for me, I don't think you and I are destined to be . . . I mean, you have wonderful qualities, and I'm sure that someone else would be honored if you—"

He put down his fork. "I'm not interested in you, Ally."

She blinked, taken aback. To her surprise, she felt a little disappointed. Having him charge up here out of lovesickness had given her a bigger ego boost than she'd thought. But now he'd claimed he wasn't interested, so that was the end of that. She couldn't call him a liar.

Then she figured out what was going on. He was rejecting her before she could reject him, to save his pride. Fine with her. Let him take whatever way out suited him.

"I must have misunderstood," she said. "Jet lag messes everyone up, doesn't it?" She gave him a big smile to show that they could move on and forget all about this awkward situation. At least now that he realized there was no hope, he would leave once the blizzard was over.

"I told Betsy I was interested in you in order to sidetrack her. She seemed determined to get me into that Murphy bed."

"She sure did!" Ally managed a hearty laugh, although she felt sort of depressed that he could so easily come up with a cover story to explain away his obvious infatuation. "That Betsy's hot to trot, isn't she? Okay, time for one of us to test this moose-meat pie!" She stuck her fork into the mixture on her plate, which looked a lot like beef pot pie.

"You don't believe me."

"Of course I believe you, Mitchell." She took a tiny taste of what she had on her fork. "You know, this isn't as bad as I thought it would be. Forget where it came from and try it."

He left his fork on the table. "You don't believe me. I can tell. But I grabbed the first excuse that came my way. Then when I was worried that you might be getting involved with Rudy, I decided to use the same tactic to get him to back off."

"Wait a minute." She paused with her fork halfway to her mouth. She'd been willing to cut him some slack, but he'd just managed to hang himself with all that extra rope. "Are you telling me that you *disapprove* of Rudy?"

"Not in general. He's a great guy, but if you're talking about hooking up permanently with him, then—"

"Hey! Time out!" Now that she'd sobered up, she didn't think Rudy was an appropriate boyfriend, either, but she'd defend to the death her right to make that decision for herself. "I don't know if you're interested in me or not. You say you're not, but I can't think of any other reason why you're here."

"I'm here because—"

"But whether you're interested is not the issue on the table." She barreled on, pointing her fork full of moose meat at him for emphasis. "You are my grandmother's personal assistant. You are *not* in charge of choosing which men are appropriate for me and which are not. End of discussion. If I want to date Rudy—hell, if I want to *marry* Rudy—I will!"

He gazed at her, his expression unreadable. "Are you finished?"

An adrenaline rush made her long to toss the moose-meat pie in his face. But she was sober now, and she couldn't override years of training in the social graces in order to do it. Besides, the food was actually pretty good. The onions, potatoes, and carrots added a lot to the mix.

Giving herself time to calm down, she took a bite, chewed, and swallowed. "What do you mean?"

"If you've said your piece, I'd like to say mine."

"I may not stick around to listen." But if she left, she was taking her plate with her.

He nodded. "You're right. You're your own boss. I

can't choose your dates or your husband. And you're also worth a hell of a lot of money."

"That's not important to me." She speared a potato wedge and popped it into her mouth.

"Meaning you plan to take no responsibility for it? Because that's the message I've been getting for weeks, and I need to know if that's the case."

Well, damn. He had her by the short hairs, now. He was coming off as Mr. Reasonable and Responsible, while she was coming off as Ms. Spoiled Brat who didn't appreciate the privileged position she'd been given and didn't want to have any obligations as a result.

She did appreciate it. Because of Grammy's generosity, she had the financial freedom to pursue any career she wanted, or no career at all. She'd chosen wildlife photography, and she had the money to stay in Alaska for as long as she wanted while she took pictures and learned her craft. Most people would have to juggle that with a day job. She didn't have to.

Swallowing her food, she looked at him. "I don't intend to waste the opportunities available to me. You know, you should really dig in, Mitchell. This isn't half bad."

"What would you do if I decided to quit?"

She abandoned her food and launched into full-blown panic mode. "Are you considering it?" Oh, God, what if her rejection had wounded him to the point that he wanted nothing to do with her or Grammy's estate? She'd counted on the fact that Mitchell liked his job, but maybe she'd just taken all the joy right out of it.

"Never mind whether I'm considering it. What would you do?"

She'd have to find a new Mitchell. And she wasn't sure they were all that thick on the ground. He was loyal and conscientious. She'd never for a minute doubted his integrity, and that was pretty damned important. Sure, there were checks and balances built into Grammy's trust, but Mitchell was smart enough to find ways around those if he'd wanted to, and so far as she knew, he hadn't. Grammy had chosen well.

"I don't know what I'd do," she admitted. "But definitely I would have to put this photography plan on hold until I found your replacement." *If I can find a replacement.*

"Well, I'm not quitting."

She let out her breath. "Thank you. You about killed my appetite with that subject." Ready for a truce, she gazed across the table. "Go ahead and eat, Mitchell. I'm not planning to get engaged to Rudy, and you're not quitting your job. And it looks like we won't be having a wild and crazy affair, despite having a supply of condoms not twelve feet away. So there's nothing left to do but eat this moose-meat pie. Think of it as smoking the peace pipe."

His mouth twitched.

"Feel free to smile, too. It wouldn't kill you."

He did more than that. He laughed. "Since you're not gagging and rolling on the floor, I guess this meal is safe to eat."

"Nice. You let the heiress be your food taster. I thought it was supposed to work the other way around."

"But you don't want to be treated like an heiress." He took a sizable bite and stuck it in his mouth.

"You've got that right."

He chewed and swallowed. "You know, it really isn't

bad. A little gamey, but what can you expect from road-kill?"

"Exactly." She settled in to enjoy the rest of her meal. But when she'd nearly cleaned her plate, she suddenly thought of how close she'd come to disaster tonight. She glanced up. "Mitchell, please don't ever quit."

His brown gaze softened. "Don't worry. I won't."

That's when she knew for sure. No matter what he said, he had the hots for her. But he'd pretend that he didn't, and that was okay, too. She could do worse than having a secret admirer like Mitchell.

Chapter Six

Mitch wasn't entirely happy with the status quo, but at least he and Ally had managed to finish the meal and do the dishes together without getting in a fight. She still thought he wanted her, and maybe that was okay. For one thing, he did want her, and he was having a tough time pretending not to.

Women had a sixth sense about these things. No matter what he said, she'd picked up on his lust vibes, and he didn't know how to block those. Her bulky red sweater and jeans didn't entirely disguise the curves that he'd spent way too much time thinking about.

True, he had to pay close attention to catch the moments when the sweater shifted to reveal the line of her breast. He had to keep his eyes open so he wouldn't miss the times when she leaned over to put away a pan and her jeans would pull tight over her ass. He didn't miss anything. He tried to rationalize it as his PI training kicking in. Yeah, right. What he was doing was engaging in covert ogling.

Not covert enough, either, because he felt certain she was aware of his thinly veiled obsession with her body. She probably liked it, the little tease. Matter of fact, he was convinced she liked it, because her green eyes got all sparkly during their dishwashing episode.

"So where did you learn to wash dishes?" he asked, as she finished wiping down the counters.

"In college."

"You took home ec?" If so, he'd missed that piece of info when he'd briefed himself on her past.

"No, I joined a sorority. As a pledge, I had to do chores around the sorority house. I was bad at it, but eventually I learned out of self-defense." She set the sponge on the back of the sink.

He knew about the sorority gig, and that she'd graduated with honors. "Because they'd make you do it over?"

She stuck her hands in the back pockets of her jeans. "No, because they'd make fun of me for being a rich bitch who didn't know how to do anything useful."

"Ouch." He tried to concentrate on what she was saying. He needed to ignore the way her breasts thrust forward, pushing against the red sweater.

"Being Madeline Jarrett's granddaughter hasn't always been a bed of roses."

"I'm sure it hasn't." He pictured her lying naked in a bed of roses, while he scooped up a handful of petals and let them drift over her skin . . .

"I don't know which was worse, the people who did

mean things out of envy, or the ones who spent all their time sucking up."

"It must have been hard to know who your friends were." And speaking of sucking, he had another image going in his fevered brain.

"Very hard."

And if he didn't get out of this kitchen soon, he would be, too. He faked a yawn. "You know what? I'm bushed. I think I'll turn in."

Ally glanced at her watch. "It's barely nine o'clock."

He knew that, but he figured the safest place for both of them was in their own bedrooms. Hanging around in this empty lodge with Ally wasn't a good idea. And he couldn't face the prospect of battling their way back through the wind and snow to the Top Hat.

Besides, he needed some privacy to read his e-mail. He'd probably run up a hell of a long-distance bill, but that couldn't be helped. "Yeah, I know I sound like a wimp, but it's been a long day and I'm ready to hit the hay." He started toward the lobby.

"Then I guess I will, too. Maybe we should turn out some lights." She flipped the switch on the wall and the kitchen went dark.

In the lobby, Mitch walked over to the front door and turned off the overhead there. "We'll leave that Tiffany lamp on by the registration desk, so it's not completely dark in here if Betsy comes back."

"Okay."

The glow from the lamp gave the lobby just enough jeweled light to make it very romantic. Inviting. Ally looked way too appealing standing by the stairs. In another era, she could have been a lady of the night, waiting to go upstairs with a client.

Mitch shook his head, as if that could derail his one-track mind. "I guess that's it. The place is shut down for the night."

"Time for bed." Ally stretched, arching her back like a cat.

He swallowed a whimper of longing. "You can have the bathroom first."

She paused in mid-stretch. "Oh. That's right." She gave him a wary look. "I guess we need to give some thought to logistics."

"Just lock the door that opens into my room. When you're finished, unlock it. I'll do the same."

"That should work." She smiled and started up the stairs. "It's not like we haven't been living in the same house for months. This isn't all that different."

"I guess not." It was enormously different, but he wouldn't point that out. He followed her up the wooden stairs, their footsteps creaking in rhythm. He shouldn't be watching how her cute little butt moved as she mounted the steps ahead of him, but he was a guy, and guys did that.

He'd always thought that this supposedly polite behavior of allowing women to go upstairs ahead of men had nothing to do with manners. The whole "after you" game was designed to give men a better view as they contemplated whether or not they might get lucky when they reached the second floor.

And no matter how much he tried, Mitch couldn't throw off the impression that they were about to share a bed. Maybe that was because they'd just finished eating a meal in the kitchen, washed the dishes together and turned out the lights.

"Listen to that wind," Ally said.

"I'm glad we're not out in it."

"Me, too."

He thought the blizzard outside might be another factor. They were tucked away from the wind and snow, safe in a cozy retreat. Now it was time to roll around in the sheets before going to sleep.

He'd never come close to having those thoughts back in Bel Air. For one thing, no blizzards. For another, he'd never followed Ally up the stairs at night. And they'd never been alone, not with the staff of twenty servants the mansion required.

In the mansion Mitch had been relegated to the south wing and Ally had slept in the north wing. The endless hallways that had separated them made it seem as if they lived in different zip codes. When Madeline had hired him, he'd taken a tour of the mansion and grounds to double-check the security system, and that had been the only time he'd stepped inside Ally's bedroom and attached bath.

The Loose Moose was quite a change from what she'd been used to. And yet she hadn't said anything that made him think she missed all that luxury. Instead she seemed to relish her new and unfamiliar surroundings.

He could see this plan working for her, if he didn't suspect that Kurt Jarrett figured into it somewhere. If Ally had come up here on her own for on-the-job training in wildlife photography, he wouldn't be particularly worried. Yes, she might get in over her head in some wilderness situation, or misjudge the danger of stalking certain animals with only a camera to protect her, but those were acceptable risks, in his book. People had to live, after all.

Madeline hadn't foreseen that kind of danger, anyway. She'd focused on the twin issues of men who would want to marry Ally for her money, and Kurt, who might do anything to get the inheritance he thought he deserved. Mitch needed to read the latest report on Kurt from a PI in Anchorage and find out if Ally's uncle had been up to anything special.

"See you in the morning," Ally said as she walked down to her room and opened the door. "Let's hope it's stopped snowing by then." She paused, her hand still on the doorknob. "I'm sure you're eager to get back to L.A."

So she'd had to get in one last dig. "I really do have papers for you to sign," he said. But they weren't anything important. She'd know that the minute he dragged them out.

"How about I do that now?"

"Tomorrow's soon enough." He wanted to delay showing her the piddly documents he'd come up with on short notice. A person would have to be incredibly anal to think those papers mandated a flight to Alaska. Either anal or in love. Ally probably thought he was both.

"Then I'll see you tomorrow." She went into her room and closed the door.

He had the oddest feeling, as if a light had just snapped off. He hadn't realized how much energy surrounded her and how empty the air felt without it. Telling himself he was only doing his job, he walked into his room and activated his recorder so he could hear what was going on in her room.

Then he smiled. She was singing an old Bee Gees tune from *Saturday Night Fever.* She was way off-key and her fake falsetto was horrible, but the subject of the song was perfect. She was singing "Stayin' Alive." He'd drink to that.

Pulling his laptop out of its case, he took off the glasses he didn't need, plugged a phone cord into the jack beside the bed and logged on to the Internet. The dial-up chugged along, taking forever, but eventually he got on. Sure enough, there was a message from Pete, the PI he'd hired in Anchorage to keep an eye on Kurt.

Through that contact he'd learned that Kurt lived with a woman named Vivian Altman. Vivian was in real estate and Kurt sold used cars. At least that was his most recent job. He'd never hung on to a job for long.

From purchases Kurt had made at an X-rated shop, Pete figured Kurt and Vivian were into S and M. Normally Mitch was ready to live and let live when it came to kinky sex, but the S and M connection fit in with Madeline's estimation of her stepson, so it was important information.

He opened the latest e-mail from Pete as Ally wound down her rendition of "Stayin' Alive." He wondered if she added dance steps to the tune. After seeing her on top of the bar this afternoon, he wouldn't doubt it. But the show was over, and she was rustling around, gathering something together. Moments later he heard footsteps indicating that she was headed into the bathroom.

The lock on his door into the bathroom clicked. Then the pipes squealed, followed by water drumming on the sides of the metal shower stall. And thanks to Betsy's comments earlier, he now pictured Ally stripping off her clothes and stepping naked into the spray.

He forced his attention back to the e-mail, dated to-day. *Jarrett bought a new Dodge Ram truck, silver, and a fully equipped fifth wheel at 9 A.M. Weather coming in should prevent him from taking it anywhere real soon. More later. Pete.*

Now Ally was singing in the shower, and he didn't need a listening device and receiver to hear it. She'd switched to the theme song from *The Secret of My Success,* "Walking on Sunshine." She couldn't carry a tune in a bucket, but what she lacked in skill she made up for in volume.

Damned if he wasn't plagued with a vivid image of her soaping up in time with the song. He wondered if she used a washcloth or just the bar of soap. The bar of soap painted a far more erotic image, especially when she moved it down between her legs . . .

And here he sat with an erection and his long-distance minutes going right down the drain, along with Ally's soapy water. With a snort of frustration, Mitch keyed in his response. *If Jarrett leaves Anchorage with truck and fifth wheel, call me at this number.* Mitch checked his electronic daybook and typed in the number of the Loose Moose. *Apparently cell phone reception lousy in Porcupine. Will have to use land line. Mitch.*

He signed off, irritated to think he'd used Internet time to fantasize about Ally. He'd have to get a grip, and fast.

Before she stepped in the shower, Ally heard the click of computer keys in Mitchell's room. Following her up here had probably played hell with his usual schedule, but if she knew Mitchell, he'd found a way to keep track of everything, even from this small town in Alaska. Even a serious infatuation wouldn't alter Mitchell's course for long.

She'd thought of bringing a laptop, but in the end she'd chosen to travel light, as Uncle Kurt had suggested. He'd promised to find her good deals on all the equipment she'd need—top-of-the-line cameras, a new laptop, and the right printer. He was researching good processing labs, too, for those times when she didn't want to go digital.

But without a laptop, she couldn't keep up her e-mail correspondence with him, and she missed that. They'd exchanged e-mails for years, ever since he'd paid that surprise visit during her sophomore year in college. She'd been fascinated to finally meet the mysterious Kurt, her grandfather's son by his first wife.

Back when her grandmother and grandfather had married, Kurt had been eighteen, and Grammy's son—Ally's father—had been ten. Ally's father had been adopted and given the Jarrett name, seemingly replacing Kurt, who'd chosen to live with his mother. Ally had always been curious about this stepuncle, but for reasons no one would talk about, he'd been banned from the Jarrett mansion long before she'd been born.

At last she could ask Kurt about those reasons. He'd explained that Grammy couldn't bear to look at him because he reminded her that her beloved husband had once shared a bed with another woman. Because it was the only explanation Ally had ever been given, she had to believe it, although she thought it was horribly unfair.

Kurt still got a monthly trust fund allowance, and he'd admitted that he'd lose that if Grammy knew he'd come to see Ally. Not wanting him to be punished any further, Ally had suggested they keep in touch secretly through the Internet. They'd kept it up after she'd graduated.

Even though Grammy hadn't shown any interest in the Internet, Ally hadn't wanted to take any chances that someone in the household would figure out she was in touch with Kurt, so she'd arranged for him to use her college roommate's e-mail address. After Grammy died, they'd kept the same routine out of habit. Together they'd planned her trip to Alaska so that she could follow her dream with Uncle Kurt's help.

Now she just had to wait for Uncle Kurt to show up. She was eager to see him, but she'd love to get Mitchell out of town first. As she was contemplating the best way to do that, the water changed from hot to lukewarm. Uh-oh. She'd just lathered up her hair. She quickly rinsed it, but the lukewarm gave way quickly to cold, and then icy.

Without meaning to, she yelped.

Instantly Mitchell pounded on the bathroom door. "Ally! What's wrong! Ally!"

She turned off the shower and grabbed a towel. "The hot water ran—" Then she screamed as wood splintered. With a huge crash the bathroom door flew open.

Mitchell stood in the doorway, breathing hard. "What's . . . wrong?"

Gulping for air, she stared at him, unable to process what had happened. "You scared me to death!"

"You scared *me* to death! What happened?"

"Nothing that required breaking down a door! Good God, Mitchell. Betsy's going to have your head on a platter."

"But I heard you cry out!" His gaze flicked over her. "Listen, could you . . . wrap that around yourself?"

She glanced down at the towel she held in front of her and saw that it wasn't quite covering the subject. "Um, sure." She held it against her breasts and managed to get the edge of the towel around her and tucked in. But it wasn't what she'd call a generously sized towel. The bottom hem barely made it past the salient points.

Then another fact registered. "You're not wearing your glasses."

His hand went to his face, as if he hadn't realized it. "No, I guess not."

"Well, there's one good thing about this incident. You probably can't see me very well."

"Right, right," he said immediately. "You're really fuzzy. Extremely fuzzy."

"Good, because otherwise this could be one embarrassing moment."

"I think it still has potential. What was the yelp all about?"

She hated to tell him. "The hot water ran out."

"That's *it*? I broke down a door because you ran out of hot water?"

"I didn't ask you to break it down, now did I? I had a natural reaction to ice water suddenly ending up on my . . . body, and then wham! Arnold Schwarzenegger crashes into the bathroom. I thought we were being invaded!"

"I thought you were in trouble!"

"You couldn't have waited five more seconds for me to tell you about the water situation?"

"Sometimes five seconds is the difference between life and death!"

Ally sighed. She'd had no idea that Mitchell was wound so tight, but maybe all the talk about grizzlies and the Peeping Caribou had freaked him out. And it was sort of cute that he'd come to her rescue.

"Okay, I appreciate the effort," she said. "But the thing is, Betsy's door is busted, and we're going to need a really good reason why that happened. I don't think a little yelp from me is going to cut it." She still couldn't comprehend that Mitchell had done the busting, either. She hadn't imagined he was that strong.

He rubbed the back of his neck. "Something could have gotten into the bathroom, for all I knew." He shrugged. "Maybe even a mouse."

Ally looked at the door hanging crazily by one hinge. Mitchell had really trashed that door. "Let's say it might have been a mouse. I still think breaking down the door is a little over the top. Betsy isn't going to be happy."

"I suppose not." Mitchell glanced over his shoulder at the door.

She took pity on him. "Tell you what. I'll explain to Betsy that I screamed really loud when the water turned cold, and you were sure someone was in here murdering me, and that's why you broke down the door."

"That's okay." His grin was sheepish. "You don't have to protect me from Betsy. I can take the heat. I'll apologize and pay for a new door."

She assessed the damage. "And a new doorframe, looks like. I hope that wasn't historic."

"God, do you think it was?" Mitchell turned and took a good look at what he'd done. "You know, that could be original. That's probably why it gave way so easily."

"It didn't sound like it gave way easily. You made a horrible crash when you came through." She peered at him. "How did you do that, Mitchell? It's not like you're into body building, or anything."

"It's adrenaline," he said. "Like when a kid is pinned under a car and the mother comes along and lifts the car off the kid. That kind of strength."

"And you summoned up that kind of strength to come and save me?" She was totally impressed.

"I would have done that for anybody I thought was in trouble."

She gazed at him. "Okay." But she didn't think so. She thought he had a really bad case of unrequited love. "Well, in case you didn't already know it, the bathroom's available now."

"Thanks."

"That's the good news. The bad news is, there's no hot water. Guess I'll go get into my jammies." She turned and walked back into her room, closing the door between her room and the bathroom. Then she turned back, opening it a crack and peeking through. "Oh, and Mitchell?"

He was standing in the exact spot she'd left him, as if he'd been nailed to the floor. "What?"

"That system we worked out—it's not viable anymore. Plus it seems to lead to extreme damage. We'll have to come up with a different signal. We could try whistling. Good night, now."

"Good night." His voice sounded gravelly.

Yep, Mitchell was over the moon about her. And it made him do some very un-Mitchell-like things, like spontaneously book a flight to Alaska and break down a bathroom door. She hadn't thought he was a very interesting man, but much more of this and she might change her mind.

Chapter Seven

Mitch gladly took a cold shower. After interacting with an almost-naked Ally, he was thinking he might need to stand in a cold shower all night long. But eventually his equipment returned to normal and he began to shiver, so he toweled off and headed back to his room.

As for the bashed-in door situation, he managed to prop the door against the frame, but the privacy factor was definitely compromised. Peekaboo spots all around the perimeter. Therefore he pulled on his sweatpants and sweatshirt in a hurry, in case Ally wandered back in the bathroom to brush her teeth.

So far all he heard from the bug under her bed was plenty of rustling around, and something that could be the pages of a book turning. He glanced at his watch. Barely ten.

He was a night owl, which left a lot of night left to owl around in . . . lots of time to think about Ally naked except for the haphazard drape of a yard of skimpy white terry. Between the excitement of breaking down the door and the rush of seeing her fresh out of the shower, he might not go to sleep at all.

So he'd overreacted. Better too much protection than too little, in his estimation. Besides, he'd never guarded someone in the wilds of Alaska before. For all he knew, there might be a brand of Alaskan mouse that stood three feet at the shoulder.

And there was always the danger that Kurt had given the Anchorage PI the slip and driven up here in some badass Hummer. Or hired someone else to do it. Mitch didn't have a handle on how much of a threat Kurt posed, but at the very least the guy would probably try to get his hands on some of Ally's money. At the worst, he'd decide to eliminate her and go for the whole pie.

Mitch flopped back on the double bed and wondered how to spend the next couple of hours. Finally he resorted to his old standby and pulled a worn deck of cards from a pocket in his suitcase. Sure, he had solitaire and a bunch of other games on his laptop, but he liked the tactile experience of handling cards.

At one time he'd toyed with the idea of becoming a professional gambler. With casinos sprouting up on every reservation, a gambler didn't have to headquarter in Vegas or Atlantic City anymore. Mitch liked figuring percentages and reading his opponents, some of the same skills he used as a PI. In the end he'd ditched the idea because he didn't like cigarette smoke.

But he still loved a good game of poker. Unfortunately, he needed someone to play against for that, so he was reduced to solitaire. Shuffling the cards, he laid them out on the bed and started to play.

He was about halfway through his second game when the noises coming from Ally's room changed. Her bedsprings squeaked, footsteps headed for the bathroom, and light shone through the sizable gap between the door and the splintered frame. Ally started brushing her teeth.

Turning over another three cards, Mitch continued with his game. Sort of. He wasn't really paying attention to it anymore. Instead he listened to Ally, who didn't let the water run while she brushed. She might have more money than God, but she conserved water. He liked that.

Because she was brushing her teeth, he couldn't help thinking how straight and white they were. Of course, they would be the best teeth orthodontia could buy. She wouldn't have been allowed to grow up with any flaws. Yet he was amazed that she wasn't more high-maintenance as a result of all that pampering.

He went right past a five of hearts that would have played on the six of spades because he fell into a daydream about her lips, which at the moment would be decorated in toothpaste foam. She had a great mouth, the top lip creating a perfect archer's bow and the bottom one full with a slight pouty look. Delicious.

By the time he realized he'd checked out of his solitaire game, he had a mishmash of hearts and diamonds in one of his suited piles. With a snort of disgust, he gathered up the cards, shuffled, and laid out a new hand. He needed to stop obsessing about Ally's finer points. And speaking of her finer points, her breasts were two extremely fine points. She—

"Do you cheat?"

He glanced toward the bathroom door. She'd pressed one eye to the crack and was watching him.

"No, I don't cheat." He tried to gauge whether she could see the recorder he'd been using to listen in to her activities. He didn't think so. The angle was wrong. "Do you cheat?"

"Never. If you're gonna cheat, what's the point? You haven't really beat old Sol, then, have you?"

"Nope."

"Why aren't you wearing your glasses?"

Busted. He thought fast. "My eyesight's okay up close. I need the glasses for distance."

"But whenever I came into your office back in Bel Air, and you were working on the computer, you had on your glasses."

That was part of the look your grandmother wanted me to have. "They have a special, nearly invisible tint that helps with the screen." He wondered if she'd swallow that whopper.

"I see."

He couldn't tell if she believed him or not. "At least that's what the optometrist told me. I'm not sure it makes much difference, so sometimes I forget to put them on." Maybe that would cover his lapses.

"So you're playing cards?"

"For a while."

"Can I play? I'm not even slightly sleepy, and I'm going stir-crazy in my room."

"Um, sure." He hopped off the bed, headed for the receiver. "Let me get the door."

"I can do it."

He had about three seconds to flip the switch on the recorder and throw a shirt over it. He turned toward the doorway right as she came through it wearing red plaid pajamas and a pair of thermal socks.

As a sexual turn-on, her outfit should have been a miserable flop. The flannel was completely opaque and clownishly baggy. But it looked soft, the sort of jammies that women wore over bare skin. No underwear. That was enough to jump-start Mitch's battery.

"Should we just play on the bed?" she asked.

His brain stalled. Oh, yeah, they could certainly play on the bed. Forget the cards.

"Unless you think the floor makes more sense. The bed might be a little bouncy."

Bounce could be good. Getting a little rebound action going could put some real punch in the action.

"Mitchell?" She waved a hand in front of his face. "You're spacing out on me. Maybe you're too tired to play cards, after all. Listen, if you want to go to bed, that's fine."

Oh, he did, but not alone. "I'm not tired. I was listening to the wind. It hasn't let up out there. We may be snowbound for a while."

"God, I hope not. That would be so frustrating."

No kidding. Especially considering that he couldn't let himself get involved with the woman standing there in her fiendishly sensuous flannel. "Let's play on the bed," he said, and managed to say it in a normal voice, as if he'd never thought those words meant anything other than a simple card game.

"Good choice." She climbed up and sat cross-legged

near the end of the bed. "It'll be warmer than the floor." She waited for him to sit down at the pillow end. "Now what shall we play?"

Oh, man, this was going to be hell. "Poker?" The suggestion came out as a croak. Immediately he thought about strip poker.

"I'm not very good."

Even better. He could literally beat the pants off her.

"But I think it's a fun game. We played at the sorority."

"Okay, then poker it is."

"Don't we need something to count as chips?"

It was an indication of how rattled he was that he hadn't thought of that. "I'll bet Betsy has kitchen matches." A little trip downstairs might give him a chance to get his libido under control. He slid off the bed. "Let's go see."

"Good idea." She followed him to the door. "Wait. Get your glasses. We left it pretty dark, and I don't want you falling down the stairs because you misjudged a step."

"Right." He had to pick up his orange parka to locate his glasses, but he managed to keep the recorder out of sight in the process.

They left his room and started down the darkened stairs, Ally going first.

"I haven't heard Betsy come back, have you?" she asked.

"No." But he'd been so busy listening in on Ally that he might have missed the sound of the front door.

"I don't think she's back. I wonder if that means she's staying at Clyde's for the night."

"Could be. Let's not think about that."

Ally laughed. "I can't help it."

"Personally, I'm blocking those images." Besides that, reminding himself that Betsy might not come home also reminded him that it could be just the two of them here tonight. Well, two people, but Mitch's penis seemed to have a mind of its own, so he'd almost count it as a third party to the gathering.

"I feel like a kid sneaking downstairs to raid the refrigerator," Ally said.

Mitch felt like a man ready to seduce a woman in a darkened kitchen. So he fumbled for the light switch and they both stood there blinking in the glare from overhead.

"Refrigerators are best raided in the dark," Ally said.

"I know, but we're not raiding the refrigerator."

"Maybe we should. I've always wanted to."

"So you've never done it?" Now that he thought about it, he had a tough time imagining how that would work in the Garrett mansion.

"I didn't dare. We had security cameras, you know."

He did know. He'd recommended an update. "Somebody would have busted you?"

"Not in the sense that I would have been punished, but I never could have completed a successful raid. And I would have been gently reminded to buzz the maid's quarters so that someone could fix me whatever snack I wanted. Then I would be asked not to wander around the place in the middle of the night because it got the security staff's undies in a twist."

"That all makes sense."

"But it tends to take the spontaneity out of life."

"Yeah, I suppose it does." He tried to sympathize, and wondered if he'd trade all his refrigerator raids for the chance to do whatever he wanted with his life and not have to worry about making a living at it . . . ever. Probably.

"I know that look," Ally said.

"What look?" He quickly erased all envious thoughts.

"I've seen it a million times on the faces of my friends. You're thinking that I have nothing to complain about, and you'd be right." She gave him a lopsided smile. "But you can't blame a girl for wanting to stage a refrigerator raid when she has the chance."

Her wistful expression got him right where he lived. "Let me find the matches first. Then we'll douse the lights and raid the refrigerator."

Her smile widened. "Mitchell, you're not half as stuffy as I thought you were."

That meant his disguise was slipping. And now that he'd agreed to this midnight snack, he could see the card game evolving into a full-blown party. If she spent too much time in his room, she might find his recorder. She might even, given enough time, find his gun.

But she'd just handed him the perfect excuse to move the festivities to her room. "I'm at least as stuffy as you think I am," he said. "We're eating this late-night snack in your room because I can't stand crumbs in my bed."

Well, so he was persnickety about crumbs in his bed. Ally didn't think that was so unusual. She didn't know how she felt about that subject, having never slept in a crumb-filled bed. Eating in bed had been reserved for times when she was sick, and then the linens had been changed immediately after she finished.

At least Mitchell had enough experience to know he didn't like crumbs in his bed. She wondered if he'd discovered that on his own or when he was sharing a bed with a woman. Until very recently she hadn't imagined Mitchell with a love life.

Now she could sort of see it. He obviously had the capacity to be spontaneous, possibly even wild. A totally controlled person wouldn't break down a door.

His appearance had been greatly improved by those gray sweatpants and sweatshirt, too. When she'd first seen him sitting on his bed playing cards, with no glasses and his hair sort of messed up and that cute cleft in his chin, he'd looked almost studly. Thinking of Mitchell as studly made her laugh, but he had looked that way.

Yes, he was still the guy who'd bought himself an orange parka and a matching knit cap with a yellow pompom on top, but he wasn't wearing either of those things right now as he rummaged through Betsy's kitchen drawers looking for a box of matches.

"Got 'em!" He held aloft the box of kitchen matches.

"So lights out?"

"Lights out."

She hit the switch, and the kitchen went black. The light from the Tiffany lamp in the lobby was too faint to reach the kitchen and the storm had blocked the window with snow and ice. "Tactical error," she said. "I should have opened the refrigerator door first." She groped her way toward what she thought was the refrigerator.

"Here, let me get it." He reached out and got a really tight hold on her breast. With a gasp he backed up and bumped noisily into something, probably the kitchen table.

Once she got over the shock, Ally started to laugh.

But Mitchell wasn't laughing. "Ally, I'm sorry. I sure didn't mean to—"

"Cop a feel?" She swallowed another fit of laughter and cleared her throat. "I'm sure you didn't, Mitchell. You're not the type. Besides, in the dark, boobs and refrigerator door handles look pretty much the same. At least you recognized the difference when you felt it."

He groaned.

"Oh, Mitchell, forget it. Let's get this raid started." She pulled open the refrigerator. "I know there's blackberry pie. Ah, here it is." She pulled the pie tin from a shelf. "And here are some kind of cold cuts. Don't know what, though."

Mitchell had recovered himself, apparently, because he came to stand behind her. "If you can't identify it, don't take it."

"Relax. The moose meat turned out to be okay. Here, take the blackberry pie." She handed it to him.

"I vote we don't take the meat. It could belong to something that was scraped off the road."

"We're taking it." Ally pulled out the package of sliced meat. "You can't have a decent refrigerator raid without making sandwiches. We need bread."

"Bread sounds safe. I think there was a breadbox on the counter."

"Do you have enough light to find it, or are you likely to grab my ass while you're searching?"

"Ally, I really didn't mean to grab you. It was a total accident."

"I know." She grinned at him. "I just couldn't resist." He was really quite adorable in his obvious discomfort.

Another kind of guy might have grabbed her boob by accident and then held on, thrilled by the unintentional contact and willing to use it as an excuse to start something. Not Mitchell. He was mortified.

Locating a wedge of cheese and a jar of mustard, she pulled both out and held them with one arm while she snagged a couple of beer bottles from the refrigerator door. "Did you find the bread?"

"Yep. And a knife to slice it."

"Then I think we're set. We can—" She stopped speaking when she heard the front door open. The wind blasted in with a roar, and then the door closed with a loud slam.

"Betsy's home," Mitchell said under his breath.

"I refuse to be caught red-handed on my very first raid," Ally muttered. She closed the refrigerator door gently so that they were once more in the dark.

Mitchell leaned toward her. "We'll stay right here until she goes into her parlor," he whispered.

Betsy's voice drifted from the entryway into the kitchen. "Clyde, you animal, you. Hold your horses."

A man's voice followed, but his words were muffled, as if he might have his mouth up against something soft. Ally could easily imagine what that something might be.

"I know what you want, tiger. And Betsy's gonna give it to you. But first we need to take off our boots so we don't track up my carpet."

The man's murmuring became more insistent. Ally bit her lip to keep from laughing. Betsy had found herself a live one.

"No! Clyde, you naughty man! You stop that! I

haven't even had a chance to get my other boot off . . . Oh, my goodness!" Her exclamation was followed by a solid thud. Clyde wasn't big enough to make that much noise going down, so it had to be Betsy.

"Clyde!" Betsy started laughing. "You're a crazy man. You can't just go ripping a woman's shirt off and . . . well, as long as it's unbuttoned . . ." Moans and loud sucking noises came next.

"Good God," Mitchell muttered.

Warmth spread through Ally as she realized that she and Mitchell were trapped into being voyeurs, whether they liked it or not.

"Clyde . . ." Betsy's protests sounded weaker. "We should at least get into the bedroom before we . . . oh, well . . . as long as we've come this far . . ."

The labored breathing and rhythmic slap of flesh against flesh could only mean one thing. Ally closed her eyes as the groaning and moaning grew in intensity. She was bearing auditory witness to Betsy getting some.

Sure, she was embarrassed to be caught in this awkward situation, especially with Mitchell standing right behind her. But embarrassment wasn't her only reaction. She was getting into it. She didn't want that to happen, but she seemed to have no control over her wayward body.

Most of all, she didn't want Mitchell to know that this incident was affecting her that way. That would be humiliating. She swallowed and tried to breathe normally.

Then she became aware that Mitchell's breathing had changed, too. Oh, no. It was happening to him, too. And he, poor guy, had the hots for her. Talk about your cruel and unusual punishment.

Thank goodness she didn't have a similar crush on

him. Otherwise, once they finally made it back upstairs, their midnight snack would be forgotten. They'd have far more important things to take care of first.

For a nanosecond Ally let herself imagine how much fun that would be, even considering she'd be doing it with Mitchell instead of a guy she really craved. Then she dismissed the idea. Doing it with Mitchell, when he cared and she didn't, would be unforgivable. He deserved better than that.

Chapter Eight

This is what he got for allowing himself to be sucked into unnecessary schemes like refrigerator raids. Mitch listened to the sounds of lust from the other room and tried to gain some control over his already susceptible package.

If he'd had any common sense, he would have nixed the refrigerator raid and he and Ally would be upstairs now, playing poker with matches. But no, he'd decided to go along with Ally's wish for a middle-class experience— a midnight snack swiped secretly from the kitchen without the cook's knowledge.

Now the cook was horizontal in the hall with the tap-dancing owner of the Top Hat, and Mitch had to carry on as if that sort of thing didn't faze him.

"I can't believe this is happening," Ally murmured.

"Welcome to Alaska." Mitch tried to say it in an offhand way, as if he found this mildly amusing instead of downright stimulating.

"Not so loud," she whispered back. "They might hear you."

"Are you kidding? They wouldn't hear a full orchestra playing the 'Eighteen-twelve Overture' complete with cannon fire. I'm sure we could parade right through the lobby and up the stairs and they'd never notice."

"Tell me you're not suggesting that."

"I'm not suggesting that." The mental image made him cringe. "We'd both be scarred for life."

"Probably. I can't say, never having been in this—" She stopped speaking as Betsy screamed, "*Oh, God, I'm coming!*"

Mitchell cleared his throat. "There's a chance that could be the grand finale."

"We can only hope."

But Clyde's tempo didn't change and Betsy tuned up again.

"That's two," Mitch said as Betsy announced her second Big O. "*Now* it should be over."

"Maybe not. I think she's been saving up."

And sure enough, Mitch caught the unmistakable signs of Betsy working up to another climax.

"That's three," Ally said when the moment arrived.

About a minute later, Mitch sighed. "Four."

Four, it turned out, was Betsy's limit, at least for this particular coupling. Mitch clenched his jaw as they were treated to Clyde's delayed, and definitely well-deserved, bellow of satisfaction. Then silence reigned.

Mitch was afraid to say anything, because the silence was so complete that the slightest shuffle of their feet would echo through the lodge. He hoped Betsy and

Clyde hadn't killed each other with passion. He waited, breath held, for signs that they'd recovered.

With luck they wouldn't lie there until morning, but it was always possible. Even when they roused themselves, they'd probably crawl on hands and knees into Betsy's red parlor. Neither of them were exactly spring chickens. Still, Mitch had to award grudging respect to Clyde's performance, and unless Betsy had been faking, she was one hell of a woman.

Finally, signs of life issued from the lobby.

"Get off me, Clyde. I can't breathe."

That was greeted with more muffled mumbling.

"Yes, yes, it was terrific. You're a stallion. Now move before I suffocate."

Mitch smiled. Betsy might take the sex, but she wasn't going to give her heart to the first guy who presented her with four on the floor. He had to admire her style.

After several groans and a considerable amount of thumps, rustling, and gasping, another door clicked shut.

"I think it's safe to move." Mitch kept his voice low.

"Okay, I'm heading out," Ally said. "Don't drop anything."

"I won't." Mitch followed her into the dim light of the lobby. He didn't look over toward the entryway, just in case Betsy and Clyde had left items of clothing scattered around. Or in case Betsy had left Clyde lying there, his weenie waving in the breeze. She was one tough lady.

"We probably don't have to worry that they'll hear us," Ally said. "And even if they did, I doubt Betsy would have the energy to come out and investigate." Ally started up the stairs. "I certainly wouldn't."

Mitch wished she hadn't said that. Now he wanted to know if she'd ever had multiple orgasms. It seemed to be the order of the day in Alaska. Lurleen had left Rudy because he couldn't provide them, and Betsy seemed to accept them as her due.

In Mitch's experience, multiple orgasms were a co-operative deal. The guy had to have some skill and staying power, but the woman had to be open to the idea. The combination had only worked out a couple of times for Mitch. Although the sex in each case had been great, he'd had nothing in common with either woman besides this particular achievement. Nice as it had been, it hadn't been enough to make him want to hang around.

All that had taken place pre–Madeline Jarrett. Since Madeline had hired him, he'd been too involved with the job and its heavy responsibilities to have time for women. And the heaviest of his responsibilities, despite her gorgeous little figure, was climbing the stairs ahead of him for the second time tonight. And he wanted her more than ever.

Ally opened the door to her room and walked in, leaving the door ajar for Mitchell. For good or bad, they'd just shared something that few people ever did. She felt a kinship with him.

She'd also be willing to jump his bones, but she didn't trust that feeling. She might have been willing to jump any guy after the boinkathon they'd been privy to. So she'd concentrate on food, instead. Maybe that would take the edge off.

"I'll make the sandwiches," she said.

"I could make the sandwiches."

"I know, but making the sandwiches seems like an integral part of the refrigerator raid, so I'll do it."

He glanced at her. "Do you know how?"

She put her pile of food on the dresser and turned to him. "I may be filthy rich, but I'm not totally incompetent."

"Sorority living," he guessed.

"Exactly." She went into the bathroom, grabbed a hand towel and spread it on the dresser. Then she took out bread and started in on the sandwiches.

Mitchell sat on the edge of her unmade bed and picked up the book lying there. "Tanya Mandell. I've heard of her."

"She's only the best wildlife photographer in the world, in my opinion."

"I never could understand how they get some of these shots, like this one of the bear on its hind legs, without being—"

"Noticed?" She arranged slices of meat on each sandwich.

"I was thinking *mauled*."

"You learn those things. That's what I'm here for."

Mitch closed the book with a shudder. "Let's talk about refrigerator raids, instead. Didn't you ever swipe food from the kitchen when you were a sorority girl?"

"The truth is, I never got past the pledge stage."

"Why not?"

"Oh, one afternoon I overheard a couple of seniors talking about me." She tried to sound as if it didn't matter, but thinking of the conversation still hurt. "One said,

'Thank God she's not a real pain,' and the other one said, 'I know. Because we'd have to keep her, regardless, after all the money her grandmother gave us.' See, I hadn't known about any money changing hands."

"So you de-pledged."

"Uh-huh. You should have seen how hard they tried to talk me out of it, too. I should have made those girls clean the sorority kitchen floor with their tongues." She used the carving knife Mitchell had brought up to cut slices off the wedge of cheese and put them on the sandwiches.

"I wish you had."

"Actually, I was determined to hit them where it would hurt the most. I wanted Grammy to take back the money." Slapping another piece of bread on top, she picked up both sandwiches and handed one to Mitchell.

"Thanks." He took the sandwich in both hands. "Did she?"

"No. Instead she wrote them a note saying it was a shame they'd treated me so callously, but because money seemed to be more important to them than gracious behavior, they could keep it."

"Hm." He bit into his sandwich, chewed and swallowed. "I have no idea what this meat is."

Ally sat on the edge of the bed beside him and took a bite of her sandwich.

He glanced at her. "Do you recognize the taste?"

She shook her head, still chewing. Then she swallowed. "A little gamey."

"Then we probably don't want to know what it is." He lifted the bread and studied the meat. "Are you going to eat it?"

"Are you kidding? This is my refrigerator-raid sand-wich. You bet I'm going to eat it." She took another big bite.

"Me, too." He tucked into his sandwich with gusto. About halfway through the sandwich he got up and opened both beers, twisting off the caps with his fin-gers.

"Nice job." She accepted the beer, impressed at the way he'd opened it. "I'm beginning to think you have hidden depths, Mitchell."

"Because I can twist off the top of a beer bottle?"

"No, because you can manage my grandmother's es-tate *and* twist off the top of a beer bottle. That combo is hard to find."

"Not so much." He grinned at her. "If I could twist it off with my teeth, that would be saying something."

"I'll bet Rudy can."

"Which could be another reason he's missing a few of those pearly whites." Mitchell took a swig of his beer. "So how did that work for you, that your grandmother let the sorority keep the cash?"

Ally considered that. "I thought it sucked."

"Yeah, me, too."

"I mean, maybe they all had an attack of conscience and are still feeling guilty, but I doubt it. But that was Grammy. She never wanted to descend to petty behavior. Which is why I never could understand that she—" Ally caught herself just in time. The new-found comradery with Mitch had made her forget that some topics were better left alone. Like Kurt.

She would love to know if Grammy had said any-thing to Mitch about Kurt, but she didn't want to ask.

Grammy hadn't known that Kurt was up here in Alaska, and there was no reason for Mitchell to know, either.

If Mitchell left when the snow cleared, that might be about the time that Kurt would drive up to see her. She hoped he'd bring her mentor, the person who would teach her the ropes. They might pass Mitchell going the other way, headed for the airport, which would be perfect. If Grammy had mentioned Kurt at all to Mitchell, she wouldn't have had anything good to say.

Grammy had to be embarrassed about her rejection of Kurt. When Ally had tried to get her to talk about him, her usually poised grandmother had turned bright red. She'd refused to discuss Kurt and had forbidden Ally to mention him again.

"I take it you're not going to finish that sentence?" Mitchell said.

She turned to find him watching her and knew she'd have to come up with some plausible ending to her comment. "Oh, she fired one of the staff over some little detail. But I have no right to judge. I'm sure she had her reasons."

Ally hadn't agreed with her reasons, though. A maid had put through a call to her grandmother from Uncle Kurt. Apparently the young woman had been bold enough to say that she couldn't see the harm in a stepmother talking to her stepson on the phone. Grammy had sent her packing that very day.

"She did demand loyalty."

"Yes, she did." Which meant Ally had battled feelings of disloyalty from the moment she'd started communicating by e-mail with Uncle Kurt. Grammy would have hated it. But Uncle Kurt understood Ally's need for adventure and Grammy never had. He'd encouraged her to live life to the fullest and not become a pampered society type. All this time he'd been her lifeline.

Ally decided to see if she could derail this discussion of Grammy, a discussion she'd been dumb enough to start. "Ready for some of that blackberry pie?"

"Sure." Mitchell set his beer on the floor, walked over to the dresser and picked up the pie plate. "How about forks?"

"I didn't get any."

"Neither did I."

As they looked at each other, both of them obviously considering whether it was worth going back to the kitchen, a muted moan of ecstasy drifted up from the first floor.

Mitch's eyes widened. "Again? These people are practically senior citizens! Have they no shame?"

Ally laughed. "I guess all that tap dancing has kept the guy in shape."

Escalating cries penetrated the floorboards.

"In shape is one thing." Mitchell shook his head. "I think the guy's mainlining Viagra."

"Whatever he's on, you won't catch me trundling down to get the forks."

"Me, either. The way this thing has been going, I wouldn't doubt they're doing it on the kitchen table. I'm staying upstairs until morning, and even then I don't know if it will be safe to go back down." He cocked his head as Betsy trumpeted the news of another climax. "That's five."

"Don't you have to start over with number one?"

"Any way you count it, those two belong in *The*

Guinness Book of World Records. And the night's still young."

"Which leaves us with the problem of a blackberry pie and no forks."

"I'm afraid so."

"We could eat it with our fingers." She didn't believe for a minute that Mitchell J. Carruthers, Jr., the guy who wouldn't tolerate crumbs in his bed, would go for that. Even she knew it would make a big mess.

"Okay. Why not? It's no crazier than all the other stuff we've been involved with today."

"But we need bibs if we're really going to do this." Ally went back into the bathroom, grabbed both bath towels and gave one to Mitchell. "Let's sit on the floor and tie a towel around our neck. And I strongly suggest you roll up your sleeves."

Mitchell sat down on the braided rug and put the pie plate in front of him. "There's two-thirds of a pie here. Once we dig into it, no one else will want to touch it."

"Then we'll have to finish it, won't we?" She sat across from him Indian-style and tied her towel around her neck. Then she rolled up the sleeves of her flannel pajama top.

Mitchell followed suit, pushing his sleeves up past his elbows.

To her surprise, his forearms looked muscular. Inviting, even.

He glanced at her. "After you, madam piggy."

"I have to say, Mitchell, that this is turning out to be a most excellent refrigerator-raiding experience." For all the anger she'd felt when he'd shown up this afternoon, at this moment she was kind of glad he was here.

"Even with the unplanned entertainment?"

"It added that extra challenge." She realized that without Mitchell here, she might not have raided the refrigerator, and she could easily have ended up in her room all alone, listening to Betsy and Clyde go at it.

"It's been a unique event, that's for sure." He paused to listen to the sounds from the first floor. "That's either two or six, depending on which way you want to keep score."

"I don't know how I'm going to face her at breakfast in the morning."

"Who says they'll be finished in time for breakfast? We might be on our own for days."

"Then we'd better fortify ourselves." Ally dug her fingers into the pie and came up with a gooey handful that smelled heavenly and dripped purple on her white bath-towel bib.

Pushing her fingers into the pie turned out to be an extremely sensuous experience. The thickened juice oozed through her fingers and the pebbled surface of the blackberries rolled against her palm in a moist caress. Add in Betsy's climactic vocalizations, and it was almost enough to give Ally an orgasm on the spot.

Her body humming with tension and anticipation, she started eating the pie. Then she glanced over to see if Mitchell actually had the nerve to put his hands in the middle of that dessert. Maybe not.

He was watching her, instead. Then she realized exactly *how* he was watching her, with definite lust in his brown eyes, and her already supercharged libido went into overdrive.

She hadn't meant to seduce him with this pie-eating deal. Or herself, for that matter. Yet that seemed to be what she'd accomplished. Okay, so maybe the way he was looking at her got her even hotter. So maybe she wanted him to nail her right here and now, on the floor, in the middle of eating blackberry pie.

But then what? She'd be stuck with him. If he was infatuated now, he'd be over the moon if he got lucky tonight. He would rightly assume that she wanted him to stay in Alaska. He'd still be here when Uncle Kurt arrived. He'd be in the way.

So no sex for either of them. It would only cause problems. Once he started eating the pie, she should be safe. Making a grab for her while he had his fingers covered with blackberry juice would require a level of abandon she didn't think he had, despite the door-bashing incident.

"Dig in," she said. "Before I end up eating the whole thing by myself. It's really yummy, Mitchell. You don't want to miss out."

Chapter Nine

Mitch knew exactly what was yummy, and he wasn't thinking about the blackberry pie. Ally had no clue what a temptation she dangled in front of him as she calmly ate the pie with her fingers. He felt like a long-at-sea pirate sighting his first woman in months. He ached. He drooled. He hardened.

He craved those plump lips that were stained with blackberry juice. He wanted that eager tongue that lapped thick syrup from between her fingers. He wanted that tongue to lap in other, more personal places. His personal places.

He wanted to get closely involved with her mouth and taste the blackberries she was munching with such abandon. Then he would move on, eliminating her bib, her pajama top, and especially her pajama bottoms so that he could sample fruits sweeter than any blackberry ever invented.

For one glorious moment she looked at him as though she'd go for that routine. If that look had stayed in her green eyes another second, he would have shoved the pie plate aside and deployed his eager forces. Unfortunately, her expression *had* changed, and he could guess what was going on.

Her mind had taken over the controls. Although her body might have been swayed temporarily, due to the circumstances, her mind hadn't changed its tune. Mitchell J. Carruthers, Jr., anal nerd-boy hired to do boring paperwork for her grandmother, was not the man for Ally Jarrett, Alaskan adventure seeker.

He should be relieved that she'd taken control. He'd been about to lose it, and that would definitely screw up the program. Telling himself that he was, in fact, extremely relieved, he settled for the consolation prize. He dug his fingers into the blackberry pie.

The experience made him think of sex, but in a former whorehouse with a landlady like Betsy and a next-door neighbor like Ally, he didn't have much choice. He'd naturally associate everything with sex. The place was saturated with it.

"Good, huh?" Ally gouged out another handful of pie. "I'll bet this will stain our fingernails, so Betsy will know we ate with our hands."

"Considering the fact that she offered us condoms before she left for the Top Hat, I don't think blackberries under our fingernails will shock her much." For the first time he noticed that Ally's nails weren't long and artfully polished. They were short and neat, without a trace of polish, not even clear.

Yet her grandmother had indulged in a biweekly

manicure until a few days before she died. He remembered that because she'd asked him to make his reports during her scheduled manicure. She'd been a dedicated multitasker.

"What?" She licked her fingers and gazed at him.

"I was just thinking about your grandmother's manicure sessions."

"Ugh. Don't remind me. Before you showed up she'd schedule me in there to make use of that time."

"Yeah? To do what?"

"Probably the same thing you had to do—read her the minutes of one of her endless charity board meetings or else a prospectus on some stock she was considering. Am I right?"

"Pretty much." He couldn't tell her that he'd been advising Madeline on security issues inside and outside of the mansion, plus relaying any worries about Ally's current friends, and most of all, telling Madeline what Kurt Jarrett was up to these days.

"Man, I dreaded those manicure sessions." Ally held up her hand, the nails facing him. "That's why I go bare. One sniff of nail polish and I'm comatose with boredom."

He'd never thought of not wearing nail polish as going bare. Right on schedule, his penis started to dance the tango as Mitch pictured her going bare everywhere, prancing around the room in her bare nails, her bare breasts, her bare tush. God, he was a sorry case.

"So, are we gonna play poker?"

He thought not. He'd had about all the seductive exposure to Ally that he could stand for one night. "How about we postpone it till tomorrow night?"

She looked disappointed. "There's always the chance you won't be here tomorrow night."

"With the way the storm's blowing out there, I think there's an excellent chance I'll be here tomorrow night." So she still planned on getting rid of him. He might have to bribe Rudy to put Slewfoot Sue on the disabled list. Without a shuttle to the airport, Mitch would be forced to stick around.

She gazed at him for several long seconds. "Mitchell, I'm afraid I don't believe you when you tell me that you came up here because of some important papers I have to sign. I think you really do have a thing for me."

He tried to think of a snappy response and came up empty. He was developing a thing for her, so she wasn't totally off track. And he couldn't tell her the real reason he was here, either.

"I'm not upset about that," she said. "In fact, I'm touched." Then she gave him an endearingly serious look. "But you have a job to do back in L.A., and I'm starting a new career up here in Alaska, so even if I returned your feelings, which I'm sad to say I don't, there's no way we could have a relationship."

Relationship, maybe not. Hot-and-heavy fling, definitely. He thought of suggesting it, rejected the idea. He'd continue to let her think he was infatuated, though. "I understand."

Her expression softened. "It's better if you go back, Mitchell. I don't want you to get hurt."

"I'm tougher than you think." He almost smiled when he said that, but managed to maintain his sincere-but-saddened look.

"Oh, I'm sure you are! I never meant to imply that

you were weak. It's just that having you stay on, when we both know it's hopeless, would be . . . well, awkward."

"I don't mean to make you uncomfortable." Just Fort Knox safe.

"I meant awkward for *both* of us, Mitchell. It can't be easy for you, having me near and yet knowing that nothing will ever change."

He thought plenty had already changed. She'd never entertained thoughts of sex with him before tonight. And he knew good and well she'd entertained them a little while ago.

"I know exactly what you need," she said.

"Do you?" He couldn't resist putting a little heat into his gaze.

Sure enough, she blushed. "I mean, other than that. You need to find the right woman for you, and I'm not that woman. You need someone who's . . . more like you."

"In what way?" By getting her to answer that question, he could check out how his nerd disguise was working.

She hesitated, obviously searching for a description that wouldn't offend him. "You know . . . someone quiet and methodical."

He nodded. So far, so good.

She brightened, as if encouraged that he was accepting her description. "You need someone who likes a more structured life, someone who's happy with a steady routine. I mean, look at me—running off to Alaska, abandoning the life I've known for twenty-six years, giving up all the advantages of a big city and the warmth of sunny L.A. so I can freeze my butt in a one-Bronco town like Porcupine. That's so not you, Mitchell."

"You're right about that."

"See?" She looked triumphant. "We're all wrong for each other. I'm ready for change and adventure, and you're . . . you're . . ." She seemed to have run out of sympathetic adjectives to attach to his blah self.

"Boring?" he supplied helpfully.

"No! I don't mean that. You're incredibly reliable, and that's wonderful. The world needs all kinds of people, and you're *great* at what you do."

He certainly hoped so, if that meant he could help her avoid the clutches of a guy like Kurt. "I accept the label of boring," he said. "Don't think you have to make me sound like Russell Crowe. I know my strengths and I know my weaknesses. You're not going to damage my fragile ego."

She regarded him silently for a few seconds. "That's good," she said, a new note in her voice. Was it interest? "That's very good. Self-confidence is a valuable thing. But I think hanging around here is liable to erode—"

"Look, Ally, you've made it clear that you're not the one for me. I accept that. But this sudden dash to Alaska scared the shit out of me. Before I leave, I have to establish for myself that you're going to be okay up here."

"I will be *fine* up here." The rebellious light was back in her eyes. "Perfectly fine. These are good people."

"So far, I agree with you. The ones I've met seem like good people. Fixated on sex, but good people. I haven't met everyone yet."

A muscle in her jaw worked. "It's a small town. I'll bet you could meet them all in an hour. Then off you go."

"Like I said, I care about you. For my own peace of

mind, I need to know that you're in good hands before I leave."

"Oh, for heaven's sake." She stood and used her towel to wipe the blackberry juice from her mouth. "Now you sound like an insurance company commercial. I've tried to spare your feelings in gratitude for what you've done for Grammy and for me, but the truth is—in case you've missed the message—I don't want you to stay. I don't care a whole lot about your peace of mind, to be perfectly honest."

He stood and pulled off his towel so he could wipe his mouth, too. Ultimatums weren't as effective when you had blackberry juice smeared all over your mouth, and he was about to deliver one. "Tough."

She stared at him. "*Tough?* Is that what you just said?"

"Uh-huh."

"Can I fire you?"

"I don't think so. Maybe. You'd have to come back to L.A. and talk to the lawyers who drew up the trust."

She bristled. "And wouldn't you just love that? You'd get me to abandon my Alaskan adventure and fly back to L.A. so I could be bogged down in legal details trying to get you fired, which I might not even be able to do. Probably can't do, if I know Grammy. She put some clause in there that requires me to prove you embezzled or something equally drastic. I doubt there's a provision for me to fire you because you're a pain in the ass."

He kept his face free of expression as he gazed at her. Madeline's instructions had been quite specific in that regard and Ally didn't have grounds to get rid of him. He'd make sure she never had grounds. And he would do the job Madeline had hired him for, whether Ally liked it or not.

"And here I was starting to think you were an okay guy. But an okay guy would grab a clue and leave. He would not stay and inflict himself on a woman just for his own peace of mind." She paused, as if gathering more insults to hurl at him. "Haven't you ever heard that saying, that if you love something, you should let it fly free?"

"I've heard it."

"Well? What do you have to say about that?"

"Once I've checked out your fly zone, you can flap around in it all you want. But I've been charged with administering your sizable estate. Can you imagine the truckload of paperwork I'd have to deal with if anything happened to you? I hate to even think about it."

She blew out an indignant breath. "So this isn't really about your having the hots for me, is it? It's about simplifying your job! It would be very inconvenient for you if I turned up missing. Is that what you're saying?"

"That's what I'm saying." Maybe a little hostility was healthy. Maybe then she wouldn't throw any more sexual vibes his way.

She stood with her hands on her hips, legs spread in a belligerent stance. "I'm beginning to get the picture. Before I left, you had everything running like clockwork, just the way your little anal mind likes it, and now I've thrown a monkey wrench into your neat little world."

"That's one way of describing it." He wished that he could forget that she was most likely naked under that flannel. She might not be feeling sexual desire right now, but he hadn't completely tamed his woody. He held his towel in supposed nonchalance while he allowed it to dangle protectively in front of that area.

"And you can't deal with the unexpected, can you, Mitchell?"

"I'd rather not." In his line of work, the unexpected meant he hadn't done his homework and had left an opening for the bad guys.

"Well, using your word, that's *tough*. Expect the unexpected. And now I'd appreciate it if you'd take your unwelcome presence back to your own room."

"I was just leaving. See you in the morning."

"Not if I see you first."

Once his back was turned and he was on his way to his room, he could allow himself the grin that had been threatening ever since she'd started her tirade. The exchange had actually gone very well. He'd rather have her mad at him than feeling sorry for him. Less temptation.

He'd also shored up his role as Mr. Killjoy, the nerdy wet blanket, someone who would rather see her safe than happy. He wouldn't mind seeing her both safe *and* happy, but with her current trajectory, the two seemed mutually exclusive. So he'd opt for safe, and let happy take a back seat for now.

Ally woke up in the dark to the alarm on the watch she'd shoved under her pillow. She turned it off immediately, not wanting to take the chance that Mitchell might hear it. Then she listened for the howl of the wind and the splat of snow against her window. Blissful silence greeted her.

Maybe the storm was over! On that happy note, she hopped out of bed, gasping at how cold the room was.

Shivering, she whipped off her pajamas and struggled into her clothes.

Seven o'clock. Mitchell would be sawing logs because he wouldn't yet be acclimated to how late the sun came up on winter mornings in Alaska. He'd sleep in late, just as she had on her first morning.

She wished to hell it would be his last morning here, too, but she couldn't think of a way to run him out of town. So she'd have to make herself scarce. If the storm had truly ended, she'd get out there with her camera before Mitchell even knew she was gone.

What a thrill, to anticipate a few hours of freedom without him hovering around peering behind every tree searching for the Big Bad Wolf. He was more overprotective than Grammy, and that was saying something. To think that for a brief time last night she'd imagined herself sexually attracted to him.

To think for a while she'd imagined him sexually attracted to *her*. Maybe the glare from the lamp had reflected off his glasses and she'd mistaken it for a gleam of desire. A man who needed predictability in all avenues of his life would run from honest-to-God lust. Nothing about lust was predictable, as witnessed by Betsy and Clyde last night.

She hoped Betsy and Clyde were sleeping in, too. She would prefer putting a few more hours between last night's hokey-pokey in the hallway and a face-to-face with Betsy. However, making herself a sandwich before she left for the day would mean she could avoid Mitchell that much longer.

He wasn't the type to go wandering around looking

for her once she gave him the slip. Not someone as
frightened of the unexpected as Mitchell. She'd left her
parka and boots in the hall, so all she needed was her
backpack. Grabbing it by the strap, she tiptoed out of
her room, ready to begin Operation Ditch Mitchell.

As she crept down the stairs, guided only by the light
from the Tiffany lamp on the registration desk, she heard
the sound of someone humming "Keep Your Sunny Side
Up." A female someone. A female someone working in
the kitchen. Betsy.

Ally sighed and considered her options. Number one,
it was still dark outside. Leaving early had seemed like a
great idea, but in reality she wasn't familiar with the
area and wandering around in the snow with a flashlight
didn't seem particularly productive. She wasn't prepared to take pictures of animals in the dark, wasn't
even sure how to do that.

Number two, if she planned to stay out there for
hours, she needed something to eat. All the available
food was in the kitchen with Betsy. And Ally would
have to talk to Betsy sooner or later, anyway.

Number three, the aroma of freshly brewed coffee
made Ally's mouth water. She'd had some of Betsy's
coffee yesterday, and it was ambrosia. Betsy owned a
manual coffee bean grinder and wielded it like a maes-
tro. For a hot cup of coffee on an icy cold morning, Ally
could handle some uncomfortable moments with Betsy.

She could even handle seeing Clyde in the kitchen,
too, so long as Clyde hadn't backed Betsy up against the
refrigerator. If Betsy kept humming, that was a good sign.
Most women didn't hum "Keep Your Sunny Side Up"

while having sex. Of course, with Betsy, anything was possible.

Ally walked into the kitchen to find Clyde sitting at the table with a giant mug of coffee in front of him. He'd positioned himself so that he could watch Betsy moving around the kitchen, and boy, was he watching. When she leaned over to put a pan of biscuits in the oven, his Adam's apple bobbed and he started to get out of his chair.

"Good morning!" Ally said brightly, figuring she needed to announce herself quickly before Clyde acted on his impulse and leaped on Betsy. Judging from last night, he didn't require a bed to start the proceedings.

Clyde whipped around and sat down again with a thump. To his credit, after his first look of deep disappointment, he smiled at Ally. "Good morning to you, too, Ally. How's your head this morning after all those Irish coffees?"

"Pretty good, actually." *How's your ding-dong after all those orgasms?*

Betsy closed the oven door and turned toward Ally. Her chin was red with whisker burn and her eyes sparkled. "Hey, there, Ally! Isn't this a gorgeous day?"

Ally swallowed. "Sure is! I mean, I'm sure it will be, once the sun comes up, although when it's still dark, it's a little hard to know whether it'll be a nice day or not . . . isn't it?" She tried to pretend she had no idea why Betsy was in such good spirits, and *really* tried to block out the memory of what she'd heard while stranded in the kitchen with Mitch.

"I wasn't talking about the weather." Betsy winked at Clyde. "Was I, Poopsie?"

"I don't suppose you were, Kitty-cat." Clyde gazed at her with obvious adoration.

Betsy blew him a kiss. Then she glanced at Ally. "Isn't he the cutest thing you ever saw?"

Ally scrambled for a response. Clyde, aka Poopsie, looked like a gnome, with his hooked nose, thin hair, and caved-in chest. He might be five-four if he stood up very straight.

"You're embarrassing the poor girl, Kitty-cat," Clyde said. "She doesn't know what to make of me sitting here in your kitchen."

Betsy grinned at Ally. "Oh, I think she knows exactly what to make of it. And let me tell you, Ally, he was worth the wait."

"You're the one who kept me waiting, Kitty-cat," Clyde said fondly. "I told you I was ready any time, anywhere."

Ally gulped.

"And you certainly backed up that boast, Poopsie. Ally, this man is a marvel. Such stamina."

"You bring out the beast in me," Clyde said.

"Hey, is there any more coffee?" Ally wondered if Betsy kept a travel mug around somewhere. Ally was ready to travel. A girl could only be expected to deal with so much information.

"Yeah, I'd love a cup of coffee, too."

Ally spun around. Sure enough, Mitchell stood in the kitchen doorway. "What are you doing up?" she asked.

"It's after seven. I always get up by seven."

"But it's still dark out!" She couldn't believe that her escape plan was already compromised. She also couldn't believe that he had on dress slacks, a dress shirt, a tie, and his same ugly sport coat. Surely he knew that it looked ridiculous in general, and especially ridiculous in Porcupine, Alaska.

He shrugged. "Doesn't matter if it's dark or light. As you pointed out, I'm a creature of habit. I like routine." He glanced at her backpack. "Going somewhere?"

Chapter Ten

The minute he'd heard Ally's alarm coming through the bug under her bed, Mitch was wide awake. It felt as if he'd been asleep all of two hours, and no light shone through the ice and snow coating his window, but apparently Ally was getting up. And that meant he was, too, dammit. He'd just started to feel warm.

He hit the button that lit up the dial on his watch. Seven already. She might be trying to sneak out of the lodge without him, and he couldn't allow that to happen. He shoved back the covers. Pulled them up again, shivering. God.

Okay, so his room was colder than a meat locker. Jaw clenched to keep his teeth from chattering, he climbed out of bed and grabbed his wrinkled dork clothes— slacks, shirt, tie, and jacket. Ugly though they were, he couldn't get them on fast enough.

Damn, it was cold. He'd promised himself as a kid in

Chicago that he'd never live in snow country again. Yet here he was, his nuts drawn up tight against the arctic air as he tried to get his pants on before his penis froze up and dropped off.

He needed other clothes. Warmer clothes. He needed long underwear, thermal-lined sweats, and heavy-duty sweaters. Hell, he needed his leather biker jacket and chaps. This dopey outfit he was wearing didn't work in Alaska. He'd suspected that, but he hadn't dared modify it and tip off Ally that he was someone other than who she'd thought.

So down the stairs he went, feeling the cold air climbing his pants legs while he listened to the conversation in the kitchen to make sure Ally hadn't left yet. She hadn't. Furthermore, Clyde was still in residence, and he and Betsy were to the sickening pet-name stage. Mitch braced himself and walked to the kitchen doorway.

Big surprise, Ally wasn't glad to see him. And she definitely had plans for the day because she had her backpack with her. On the one hand, he wanted them all to be snowed in so she couldn't take off on a shooting expedition, which would mean he'd have to go with her. On the other, he'd love to have a tropical heat wave that would melt all that godawful white stuff by noon.

"Nobody's going anywhere until we do some shoveling," Betsy said. "Open the front door, there'll be a wall of snow to meet you. Open the back door and step out, and you'll sink crotch-deep in drifts. Right, Poopsie?"

Mitch winced, both at hearing Clyde's nickname tumbling from Betsy's mouth and remembering how much he hated to shovel snow. Besides, no way was he going to aid and abet Ally's plan to leave the lodge.

"That's right, Kitty-cat," Clyde said. "I pried the front door open this morning when I went out in the hall to pick up the loose change I dropped last night. And there's nothing there but solid white. We'll have to go out the back way and tunnel in."

"Or not," Mitch said hopefully. He chose to ignore Clyde's reference to loose change on the hall floor, because he didn't want to think about how Clyde had spilled his money from his pockets. "I'll bet you have a chess set around here somewhere, or wait! I have cards. There's an idea! The four of us could play some poker. The snow will melt sometime, right?"

Ally glared at him. "I'd rather shovel."

"Somebody has to shovel," Betsy said. "Poopsie has to get back to the Top Hat in time to open up at ten. I have to run over to Heavenly Provisions and pick up eggs and condoms."

Clyde coughed and got red in the face. "Kitty-cat, I thought you said we didn't need to worry about that."

"Oh, not for us! I'm way past the need for them, and with you not having anything but solo sex for years, we certainly don't have to worry about disease. I'm talking about these two."

"Save your money, Betsy," Ally said. "Mitchell admitted last night that his interest in me is strictly business. He's afraid that if something happens to me, he'll have a lot of extra paperwork to do, and he would hate that. Right, Mitchell?"

Last night that assessment had seemed useful. This

morning he was uncomfortable with such a sleazy concept, especially since Betsy and Clyde were looking at him as if they'd like to feed him to the nearest grizzly bear. "That's not quite the whole story," he said.

Betsy snorted. "Didn't think so. I'd pegged you for a better man than that. I'll stock up on those condoms."

Mitch couldn't have her buying supplies they didn't need, though. "That won't be necessary," he said.

"You brought your own?"

"Uh, no, but Ally and I won't be . . . that is, we're not—"

"What he means is," Ally said, "that I would sooner bed down with a musk ox than sleep with Mitchell."

Clyde shook his head. "Lovers' spat. Happens all the time when you're itching to do the deed but holding off because you're not sure it's the right idea. Isn't that so, Kitty-cat?"

"Yep. You heard how Clyde and me argued over at the Top Hat last night. We'd been doing that on a regular basis, until we finally figured out that we wanted to get in each other's pants."

"That's, um, not our situation," Mitch said.

"You just said a mouthful," Ally agreed darkly.

Betsy clapped her hands together. "Listen to you two! You have it bad. But you'll have to postpone your fighting and making up while we get ourselves fed and then dug out of this snow. Sit down and I'll bring you both coffee."

Mitch took a seat, and Ally chose the one across the table from him.

"Here you go!" She set an Alaska-sized mug in front of both of them. "And I see Poopsie needs a refill."

"I'll take anything you got, Betsy." Clyde reached around and pinched her on the butt, and she reacted by laughing and slapping his hand.

Mitch glanced across the table at Ally, to see if she'd meet his gaze and indicate that a tiny bit of last night's bonding experience was left in her. Nope. She looked at a point just beyond his right shoulder, as if bonding with him was the single thing she planned to avoid forever.

Figuring that now was as good a time as any to confess his sins to Betsy, Mitch cleared his throat. "Uh, Betsy, there's something I need to let you know. About the bathroom door opening off my bedroom."

Betsy laid several strips of bacon in an iron skillet. "It sticks, right? I should have warned you about that. I need to get up there and plane off about a quarter inch below the lock and it'll be fine."

"Well, that's not the problem." Mitch cast another look at Ally, but she'd abandoned him. "See, it was locked, and Ally was in the shower, and I heard her squeal. Turns out it was the water going cold, but I didn't realize that, so I—" Sitting here at the breakfast table, he couldn't believe he'd done such a stupid-ass thing. And all to save Ally from a cold shower.

"Jimmied the lock, I suppose." Clyde nodded in understanding. "Wanted to check on her to see if it was a mouse or something. I would have done the same, son. I can help Betsy with that lock if it doesn't work right, now."

"The lock's no big deal," Betsy said as she began to beat a bowl of eggs with a wire whisk. "Now the door itself, I couldn't replace that. It's a hundred years old, at least. But locks are no problem. Don't worry about it, Mitchell. You have bigger fish to fry, if you get my meaning."

"The door's . . . uh . . . how old?" Mitch wondered how much snow he'd have to shovel to make up for this.

"At least a hundred years."

"The frame, too?"

"The whole shootin' match is that old. Frames and doors. That particular one sticks a mite, but the rest are perfect. I'm real proud of those doors. No warping, no cracking, nothing. As good as the day they were made. People knew craftsmanship back in those days."

"Well, the door may not be *quite* as good as the day it was made." Mitch felt completely miserable. "Not anymore."

Holding the bowl of whipped eggs against her hip, Betsy turned toward the table. "What's wrong with the door?"

"I sort of . . . broke it down."

"Whoa, Nellie!" Clyde's eyes widened.

Betsy's jaw dropped. Then she put the bowl back on the counter and turned off the flame under the bacon. "Guess I'd better see about this."

"I'll go with you, Kitty-cat." Clyde pushed back from his chair.

"I'll come, too." Mitch thought he should be there for the first viewing. Maybe it wasn't as bad as he thought.

"Me, too." Ally stood.

"That's okay, Ally." Mitch figured she was enjoying watching him twist in the wind. She probably wanted to witness the scene when Betsy laid into him. "Stay and enjoy your coffee."

She met his gaze and shrugged. "I'm partly to blame. I'm the one who squealed." Instead of mockery, there was sympathy in her eyes.

He was surprised, but he'd take whatever help he could get. "It's not your fault, but if you want to come up with us, that's fine."

"I think I should."

"Thanks." Appreciative for the show of support, he gestured for her to go ahead of·him out the kitchen door. "A hundred years old," he murmured to her as they climbed the stairs behind Betsy and Clyde. "Man, I hated to hear that."

"I know. I was hoping she'd picked it up at Home Depot."

"Yeah."

"Some places can make really good reproductions," she said.

"They can?" He valued her encouragement more than she could know. He hated damaging something in his care. Although he hadn't realized he was dealing with a one-hundred-year-old door, it had been temporarily under his care. And he'd busted it.

Betsy used a key she pulled out of her pocket to unlock his room. Then she turned on a light and stood there silently staring at the door propped against the splintered frame. Mitch hadn't realized until now that the door itself had a sizable crack in it. A good kick and it would split in two.

Turning toward Mitch, Betsy looked him up and down. "There's more to you than meets the eye, isn't there?"

He coughed and pushed his glasses more firmly on his nose, typical nerdlike behavior. Maybe then he wouldn't look quite so much like a black belt who could do serious damage with his feet. "Adrenaline. Makes people stronger for a few seconds."

Betsy didn't look convinced.

"Kitty-cat, I think we can save it."

Walking over to the door, Betsy ran a loving hand over the wood. "We can sure try. But in the meantime, you don't have much privacy, Mitchell."

"Doesn't matter. And I'll pay for the damages. Whatever you think is fair, considering the value, and the work you'll have to put in."

She ran a finger down the crack. "How are you at shoveling snow?"

"Decent."

Ally glanced at him. "How can you be good at shoveling snow? You live in Southern California."

"But I spent the first twenty-two years of my life in Chicago."

"Really? I didn't know that."

Betsy turned back to them, her expression resolute. "Okay, Chicago boy, I couldn't come up with an amount to charge you for the door, or the labor, for that matter. We tend to work a lot on the barter system here in Porcupine, so I'm putting you on snow shoveling detail."

He accepted his punishment, knowing this wasn't the kind of thing that an influx of money could fix. "Okay."

"I'll help you," Ally said.

"You don't have to," he said immediately.

"Yes I do. I feel partly responsible for this."

"Let her help. She was the one who squealed when she got hit with a little cold water." Betsy crossed her arms under her breasts. "But I would love to know something. What happened after you broke the door down?"

Mitch and Ally spoke in unison. "Nothing!"

Betsy studied the two of them like a parent who wasn't

about to swallow the story. "You break the door down like some hero in a B movie, and she's in there naked, and *nothing* happened? What's wrong with you two?"

"It's the younger generation, Kitty-cat," Clyde said. "They see it all the time on TV—bashing down doors, naked women right out of the shower, you name it. They don't get excited about things like we do."

Mitch wasn't about to correct that impression. Let all three of them think he'd been totally cool when confronted with Ally and a skimpy towel.

"And the second thing," Betsy continued. "I get up this morning to find a package of sliced caribou, a loaf of bread, cheese, and the blackberry pie missing."

"Caribou," Mitch muttered. "So that's what it was."

"That wasn't just any caribou, either," Clyde said. "That was a town institution. See, we had this caribou in Porcupine who had the habit of going around peering in people's—"

"We ate the Peeping Caribou?" Ally cried out, her expression horrified. "Eeuuww!"

"You have to admit he's delicious, though," Betsy said.

Ally clutched her stomach. "If I'd known, I never would have had any. The way you described him, I thought of him as a town character, with a personality."

"I thought so, too," Clyde said. "But some folks got sick of him putting his nose in everywhere, and finally Ziggy Berluski shot him. We divided him up."

Ally looked a little green, and Mitch's stomach didn't feel all that wonderful, either. From now on he was asking a lot of questions before he put anything in his mouth.

"We're getting off the subject," Betsy said. "I want to know how it can be that two people insist they have no intention of doing the wild thing, but one has already seen the other pretty much naked, and besides that, they obviously raided the refrigerator together, too. Now that takes some cooperative effort."

"We liked each other better then," Ally said.

"I don't dislike you, Ally."

She turned to him, her gaze hard. "No, but I'm just one of your projects, one you want to run smoothly."

"No you're not. I—"

"Enough!" Betsy raised both hands. "We're going back downstairs, because I can smell the biscuits and they're done. And I don't want to hear any more arguments from you two during breakfast. It disturbs the digestion." She started out of the room and Clyde followed.

"She knows what she's talking about," Clyde said over his shoulder.

"Damn straight I do," Betsy said as she clomped down the stairs. "And after checking out that door, I know something else for sure."

"What's that, Kitty-cat?"

"I definitely need to lay in a good supply of condoms."

After a breakfast that included bacon from a pig nobody had named or even knew very well, Ally was ready to tackle the snow-shoveling. So was Mitchell, after Betsy informed him that he would freeze his privates if he went out there dressed like that. Betsy had some outfits stored in the lodge's attic, items of clothing her various husbands had left behind.

Consequently Mitchell appeared for shoveling duty looking more studly than Ally thought was possible. He wore ski pants that hugged his butt, making her aware of that part of his anatomy, which she hadn't been until now. Nice. Buns to brag about. Who knew?

The borrowed flannel shirt in muted browns and greens complemented his dark hair and brown eyes. And Ally could really appreciate his eyes, because he'd tucked his glasses in his shirt pocket after saying that he really didn't have to see that well to shovel snow.

On top of Mitchell's new and improved outfit, he wore a tan parka with a hood instead of the orange monstrosity he'd arrived in. Ally wondered if Betsy deliberately had chosen clothes for Mitchell as a way to improve his look and his chances with Ally. Betsy seemed to have the matchmaker gene.

But she had an uphill climb if she hoped to get Mitchell and Ally together. Betsy could dress him up any way she wanted, but he would still be the overprotective anal guy who wanted Ally to make his life easier by never doing anything risky. She didn't intend to make his life easier.

While Clyde took a shower in Betsy's bathroom, Betsy addressed her two shoveling recruits in the kitchen. "The back porch is never as bad as the front, on account of we have trees to block the wind and snow." She handed Mitchell a small shovel.

Mitchell looked doubtful as he took the shovel. "This is it?"

"This is the shovel I keep in the pantry to shovel my way over to the storage shed on the far side of the porch. In there you'll find a couple of real shovels."

"And a snowblower?" Mitch asked hopefully.

Betsy laughed. "Oh, you'll find one, but you won't be able to use it. The blower's for the little storms, like what you get in Chicago, I expect. Once you get the shovels, your best bet is to see if you can walk on top of the snow down the alleyway around to the front, where you'll start tunneling in. But be careful. The snow can cave in on you."

"Wow." Ally found herself looking forward to snow like that.

"Couldn't we use snowshoes?" Mitch asked.

"Sorry. I checked my supply a week ago and a mouse has been chewing on the webbing. I got the mouse, but haven't replaced the snowshoes. Besides, I think trying to shovel in snowshoes is awkward."

Ally glanced at Mitch. "See, it could have been a mouse in the bathroom."

"You don't seem spooked about it." Mitch sounded slightly impressed by that.

"I wouldn't have been spooked. I have an affinity for all kinds of animals. I would have tried to take its picture."

"Not me," Betsy said. "I would have tried to kill its ass."

"But you don't cook them, right?" Mitch asked.

Betsy regarded him with disdain. "What do you think we are, uncivilized?" Her eyes sparkled. "We eat 'em raw, like oysters." Then she laughed so hard she had to lean over and clutch the kitchen counter for support. "You should see your face, Mitchell. You believed me."

Ally didn't want to admit she'd believed Betsy, too. She decided a change of subject was in order. "What about the main street, the one that runs in and out of town? Does some state agency plow that for you?"

"A snow like this, they're busy with the main drag, and they don't get around to us for days. So we have Ernie do it. He's the only guy in town with a tractor, and he plows when he feels like it."

Ally really wanted that road open, to give Mitchell a way out and Uncle Kurt a way in. "Do you suppose he's feeling like it today?"

"Don't think so. Saw him tossing back quite a few at the Top Hat last night. Everybody talks about taking up a collection to buy a plow for the town, one any of us could drive if necessary, but then Ernie goes on the wagon and swears he'll plow all the time, and we forget about it."

"So he's off the wagon," Mitchell said.

"I'm afraid so. See, Ernie inherited that tractor from his daddy, who used to plow all the time for the town. But Ernie's a throwback, doesn't really believe in motorized transportation. He thinks we should all travel by dogsled, like he does. Control freak, if you ask me."

"Hm." Ally eyed Mitchell, who was another one.

He lifted his eyebrows. "What?"

"I can see that you're happy there won't be traffic in or out of town today, that's all. If I didn't know you were here last night, I'd think you'd been over at the Top Hat buying rounds for Ernie."

"Ernie buys his own rounds," Betsy said. "Got a big court settlement from the state of Alaska when a bush pilot on state business crash-landed on Ernie's property, knocking over the outhouse. See, Ernie doesn't believe in indoor plumbing, either."

Mitchell stared at her. "He got big money for an out-house?"

"He was in it at the time. Claimed all sorts of injuries, including the fact that he now has fear of elimination, due to the trauma. Anyway, all this gossip isn't getting the snow shoveled. When you get to the front door, give us a little jingle-jangle on the doorbell so we know Clyde's got access to the street."

"But won't his front door be piled high with snow, too?" Mitchell asked.

"Dave will probably be out there clearing a path to the Top Hat. Feel free to help him out if you get finished and he's still working. Here in Porcupine we generally do for one another like that. Well, except Ernie, who marches to a different drummer. But even Ernie's been known to help out in a pinch. There's nobody in Porcupine who's all bad."

"Who's Dave?" Ally didn't remember anyone by that name working at the bar. Then again, in her condition she might have missed somebody, or half the town, for that matter.

"Oh, that's right. You didn't meet Dave. We were in a hurry to get you back here for your private meal." Betsy's eyes took on a gleam of anticipation. "If you don't run into him while you're shoveling, I'll make sure you meet him tonight. You'll want to get to know Dave."

Now Ally was curious. "Why?"

"Oh, honey, once you've laid eyes on the man, you won't ask why. He's the hottest thing to hit Porcupine in years. Does chain-saw sculpture by day, tends bar for Clyde by night. A chain-saw sculptor." Betsy sighed dramatically. "How's that for the perfect combination?

The soul of an artist and the tools of a manly man. *Rrrrrowww.*"

"So does he sell any of that chain-saw art?" Mitchell asked.

Ally rounded on him. "How typical of you to ask. In your book, nothing's worth doing if it doesn't make money. Maybe he does it for the joy of creating something beautiful."

"It's a reasonable question." But Mitchell's jaw was set at a belligerent angle. He was spoiling for another fight, and she was just the woman to give him one.

Chapter Eleven

"Okay, Viv, time to get into your photog duds." Kurt snapped his cell phone closed. "The snowplows are clearing the roads."

Vivian continued to flip through the elaborate coffee-table book she'd been studying as she sprawled on Kurt's white leather sofa. Books on wildlife photography lay scattered on the floor and two very expensive cameras sat on the table beside her.

Impersonating Alaska's reclusive wildlife photographer Tanya Mandell had been Vivian's idea after Kurt had told her Ally admired Tanya's work. Kurt had to admit the impersonation idea was brilliant. Tanya's photographs were famous throughout the world, but the artist herself stayed out of the limelight, a person no one would recognize on the street. Vivian had bought a bunch of Tanya's books, plus two very nice cameras, plus a wardrobe that fit the occasion.

As Tanya Mandell, Vivian would be able to talk Ally out of huge chunks of money. At least that was Plan A. Kurt didn't want to think about Plan B, although Vivian had forced him to map it out, just in case. She'd insisted that he consider the fact that removing Ally from the picture would allow him to inherit everything.

Vivian had done her research and had reported to him that if Ally should happen to die, the trustees would have to give him all the money, because he'd be the only surviving relative. But Kurt didn't want anybody getting killed. He had every confidence in Plan A. Equipment, lessons, even a joint publishing project could have Ally writing checks like crazy, all to a special account Kurt had set up for this purpose.

"Did you hear me, Viv?" he asked a second time. "Let's pack up and go. We can leave for Porcupine."

She didn't look up. "I heard you." She untied the sash of her black silk robe and let the lapels hang open. As she continued to glance at the pictures, she carelessly fondled herself. "I'm not finished."

"You can read those on the way up there." He tried to ignore the way she flaunted her body. She knew it distracted him, which was why she did it, to keep him constantly off balance. "We need to get on the road."

"I didn't mean I wasn't finished reading." Her gaze locked with his as she settled into a more focused program, her burgundy-tipped finger moving steadily over her clit.

He started to get hard. "We don't have time for that."

"I do." She sighed and adjusted her position so that he could see her better.

"I don't." But he couldn't look away. "I'm going to get the suitcases."

Her voice sharpened. "Stay right where you are. I want you to watch."

"Viv, you know what that does to me."

"Yes, I do." She smiled. "And it's painful, isn't it?"

"It is when you won't let me finish."

"Good, because that's how it will be this time. You were ordering me around just now, and you know how I hate that."

Kurt groaned. "I didn't mean to order you around. I just want to get going."

"When I'm ready, we'll leave for this backwater place called Porcupine. I'm not ready yet. Now unzip your pants and show me what's happening with your little swizzle stick. I want to make sure you maintain your self-control, like a good boy."

His heart drummed faster as he fought not to get aroused. But humiliation always aroused him. "Viv, no. Please."

Her eyes narrowed and her breath hissed out. "Do it!"

He unzipped his pants, reached in and pulled out his dick, which was stiff as a walrus tusk. He knew better than to disobey her when she got like this. She was right—he'd been too demanding, and now he had to pay for it. If he didn't pay now, it would cost him more later.

"Now don't you dare look away," she said. Her eyes were like lasers, making sure that he stood perfectly still while she made herself come. She deliberately took her time about it, drawing out the moment and putting him through exquisite torture.

Watching her busy fingers as he'd been told, listening to her moan and gasp, he clenched his whole body against the urge to erupt. He'd developed amazing control, and yet every time she put him through this, he was sure he'd never make it.

At last, with a throaty groan, she shivered and was still. Then, with a sly smile, she raised her hand to her mouth and began to lick her fingers. "I should do it again," she said. "Just because you've been such a bad boy."

He held his breath, ready to burst. If she went for round two . . .

"But I won't." She rose languidly from the sofa and walked toward him. Curling her forefinger under her thumb, she released it with a snap, flicking her nail against the head of his penis.

He bit the inside of his cheek and managed not to come.

"Very *good*, Kurt, baby. Now stand like that while I go change into that ugly photographer's outfit. God knows why this woman always dressed in khaki. It's so unattractive." She started out of the room, but then she turned, put her finger against her chin and looked him up and down. "You know what? This whole photography gig is giving me ideas."

"What do you mean?" He watched nervously as she wandered back to the table and picked up one of the cameras.

"Say cheese." She pushed a button and the camera flashed.

"Did you really take a picture?" He thought briefly of the blackmail possibilities, but she already had so much on him she wouldn't need a picture of him standing with his ding-dong hanging out to blackmail him. They'd been planning this caper for two years, ever since he'd hooked up with her at a Vegas S and M club and had mentioned that his wealthy stepmother had a brain tumor.

"Of course I took a picture." The telephoto eased out with a little whine and she pointed it right at his crotch. "Oh, my, we seem to have some shrinkage. Don't tell me you're camera shy."

"Don't do this."

She lifted her eyebrows. "Did you just give me another order?"

"No. Not an order," he said quickly. "A suggestion. Only a suggestion."

"I'm so glad it wasn't an order. Now get it up again for mama, so I can take its little picture."

"I can't. Not when you have that camera pointed right at it."

"Sure you can. All you have to do is think about last night, and how you felt when I slapped those reins against your buns, and then how you enjoyed the fun you had later on, after you fetched that joystick in your teeth. Remember how much you liked what happened next, and how much you'd like that to happen again?"

He clenched his teeth.

"Ah, there we go. That's better. Much perkier. Now you're ready for your close-up." She clicked the shutter several more times.

At last she lowered the camera. "There. I've taken my first wildlife pictures." Then she walked into the bedroom, leaving him standing there with his own personal telephoto fully extended.

Mitch stepped out the back door onto crunchy white stuff that he'd hoped never to deal with again. As he proceeded to shovel a path to the shed where the giant shovels lived, he thought about the new danger posed by Dave, the chain-saw sculptor. Nothing like a starving artist to prompt a woman like Ally to empty her pockets, and her pockets held a considerable amount of moolah.

At least Kurt Jarrett and his fifth wheel would be delayed if the roads into Porcupine wouldn't be plowed in the near future. Good old Ernie could stay soused as far as Mitch was concerned. Given a choice, Mitch would rather tilt at his windmills one at a time.

"Mitchell, look!"

"What?" Mitch's head came up and he switched immediately into fight-or-flight mode as he glanced warily through the trees. Ally might promise that the grizzlies were taking a long winter's nap, but nature always had exceptions to the rule.

"There! Look at the mountains!"

His shoulders sagged in relief. She was pointing out scenery, not a thousand-pound combo of big claws and big teeth. He looked at the horizon, and sure enough, the landscape was one big postcard. The sky had cleared to faded-denim blue, and jagged peaks dressed all in white reminded him of the whipped meringue on a lemon pie.

"That takes my breath away," she said. "Well, that's obviously just an expression, since every time I talk, I can see my breath. I could probably blow smoke rings, there's so much breath to see."

He turned to glance in her direction as she tried to do exactly that and was ambushed by pink cheeks and smiling lips as she tried to puff out perfect little rings. Damned if she hadn't reverted from being a pain in the ass to someone he desperately wanted to kiss.

"Can't do it," she said. "But really, doesn't the view leave you speechless?"

"Not exactly." He had to remember that he wasn't supposed to see that well. "It's kinda fuzzy, but I guess it's pretty." He'd rather look at her any day.

"Maybe you should dig out your glasses so you can see it better. *Pretty* doesn't even come close."

No, it doesn't, he thought, completely absorbed in watching her. *Pretty* was a word for a girl in a nice dress, one with a measured smile and carefully styled hair. Ally had none of that going for her.

She wore a bulky parka that eliminated all curviness, a knit cap pulled down over her ears, and a grin that made her seem more alive than any woman he'd ever cared about. She wasn't pretty. She was gorgeous.

"You know, I came out here ready to have an argument with you about the value of art for art's sake, like Dave with his chain-saw sculpture." She continued to gaze at the mountains, which were beginning to glow pink where the sun touched them.

"I'm not against art." Every sentence was accompanied by little puffs of fog. It was far too cold out here. "But I think a guy like Dave, who's scraping along on tips from the Top Hat Bar, might think of you as a sugar mommy. I'd hate to see anyone take advant—"

"Stop right there." She held up a hand. "I said I came out here ready to argue, and you're tempting me, but I don't want to fight. Not in the face of that view. Even you have to admit that it makes our problems seem tiny."

He chose to ignore the *even you* part of her comment. After all, she was supposed to think of him that way, the kind of guy who deserved an *even you* now and then. "I know what you're saying, but I think you and I have a different perspective on snow."

She turned back to him. "You mean because you grew up in Chicago and I grew up in Bel Air?"

"Uh-huh." And he remembered too well the frozen eyelashes and numb fingers and toes. "I shoveled snow for my folks. I shoveled snow for my grandma who lived two blocks away. I shoveled snow to save money for—" He caught himself before saying *the police academy*.

"For school, right?" she said.

"Right. For school. Anyway, when I finally was in a position to choose where I would live, I came to Southern California and vowed I would never shovel another flake of snow or go out in weather where I could see my breath."

She looked him straight in the eye. "Mitchell."

"What, Ally?"

"Go home."

"Can't."

"Of course you can. I will be *fine*. I love this snow! And what could possibly happen to me?"

"A million things." Above them, the house seemed to creak and groan as it cast off the buildup of ice and snow. Surely she could see what an alien environment this was. She had to understand that guys would covet her money, even if they didn't know the full extent of her wealth. She obviously wasn't a pauper and many of the residents of Porcupine . . . well, they weren't exactly in league with the Kennedys.

Ally blew out a breath, creating even more vapor. "I'll survive the weather, no problem. And as for the men around here, you don't give me enough credit. I won't let myself be sweet-talked by a guy who's only after my money."

"You might!" Betsy called from the open window of Mitch's bedroom upstairs. "If he's hung like a horse!"

Mitch glanced up and realized part of the creaking and groaning had been Betsy opening a window to eavesdrop. Ally laughed at Betsy's remark, but Mitch didn't laugh. He was too busy wondering what the hell he'd do if Betsy was upstairs poking around in his stuff. He'd tucked both the recorder and his gun in his suitcase, so she'd have to really snoop to find them. He didn't think she would, but he wasn't willing to bet on it.

"You two are hereby awarded the booby prize for shoveling!" Betsy said. "In the time you've been out there yakking, Clyde and I have enjoyed a private moment, he's taken the busted door off the hinges to see if he can repair it, and I'm halfway through my morning chores!"

Ally waved a gloved hand. "We'll be done before you know it!"

Betsy snorted and closed the window.

"Where do you suppose they had their private moment?" Mitch cleared away the last of the snow from the front of the shed, unhooked the rusty hasp and yanked the door open.

"They wouldn't do it in your room . . . would they?"

"I dunno, but she said he was taking the hinges off the door, and she's up there making the bed. Clyde's a regular firecracker. I think it adds up to funny business." He reached in and found two super-sized snow shovels. "Here's your weapon."

She took the shovel. "I feel like we're chaperones at a college dorm."

"Me, too, but I try to look on the bright side." He started across the porch toward what might have been steps if the whole area hadn't been blanketed by snow. "If she's occupied with Clyde, she's not after me."

"And she would definitely be after somebody," Ally said. "Seven husbands and working on number eight. She's a force of nature. She's—"

"Hold it." Mitch held out his arm, stopping her from walking on what appeared to be level snow. "Betsy warned us to watch out for cave-ins. Better let me go first."

"No, I should go first. I'm lighter."

He looked at her. "I don't see the logic. If it supports me, then you're a shoo-in. If it supports you, I'm still an unknown quantity."

She shrugged. "So I want to be the test walker. This is a brand-new experience for me."

He was beginning to think nearly everything was a brand-new experience for her. After Madeline had lost her only son and beloved daughter-in-law when they died on a scuba-diving vacation, and her husband Clayton had keeled over three years later of a massive heart attack, Madeline had drawn a protective net around Ally, the only one left to love.

From reading Ally's file, Mitch knew that she'd never gone skiing, never tried surfing, and had never ridden on a motorcycle. Some kids would have rebelled and done those things anyway, but not Ally. Apparently she'd understood the agony she'd cause her grandmother, and she'd reined herself in.

Now Mitch had been assigned Madeline's role, and in some ways, he didn't much like it. "Go ahead." He gestured her toward the blanket of snow. "Test it out."

Ally supposed it wasn't much of a concession. A significant concession would have been Mitchell leaving Alaska to let her explore her options on her own. But that might be too much to ask of a worrywart like Mitchell. So she'd take this opportunity to walk on a crust of newfallen snow and find out whether she fell through.

Holding her shovel like a pole used by a tightrope walker, she started out, placing one foot gingerly in front of the other. Her boots crunched about an inch into the snow, but that was it. This test walk wasn't a huge deal, anyway. Even if she fell through, she guesstimated she'd only fall about six feet down, through soft snow.

Mitchell knew that, of course, which was why he'd let her have her way. If she'd told him she planned to spend the afternoon on the outskirts of town searching for signs of wolves, he'd probably pitch a fit and insist on tagging along. So that's why she didn't intend to tell him where she was going later on today.

"Okay," Mitchell called after her. "I'm going to follow you."

She turned back to watch him step out on the snow,

putting his boots down in her footsteps. "It should be doable. Think of it. When we're not here, Betsy's the one who has to walk around and dig through to the front door."

"Exactly." He moved more confidently now. "And it's only snow. I mean, even if it gives way, how bad can it—" He yelped as the snow crumpled like tissue paper under him. He threw his shovel off to one side before he completely disappeared.

"Mitchell!" Ally tossed down her shovel and ran back, no longer thinking of whether the snow would hold her or not. Naturally when she reached the edge of the hole he'd made, she crashed right through the crust and landed on top of him.

He groaned, and his voice was muffled. "Ally . . . move your boot. It's right on my . . ."

"Your what? Mitchell, is anything broken?"

"Not yet. Lift your leg. No, the other one."

She floundered around in the snow, trying to figure out which way he was facing. Snow was in her mouth and eyes. "Mitchell, hang on. I'll save you."

"Don't save me." He sounded desperate. "Just get off me."

"I'm trying!"

"Stop wiggling around!"

She cried out in surprise when his hand clamped onto her thigh. For a guy who pushed papers all day, he had an amazing amount of strength. With only that one grip on her thigh, he managed to flip her over on her back, where she sank down in the fluffy snow and decided to lie there for a minute and catch her breath.

"That's better." Next to her, Mitchell sat up and

brushed snow off his face. "Much more pressure from the heel of your boot and I'd have been singing soprano."

"I'm sorry." She gazed up at him. "I didn't mean to." The hood of his borrowed parka had been shoved back by the fall, and his hair and eyebrows were crusted with snow.

He grinned. "Are you quite sure about that?"

"Of course I'm sure! I might get irritated with you from time to time, but I wouldn't ever knowingly kick you in the balls! What kind of woman do you think I am?"

His grin gentled to a soft smile. "A snow woman." He leaned down and brushed at her eyebrows. "You look like one of those ads for a retirement community, where the people look about thirty, but they all have the PC white hair, by golly."

"So do you." And for some reason, her heart had started racing again. The excitement of the fall was over, so why was her pulse rate so high? Surely not because Mitchell was leaning over her, wiping the snow from her face.

And yet it was sort of silly, for him to be concerned about getting the snow off. They were lying in a snowy hole and would probably get covered all over again when they tried to work their way out. They'd have to dig out with their hands because neither of the shovels had made it into the hole with them.

She was enjoying this little interlude they were having, though. Mitchell's brown eyes glowed with a tenderness that she'd never seen before. Maybe he'd looked at her that way in the past, but if so, the light reflecting off his glasses had disguised his expression.

Nothing disguised his expression now, and she found herself growing really fond of it.

In fact, shock of shocks, she discovered herself thinking that he was almost handsome. No, not just *almost*. He was definitely handsome, especially with that certain glow in his eyes, a glow that seemed to be getting hotter by the minute.

A curl of desire started low in her belly and branched out until she began to tingle everywhere, especially in areas that she wouldn't normally associate with thoughts of Mitchell. She couldn't come up with any excuse for it. They weren't currently listening in on Betsy and Clyde, and they weren't eating sensuous globs of blackberry pie.

He leaned closer.

His mouth had never looked better to her than it did right now. She decided to take the guesswork out this episode. "Mitchell, are you going to kiss me?"

"Yes, Ally, I am. Any problem with that?"

"None whatsoever. I'm totally in the mood. Lay one on me."

Chapter Twelve

Many times in his life, Mitch had realized he was about to make a mistake and had barreled ahead, anyway. This was one of those times. He wanted to kiss Ally more than he wanted to follow the path of right living.

Her lips were so plump, so pink, so incredibly inviting. Her mouth was open just the tiniest bit. Mitch longed to find out if the tip of his tongue would fit right in that opening.

He was sexually educated enough to know that the urge to put his tongue in her mouth was related to the urge to put something else in a different opening belonging to Ally. He knew that once he kissed her, he was headed down a slippery slope. But he couldn't help himself.

So he made contact, putting his cold mouth against her cold mouth. She sighed, wrapped her arms around his neck, and opened her mouth a little more. His heart slammed into high gear. She was thinking along the same lines that he was. Bring it on.

Not about to let that kind of invitation float away unnoticed, he made a gentle foray with his tongue to see what kind of reception he might get. Ah, man, she threw open the door and pulled him right inside. Did he feel special!

His lips were no longer cold. Neither were hers. Warm lips, warm mouth, warm tongue—what a trio. He could hang around here all day. Kissing Ally was way more fun than he'd thought it would be, and that was saying something.

His only problem, and it seemed relatively minor, was that he was running short of breath. But then again, if he couldn't breathe, he might pass out, which would not be a good thing. This kiss was building into something pretty damned wonderful, and he needed a second wind so that he could dive in again.

Lifting his head, he gulped for air while clouds of vapor swirled around them.

"Don't stop," she moaned, and pulled him back down.

"Not going to." He picked up right where he left off. The kiss got wetter and sloppier and he started wanting something to do with his hands. At this stage in a kiss, a guy usually developed the urge to fondle, but Ally seemed to be covered in the equivalent of bubble wrap.

At the moment he reached for the zipper of her parka, an alarm sounded in his brain. It was as if his conscience had picked up a bullhorn. *Hands off the zipper. Back away from the zipper.*

Wrenching his mouth free, he sat up, and became

aware upon doing so that he was sporting a real dandy of an erection. Fortunately his parka covered the evidence.

What had he been thinking? He'd been ready to unzip her coat! And he probably wouldn't have stopped there, either. One zipper down, one sweater and a bra catch to go, and before long he'd have been in, touching the merchandise. And it was freezing outside. But down in this little cave of snow, it wasn't quite so cold, and the waves of body heat made unzipping her coat seem logical.

He still wanted to.

And obviously she was of the same mind. "You quit!" Her tone was accusing.

"One of us needed to exercise some restraint." That sounded sufficiently anal. He should get back in geek mode, and fast.

She gazed up at him, her chest heaving. "I suppose I could have guessed it would be you exercising restraint."

Although she'd hurled it like an insult, he took it as a compliment. "Thank you."

"Oh, well." She sat up. "I wasn't having all that much fun, anyway."

He didn't contradict her, didn't dare look at her for fear he'd grab her and start all over. "Yeah, me, neither."

"Ha. I could feel your woody all the way through the layers."

"Oh, yeah?" He gave her a quick glance. "I could feel your nipples getting hard. So there." It was a lie. He couldn't really feel her nipples through three inches of padding, but he would bet that if he *had* been able to feel them, they would have been as hard as acorns. And not just because it was cold outside.

"Mitchell."

Instead of meeting her gaze, which would lead to more kissing, he picked at a thread on the stitching of his gloves. "What?"

"This is embarrassing to admit, but . . . you did turn me on."

He nodded. "I thought so."

"I mean, talk about an unlikely source, but there you have it. You're excellent at this kissing business."

His penis strained against his pants, wanting out, wanting action. "You're not so bad, yourself."

"Let's do it some more."

Oh, God. "Ally." He still couldn't chance looking at her. The temptation was way too strong right now.

"What?"

"I thought you didn't want to have anything to do with me? I thought you wanted me to go back to L.A. and leave you alone?"

"Well, that's true."

Finally he turned to face her. "Then what in the hell are you doing, kissing me like . . . like you wanted to have sex with me?"

She blinked, as if surprised that he'd even ask the question. "Because it seems I do want to have sex with you! That doesn't mean I don't want you to go back to L.A. and leave me alone. People can want plain old sex, can't they?"

He didn't think there would be anything plain about it. "So you want to have sex?"

"Yes, but we're not going to. I mean, that would be like I was using you. I couldn't do that."

Oh, go ahead. "I guess not." He gazed at her as the

concept of her using him for sex settled into his brain and started fooling with his body parts, getting them even more excited.

She had scruples about using him, but what if he was willing to be used? She wasn't talking about a relationship, the kind that would make him look like an opportunistic, gold-digging four-flusher of a cad. She was talking about straightforward sex, a healthy exchange of goodies between two consenting adults.

Having sex with Ally would have several advantages besides the obvious one that it was more exciting than skydiving. She wasn't the sort of wild girl to have sex with more than one guy in a given period of time. So if Mitch was having sex with her, nobody else in Porcupine would get to.

In addition to that, having sex would mean they'd necessarily have to spend lots of time together. She'd have fewer opportunities to sneak out on him and get herself into trouble with wild animals or Kurt Jarrett. Mitch might not even need that bug under her bed.

He'd have to take it out of there if they actually had sex. She could get really ticked off if she ever found out he'd recorded whatever they did on that bed. However, he'd have more chances to drop the little transmitter into her backpack, which might prove very useful if she should happen to give him the slip.

"And I wouldn't use you in that way, Mitchell, but let's face it, you're the kind of guy who might be able to handle such an arrangement."

"Why's that?" He had some ideas. For one thing, he'd know going in that he couldn't expect more than this. False expectations were killers, but he wouldn't have any.

Still, he was curious as to why she thought he'd be perfect for uncommitted sex.

"It would work because you have such a methodical mind," she said. "You could view sex as a practical application of resources, an activity to be enjoyed while you're here and dropped when you leave."

She was painting a picture that he didn't quite agree with, but her image of him suited his purposes. She might say no now, but he didn't want to screw up a future opportunity by telling her that he wasn't quite that businesslike about sex.

"And there's another point in its favor," she said. "We're in the middle of nowhere."

"So it's not like the servants will talk."

"Nope, and we'd make Betsy really happy. But I still don't think I should take advantage of you like that."

"Wait a minute. Let's suppose you change your mind and decide to take advantage of me, after all. You wouldn't tell Betsy about it, would you?"

She smiled. "You've heard the acoustics at the Loose Moose. It would be impossible to keep it a secret."

"Um . . ." As much as he would love to have sex with Ally, the prospect of an audience listening from the first floor didn't appeal to him at all.

"Then again, maybe you don't make any noise." She looked him up and down. "I suppose that's possible, knowing you. But it's not only the moans and groans that would give us away. There's the rocking back and forth part. My bed squeaks."

"I know." Then he hurried to cover up his flub. "I mean, it squeaked when we sat on it eating sandwiches. A mattress on top of squeaky springs." When she nodded in agreement, he relaxed. But then, she'd never suspect him of installing listening devices under her bed.

"Well, it doesn't matter whether the beds squeak or not, because my conscience wouldn't let me use you for my own selfish purposes."

Letting her use him for her own selfish purposes was the best idea he'd heard in years. "You know what, Ally? I think maybe you should—" He stopped talking when he heard footsteps crunching in the snow.

"Is somebody down there?" called a deep male voice.

Because Mitch knew that the voice didn't belong to either Clyde or Rudy, and because Betsy had alerted them that Dave might be shoveling nearby, Mitch was sure it had to be the wondrous manly chain-saw sculptor. How lovely. Caught looking stupid by Dave, who managed to stay in touch with his softer side while still hanging on to his rugged, studly side. Mitch figured he'd hate the guy on sight.

"We fell through!" Ally called out. "And we lost our shovels in the process!"

"Blabbermouth," Mitch muttered. He would rather carve out an exit with his bare hands than have Dave the Magnificent know they were semi-stuck down here.

"I saw the shovels." From the flutter in his voice, the guy obviously was right on the verge of laughing. "I'm Dave, by the way, from over at the Top Hat."

"Thought so." Mitch ground a little bit of enamel off his back molars. "Just toss me a shovel," he said. "I'll dig us out." But the sound of a shovel blade biting into the snow told him there was no saving this situation. Dave was going to play hero.

That was confirmed with another cheery message. "Sit and relax. I'll have you out in no time."

That's good, because Ally and I were discussing whether or not we should have sex. Put that in your pipe and smoke it. How Mitch longed to set Dave straight. But if Ally was unwilling to use Mitch for selfish purposes, she wouldn't use Dave, either. If anybody was going to be used, Mitch intended for it to be him.

And he'd be damned if he'd sit there and let *Dave* dig them out all by his lonesome. "I'll dig from this side," he said. Then he got to his hands and knees and started scooping snow out of the way.

Ally thought it was cute the way Mitchell got all grumpy and competitive after Dave showed up. His Dudley Do-Right chin with the adorable cleft got all rigid and his mouth settled into a straight line. Digging away like that, he looked like a dog trying to bury a bone.

She'd be happy to help him, but there wasn't enough room, and besides, she thought he was being silly. Dave would make much faster progress with a shovel, and Mitchell was wearing himself out for nothing.

She understood how a guy like Mitchell would be threatened by a guy like Dave. Mitchell might be a terrific kisser, and Ally wasn't kidding about wanting to go to bed with him. There was amazing chemistry between them. Too bad she didn't believe in using someone for her own gratification.

And that's what it would have to be, because Mitchell was not a guy she'd ever get serious about. He was one-dimensional. He seemed to have no outside interests whatsoever. Work, work, work—specifically his job tending Grammy's estate—was his life.

"Betsy's going to wonder where in the world we've been," she said. "And why the front door's still blocked. She was eager to go shopping."

"At least she has Clyde to amuse her. And she doesn't need to go shopping in order to have tons of fun with Clyde."

Ally laughed. "Right."

"That reminds me." Mitchell kept digging, building a little ramp as he went. "About that item she planned to pick up, I—"

"You mean eggs?" She couldn't resist. She knew he didn't mean eggs.

"No, the other thing." He scooped snow in a steady rhythm.

She remembered his finger tapping ever so subtly on the table when they'd been watching Clyde's tap-dancing routine. Thinking about Mitchell's sense of rhythm got her hot and bothered again.

She wondered if he'd turn out to be as talented as she thought he might be. She didn't care if he moaned and groaned or not. She just wanted him to pay attention. From all that she knew of him, he seemed to be the kind of guy who would pay very close attention. He was into detail, after all. But she wasn't going to find out.

"So what about this other thing?" she asked.

"If you should change your mind, I wouldn't use Betsy's supply. I'd buy my own."

"Oh. Okay." She liked that kind of assertiveness. "But you don't need to bother. I won't change my mind."

"Just letting you know, in case you do. Maybe I should pick some up, anyway. To have on hand."

"Trust me, I respect you too much." Warm squiggles of desire shot through her system. It would be fun to test the sexual skills of Mitchell J. Carruthers, Jr. "I don't suppose you'll be telling Betsy that you're buying your own."

"No, I won't be telling Betsy. I'm just telling you. In case you change your mind."

"Okay, but it's a waste of money." She pictured him going to the store and picking out the item in question. "And you do realize this is a small town."

"I'm sure even small towns keep a supply in stock. Especially this small town, which seems to be focused on the subject."

"That wasn't why I mentioned it. I—" But she didn't get to explain that buying condoms at Porcupine's general store might be similar to putting up a billboard announcing *"Mitchell J. Carruthers, Jr., the new guy in town, is hoping to get lucky."*

She couldn't finish the sentence because Dave suddenly appeared, and Mitchell had to leap backward to keep from scraping his knuckles on the blade of Dave's shovel.

"And there you have it!" Dave smiled, flashing what looked like a perfect thirty-two, polished within an inch of their lives. "You can climb right out of there. The rest of the alleyway is safe. I tested it, poked a few holes in the crust with a section of rebar. You're good to go."

Dave's smile was dazzling, no doubt about it. Ally imagined little points of light sparkling from those very white teeth. Or maybe the teeth seemed whiter set against his neatly trimmed black beard and mustache. His eyes were such a startling shade of blue that she wondered if he wore tinted contacts.

He might, judging from the perfection of his beard. He'd thrown back the hood of his parka, as if disdaining the need for warmth, but it might have been to show off the luxurious hair he'd pulled back in a ponytail. Dave obviously took pains with his look.

To Mitchell's credit, he got to his feet and stuck out his hand. "Thanks, Dave. Appreciate it. I'm Mitchell Carruthers, by the way, and this is Ally Jarrett."

Ally stood, too, impressed with Mitchell's manners. But of course he would have good manners. Grammy wouldn't have hired a person lacking in manners.

"Glad to meet both of you." Dave stepped down into the hole and shook Mitchell's hand, but he made it quick. He took a lot more time shaking Ally's hand. "I heard about Betsy's new guests. So, Ally, I understand you're up here to take wildlife photos?"

"That's right."

"I don't know much about photography, but I'm a great guide. I know this area like the back of my hand, and I'm available during the day."

"Thanks for the offer." If Uncle Kurt didn't get here soon, she might need to take Dave up on it. She didn't want to waste time waiting for Ernie to sober up and start plowing.

"Anytime," Dave said. "And I'm not a photographer, but I have a fair eye for what would make a good shot. I don't know if Betsy mentioned that I do some sculpture." He said it with exactly the right touch of modesty.

"Betsy mentioned that. Chain-saw sculpture." Ally thought about the advance billing that Betsy had given Dave, and so far she could see why he'd make some women sigh with longing. Strangely enough, he had zero effect on her.

There was something a little too calculated in the way Dave came across, as if he'd put together a package designed to impress. She wondered if his chain-saw art was any good, or if it was part of his image.

"What kind of market is there for that type of sculpture?" Mitchell asked.

Dave shrugged. "I don't really worry about that. If someone likes what I do and wants to pay me for it, that's fine. If not, it doesn't matter. Doing art gives me pleasure. I don't feel the need to sell it."

Ally wondered if she'd been hanging around Mitchell for too long. An hour ago she'd argued this very point with him. She believed what she'd said, that artists should be free to create for their own pleasure. But with Dave, she sensed an agenda. She'd bet that chain-saw sculpture wasn't his creative outlet so much as his claim to being different and slightly superior.

"Well, thanks again for getting us out of here," Mitchell said. "We'd better head around to the front of the Loose Moose and get that door freed up."

"It's done."

"Done?" Ally stared at him.

"Yeah, no big deal. I finished at the Top Hat, and noticed the Loose Moose was still socked in, so I got Betsy all squared away. Then I rang the doorbell, to let her know, and she said you two might be stuck somewhere, so I came looking for you."

"Uh, then I guess we owe you a drink," Mitchell said. "Thanks for taking care of all that."

"Not a problem. If you stick around a while, you'll get the hang of things before you know it."

Ally glanced at Mitchell and noticed a muscle twitching in his jaw. If this were a cartoon instead of real life, steam would be coming out of his ears, too. He obviously didn't appreciate being patronized by the resident chain-saw sculptor.

She turned back to Dave, determined to be polite, even though she'd been looking forward to tunneling into the Loose Moose's front door with Mitchell. It would have been fun. "Yes, thank you very much, Dave. The drinks are definitely on us."

"Unfortunately, I don't drink."

"Oh."

"But maybe you'll give me a photography lesson sometime, Ally. I'm always up for learning new things." He winked at her.

"That would be fine, except I'm not good enough to be giving lessons," she said.

"Oh, I doubt that." He oozed gallantry.

"No, she's telling you the truth," Mitchell said.

"Hey!" She turned to him. "Since when have you seen my pictures?"

He looked like a little boy caught with his hand in the cookie jar. "Uh . . . okay, I haven't actually seen your pictures. I was going on what you said, that you still had a lot to learn."

"Which I do." She understood that he was grabbing any excuse to get rid of Dave, even if it meant trashing her photography skills, so she kind of forgave him.

"Anyway, Dave, I guess you'll have to accept our gratitude, because there doesn't seem to be anything else we can do for you."

"You could come out and take a look at my sculptures sometime." He directed that comment straight at Ally, not even bothering to include Mitchell in the laser beam of his gaze.

"Thanks," Mitchell said. "We'll certainly do that." He took a deep breath. "Well! If we're all done here, I'm in favor of heading back inside. How about you, Ally?"

"Sounds good."

"I'll lead the way." Dave climbed effortlessly out of the hole. Then he turned back and held out a hand to help Ally up the snow ramp he'd created.

To refuse his help would have seemed ungracious, and she'd been raised to be gracious. She put her hand in his. He was strong, she'd give him that. He had her up on top of the snow in no time. Then he gave her hand an extra squeeze before releasing it.

Next he held out his hand to Mitchell.

"Got it, thanks." Mitchell ignored Dave's outstretched hand and scrambled out by himself. "See you around, Dave. You coming, Ally?"

"Yep, sure am." So maybe Mitchell's manners only went so far. Ally hid a smile as Mitchell headed out.

"Ally, hang on a sec," Dave said.

She saw Mitchell hesitate. She didn't want to hang back and talk to Dave, but the guy had dug them out of a snowbank, after all. "What's up?" she said, and watched Mitchell's shoulders drop. Then he continued on.

He probably thought she was entranced by Dave,

when nothing could be further from the truth. Mitchell might be used to playing second fiddle to the likes of Dave. He had no way of knowing that wouldn't happen this time.

"You mentioned going inside to get warm." Dave came alongside her, his smile flashing brighter than the snow at their feet.

If he was going to make a pass, she didn't want to be caught standing still. She started walking. "That's the plan."

He fell into step beside her as they navigated the alleyway. Mitchell had reached the street and hopped down to the sidewalk Dave had recently shoveled. Ally moved faster, wanting to catch up. Dave was giving her the heebie-jeebies.

"I was thinking you might as well come on into the Top Hat." Dave lengthened his strides. "Clyde's over there getting ready for lunch, and I'm sure we could round up a cup of coffee or hot chocolate for you. I think he has some doughnuts, too."

"Thanks, but I have a few things I need to do." She watched Mitchell disappear around the front of the Loose Moose.

"Anything I can help with?"

"No, not really. But I appreciate the offer." She figured that if she gave him an inch, he'd take about twenty miles.

"All righty, then. If you're sure there's nothing I can do to make you feel more welcome in Porcupine." He sounded slightly baffled because she was resisting his manly charms.

"I feel very welcome."

"That's good. That's very good. So I guess I'll go visit Ernie and see if he'll let me use his plow. We won't even get mail delivery today if the road into town isn't cleared in the next couple of hours."

She got the message. Dave was off to do more good deeds and she was supposed to be mightily impressed. "Good luck with that. 'Bye, now." She hopped down to the sidewalk.

"See you at the Top Hat tonight!" Dave called after her.

She waved again, not willing to give him a definite answer on that. Dave was not her type. Neither was Mitch, really, so it was very unsettling that she wanted so desperately to get naked and jump him.

Chapter Thirteen

Mitch had never resented playing the nerd more than he did right now. He was already at a disadvantage against guys like Dave simply because Dave knew the territory and Mitch didn't. But add in Mitch's supposed geekiness, and he was completely outgunned.

Childish though it was, he wanted to put on his snug black T-shirt, his black leather jacket, his black chaps, and his motorcycle boots. Then he wanted to ride into town on his Harley as Mitch Carruthers, PI/bodyguard, and see how Chain-saw Dave liked *them* apples. But that wasn't happening, so his mood was not good as he walked in the front door of the Loose Moose.

Betsy was behind the registration counter getting money out of an antique cash register, most likely in preparation for her proposed shopping trip. She glanced up and grinned. "Fell through, did you?"

"Yeah, we both fell through, but Dave the wonder boy

got us out." Mitch unzipped the parka Betsy had loaned him. "This coat worked great, though. Thank you."

"Keep it. My closets are stuffed with all the clothes my husbands left behind. I wish they'd left some money in the pockets, too, but no such luck. That coat doesn't fit me and it would swim on Clyde, so you might as well have it."

Mitch hung the parka on one of the many hooks by the front door. "That's a generous offer, but I won't need a heavy coat like that once I leave here, so it would be a waste to give it to me." He sat down on the bench under the row of hooks and started taking off his boots.

"And how soon would you be thinking of heading out?"

He looked over at her. "That depends."

"On Ally?"

He blew out a breath, not wanting to take that line of questioning any further. "What do you know about this guy Dave?"

"Why, are you jealous?"

"Of course I'm not jealous. I just wondered if his overgrown Boy Scout act is for real."

Betsy smiled. "Yep, you're jealous. Is Ally with him right now?"

"I most certainly am not jealous, and yeah, she is. I'm asking about him only out of concern for Ally. I'd hate to have some operator like Dave take advantage of her, that's all."

"You think he's an operator?" Betsy gazed at Mitch with great interest.

"Don't you? I mean, the perfect beard, the tinted contacts, the ponytail, the whole chain-saw-artist thing he's got going on. I think he's looking to marry well."

Betsy laughed. "You could be right about that."

"So why did you give him such a glowing report when you mentioned him to Ally? What if that turned her into a sitting duck for this opportunist?"

Propping an elbow on the registration desk, Betsy rested her chin in her hand as she studied Mitchell. "You really like her a lot, don't you?"

"It's not a matter of liking her. I want to make sure she's okay."

"Oh, I think your feelings go way beyond making sure she's okay, but you're not admitting to anything, so I won't push. I got what I wanted out of my advertising campaign when you started worrying that he might be competition. I didn't want you getting complacent, and I can see that worked out beautifully."

He stared at her. *"What?"*

"Don't look so offended. You have to understand that the winters are long and boring around here. When you and Ally showed up, I decided to have a little fun messing with you."

"That's outrageous, Betsy. You can't play with people's emotions to keep from being bored!"

"Oh, please. It's for your own good."

"It's not—"

"And in case you haven't figured it out, I *am* outrageous. Alaska tends to attract eccentric people. And if you're not eccentric when you arrive, you get that way sooner or later."

"So you admit that you're trying to play Cupid for me and Ally?"

She shrugged. "Why not?"

He could think of several reasons having to do with Ally's fortune and his lack of a fortune, but he wasn't about to share all that with Betsy. "Because we're completely incompatible."

"I don't see that. And look at you. You're all upset because she might be interested in another man."

"Because he could take her to the cleaners!"

"Ah." Betsy flapped her hand in the air. "I wouldn't worry about Ally. She won't be sucked in by Dave's routine any more than you were."

"I'm not so sure. I—"

The front door opened, and Ally walked in. Alone. She looked happy to see him, which was a good sign. "Hi, Mitchell."

"Hi, Ally." He was ridiculously happy to see her. He was even more glad to see her without Dave.

She unzipped her parka, and he remembered how he'd almost done that for her back in the snow. Just looking at her taking off that coat made his mouth water. Too bad she respected him so damned much.

Ally hung up her coat beside his, and in the process of reaching for the hook, she came close to touching his cheek with her breast. She came close enough to give him the shakes. He could smell something flowery—it could be perfume, deodorant, powder, or Ally's own skin. He wanted to smell it some more, whatever it was. He wanted to bury his nose against her sweater and nuzzle around until he reached something interesting.

Then she turned and sat down next to him on the bench to take off her boots. "You know, Betsy, I'm not so sure about Dave."

Mitch hated to hear the guy's name coming out of her mouth, but the context in which she'd used it sounded promising. He breathed in more Scent-o-Ally and waited to find out what bothered her about good old Dave.

"What about him?" Betsy asked.

"He's kind of obvious, don't you think? It's like he's created this persona for himself because he thinks that will get him somewhere."

Yeah, like in your bed. But Mitch was delighted to hear that she hadn't been swept off her feet by that toothy grin and fake blue eyes. The guy probably had caps on those teeth.

"Well, we all want to get somewhere," Betsy said.

"I know." Ally tucked her boots under the bench and stood. "I want to get somewhere in wildlife photography. But I'm not invested in trying to look like a photographer, just so you'll think I'm the real deal."

Mitch was exceedingly happy to hear that her evaluation of Dave was the same as his.

"Well, poor Dave." Betsy shook her head sadly. "He's one of those guys who can't figure out what to be when he grows up. Before he moved to Porcupine to wait tables and sculpt with a chain-saw, he tried to kick-start a franchise selling mooseburgers. He called it McMoose's."

"Let me guess," Ally said. "It didn't work."

"Nope. He put up one restaurant down in Anchorage, shaped it like an igloo, and dressed his help in fake fur, which was miserable in the summer, when most of the tourists show up. It didn't catch on."

Mitch figured he was safe to ask a question. "Are his sculptures any good?"

Betsy hesitated. "I'm no judge of art."

"But you know what you like," Mitch prompted, remembering her red room.

"Yes, I do know that, and generally I like my nudes to look a little more real. Maybe he's trying for something symbolic, but when the boobs don't match, I—"

"Wait a minute," Ally said. "I assumed this chain-saw art was stuff like bears and eagles, maybe even a totem pole or two. Are you saying his sculptures are nudes?"

"Uh-huh."

"Male and female?" Ally asked.

"He tried to do both at first, but he kept accidentally looping off a significant body part on the guys, so he gave that up and just does women now. Supposedly the model is Serena, who runs the general store. But I'm pretty sure Serena's boobs match. In summer she goes braless, and so I'd be able to tell if they didn't."

Mitch glanced at Ally. "No wonder he wanted you to come over to his place and look at his sculptures."

"You don't have to go out to his place to see them," Betsy said. "Serena has several for sale at Heavenly Provisions." She came around from behind the registration desk. "I'm heading over there, if either of you want to come with me."

"I'm curious, now," Ally said. "I'll go. But first I want to get my backpack."

"Yeah, I'll go, too." Mitch figured sometime during the shopping expedition he might be able to slip the tiny transmitter into her backpack. He also had an errand to run over at the store. He'd hate being caught unprepared if Ally had a change of heart. Maybe this was the perfect opportunity to stock up.

He could be subtle when it was required. While Ally and Betsy were looking at the chain-saw nudes, he'd have a chance to pick up the item he needed, just in case

Ally lost a little bit of respect for him and climbed into his bed.

A few minutes later the three of them trudged up and over two-foot drifts to get to the store across the street. No traffic moved along the main drag. The pickups and SUVs that had been parked there the night before were shapeless lumps under a blanket of snow. A few people were out navigating the drifts just like Mitch, Ally, and Betsy.

Mitch had put his glasses on again because he had no excuse not to wear them. They were going to the store, after all, and he was supposed to need them to see details. But they felt uncomfortably cold sitting on the bridge of his nose.

The road was seriously blocked. When he glanced toward the end of town, where no buildings stopped the wind, the drifts were even higher. The country road that linked Porcupine with the main highway was obviously impassable. He'd love for it to stay that way a while. The more familiar he became with the town, the more easily he could protect Ally if the need should arise.

"It sure is quiet without any cars or trucks going by," Ally said. "I like it."

"I do, too," Betsy said. "Once Ernie sobers up, he'll probably be out here on his dogsled. 'Course, he's been known to be out here on his dogsled when he wasn't sober, too."

"Assuming he's sober, I'd love to hitch a ride," Ally said. "I've always wanted to try that."

"It's fun," Betsy said. "My third husband had a team of dogs, even raced the Iditarod. But he kenneled those animals out behind the Loose Moose, which wouldn't have been so bad except that he wouldn't clean up the dog poop. In the winter it froze, so you couldn't smell it, but in the summer, Stink City. He was good in bed, but not that good."

Mitch kept quiet. He had no interest in riding on a dogsled, because a dogsled required snow, and he was no more in love with it now than he had been as a kid in Chicago. Sure, the mountains were pretty, and there was a certain peaceful feeling that came after a new-fallen snow, but the temperature was still below freezing, and that was about fifty degrees too cold for Mitch.

The snow's only saving grace was its apparent ability to delay Kurt.

Then the sound of a tractor motor ripped through the silence.

"I guess Dave must have convinced Ernie to let him use his plow," Ally said, as a rusty orange tractor appeared on the far end of town and started scooping drifts out of the way. "That's great."

"Yeah, just great," Mitch said. As of this moment, the snow had zero value.

Nothing like a new vehicle to make a man feel great. Kurt breathed in the new-car smell that permeated the cab of the truck. He'd picked one with all the bells and whistles, too—onboard GPS, top-of-the-line CD player, power windows and steering, leather upholstery. Vivian was partial to leather, so he'd chosen that specifically to please her.

Kurt was proud of the RV option he'd chosen, too. He loved how a fifth-wheel trailer hitch bolted right into the bed of his new truck. He'd never trusted those flimsy hitches attached to the back bumper. With those, the slightest wind could blow the trailer around, but the fifth wheel felt good and solid gliding along behind them.

"How do you like the new truck, Viv?" He glanced over to see how she was enjoying the ride.

"I think I forgot my vibrator."

"Oh." He hoped to hell she wouldn't make him go back. They were almost to the turnoff for Porcupine. If they had to reverse direction and go home again, they wouldn't make it back here until after dark.

"Pull over and go look in my suitcase."

He eyed the shoulder of the road, which was filled with snow and slush. "This isn't the best place to pull off, Viv. Let's wait until we get there."

"Pull off right now, Kurt! If we wait until we get there, and I don't have it, then what am I going to do? I'll be stuck in some stupid lodge by myself, and I seriously doubt that this podunk town we're heading for has an adult toy store."

Most of the time Kurt was glad that Vivian was so highly sexed. But not right now, when it was screwing with his plans. His instincts had been right, buying this fifth wheel so he wouldn't be staying at the hotel with Vivian. She would have tried to sneak into his room, for sure. "Couldn't you make do without your vibrator, just this once?"

She unbuckled her seat belt, reached over and grabbed him by the balls. "Pull over."

He swerved the truck to the shoulder and the fifth wheel fishtailed. Brakes screeched and horns blared, but

Kurt was too worried about the grip Vivian had on his jewels to care if anybody clipped the fifth wheel, or vice versa. When they were pretty much off the road, he slammed on the brakes.

"That's better." With one sharp squeeze that made him yelp, she turned him loose. "Now get back there and look for it. And if it's in the suitcase, bring it to me. If it's not, we're turning around."

Praying he'd find the vibrator, Kurt opened his door. He didn't have much room to climb out without danger of getting hit by oncoming traffic, so he took it slow.

"Come on, come on. You're letting cold air in here!"

Gauging the space between oncoming vehicles, he leaped out and slammed the door. He landed in about six inches of gray slush. Cold water soaked his pants leg and worked its way inside his shoes. He hated to drive in boots and hadn't expected to get out until he was on dry ground again.

But that wasn't the worst part. As he was standing there, a semi blew past and coated him from head to toe in muck. He wiped his face and brushed off what he could as he worked his way around to the back of the fifth wheel. He'd mess up the brand-new carpet by tromping inside like this, but it couldn't be helped.

Once he made it inside, he headed straight for Vivian's black leather suitcase, not wanting to stain the carpet any more than necessary. He loved the inside of this fifth wheel, which had been, until now, blemish-free. With the money he planned to weasel out of Ally, he could buy new things all the time. Buying new things gave him almost as much of a charge as sex with Vivian.

He zipped open the suitcase and searched for the

vibrator. He found her ben wa balls and her nipple clips tucked in with her crotchless panties. Just handling that stuff got him hot, but he had to forget about sex and find the vibrator. Not here, dammit.

Then he remembered a zippered pouch on the outside of the suitcase. Ah, thank God. He pulled out the vibrator, a specialty job with one part that went inside and a second part that buzzed against her clit. The whole business was a startling neon green.

Now all he had to worry about was battery life. He switched it on and everything worked. The hum of it plus the tremors moving through his hand brought back fond memories, but he had places to go and people to see. He turned it off again.

Clutching the vibrator, he stepped back down to the slushy shoulder of the road just as a cop pulled in behind him. He quickly stuck his hand behind his back. It wasn't like this toy was illegal, but he'd rather not be confronting an officer of the law while holding a neon-green, two-part vibrator.

The officer stepped out, and damned if it wasn't a woman. He would much rather deal with a guy if he had to be caught with a vibrator. Cops always made him sweat, though. Although he'd never done jail time, he'd come too close for comfort.

Today, though, he couldn't think why they'd hassle him. The truck and fifth wheel were his, or at least as long as he kept up the payments. He had no outstanding tickets that he could remember. And he definitely hadn't been speeding, considering the weather and the fifth wheel he was pulling.

The officer approached warily. Although she was

bundled up, there was no doubt she was a woman—a short, stocky, jock type of woman. She rested her right hand on the butt of the gun at her hip. "Sir, I need you to bring both hands out where I can see them," she said.

Reluctantly, he produced the vibrator.

The officer's eyes widened. "What the hell is that, some kind of newfangled club for the steering wheel?"

"It's . . . a . . . a . . . personal product, Officer."

After studying it for a few seconds, she nodded. "Okay, I get it. Never seen one shaped quite like that, and definitely not in lime green."

"It was a special order."

"Uh-*huh*." She glanced up toward the truck. "You have a passenger in there?"

"Yes, yes, I do."

She cleared her throat. "I recommend that you and your passenger not make use of that device while the vehicle is moving. Cell phones are enough of a distraction these days, without adding in . . ." She gestured toward the vibrator. "That."

"Right. I was only . . . she wanted to make sure we hadn't left it at home."

"I see." She pressed her lips together real tight, as if she might start laughing if she didn't.

A trucker went by and leaned on the horn. Kurt figured the trucker had recognized the item in his hand and was getting a kick out of letting him know that. Then another car beeped, and Kurt realized that plenty of other people would recognize what he was holding, even if the officer hadn't known right away what it was.

He was really tired of standing there on the open road gripping this neon-green vibrator, to be honest. "Was there a problem, Officer?" he asked, hoping to get the whole episode over with.

"I stopped because of the way you're parked, sort of jackknifed onto the shoulder. It appeared as if you'd pulled off the road in a hurry. I thought you might be in trouble."

"Nope, no trouble."

Her lips twitched. "Just an urgent need to make sure you were packing your personal product?"

"Exactly."

"Let me give you some free advice. In the future, it'll be a whole lot better if you don't put your hand behind your back when approached by a police officer. We tend to get nervous when you do that."

He couldn't imagine a repeat of this situation in a million years, but he nodded, as if taking her comment to heart. "I understand. Am I free to go now?"

"Just be careful pulling back into traffic, and make sure that fifth wheel doesn't end up in the ditch. We have vehicles stuck all up and down this road today. I'd hate for you to be one of them."

"Thank you, Officer." Tucking the vibrator under his arm, he made his way back to the cab and tried to get as much slush off as possible before climbing into the blissfully warm interior. He handed the vibrator to Vivian.

"Finally!" She took the vibrator and switched it on. "I thought you'd be standing out there forever! What did that cop want, anyway?"

"She thought we might have some trouble because it looked like we'd pulled off the road abruptly."

Vivian smiled and ran the vibrator along his thigh. "Did you tell her I had you by the short hairs?"

"What do you think?" He watched the vibrator and found himself responding, whether he wanted to or not.

"I think you didn't say that. I'll bet you had no idea what to say when you were caught out in broad daylight with a bright green vibrator in your hand."

"Look, I have to pull into traffic, and she's going to be back there watching. You'd better turn that off."

"Why? Does she have X-ray vision?"

"She said we shouldn't operate it while the vehicle is moving."

"Oh, really?"

"Vivian, stop looking like that. She wasn't giving an order, just making a suggestion."

"Just drive, Kurt, baby."

"Are you going to turn it off?"

"Maybe. Maybe not." She jabbed him in the crotch with the vibrator, which made him jump. "Get us out of here."

Checking quickly for traffic, he gunned the motor and the truck lurched forward onto the pavement. The fifth wheel jerked sideways, but then it followed, thank God.

The hum of the vibrator continued, but at least Vivian wasn't running it along his thigh anymore. He glanced in the side mirror and, sure enough, the cop was tailing them. He'd have to drive like a damned saint until the cop got bored and peeled off.

And driving like a saint wouldn't be easy. Vivian had unzipped her khaki cargo pants. He should never have told her the officer had advised against using the vibrator when the vehicle was moving. Being Vivian, she intended to do exactly that.

Chapter Fourteen

Ally wondered if there was any way during this store visit that she could skip out to take some pictures. Alone. Maybe Mitchell would get absorbed in looking at the chain-saw nudes. She'd never met a man yet who wasn't intrigued by nude sculptures, no matter whether the boobs matched or not. Then again, she was dying to know if he'd try to buy condoms, and if he could accomplish it without causing a stir.

But if she wanted to escape to go tramping around on the outskirts of town looking for critters, she'd have to give up the potential of watching him fumble his way through the condom situation. And she did want to go tramping around. That's what she'd come to Alaska for. She needed to remember that no matter how Mitchell tempted her, she hadn't come to Alaska for sex.

Betsy led the way into Heavenly Provisions. "Hey,

Serena," Betsy called out, as if she were dropping in on a neighbor. "I've brought you some customers."

"Be right there!" A woman's voice drifted from a back room. "I have to finish setting the candle wicks!"

Ally unzipped her coat and pushed back her hood as she glanced around with interest. Grammy would have turned up her nose at the musty old place, but Ally liked it. If she weren't so eager to get outside and take pictures, she could prowl around in here for hours.

Everything was so different from what she'd known in Bel Air. She'd never been in a place where the walls were decorated with animal skins. Even the hunting and fishing gear fascinated her. She wasn't into that, but the colorful paraphernalia would make a cool photo collage.

Three sets of free-standing shelves in the middle of the store held the bulk of the grocery-store part, although Ally noticed boots and hats interspersed with crackers and canned veggies. Heavy knit sweaters hung on a rack in one corner. A glass case under the front counter was filled with Native Indian jewelry, much of it with a Porcupine theme, plus several colorful pillar candles, which probably explained Serena's comment.

The chain-saw nudes paraded across a ledge behind the counter. They were of varying heights, with the average being about four feet. These girls had serious problems, and matching boobs were the least of them. For one thing, none of them had necks, or even much in the way of faces.

Their chest measurements were substantial, but as Betsy had noted, no two breasts were alike. Each one jutted out independent of the other, a rough-hewn cone reminiscent of Madonna in her early days. The size of the boobs would have caused the sculpture to tip over, except the artist had given each nude sumo-wrestler legs and feet the size of snowboards. Dave either needed a few lessons or a truckload of therapy.

"Here I am, here I am." The store's owner swept out of the back room wearing a wool caftan with more colors woven into it than Ally could count. From her feathered earrings and burgundy hair to the beaded moccasins on her feet, she proclaimed herself a free spirit. "This must be Mitchell and Ally, Porcupine's newest arrivals! Welcome!" She came toward Ally, hands outstretched.

For a minute, Ally thought Serena might pull her in for a big hug. Instead she simply gave Ally's hands a tight squeeze. Then she did the same thing with Mitchell, who didn't seem to know what to make of her.

"You two have come to Porcupine at the perfect time," she said.

Mitchell looked doubtful. "How's that?"

"It's the slow season, so everything in my store is fifty percent off! Look around, find what your heart has been yearning for, and let's make a deal."

Betsy sauntered over to a shelf and picked up two boxes of condoms. "Fifty percent off on these?"

"Oh, why not?" Serena turned to Ally. "Although that's an item that sells like hotcakes during the winter. I think it's nature's way of balancing our moods up here. We don't get as much sunlight as we need to stay cheerful, so we compensate with lots of sex."

"Makes sense," Ally said. But the constant focus on the subject blew her away. She'd never heard so much open discussion of sex in her life, not even in the sorority house.

Maybe that explained her sudden attraction to Mitchell. She was compensating for the lack of sunshine.

Glancing over at the current object of her affections, she found him studying the chain-saw nudes, just as she'd predicted.

Serena obviously noticed, too, and moved closer to him. "I can give you a really good price on one of these fine pieces of interpretive sculpture," she said. "The artist, David Beedleman, is local. We're so lucky to have him living and creating his fine works right here in Porcupine."

"Out of curiosity, how much are they?" Mitchell asked.

"Normally, they sell from one thousand up to three, but I'll—"

"A thousand *dollars*?" Mitchell's jaw dropped.

Serena moved smoothly past his astonishment. "That's what something this unusual would go for in a sophisticated environment like New York City. But you're lucky because you're buying practically straight from the artist, who is a personal friend of mine."

"I'm not really interested in buying. I just—"

"Ah, but you asked a buying question," Serena said brightly. "David would want me to give you a special price, because you're a visitor in his hometown. Why don't you tell me what you'd be willing to pay for such a fine piece?"

Mitchell had a deer-in-the-headlights look. "The thing is, I wouldn't have a way to get it home."

"I'll ship it. Just pick out the one you want."

"You know, actually, I don't have a spot for it, either."

"These will go *anywhere*."

Mitchell sent Ally a pleading glance, as if asking her to throw him a line.

She just smiled. He was on his own, although she

thought his consideration for Serena's feelings was very sweet.

Clearing his throat, Mitch turned back to Serena. "In my current living situation, I wouldn't exactly feel comfortable adding a piece of sculpture."

"But when will you have this kind of opportunity again?" Serena asked.

The sound of a tractor outside, no doubt Dave plowing the street in front of the store, made it hard to hear Mitchell's answer. Entertaining though the exchange had been, Ally had listened long enough, anyway. She had other fish to fry.

She walked over toward Betsy, who was taking a carton of eggs out of a refrigerated case. "Are those from Rudy's chickens?" she asked.

"Uh-huh. He used to give the eggs away, but I convinced him to have Serena sell them, so they both can make some money. I know Rudy keeps the chickens for pure enjoyment, but he needs to make a little something to keep him in chicken feed. The shuttle service doesn't bring in enough to keep him going."

"Then I'm glad you suggested it." Ally glanced over toward Mitchell. Serena had taken one of the smaller nudes and handed it to him. He held it awkwardly, one hand clutching a boob and the other a thigh, while Serena continued to talk, probably heaping praise on Dave's artistic merits.

Watching him standing there clutching the ugly nude, Ally had the oddest rush of tenderness, which was really weird. Then the tender feeling was followed by a zing of sexual heat. She hoped she wasn't getting hooked on Mitchell. That would be very inconvenient.

"She's going to sell him one, yet," Betsy said.

"She might, at that." As the tractor noise outside the window grew louder, Ally turned back to Betsy. "Listen, I think I'll leave you and Mitchell to finish up the shopping while I go take a few pictures." She needed some distance between her and this guy, needed to get back on track with her original purpose in being here.

"You don't want Mitchell to go, too?"

"To tell you the truth, I'd rather go by myself. He's not really into it, and I've been dying to get out and roam around ever since yesterday."

Betsy glanced at an antique Regulator clock on the wall. "It's almost lunchtime. I thought we'd stop by the Top Hat for something to eat. You could go after that."

"I could, but I'd rather go now, while Mitchell's involved in something else. Tell you what. I'll meet you two at the Top Hat in an hour or so."

Betsy gave her a woman-to-woman glance. "Girl, I know what you mean about doing some things on your own. Sometimes we need a little time to ourselves, don't we?"

"Yes, we do. I'll meet you guys at the Top Hat." She headed for the door. But before she reached it, Mitchell turned, the nude in both hands. "Ally?"

She paused. "What?" She noticed that the tractor motor had been turned off, as if Dave had parked the thing right outside. She hoped she wouldn't have to deal with him once she slipped out the door.

"These sculptures are made from cedar," Mitchell said. "They smell really great."

"Interesting." She wondered if she'd just lost her chance to escape. And something was definitely going on outside with Dave. She could hear loud voices.

Mitchell seemed to be totally involved in this sculpture decision, though. He looked at the three-foot nude he now held by the waist. "So I was thinking that maybe—"

Whatever he'd been about to say was cut short as the door flew open and Dave hurtled through it, followed by a short man who was hollering and waving his arms.

"I never said you could use my tractor!" the little guy yelled. "You stole it! You're using up my gas! I bought that gas! I'm gonna have you arrested!"

Dave glanced frantically around and spotted Ally. "There you are! I thought I saw you come in here. Tell this lunatic that all I wanted to do was *borrow* his tractor. That's what I told you this morning, right?"

"Right. But—"

"Right! Hear that, Ernie? The word is *borrow,* not *steal.*"

"But you didn't even ask me!" Ernie bellowed. "I get up from my nap, look out the window, and my tractor is *gone*! Is that stealing? You bet your sweet bippy!"

"You were passed out! How could I ask if you were comatose?"

"I was not!" Ernie advanced on him, face contorted. "Forget the police. We're snowed in, so nobody could get here to arrest you, anyway! I'll take care of it my-self." With that he launched himself at Dave.

"You idiot!" Dave tried to fight him off. "That's why I had to plow, so we could have the roads open for an emergency!"

"We're about to have one!" screeched the little guy, going for Dave's throat.

"Stop, stop!" Serena started toward them. "There's no fighting allowed in Heavenly Provisions!"

"That's enough!" Mitchell put down the nude. Grabbing hold of Ernie, he pulled him, kicking and screaming, off Dave. "You are not going to trash this woman's place of business."

Ally was torn. On the one hand, she would love to see how Mitchell handled this matter. On the other, Dave and Ernie had given her the perfect cover for skedaddling out of the store. After all, she'd told Betsy where she was going and Mitchell seemed to be in control of the situation. Edging toward the door, she slipped outside.

Freedom.

Mitch hadn't wanted in on this altercation, but he couldn't stand by while one man assaulted another, especially in a store where damage could be done to the merchandise. He was touched by Serena's devotion to her place and its contents, and he didn't want Dave and Ernie making a mess.

So he grabbed Ernie in a bear hug and pinned his arms to his body. "Get his legs, Dave."

"Will do." Dave latched on to his legs and helped wrestle him to the floor.

"I'll sue the lot of you!" Ernie struggled to get up. "Can't steal a man's tractor and then act like it's nothing! I don't care if this is Alaska. We have laws here, too, you know!"

"I have a suggestion," Betsy said, pitching her voice loud enough to be heard over Ernie's caterwauling.

Mitch glanced up at her. "What's that?"

"Try the hair of the dog. Carry him over to the Top Hat and get some beer into him. I guarantee he'll settle down."

"I don't want no beer!" Ernie said. "Let me up so I can teach this yahoo a lesson!"

"Beer would probably work," Serena said. "Mitchell, before you go, would you like to have me wrap this sculpture for you?"

"Uh, well . . ." Now that Mitch had some distance from her sales pitch, he realized he'd been about to buy the sculpture because he'd felt sorry for Serena, who so obviously believed in the value of those hideous things. He'd justified it because at least they smelled nice, but that was sort of dumb, even if Serena had brought the price down to ten bucks. He could get a can of Glade for a lot less.

"You're going to buy one of my sculptures?" Dave's face lit up. "Wow, that's awesome! I've never—" He stopped speaking and coughed. "I've never sold one in February. It's a slow time of the year."

Mitch guessed that Dave had never sold one, period. That wouldn't be surprising. They were incredibly ugly. But now he was caught, hooked in by Dave's excitement over making his first-ever sale.

He didn't even like the guy, but dousing that glow of joy on Dave's face seemed like intolerable cruelty. And the wood did smell terrific. Having it in his room, or Ally's room if she wanted it, might be kind of nice.

Ernie kept raving. "I don't give a good goddamn whether you sell one of your precious sculptures, you tractor thief! They're not good for nothin' except if I can use one to whap you upside the head."

"Sure, wrap it up," Mitch said. "I'll come back for it later." That way, he could buy condoms when he picked up the sculpture.

"That's okay," Betsy said. "I'll carry it over to the

lodge for you. I have to take my stuff back home, any-way. I'll meet you all at the Top Hat."

"Wait, wait," Dave said. "Serena, how about if you closed for lunch and took it over to the Top Hat un-wrapped? I want to show Clyde which one I sold."

Serena nodded, smiling at him. "I can do that, David."

Mitch wasn't crazy about everyone at the Top Hat knowing he'd been sucker enough to buy one of these monstrosities, but he couldn't think of a good reason to object. "Then let's go. Dave, we'll pick him up on three. One, two, *three*."

"Did you *ask* me if I wanted a beer?" Ernie railed. "No, you did not. Just like you didn't ask if you could use my tractor! Put me down!"

Mitch ignored him, but as they started out the door, he realized that Ally wasn't with them. Maybe she'd gone to the back of the store to look at something. He glanced over his shoulder. "Ally? We're leaving!"

"She's not here, Mitch," Betsy said, walking behind him out the door.

He nearly dropped his half of Ernie. "What do you mean, she's not here?"

"She told me a while ago she wanted to spend some time alone taking pictures, so I guess when all this started, she decided to cut out and get that done."

"Take pictures where?" By now they were out the door and headed across the street, with Dave leading with Ernie's feet. Mitch scanned to his left and right. He tried not to panic. "You mean right around here?"

"She said she wanted to wander a bit," Betsy said. "Don't look so worried, Mitchell. It's still daylight and Porcupine is perfectly safe."

"Is not!" Ernie yelled. "The place is full of bullies and tractor thieves!"

Mitch kept checking the area for signs of Ally while navigating a street that had been only partly plowed. "You don't happen to see her, do you, Betsy?"

"Mitchell, the way you're acting, it's no wonder that girl took off. Women need some breathing room. You'll get nowhere if you crowd her. Lighten up."

"Um, yeah, I'm sure you're right, Betsy." Dammit. No doubt Ally had slipped away from him on purpose, to demonstrate that she was her own person. She probably thought she was perfectly justified in sneaking out to do her thing. She didn't know yet that it could be dangerous. And he didn't know how to warn her.

Ally took a deep breath of the cold air. Now this was what she was talking about, following a trail of animal tracks through the snowy woods, her camera out and ready to go. How she'd dreamed of this. She'd taken pictures at the zoo and at San Diego's Wild Animal Park. She'd brought her best shots with her, to show Uncle Kurt, but she knew they wouldn't compare with what she could take here. This was wilderness.

She'd found the trail in back of Heavenly Provisions, but now the trees blocked any view of civilization. Her heart pounded faster as she went deeper into the woods, following a little groove in the snow that had been made by four-footed creatures. Overhead a branch rustled, sending snow cascading down.

She jumped out of the way and tucked her camera under her arm. Damn, she'd made too much noise doing that. She looked up to see what had caused the branch to rustle and thought she saw the flash of a squirrel's tail, but she couldn't be sure of it.

Setting her feet down carefully as she continued following the path, she tried not to crunch the snow under her boots. The woods were so quiet, and if she was close to something wild, she didn't want to scare it away with her footsteps. Once in a while she saw a clear paw print in the snow.

From the shape of the print, she could be following a large dog, somebody's pet out for some exploration in the woods. A town like Porcupine didn't seem like a leash-law kind of place. But instinct told her the paw print hadn't been made by a dog.

Every once in a while she'd pause to listen, but she heard nothing except the soft sighing of the wind through the trees and the plop of snow as it dropped from the branches to the ground. The wind was to her back, and that probably wasn't ideal. It would carry her scent toward an animal ahead of her, maybe scaring it away.

Oh, well. She'd figure everything out eventually. For now, she was experimenting. The large pines cut out most of the sunlight, so it was dim there under the trees. She searched the spaces between the trunks, hoping for a glimpse of movement. Nothing.

She shouldn't expect much, considering she didn't know what she was doing. Besides, a wildlife photographer had to learn patience. Once she understood where to go, where to set up blinds, what equipment to take, she'd be far more effective. At Uncle Kurt's advice, she'd held off buying anything until after she'd talked to his contacts.

Bless his heart, he'd been working so hard trying to

find a wildlife photographer in Anchorage who would be interested in mentoring a rank beginner like Ally. She'd given him permission to offer them decent compensation for their time. She had the funds, so she might as well use them for private tutoring.

Meanwhile, she'd have some fun with her digital camera. She might even get lucky. Sometimes a good shot was a matter of luck—even Tanya Mandell had admitted that in the foreword to the book Ally had brought with her.

She glanced to her left, once more scanning between the trees for something, anything, that didn't quite fit the pattern. Wait a minute. There. No, maybe not. Yes! A dog? She began to tremble. That was no dog.

Through the trees, nearly camouflaged in the shadows, stood a wolf, staring at her. He was light gray, almost white, which helped him blend into the snow, as well. She was shaking so much the camera wobbled in her hands as she brought it up. The woods were completely silent except for her heartbeat and her quick breaths.

She wanted to use the telephoto, but was afraid the whine as it extended would scare the wolf away. Instead she'd take the first one without, and if the wolf stayed there, she'd chance using the telephoto. But she had to stop quivering or the whole thing would be a blurred disaster.

She averted her gaze slightly, watching the wolf from the corner of her eye. A direct gaze was supposed to make most animals nervous. She'd read that, too. Then she took a long, slow breath. In . . . and out. The wolf stayed put.

Steadier now, she raised the camera until the wolf appeared in the center of the digital screen. The click of the shutter seemed to echo in the forest. She thought for sure the wolf would bolt, but only a slight movement of one ear indicated any response.

No doubt the wolf had picked up her scent and had decided to circle back and check her out. If she remained right where she was, they might stand there watching each other for a long time. She should take a chance on the telephoto.

Holding her breath, she pushed the button that extended the lens. The high-pitched hum seemed way too loud, certainly enough noise to spook her subject. And yet the wolf didn't move.

She'd heard that meeting an animal in its native habitat was a completely different experience from seeing one in a zoo, and now she knew how true that was. This wolf had such presence, such dignity. From the size, she'd guess it was a male, and his winter coat was thick and luxurious.

She put her finger on the shutter button and was about to squeeze off the shot when footsteps crunched through the snow behind her, coming fast.

"Ally! Don't be afraid! Don't make any sudden moves! I'll be right there!"

The wolf melted into the shadows and was gone.

She gritted her teeth and turned to see Mitchell running toward her. Good thing she had her precious camera in her hands. If she'd had her hands free, she might have strangled him.

Chapter Fifteen

As he approached, Mitchell could tell Ally was furious. He didn't really give a damn, either. He'd thought she'd been standing there frozen with fear, when instead she'd been concentrating so hard she'd been oblivious to the danger. Either way, he didn't regret what he'd done for a minute.

"Dammit all, Mitchell, why did you come charging in here like that? I wasn't afraid! I was trying to get a picture!"

Heart pumping with adrenaline, he stopped and gasped for breath as he took a survey of the area. "Of which one?"

She glared at him. "What do you mean, which one? There was a wolf standing there. He was gorgeous, and I was about to get a perfect shot with my telephoto, when you started yelling and ruined everything."

"So you didn't see the others." He'd left the Top Hat

the minute he'd felt certain that Ernie was under control. Then he'd had to go back to where Ally had started her trek behind Heavenly Provisions and follow her trail into the woods. He'd taken classes in tracking but he was no expert, and it had been damned slow going. He needed to plant that transmitter in her backpack ASAP.

"There were no others!"

"Yeah, there were, Ally." He waved his arm to the left. "Over there I saw three, and over there—" He pointed to the right. "Four more. They were hard to see through the trees, but they were there, and it looked like they were starting to close in."

"I think your imagination was playing tricks on you." But a tiny flicker of uneasiness showed in those gorgeous green eyes.

"Ally, they were there. Seven more wolves. The one in front of you was stationary, but the others were gradually moving closer."

She obviously didn't like being caught unawares. Her chin came up. "Even if there were more wolves, I wasn't in danger. They don't attack people. They're victims of bad press."

"And in the press is where I want my future contacts with a pack of wolves. I'll be happy to read all about them. I'd rather not encounter them in their own territory, which they know a hell of a lot better than I do."

"News flash, Mitchell. I didn't ask you to come out here in the woods looking for me." Then she paused and her eyes narrowed in suspicion. "How did you find me, anyway?"

He shrugged. "Lucky guess."

"I could have gone off in the woods in any direction."

"I tried to think like you."

"Ha. If you'd been thinking like me, you would have crept up the trail very silently, so you wouldn't *scare the wildlife*. Sheesh. I still can't believe I missed that shot."

He refused to apologize. So he'd come charging into a situation where he saw her surrounded by a pack of wolves. He'd do it again.

She sighed. "We might as well go back. I'm sure they're gone. I'm sure after all that ruckus every living creature except us has left the area." She shut down her camera and shrugged out of her backpack so she could put it away.

"I'd be glad to carry that for you." And in the process he could slide the transmitter into the bottom of the backpack where she'd never find it.

"Thanks. I've got it." She swung the pack over her shoulder and started back the way she'd come. Her expression was not the least bit friendly.

It occurred to him that the condom issue, which he had yet to resolve, might be a moot point. But he had to do his job, had to protect her from the wolves, both four-legged and two-legged. If that ticked her off so much that she forgot she'd ever been attracted to him, so be it. The sex was an iffy proposition and would have been an unexpected benefit, anyway.

The trail was only wide enough for one person, so he brought up the rear. He resisted the impulse to look over his shoulder and see if a man-eating wolf was gaining on them. Okay, so she might be right that they weren't dangerous, but he hadn't liked the look of that situation.

The bottom line was, he didn't care for the whole idea of her wandering out in the wilderness by herself.

Yet that was exactly what she had in mind with her photography gig. "This Tanya Mandell," he said. "The photographer whose book you have up in your room, does she have a sidekick?"

"Sometimes. Not always." Ally still sounded ticked off. "What's your point, as if I didn't know?"

"I just think it would be a better idea to utilize the buddy system, that's all."

"That's not always practical. And besides, I like being on my own. It's a treat Grammy hardly ever allowed."

"Okay, but do you have to be on your own out in the woods, where stuff can have you for lunch?"

She adjusted her backpack strap. "Mitchell, you are so melodramatic. Face it, this isn't your thing. There's no way you will ever understand my need to get out here with nature, one-on-one, and capture the spirit of wild animals with my camera. You'll never get it."

"I might get it, but that doesn't mean I have to like it." The words had a familiar ring, and yet he'd never said that before. Then he remembered why they sounded so familiar. His father had told him that very thing the day he'd come home with his first motorcycle at the age of seventeen. Yikes. Now he was sounding like a parent.

His father had threatened to make him return the bike to the dealership. Mitch had threatened to leave home, taking his precious bike with him. In the end, they'd come to a compromise. Mitch had enrolled in a course on safe motorcycle practices, and his dad had let him keep the bike.

Mitch didn't want to act like a parent with Ally, and yet that seemed to be the way he was behaving. Madeline had put him in a crummy position, when you came right down to it. She'd hired him to watch out for Ally but she'd given him no power. He hadn't really figured that out until now.

He could quit, of course. But as recently as last night he'd promised Ally he wouldn't do that. He'd also promised Madeline that he'd keep Ally safe. He needed to stop being so damned free with his promises, because unfortunately for him, he was the kind of guy who believed in keeping them.

The closer Ally came to the back end of Heavenly Provisions, the more certain she was that the tractor was running again. A cleared road would be a good thing for Uncle Kurt, so she hoped the tractor was operating. She'd wondered if he knew about the iffy road conditions around Porcupine. If he'd given her a telephone number, she would have called to let him know.

But Uncle Kurt wasn't a telephone kind of guy, as he'd told her. To him, telephones tied you down. You had to interrupt whatever you were doing to deal with a telephone call, and he didn't like that. He preferred e-mail.

She didn't really want to talk to Mitchell, because she was still mad at him, but she was curious about the tractor situation, and he might know the story, considering that she'd last seen him pinning Ernie to the floor. "I think someone's plowing the road," she said. "Do you know anything about that?"

"Nope. I just hope to God it's not Ernie. Last I saw, he was putting away the beer like it was going out of style. If he's both plowed *and* plowing, we'd better make a run for the Top Hat before we get scooped up in his shovel."

"Who said I was going to the Top Hat?" She didn't want him making assumptions about her schedule, although she was getting very hungry, and the Top Hat was the only game in town if she wanted lunch.

"So you're not going to the Top Hat?"

With the limited options in Porcupine, a girl had a tough time making an unpredictable move. "I guess I am."

"Me, too. I need some food and I have to pick up my sculpture."

"So you bought one."

"I did." He didn't sound very proud of his purchase.

"Why is it at the Top Hat?"

"Dave wanted to show Clyde which one I bought, so Serena took it over while Dave and I carried Ernie."

"I'm sorry I missed that." She walked down the narrow alleyway between the store and the building next to it, a combination beauty parlor and barbershop.

"Yeah, we made quite a procession. You should really stick around instead of wandering off into the woods by yourself. No telling what will happen next in Porcupine. Maybe you could switch to human interest photography."

"Nice try. Ain't gonna happen. But if it makes you feel any better, I should be getting a mentor soon." She stepped onto the snow-covered sidewalk. Sure enough, the tractor was working about a block down from where she stood.

Mitch came up beside her. "Whoever that is, he doesn't act drunk."

"I wouldn't know. I've never seen anybody plow a road before, drunk or sober."

"Well, I have, and my money's on Dave being the operator of that machine. I think it's safe to cross." He started toward the Top Hat.

Ally fell into step beside him. "Speaking of money, if you don't mind my asking, how much did you end up paying for your nude?"

"Let's put it this way. For a room freshener, it was expensive. For original sculpture, it was a bargain."

She'd wanted to stay mad at him. She really hated the way he'd interrupted her wolf adventure. But remembering how he'd acted so adorably helpless in the face of Serena's sales pitch, she lost her grip on her anger. "Did you really think I was about to be attacked by wolves back there?"

"I wasn't sure. But I didn't like the way they were looking at you."

She laughed. "Exactly how should a pack of wolves look at me so that you would approve?"

"Definitely not like that, as if they were considering you as an entree."

"I'll bet you read *Little Red Riding Hood* at an impressionable age."

"Maybe. I've never been crazy about wild animals with big teeth."

"I have." She stepped over a furrow of snow that Dave had missed. "And faraway places where most people never go."

"Because your grandmother wouldn't let you out of her sight?"

"Partly. But that's not the main reason." She stepped onto the sidewalk in front of the Top Hat and paused, turning toward him. "It's more because of my mom and dad." The explanation popped out, and why she'd told Mitchell was anybody's guess. She'd never talked about her parents. Grammy had never been able to, not even after years had passed.

"I'm not sure I understand. I thought you were very young when they . . . when they . . ."

"Died? It's okay, Mitchell. Grammy was sensitive about it, but I'm not. It was a diving accident off the coast of Jamaica. I was three, too little to go on a trip like that. They were searching for sunken treasure. A storm came up, and they couldn't get back to the boat."

"That's terrible."

Maybe that's why she didn't tell people about it. She was afraid they'd look at her the way Mitchell was looking at her, as if she should be pitied. "I don't think it's terrible. They died doing what they loved."

"Yeah, but you missed out on so much."

"I can't be sad when I barely remember them. I look at pictures, and it brings up this vague feeling of tenderness, but they don't seem like real people. More like a movie I've seen a long time ago, one I'm sure I liked although I don't really remember the story."

Mitchell shook his head. "I can't imagine. My parents were always there. They're *still* there, living in Arlington Heights. A fixture. A huge part of my life, my memories."

She thought that explained why he was such a conservative guy. "Sometimes I envy people like you, who have that continuity. But even though my parents died when I was very young, it's okay, because I feel connected in a weird sort of way. I'm like them, Mitchell. I plan to live that kind of life, taking risks, going to exotic places. I'm carrying on the legacy."

He held her gaze for a long time. "Ally, I have to tell you, sometimes you scare the shit out of me."

They'd dressed Mitch's nude and given her a name worthy of a town called Porcupine. Quillamina Sharp stood on the bar wearing a bar-towel sarong and a tiara made of toothpicks and straws. He should have known that leaving the sculpture at the Top Hat posed certain risks.

The bar was crowded. Glancing around, Mitch was relieved to see Ernie over in a corner with another beer at his elbow. At least the little guy wasn't out scooping snow and ramming into parked cars along the way, which meant the tractor operator was most definitely Dave.

Mitch and Ally joined Betsy and Serena at a table near the bar. The two women were finishing their sandwiches, along with a beer for Betsy and a glass of wine for Serena.

"So Dave's out plowing?" Mitch asked Betsy.

She nodded. "After a couple of beers, Ernie calmed right down. Invited Dave to be his guest and plow the entire county if he wanted."

"That's amazing." Ally glanced toward the corner where Ernie sat. "I thought they were going to kill each other."

Mitch didn't trust the supposed truce, either, and he wanted to avoid dealing with Ernie again. Too much of that macho stuff and people would start to suspect he had some law-enforcement training.

Besides, he had a ton of other things to worry about, like Ally carrying on her parents' legacy. "So what happens when he sobers up?" he asked. "Won't he start raving about his stolen tractor all over again?"

Serena smiled. "Clyde has that covered. As a public service, he'll supply Ernie with beer until David finishes, which should be before it gets dark. In fact, I think Clyde plans to keep Ernie well oiled into the evening. That gives David plenty of time to return the tractor. Someone will take Ernie home tonight, and when he wakes up in the morning, the tractor will be in the shed right where he expects to find it."

"Until the next snowstorm and the game starts over," Mitch said. "I realize I'm an outsider, but I think the town needs to buy its own snowplow." He glanced up as Clyde appeared at the table, order pad in hand. "Don't you think the town needs its own plow?"

Clyde grinned. "Nah."

"But you know this will happen again."

"Exactly. We gotta have something to see us through the winter besides my tap routines on the bar. We get a lot of entertainment out of betting on whether Ernie's going to be sober enough to plow the streets and then coming up with a plan if he's not."

"Poopsie's right." Betsy put a hand on Mitch's arm. "Sometimes the logical solution isn't the best solution for Porcupinians. You won't understand that until you've spent a few winters here."

Her implication that he would spend more winters here made him shudder. If he believed that, he'd slit his wrists. "I'll take your word for it, Betsy."

"You'd be wise to do that," Clyde said. "Now, what'll you folks be having?"

Mitch ordered a sandwich after Clyde's assurance that it contained actual commercial chicken and not some animal that had suffered a highway accident. Ally ordered the special, which Mitch figured could be anything. But that was Ally, ready for adventure.

Anyone who knew his choice of profession would think he had a taste for adventure, too, but they'd be wrong. He had chosen to become a PI and bodyguard not because he wanted adventure, but because he wanted control over the outcome of situations. He wished to hell he had more control over this one.

By the time they were halfway through their lunch, Serena had left to tend her store and Betsy had returned to the lodge. That left Ally and Mitch in a cozy twosome. He started thinking about the condoms he hadn't bought yet, and whether her mood was softening toward him enough that he needed to find a way to quietly acquire that item.

He noticed she kept glancing at him, and each time her cheeks would get pink, but she didn't say anything, just kept eating her sandwich.

"What?" he finally asked.

"I was just wondering something."

"What's that?"

"Well, you bought the nude while you were over at Serena's." She tipped her head toward the bar, where Quillamina was being toasted by a couple of burly guys who kept lifting up her sarong and then collapsing into fits of laughter.

"Yeah, I sure did buy a nude. And now I'd better get her out of here before Dave comes in. I think he'd be insulted that the guys felt compelled to give her an outfit and a name."

Her eyes widened in surprise. "You care if he's insulted? I didn't think you liked him!"

Mitch sighed. "It's not like I'm ready to be his best friend or anything, but you should have seen the expression on his face when I bought it. You'd think I'd handed him the moon."

"Mitchell, you're quite the softie, you know that?"

"I'm a sucker, is what I am." But he enjoyed the way she was looking at him, as if she wanted another kiss like the one they'd had back in the snow. And her knee had come to rest against his knee. She didn't move it. He started getting warm all over.

She fiddled with the toothpick Clyde had stuck through the center of her sandwich. "Did you . . . um . . . get the other thing?"

Hot damn. His body reacted instantly. Maybe she was changing her mind. And he was still minus what he needed to make something happen. "No, I didn't. With everyone around here so chummy, I'm not sure how to buy them without the whole town being in on it."

"But you don't want to take Betsy up on her offer."

"No. That's almost as bad." But if Ally really wanted to go through with this, he'd go back to Heavenly Provisions. Hell, he'd hitch a ride to Fairbanks to buy them, except that he couldn't leave her for that long. "Ally, are you rethinking your original decision?" He crossed his fingers under the table.

She sighed. "Mitchell, I have this terrible problem. The more I'm around you, the more I think about having sex with you."

"But you don't want to."

"It wouldn't be fair to you."

He couldn't stop looking at her lips. "Maybe you should let me be the judge of that." His heart thumped crazily as he remembered how those lips had felt on his.

"Look, I'm not saying that I'm changing my mind. I think giving in to this would show weakness on my part. But the chemistry between us is really strong."

"Uh-huh." He kept his fingers crossed tight.

"We could suddenly snap."

"Uh-huh." He was close to the snapping point right now.

"And I was thinking . . . I'll bet they have a vending machine in the men's room."

"Oh." He mentally slapped his forehead. This was a bar. A bar in Porcupine, where sex was the favorite winter sport. Of course they would have a vending machine in the men's room. He should have realized that immediately.

Seeing the gleam in her eyes and knowing that she'd given it enough thought to come up with a solution pumped up his inclination even more. He'd better check out the men's room while he could still stand without embarrassing himself.

He pushed back his chair. "I'll go find out," he said.

"Okay."

Oh, boy. She was talking his language now. They'd be upstairs at the Loose Moose all night, with only a bathroom between them. He wanted to be ready for the moment she snapped and came knocking at his door. He wished the day would end right now. At least night came early in Alaska in the wintertime. It couldn't come soon enough for Mitch.

Chapter Sixteen

Ally couldn't quite believe she'd told Mitchell where to pick up a condom or two. She'd never been so bold in her life. But the longer she hung around Mitchell, the more she thought of cool sheets and hot sex. She didn't want to be caught in a situation where their hormones went crazy and they had no supplies. Maybe she'd maintain her self-control, but she wasn't so sure about it.

While she was visualizing what tonight would be like, sleeping only a bathroom away from a man she wanted naked, Rudy walked into the Top Hat, all two hundred and eighty pounds of him.

"I was hoping I'd find you here!" He pulled up a chair and sat down. "Seein' as how Mitchell said he'd help me find Lurleen, I wanted to do something for the both of you."

Ally couldn't figure out how the heck Mitchell could

help locate Rudy's ex-girlfriend. He was no private investigator. "That was nice of him."

"Yeah, it was. Here he comes, now. Hi, there, Mitchell! Say, does anybody ever call you Mitch?"

Mitchell shook Rudy's outstretched hand before sitting down again. "It's happened before. Why?"

"I just like Mitch better, is all. No offense, but when you say the whole thing like that, I picture some dorky guy, somebody in government, maybe."

"Oh, I don't," Ally said. She actually did, but she wanted to protect Mitchell's feelings. People could be very sensitive about their names. "I think of somebody who's efficient, thorough, resourceful . . ." She glanced at Mitchell and tried to read from his expression whether he'd scored any condoms. She couldn't tell.

"Well, sure," Rudy said. "Efficient, but maybe too efficient, if you know what I mean. Now *Mitch,* that's a guy who gets things done, but he's sorta cool about it. So if it's all the same to you, I thought I'd go with Mitch."

"That's fine," Mitchell said.

But Ally was still concerned that his feelings were hurt. "Not me," she said. "I like saying the whole thing. Mitchell. It has a nice lilt to it."

She wondered what she'd call him if they ended up in the same bed. Mitch was a shorter name, and at moments like that, you didn't want to waste your breath on extra syllables. Having sex with a guy named Mitch did seem a shade more exciting, come to think of it. And she was definitely thinking about it.

"So as I was telling Ally," Rudy said. "I want to do something for you guys since you're gonna help me locate Lurleen."

"Yeah, how are you going to help Rudy locate Lurleen?"

"Through the Internet," Mitchell said. "It's amazing what you can do with the Internet these days."

"I suppose so." She laughed. "For a minute there, it sounded like you were getting into the PI business."

"Me?"

"I know. Far-fetched. But it ran through my mind."

Rudy looked at them expectantly. "So aren't you gonna ask me what special thing I'm gonna do for you?"

"You could surprise us," Ally said.

"No, he couldn't," Mitch said. "I like knowing what's coming. What's the plan, Rudy?"

Rudy beamed, showing off his gap-toothed smile. "Snowmobiles, that's what!"

"Yeah?" Mitch sat up straighter. "You have snowmobiles?"

"Two of them. I rode one in and towed the other one." He turned to Ally. "Wanna go for a ride?"

She hesitated, not really crazy about the idea. But Rudy seemed so eager, and even Mitchell looked interested. "It sounds like fun, but . . . doesn't it scare the animals?"

Rudy blinked as if he'd never considered that. "I suppose you could, if you ran right into a herd of caribou, but I didn't have that in mind."

"I'm sure you didn't," Mitch said. "It's all about operating them sensibly, right?"

"That's what I do. Operate 'em sensibly. Now once in a while, you might have to jump over a drift, but I know what I'm doing."

"Right." Mitch nodded. "It's all in the technique."

Ally wasn't fooled for a minute. They both could hardly wait to get those machines up to top speed and try all sorts of fancy-dancy maneuvers. They didn't care if they terrified whatever creatures might be in the vicinity.

Even stodgy Mitchell was salivating at the idea. Ally decided she'd better go just to keep those two in check. She'd take her camera along, on the rare chance they didn't scatter all the animals as they charged over the snow.

"I never try to hurt nothin'," Rudy said. "It's just for fun. See, I have two snowmobiles, on account of I bought Lurleen her own, and she left it here in Porcupine." He paused. "She left a lot of stuff. All she really took was . . ." He cleared his throat. "My heart."

"Oh, Rudy." Ally put her hand on his arm and gave it a little squeeze. "I have a strong feeling that Mitchell will locate her for you. I'm sure this story will have a happy ending."

"I'll do my best, buddy," Mitchell said.

"I hope when you find her she still has that heart," Rudy said. "I paid Serena a pretty penny for it."

Ally did a double take. "Excuse me?" She glanced over at Mitchell, who shrugged as if he had no clue what was going on.

"It was a thing of beauty," Rudy said. "Polished so nice, made out of rose quartz. It was supposed to be a paperweight, but I don't have any papers. I just liked holding it, you know? It felt good in my hand. I miss that heart."

Okay, so Mitchell needed to find Lurleen and see if

she still had Rudy's paperweight. The job seemed a little less urgent than it had a moment ago.

"Anyway," Rudy continued, "I can take Ally up behind me and let Mitchell handle his own if he thinks he can do that. Want to try them out?"

"Definitely, but I should do something about Quillamina Sharp," Mitchell said. "I don't want Dave to come in and discover his interpretive art has been compromised."

"Go on over and settle your bill, and while you're at it, ask Clyde to take her up to his room over the bar," Rudy suggested. "You can get her later."

"I'll do that." He stood and walked over to the bar where Clyde was polishing glasses. In no time, Quillamina was undressed and whisked upstairs.

"Mitch seems excited about the snowmobiles," Rudy said.

"Yes, he does."

"But you're not so excited, are you? Lurleen wasn't, either."

"Maybe it's a guy thing."

Rudy looked worried. "But you'll go, right?"

"Of course. I wouldn't miss it."

He grinned. "You'll like it better'n you think, Ally."

Moments later, they were headed out the door with Rudy. But Ally still didn't know if Mitchell had found an operational vending machine during his visit to the men's room.

Letting Rudy go ahead, she paused and turned back to Mitchell. "By the way, any luck with that other matter?"

"I managed to get one, and then the machine jammed."

So he had one. That was enough to affect her pulse rate. "It's only insurance, anyway. One's plenty."

He gave her a long look. "Ally, if we end up using that insurance, one won't be nearly enough."

Her pulse rate shot off the charts.

"So here we are, and this backwater town hasn't even plowed the road!" Vivian sat staring out through the windshield at the drifts across the country lane leading to Porcupine. "Now what?"

Kurt hadn't counted on this. An unplowed road into a populated area didn't make sense. "I can't understand why it's not plowed," he said. "They must need to get in and out. They must want their mail, for God's sake."

"Maybe everybody *died*."

"That's gruesome, Viv. I'm sure they didn't all die. They just have a problem with this road, for some reason."

"And we have a little problem, too, don't we? Once again, we're sitting on the shoulder of the road. You're lucky that cop gave up following you, or she'd be sitting behind us, twirling her cute little lights and wondering whether or not we operated our vibrator while our vehicle was moving."

Kurt groaned. "Don't remind me." He'd driven for twenty long miles with the cop behind him matching his speed and Vivian beside him moaning and writhing on the seat. Twenty miles with a hard-on and no place to put it. Finally the cop had passed them with a wave. Vivian had waved the vibrator. Kurt could only hope the cop hadn't noticed.

"It's too late to go back," Vivian said. "I've had

enough traveling for one day. I want French cuisine, a hot bath, and a rubdown."

Kurt decided not to mention that even if they made it to Porcupine she wouldn't be getting any of those things. He'd been deliberately vague about the amenities at the Loose Moose Lodge. Vivian wouldn't be happy that there were no tubs, only shower stalls in each bathroom.

In tourist season she might have had to share the bathroom, something she'd never do. But at this time of year Kurt was sure she'd get her own, especially after he introduced her as Tanya Mandell.

"Well, Kurt? Any bright ideas? We can't just sit here. I need to relax."

He studied the drifts. His truck had snow tires, and on TV they'd shown this very model charging right through drifts, spraying snow everywhere. There had been that disclaimer about it being a closed course, but still, the snow hadn't stopped the truck.

If he barreled through the snow and made it to Porcupine because he'd been smart enough to buy this badass truck that could take on anything, that would impress Vivian. He needed to get on her good side before he checked her into the Loose Moose. If she went into this situation convinced that he had his shit together, that would be a good thing.

He put the truck in four-wheel drive and stepped on the gas.

"Kurt! What in God's name are you doing?"

He narrowed his eyes and gripped the wheel. "I'm going through." The front tires hit the snow with a satisfying crunch, sending out eight-foot plumes on either side, just like on the commercial.

"Are you insane? We can't make it through all that snow!"

"Just watch me, baby." The truck roared, the snow sprayed in all directions, and then . . . they stopped. He stepped on the gas and the tires whined as they spun uselessly against packed snow. He glanced in the side mirror. They were buried up to the top of the wheel well.

"That certainly was brilliant. What do you do for an encore?"

Kurt hit the steering wheel with both hands. "False advertising, that's what it is! They shouldn't be allowed to show things on TV unless the average guy can do it! When we get home I'm suing the bastards!"

Vivian sighed and leaned back against the headrest. "I'm trapped in a truck with an idiot who believes what he sees in commercials. It would serve me right to freeze to death out here, because I *knew* you'd find a way to screw this up, Kurt Jarrett."

"Nobody's going to freeze to death."

"Oh, no? You don't have enough gas to run the heater all night."

Kurt fought a sense of panic. "Someone will come along."

"Kurt, the road's not plowed. If this road's not plowed, we can't expect anyone to come along, now can we? Besides, it's starting to get dark. People with any sense have gone home by now, so they don't have to deal with the ice."

"We'll stay in the fifth wheel." He felt better knowing that the fifth wheel was back there, even though the fifth wheel might have been the reason the truck didn't fly through the snow, now that he thought about it.

"The fifth wheel is heated by electricity, remember? You have to hook up to an electrical supply. See any plugs? We could tear pieces off the furniture inside the fifth wheel and burn it, but I'll bet you it's not real wood. Burning it will probably give off gases that can kill you. So we have a choice of freezing to death or being asphyxiated. Which method do you prefer?"

"I think I hear something."

Vivian blew out a breath. "You're grasping at straws. There's nobody out here but us, hanging out right here in the lovely white snowdrift. At least I have my vibrator. Maybe that's how I'll go out, making myself come until I croak. I wonder if anyone's ever—"

"Shh! I think there's a tractor working around that bend in the road."

"Watch your language, bud. That sounded like an order."

He was concentrating so hard on what might be a tractor that he didn't let himself worry about whether he'd given her an order or not. "Don't you hear it?"

She tilted her head to listen. "Now that you mention it, I do. Maybe we're both delirious."

"For crying out loud, Viv. We've been stuck here about five minutes."

"Don't get uppity with me, mister! You're the one who's put us in harm's way, and don't think Vivian's about to forget this, either. Assuming that really is a tractor and we're going to get out of here, you'll have some big debts to pay to Vivian. Yes, you will."

Kurt shuddered. Whenever Vivian started speaking about herself in the third person, he was in for it. He might be on sexual detention for the next month. But the noise of a motor got louder, so at least he wouldn't end up frozen in a truck cab with a woman welded to her vibrator.

Finally the tractor appeared around the bend. Kurt lay on the horn.

Vivian covered her ears. "Was that really necessary? I think he could probably see us. We're considerably bigger than a breadbox."

"I wanted him to know we need help."

"That's obvious, isn't it? Not many people sit here up to the fenders in snow because they intended to do that." She leaned forward and peered at the tractor driver. "He looks sort of cute."

"Vivian, do you remember what we read about Tanya Mandell's sexual preferences?"

"You mean that she's gay? Of course I remember."

"That means you can't be making eyes at any of the men in Porcupine." Kurt had been quite relieved to find out Tanya Mandell's sexual persuasion. Vivian couldn't have sex with him while they were here, but she couldn't have sex with any other guy, either.

She gave him a sly smile. "Then maybe I'll hit on your niece."

"That would *not* be a good idea."

"Why not? I've always wondered if I could swing both ways. Now's the perfect time to find out. For all you know, she'd welcome my attentions."

"I know you're only pulling my chain. You wouldn't really put the moves on Ally." He glanced over at her. "Would you?"

"I don't know yet. I'll see what mood I'm in when we finally get to this godforsaken place. I might be in need of some extra entertainment, and like I said, I've never done it with a girl. That's probably a gap in my education."

Kurt clenched his jaw. He wouldn't mind watching her try that sometime, but this wasn't the right setting. Sometimes he didn't know if Vivian was more of a liability than an asset. She was such a loose cannon.

But then he'd remember how she looked in one of her black leather dominatrix outfits and he couldn't imagine splitting up. The population of Alaska was small, and the frontier atmosphere suited him. But that also meant he didn't have a large pool of S and M folks to draw from. If he lost Vivian, he'd have to make another trek down to Vegas and hang around the S and M club there, knowing his chances of finding someone as wild as Viv were small. She was unique.

He knew she only stayed with him because that first night he'd told her that Madeline's brain tumor would probably be fatal and he'd established a connection with Madeline's heir. Vivian liked him okay, but without the lure of the Jarrett money, she'd be gone. He knew that, which was why this operation was so critical. He wanted the money, too, but he also wanted to hang on to Vivian.

The tractor pulled up alongside the truck, and Kurt rolled down his window. "Can you get us out of here?"

"Be glad to!" The guy showed off a set of startlingly white choppers. "But first let me clear the road so that once you're free, you'll be able to drive right on in to Porcupine."

Vivian leaned across Kurt. "What's your name?"

"I'm David Beedleman. I'm doing this as a favor to the town. I'm actually a sculptor. Just sold one of my pieces today, as a matter of fact."

"Good to meet you, David!" Vivian said.

Kurt sensed way too much enthusiasm in Vivian's voice. If he knew her, and he did, she was already planning a seduction. Time for some action on his part. "I'd like you to meet Tanya Mandell, the wildlife photographer," he said. He wished he could have called her "the *gay* wildlife photographer," but that would sound offensive.

David Beedleman looked impressed. "Wow. Awesome. I admire your work."

"I admire yours, too," Vivian said.

"But you haven't seen it."

She laughed. "I meant your work on the road."

"Oh! Right! Let me get back to it. We're burning daylight!" With another flash of those searchlight-bright teeth, he chugged away on his orange tractor.

"Why does Tanya have to be gay?" Vivian whined. "It's not fair."

"Keep in mind the kind of money we're talking about," Kurt said. "Pretending to be gay for a little while shouldn't be that tough when you remember what's on the line."

"Tell me again. I'll bet David Beedleman's hung like a horse. I need to know all the reasons why I'm ignoring him."

Kurt was used to this routine. She salivated over other guys all the time. He always used the promise of riches to bring her back. "Once we tap into the Jarrett fortune, you'll be able to fly to Paris for lunch."

Vivian closed her eyes. "More, more."

"You'll be able to buy a new Jag as soon as the old one needs washing. You'll be able to have a villa in the south of France. And a private jet to take you there."

Eyes still closed, Vivian flapped her hands in frustration. "I want all that *now*."

"It's closer than ever before. We've waited months. Now we're ready to make contact and start milking that cash cow."

Vivian's eyes snapped open. "Okay, so I'm gay. Happy, now?"

Chapter Seventeen

Mitch took to snowmobiling like a nerd takes to chaos theory. If he could spend all his time on a snowmobile, he might come to enjoy Alaska a little bit. Roaring along on that baby was like being on his Harley, only maybe a tiny bit better. That was tough for him to admit, because he loved his hog. But out here a guy could go full throttle and there wasn't a thing to stop him if he stayed away from the trees.

Well, maybe it wasn't quite that freewheeling. Before they left, Rudy had explained that he'd lead the way, because this time of year you had to be aware of avalanches. You didn't want to start one or get in the way of one that was already started.

But other than that, the world was his snow-covered oyster. A helmet, a pair of goggles, and he was a happy man. On a snowmobile, he could outrun anything, even a *bear*. Or a pack of wolves. That's what he was talkin' about. A snowmobile was the equalizer in this country.

As luck would have it, Ally didn't seem to care much for snowmobiling. He didn't see her smile until they spotted a herd of caribou on the horizon. But when they tried to get near, the noise of the engines scared the animals away. She only pulled out her camera once, when they stopped on a rise to take in the view.

He'd scored a small victory then. During that short break she'd taken off her backpack and left it propped on the snowmobile. Then she'd snapped pictures of what was admittedly a breathtaking scene of snowy mountains with a frozen lake nestled in the foothills. During that time Mitch had slipped the transmitter into her backpack. If he ever needed to track her, he could follow the signal. He doubted she'd ever discover it.

As the light began to fade, they headed back toward Porcupine. Rudy suggested Ally ride with Mitch on the way home, so she climbed on behind him and wrapped her arms around his waist.

He'd given many rides on his Harley to many women. He'd been sexually involved with several of them. Yet he'd never felt such a visceral connection as when he and Ally rode together on that snowmobile.

Maybe it was the cold whipping at them. Where she pressed against him, he was warm, so warm. But it was more than that. She molded herself to his back as if she relished the perfect fit, too.

Women had different styles when it came to riding behind a guy on a bike. Some women held themselves apart, and some didn't mesh, even though they tried. Ally meshed without even trying.

He made the trip home semi-aroused. Too bad Ally

hadn't loved the snowmobiling, because with her nestled against him, he felt as if he could drive until the gas ran out. The only reason not to do that was the condom that he'd tucked in the pocket of his pants and the possibility that the ride had eliminated the last of her resistance.

But as they turned down the main drag of Porcupine, his elation over the excellent snowmobile trip and the possibilities for the night ahead vanished. A silver truck pulling an ostentatious fifth wheel was parked in front of the Loose Moose. No doubt about it, Kurt Jarrett was in town.

He felt the change in Ally immediately. She went from relaxed and in tune with him to stiff and distant. In that moment he knew that she'd been expecting Kurt all along, and she hadn't wanted him to know anything about it. She might have hoped he'd leave before Kurt showed up.

Dammit. She had been in contact with Kurt and Mitch hadn't picked up on that. He felt the prick of failure. He'd monitored her calls, her mail, even her e-mail. Obviously not well enough. She, and possibly Kurt, had deliberately covered up whatever communication they'd had in the past few months.

Okay, the gloves were off now. She might have been playing sexy little games with him, but she hadn't trusted him with the most critical information, that her stepuncle was due in Porcupine the minute weather permitted. She'd guessed correctly that he wouldn't welcome that information.

"That's a real fancy rig," Rudy said as they parked the snowmobiles in front of the Top Hat.

There was no room to park in front of the Loose

Moose. Kurt had pulled in parallel to the curb, taking up at least five diagonal parking spaces. Mitch thought that said something about the guy.

Ally hopped off the snowmobile the moment Mitch brought it to a stop. "I . . . think I know who might own that truck and fifth wheel," she said, not looking at him. "If you'll excuse me, I'll go see if I'm right. Thanks for the ride, Rudy!" She hurried off, her steps eager.

Rudy gazed after her. "What's that all about?"

"Long-lost relative, I expect."

"You don't look so happy about it, Mitch."

Mitch glanced at him, thinking he could use some friends in this struggle. "Sometimes relatives take advantage."

Rudy nodded. "I've known that to happen. So you think whoever drove this outfit into Porcupine might try to take advantage of Ally?"

"He might. Before Ally's grandmother died, she warned me about this guy. She was afraid he might be a problem."

Rudy seemed to puff up and grow bigger, like an animal under attack. And because Rudy was big to begin with, a puffed-up version was very scary. "He'd better not be a problem," Rudy said. "No offense, Mitch, but I'm not sure you're up to the challenge. I think you need me to handle this dude."

"You know, Rudy, I'll take all the help I can get. Thanks for the offer."

"Just say the word, Mitch. I'm meaner than I look."

"That's good to know." In that case, Rudy would be unstoppable. Mitch was glad to have the guy on his side.

"Don't worry about the snowmobiles," Rudy said.

"You just go on in there and check out what's happening. I'll head over to the Top Hat. If you need me, you know where to find me."

"I appreciate that, Rudy." Mitch climbed off the snowmobile. "And thanks for the ride. I loved it."

"You ever ride a motorcycle?"

"Why would you say that?" Mitch didn't want to admit to anything that would possibly get back to Ally.

"Just the way you sat the snowmobile. Like you were right at home. I thought maybe you'd straddled a hunk of machinery like this before, either one of them waverunners or a motorcycle, didn't know which."

"You can't be a teenager in America without taking a few motorcycle rides."

"I guess that's true. I rode my share. Anyway, you looked good out there."

"Thanks." But the compliment didn't make up for his sense of failure where Ally was concerned. He hated playing catch-up. Mentally sweeping any cobwebs from his brain, he headed for the front door of the Loose Moose. He didn't plan on getting a warm greeting from either Ally or Kurt. In fact, he expected to be as welcome as a turd in a punch bowl.

Betsy held forth behind the registration counter. Ally stood in front of it next to a man who was probably in his fifties. If the man was Kurt Jarrett, Mitch knew exactly how old he was—fifty-nine.

The guy was dressed like everybody else around here in a big quilted coat. But he didn't have on boots, and Mitch noticed water stains on the bottom of his pants. His pricey shoes looked as if they'd taken a hit, too. According to what Mitch knew about Kurt, he was more comfortable in the city than in rural areas like Porcupine. It might be the single thing that Mitch had in common with him.

But the most interesting part of this gathering in the lobby of the Loose Moose was Kurt's companion. Mitch hadn't expected anyone else, and here was a woman, tall and slim with a blond braid hanging down her back. She also wore a heavy parka and carried a large but narrow tote over her shoulder. Girlfriend? She didn't act like one. No touching or familiarity between her and Kurt.

Ally—and Betsy, too, for that matter—seemed awestruck by this blond woman. They were so absorbed that they hadn't even noticed him come in the door. Considering the blast of cold air that came along with him, that was saying something.

Oddly enough, it was the blonde who became aware of him first. She turned her head, glanced in his direction and smiled. "Hello, there," she said.

He caught a quick flash of something predatory and sexual in her eyes. Or at least he thought he did. Why she'd be preying on a geek with glasses he didn't know, unless she got excited about anybody who buttoned his shirts from the opposite side.

Ally glanced his way. If she didn't look happy to see him, she at least looked resigned to his presence. "Mitchell, I've just had the most wonderful surprise! This is my uncle Kurt, and he's brought with him, if you can believe it, Tanya Mandell."

She said the name the way Mitch might have said *Michael Jordan,* as if she couldn't believe this person was standing right next to her. Then she gestured toward Mitch. "This is Mitchell J. Carruthers, Jr. He's . . . he was Grammy's personal assistant."

"Nice to meet you." Mitch stepped forward and shook hands with Tanya first, and then Kurt. He got a strange reading from both of them. He'd never met a world-renowned wildlife photographer before, so maybe his expectations were off. But the sexual-predator thing seemed stronger now, and he'd have thought that someone with her reputation would have a classier approach.

Kurt might have been good-looking once, but he hadn't aged particularly well. What could have been a boyish, even cherubic face thirty years ago had become pudgy. His eyes seemed too small and he'd acquired a couple of chins he probably wasn't too happy about. Kurt didn't look particularly happy, period.

But he made an effort to smile and be loving whenever he turned to Ally. "I've waited years to reunite with my niece," he said, putting an arm around her shoulders. "This is a dream come true for me."

"Me, too," Ally said, smiling up at him.

Reunite? Sounded like the jerk had made contact with Ally some time in the past. Mitch fought the urge to go over and remove Kurt's slimy hand from Ally's shoulder. He'd checked out Madeline's story with the only other person who would know the truth, a maid who'd been a young employee at the mansion during the brief time Kurt had been welcome there.

The maid had been reluctant to talk to Mitch. Years ago Madeline had told her she'd be fired if she ever mentioned Kurt, and she'd seen how quickly another employee had been sacked for allowing a phone call from the black sheep of the family. But eventually she'd told Mitch what she knew, and it had jibed perfectly with Madeline's account.

Mitch wouldn't be ready to judge a guy for one bad incident, but Kurt's years following that hadn't been sterling, either. He'd been involved in several shady business deals, although he'd managed to avoid doing jail time. When his father had died twenty years ago, Kurt had continued to receive his monthly allowance, but the rest of the estate had gone to Madeline.

Considering how much money that represented, Mitch figured Kurt had been nursing a grudge ever since. Madeline's fears for Ally seemed totally justified. And yet the guy had brought Ally the perfect gift, a world-renowned wildlife photographer as a mentor. Gestures of family feeling didn't get much grander than that.

"Ally's uncle will be using his fifth wheel accommodations," Betsy said. "But Ms. Mandell will be staying here with us at the lodge." Betsy spoke the photographer's name with the same reverence Ally had used. "Under the circumstances, I've decided that she should have the parlor suite."

Mitch glanced at Betsy in surprise. "But that's your—"

"Our finest room, that's right," Betsy said, warning him off with a glance. "And that's what someone like Ms. Mandell deserves."

That parlor might suit the woman with the predatory stare perfectly, Mitch thought. Talk about your wildlife habitat. "Will the fifth wheel be staying where it is, then?" he asked. He didn't have any stake in all those parking spaces being blocked, but he objected to greedy people in general.

"No, no. I'll be moving it," Kurt said. "I just need to

get Tanya's things unloaded." Both he and Tanya stood there as if expecting a bellhop to appear.

Betsy suddenly snapped to attention. "I'll be glad to bring them in for you if you'll show me where—"

"No, no, I'll help," Ally said. "It would be an honor."

"*I'll* help," Mitch said. "Betsy and Ally, stay inside where it's warm." He started for the door, cutting Ally off at the pass. For some reason the notion of Ally groveling at this woman's feet made him cranky. Tanya might take marvy pictures, but after only a few minutes in her presence, he had reservations about her as a human being.

In his view, a person who schlepped herself around the wilderness taking pictures of savage beasts would be the kind of self-sufficient person who would carry her own luggage into the hotel, luggage that probably included several valuable cameras. If he made his living with equipment like that, he'd want to be in charge of it. But not Tanya, apparently. She stood there and let everyone else rush around getting her stuff.

Even Kurt hurried toward the door. "I'll show you what belongs to her. It's in the fifth wheel."

So Mitch ended up going out to the fifth wheel with Kurt, who was obviously bursting with questions.

"Madeline's personal assistant," he said the minute they were out the door. "Not to be rude, but why are you still hanging around? I would figure your job ended when Madeline died."

"Not exactly." Mitch zipped his coat against the bitter cold and put his gloves on. "My contract with Madeline called for me to handle the details of the estate after she died. She knew Ally would be too upset to deal with it."

"Yeah, I bet. Poor kid." Kurt opened the back door of the fifth wheel. "I'm sure it was rough on her."

Where was a lie detector when you needed one? Mitch wanted Kurt to repeat those words of concern while Mitch watched the needle jump.

"But that still doesn't explain why you're in Alaska." Kurt paused and turned back to Mitch. "I assume all the details you were hired to handle are back in Bel Air."

"I had a few things come up, things that required Ally's signature. I decided not to trust the mail."

"Hm." Kurt's expression said he wasn't buying it. "FedEx would've been a hell of a lot cheaper. But maybe price is no object. Then again, maybe you had other reasons for coming up here."

"Strictly business." He kept his expression blank as he met Kurt's gaze.

"That better be all it is." Kurt's eyes glittered. "Because if you have some idea of marrying into all that money, think again. I'm looking out for her interests, and no gold diggers are getting past me."

Talk about the fox guarding the henhouse. Mitch had to work hard not to laugh in Kurt's face. "Or me," he said.

"Then I guess we both want the same thing."

Not even close. "Let's hope so," he said. "For the record, I think it's great that you arranged for Tanya Mandell to work with Ally. I know how much that will mean to her."

"It's the least I can do for my only living relative." He climbed into the fifth wheel. Soon he returned with a black leather suitcase and a large backpack with all sorts of zippered compartments, obviously for camera gear. He handed that to Mitch and climbed down holding the suitcase.

Mitch hoisted the heavy backpack to his shoulder. "So this is what helps make the magic?"

"Excuse me?" Kurt locked up the fifth wheel and turned to him. "What magic?"

"The award-winning photography. I assume her equipment is in here."

"Oh! That magic. Yep, that's her camera bag."

"Looks really new. You'd think after she'd hauled it all over the world it would be kind of beat up."

Kurt grunted as he picked up the leather suitcase. "She got rid of her old one and bought herself this new job just the other day."

"Sounds like you know her pretty well." Mitch was having a tough time making it all add up. The scoop on Kurt was that he generally hung around with shifty characters, none of whom were world famous. Mitch couldn't imagine Kurt moving in the same circles as a woman like Tanya Mandell.

"Yeah, we're good friends."

"How did you happen to meet her?"

"At a party."

If that wasn't a non-answer, Mitch had never heard one. He needed to check with Pete and get some info on Tanya Mandell. Maybe once he knew more about her, he'd understand the connection. Right now, it was a mystery.

They returned to the lobby, Mitch well ahead of Kurt, who was struggling along with the heavy black suitcase. Mitch didn't have much sympathy for him. He'd chosen which of the two he'd carry.

When Mitch walked in, the parlor door was open and he could hear women's voices. Betsy must be introducing Tanya to her new digs. This he wanted to see.

He carried the camera bag straight in there. "Here's your equipment, Ms. Mandell." He laid the backpack on one of Betsy's red velvet settees.

"Please call me Tanya," she said, giving him the once-over. Then she returned her attention to the Murphy bed that Betsy was pulling down from the wall. "Had you seen this room before, Mitchell?" she said without looking at him.

"Uh, yes, I did see it."

"Holy shit!" Kurt staggered in through the door and put down the suitcase with a thud. "This looks exactly like—"

"That's what it is," Tanya said, turning to him. "Betsy's been filling me in on the colorful history of the Loose Moose. I had no idea."

And she loves it, Mitch thought. The world-famous photog has a kinky side. Oh, well. People were complex. He'd learned that much during his career as a PI.

"It's all ready for you," Betsy said. "I changed the sheets this morning."

Mitch just bet she had, after the night she'd spent with Poopsie, the orgasm king.

"I'll double-check the bathroom, to make sure everything's ready in there, and we'll leave you to get settled in," Betsy said.

"And I would love to buy both of you dinner over at the Top Hat," Ally added.

"The Top Hat?" Tanya smiled. "Sounds very nice. I assume that's the best restaurant in town?"

"It's the only restaurant in town," Mitch said. "But it's very good," he added quickly, feeling a surprising loyalty to Clyde.

"Then if we're already talking about dinner, I'd better get going and set up for the night, myself," Kurt said. "David, the sculptor guy who pulled us out of the snow, said I could hook up to his electricity while I'm here."

"David said he uses a chain saw to sculpt nudes." The sexual gleam was back in Tanya's eyes. "I'm dying to see his work."

"Mitchell bought one of his nudes today," Betsy said.

Mitch could have done without that announcement. Buying the nude in the first place was embarrassing enough, without Kurt and this Tanya woman finding out about it. "Dave calls it 'interpretive sculpture,'" he said. "Quite unusual. Sort of what you'd imagine Picasso might do if somebody had handed him a chain-saw and a chunk of cedar."

"Sounds fascinating," Tanya said. "Where is it? Up in your room?"

"No," Ally said quickly. "It's not."

Well, knock him over with a feather. Ally had sounded territorial right then, as if she'd picked up on the sexual vibes coming from Tanya and she didn't want this woman, mentor or not, encroaching. Maybe all was not lost in that department.

"She's . . . I mean, it's over at the Top Hat," Mitch said.

"The bathroom's set!" Betsy emerged from that room with a smile. "Let's leave Ms. Mandell to herself, so she can freshen up. Then we can all meet at the Top Hat and celebrate."

Kurt glanced at Ally. "You'll be going over, right?"

"Absolutely."

"Good. I have some great ideas I want to discuss with you."

Mitch decided no matter what, he needed to be within hearing distance of that discussion. Kurt might have produced Tanya Mandell, but even that move was suspect. And when it came to Kurt proposing ideas to Ally, Mitch would bet they'd have *scam* written all over them.

Chapter Eighteen

Ally kept pinching herself to make sure she wasn't dreaming. Apparently she was actually sitting at the same restaurant table as Tanya Mandell, because every time she pinched herself, she felt the sting. Uncle Kurt had come through like a champ. If Ally couldn't learn how to be a wildlife photographer from this woman, she would never learn.

But Tanya, who sat on her left, wasn't doing much talking tonight. Uncle Kurt, on Ally's right, was the gabby one of the foursome. Mitchell sat across from Ally, watching and listening, saying very little. She'd been able to tell from his lack of surprise when he'd walked into the Loose Moose lobby that he had prior knowledge of Uncle Kurt. Grammy must have said something.

From the way Mitchell was studying her uncle, Ally could guess that Grammy's comments had been negative. Mitchell was on full alert. He'd barely touched his beer.

Tanya, it turned out, spent most of her time looking at Mitchell. She seemed to find him fascinating. That didn't make sense to Ally, who'd read that Tanya Mandell preferred women. Yet when Tanya gazed at Mitchell, she showed definite sexual interest.

Maybe Tanya liked both girls and boys. Maybe she had an open relationship with her partner. Creative people sometimes walked a different path from the mainstream.

Ally told herself not to think about it. If she worried about whether Tanya would hit on Mitchell, then she wouldn't be able to concentrate on learning every trick of the trade from the most talented photographer in Alaska. In any case, she shouldn't care if Tanya made a play for Mitchell.

She shouldn't care if Mitchell responded, either. That would make it easier for her, because she wouldn't be tempted to scratch that particular itch anymore. Maybe he'd scratch his itch with Tanya. Ally was so indebted to Tanya for taking time out of her life to help a novice that giving up Mitchell for the cause should be a snap.

Well, it wasn't. Ally was so busy noticing Tanya noticing Mitchell that she barely heard what Uncle Kurt was saying. Besides that, conversation was difficult in the Top Hat tonight. Serena was the entertainment, and she was playing the zither. Ally hadn't heard much zither music in her life, but she didn't think it was supposed to sound quite so much like cats fighting.

"What do you have to show us, Ally?" Uncle Kurt took a sip of his Scotch. They'd decided to have drinks before ordering dinner, although Tanya didn't drink. She'd asked for Perrier with a twist of lime, and she'd been forced to settle for Sprite with a lemon drop.

Ally couldn't remember what Uncle Kurt had been talking about and she was starting to feel the effects of the Irish coffee she'd ordered. Tonight she'd stop with one. "To show you? I'm not sure what you mean."

"Your sample pictures. I advised you to bring some. Do you have them with you?"

"Oh!" She did, but the thought of taking that envelope out of her backpack and displaying her amateur efforts in front of Tanya made her cringe. "Uh, well, I—"

"Don't be shy," Uncle Kurt said. "That's the first thing you have to learn. Demonstrate confidence in your work. It impresses people. Tanya wants to see what you've done, right, Tanya?"

"Of course."

Feeling more than a little nervous, Ally reached for her backpack, unzipped it, and pulled out a manila envelope. Her hands shook slightly as she took out the five pictures she'd brought and spread them on the table. She hoped Tanya wouldn't laugh and dismiss them as hopeless.

Everyone leaned forward, including Mitchell. "Very nice," he said. "Very nice. I really like that lion."

She appreciated his support, but his wasn't the opinion that mattered.

Tanya glanced over the photographs. "Definite talent," she said.

Ally felt as if she'd won an Academy Award. Her skin warmed with pleasure. Life didn't get much better than having her work praised by Tanya Mandell. "Thank you," she murmured.

"See?" Kurt looked pleased. "You're ready to leap right into it. Think about this. Everyone else has to build a name and find a publisher in order to be recognized. Photographers can be excellent, but until they've collected some photo credits from major magazines, they have trouble selling a publisher on a coffee-table book."

Ally remembered why she'd zoned out on the discussion in the first place. She'd thought the idea of publishing something this soon was ridiculous. "I'm a long way away from a coffee-table book, Uncle Kurt." She gathered up her pictures and put them back in the envelope.

"That's where you're wrong, missy."

She wasn't crazy about being called "missy," either, but Uncle Kurt meant it in a good way, so she decided to let it go. "Seriously, I need to get a lot of basic training before I'm ready to submit to magazines. I'm hoping Tanya can give me a crash course in technique. Then it's up to me."

Uncle Kurt leaned closer. "Tanya can tell you exactly how to take those pictures, so that your first efforts are more than adequate to create a coffee-table book. And we don't look for a publisher, we publish it ourselves! I have great contacts in that area. Distribution will be a snap. We'll flood the media with advertising. We'll—"

"Hold on a minute." Ally put a hand on his arm. He meant well, but he didn't understand. "This is sounding a little bit as if I'm going to buy my way in."

"And what's wrong with that?" Uncle Kurt laughed. "Let the other poor slobs dink around for years. Take your God-given talent and head right for the top!"

Ally took a long, shaky breath. She'd known Uncle Kurt was a go-for-the-gusto kind of guy. That's why she'd been so eager to hook up with him after Grammy died. She hadn't counted on this attitude, though. He wanted her to cut corners on her way up.

"See my point?" He beamed at her. "Good God, Ally, you're richer than God! Why not use some of that money to get what you want?"

She clutched his arm and lowered her voice. "I don't want people around here to know about the money," she said.

"Yes, for heaven's sakes, Kurt," Tanya said. "That isn't the sort of information you broadcast. No telling who might be listening. Next thing you know, all sorts of people will be pestering the poor girl for money."

"I could handle that," Ally said, still keeping her voice low. "But what I couldn't handle is people treating me differently. I came up here to escape the heiress label." She glanced at Mitchell. "Which hasn't been easy."

"Why escape it?" Uncle Kurt looked puzzled. "Why not use it to get where you want to go? Wouldn't you agree, Tanya?"

Ally turned to her, hoping that Tanya would see it her way. "You worked your way to the top. Don't you think there's a basic integrity to doing it that way? Aren't you more confident, knowing you perfected your craft before hitting the big time?"

Before answering, Tanya glanced disapprovingly at Serena, who was still torturing the zither. Then she turned back to Ally. "If I'd had your resources, I wouldn't have spent all those years in the trenches, believe me. Why do that when you don't have to?"

"But I want to," Ally said. "I think trench time is a good thing."

"Trench time is highly overrated." Tanya had one hand on her glass, but the other had disappeared under the table. "Public perception is everything. Put out a slick package of your photographs, spend enough on publicity, and you'll be launched. You could have it happen by next year, instead of working like a dog for ten or fifteen years, like I did."

Mitchell abruptly scooted his chair back. "Excuse me a minute. I'm going to get another beer. Anybody else need something?"

"More nuts." Tanya's hand reappeared as she reached for some peanuts in a bowl in the center of the table. "I do love nuts."

Ally was flabbergasted. Although she couldn't prove it, she thought the great Tanya Mandell had just made a grab for Mitchell under the table. Judging from her comment, Ally had a fair idea what she'd grabbed for.

The good news was that Mitchell hadn't been happy with the move. He had more than half his beer left, so he definitely didn't need another one. The bad news was that Ally wanted to slap Tanya silly. And this was the woman who was supposed to help her realize her dream.

Ally got up, too. "I could use another Irish coffee," she said. "I'll be right back."

"Isn't that what the waiter is for?" Uncle Kurt asked.

Ally glanced over to where David stood holding an empty tray while he talked casually with Betsy and Rudy. "He's very busy," she said, and hurried over to the bar to join Mitchell.

Kurt leaned across the table. For once he was glad the hippie woman was playing the damned zither, because the noise gave him some cover for the conversation he needed to have with Viv. "What did you do just now?"

"Nothing." She cracked open a shell and popped a peanut into her mouth.

"I don't believe it was nothing. I think you tried to grab Mitchell's balls under the table."

"What if I did?" She chewed the peanut and swallowed. "I like that whole nerdy look he's got going. Makes him more of a challenge than the sculptor."

"Vivian, how many times do I have to say this? You're supposed to be *gay*."

"I think this trip will mark my conversion to bisexuality."

Kurt fought for control. He couldn't lose it in the middle of this godforsaken little bar, because then he'd blow any chance of bringing Ally around to his way of thinking. "Viv, we have to concentrate on the goal."

"I am concentrating." She cracked open another peanut. "Mitchell J. Carruthers, Jr., is in our way. Did you happen to notice that?"

"Yeah, but he's a nerd, like you said. I'm pretty sure he's after Ally, but she wouldn't get hooked up with a boring guy like that. I'm not worried about him."

"Ally likes him. And he doesn't much like you. Plus, I don't think he's as boring as you imagine. He could be more of a problem than you're counting on."

"And you're going to solve it by grabbing his crotch? Jesus, Viv."

"It's a start. But I have the feeling that Plan A is doomed, anyway."

A trickle of cold sweat slid down Kurt's backbone. He liked Ally. He didn't want to see something happen to her. "No it's not. Give it time."

"How much time? Ten years, until she feels ready to

do that coffee-table book? You said we could get her to hand over the money for the printing right away, but I don't see that happening. She loves the trenches."

"Forget what she said. Trust me, before long we'll see naked ambition."

"I wouldn't mind seeing a naked nerd."

Kurt groaned. He'd often wondered if Vivian had ADHD because she was so easily distracted. Now he was sure of it. "Look at what we've accomplished. She's forked over a check for your mentoring fee and your expenses for coming up here. Tomorrow she'll order camera equipment through your favorite catalog and give you the money for that."

"That's right." Vivian tossed a shelled peanut in the air and caught it between her teeth. She crunched down and the peanut cracked. Then she chewed the peanut and swallowed it. "I need to remember to get that catalog out of my suitcase."

"That suitcase weighs a ton. What's in there, anyway?" He took a swallow of his drink.

"My gun, for one thing."

He choked on his Scotch.

"You didn't know I brought a gun?"

He coughed into his napkin. "No, Viv, I didn't know you brought a gun." And suddenly his stomach got queasy. He didn't have to ask why she'd brought it. Plan B.

He'd have to make sure she never had a reason to take that gun out of her suitcase. "So anyway, adding up where we are, you already have the money for your fee and expenses, and tomorrow you'll get the check for the camera equipment. Then in a couple of days you'll get a call about a lucrative assignment, which you'll refuse. She'll feel honor-bound to replace the money you turned down."

"It's the honor part of her makeup that worries me. You didn't tell me she was ethical, Kurt. How are we supposed to work with someone who has ethics?"

"I don't know. I've never had to before. But I'm sure there's an angle to play. I'll figure out what it is."

On her way over to where Mitch was standing at the bar, Ally was stopped by Betsy.

"How's it going, toots?"

"Great." Ally hated to tell Betsy that Tanya Mandell, the woman to whom Betsy had given her beloved parlor for the duration of her stay, was into groping men under the table. Betsy might have sex on the brain, but she wouldn't do something like that, at least not to a man she barely knew. "I appreciate all the trouble you went to, giving up your room and everything."

"It was nothing. I knew the minute your uncle Kurt introduced her that I'd need to put her in the parlor instead of a regular room. I'm just glad you showed up to cover for me while I ducked in there and emptied the armoire of my duds."

"No problem. Tanya seems really happy with the parlor." A little too happy, in Ally's opinion. She'd never pictured Tanya as a nympho.

"I'm glad she is. And I'll be over bright and early in the morning to cook breakfast, so don't worry about that."

"So where are you staying, Betsy?" Rudy asked.

"Upstairs with Poopsie, but don't let that get around.

It's temporary. I'm not living with a man until I have a ring on my finger. But I can't stay in a regular room at the lodge or Tanya will figure out she's in my room." She motioned Ally closer and lowered her voice. "Do you think Tanya's after Mitchell? I thought she liked girls."

"Who knows? But speaking of Mitchell, I need to go talk to him. See you guys later, okay?" She hurried over to the bar and caught Mitchell as he was about to head back with a full glass of beer.

She lounged against the bar and batted her eyelashes. "Buy me a drink?"

He looked her up and down and smiled. "You sure about that? You still have most of your first one."

"So do you."

"Yeah, well, I wanted to guarantee I had a spare. In case Dave got busy."

She gazed up at him. "Or maybe something was happening under the table that didn't appeal to you."

His eyes widened. "You saw that?"

"Not literally. I'd have had to be sitting on the floor to see it, but I noticed her hand disappearing and then you reacted like a man who'd been the unwilling victim of a grope."

Mitch adjusted his glasses and cleared his throat. "Maybe it was a mistake."

"But you don't think so."

"I want to think so, for your sake. Not that what she does regarding men has anything to do with what she can teach you, but—"

"I know. I told myself the same thing. And I still intend to learn a great many things from her. This is a terrific opportunity."

"Yes, it is, and you deserve this chance. I meant what I said about those pictures. They're wonderful."

"Really?" Maybe his opinion mattered more than she'd thought.

"Yeah, really. I know I've been trying to discourage you, but I can see now that this is what you should be doing with your life. I want you to get some coaching from Tanya."

"Thank you, Mitchell. That means a lot to me." She looked into his eyes. "But I still don't like her behavior. It's icky. And I especially don't like her trying something like that with you."

He didn't say anything for several seconds, but his eyes did plenty of talking. They grew all warm and soft, like chocolate left out in the sun. "I appreciate that."

She shrugged. "She's my ticket to breaking into this business, but when she starts putting the move on you, I can't seem to look the other way. The truth is, I have no right to care what happens between you two, but I do."

"Ally, I'm not even slightly attracted to her."

"You didn't have to say that, but thanks." Her whole body thanked him. Significant parts started dancing with joy at the news.

He took a deep breath. "I'm attracted to you."

"Yeah, same here. Sex 'R' Us." She was amazed at how possessive she felt about him.

"I thought when your uncle showed up with Tanya, you'd forget all about that."

"I thought I would, too. I guess my curiosity is getting the better of me."

His gaze heated. "Only curiosity?"

There it was, the look that turned her legs to licorice

whips and made her want to strip him down and climb aboard. "Maybe something more than that. You're a great kisser."

"You're a great kissee."

She laughed, feeling tons better. "I'm really starting to like your brand of humor, Mitchell."

"If you think I'm funny now, you should see me naked. Talk about hilarious."

She looked him over and smiled. "Somehow I doubt that. Besides, I want to get you alone so I can find out what Grammy said to you about Uncle Kurt."

"Ally, you don't really want to—"

"Never mind. We'll talk later. Now, about that drink you're going to buy me . . ."

Mitch didn't eat a whole lot of his meal. Between listening to the schemes Kurt was laying out, anticipating some alone time with Ally tonight, and making sure Tanya kept her hands to herself, he didn't have a chance to deal with food. At least Ally didn't seem to be going for Kurt's plan of publishing an expensive coffee-table book right out of the gate.

He hoped one day he'd see a book of her photographs, though. Those five pictures she'd brought with her had blown him away. Until now he hadn't fully appreciated that this was far more than a hobby. Ally had the makings of a star. But the coffee-table book idea sounded fishy.

Although Mitch didn't know much about publishing, he could imagine how someone like Kurt could embezzle thousands while he handled the details of the project. Ally wasn't into spreadsheets and cost estimates, and her grandmother had never insisted that she become informed.

In that respect, Mitch disagreed with Madeline's approach. He'd like to see Ally more involved in the financial picture. But when he'd tried to coax her into taking a look at some balance sheets back at the mansion, she'd found excuses not to. Now he understood why—she'd planned to leave it all for him to do while she pursued this photography career.

But that left her open to being swindled by the likes of Kurt Jarrett if she wasn't in the habit of checking the bottom line. Now that Mitch could see that was a real danger, he'd try to convince her to take a greater interest in the business side of things. He could always ask to look over Kurt's records himself, but she might not go for that. In any case, she needed to become better informed.

He wasn't sure how and when he'd broach the subject. Once they were alone, chemistry could take over and financial information would be the farthest thing from his mind. He didn't know how a person moved from lust to ledgers.

And speaking of lust, Tanya's agenda was becoming increasingly obvious. Twice he'd had to grab her wrist as she'd started walking her fingers along his thigh.

The second time, as the meal was nearly over, she stuck out her lower lip in a pout. "You're no fun," she murmured under cover of Kurt and Ally's conversation about career strategies.

"You've got that right." He guided her hand back to her lap.

She grasped his wrist with her free hand. "Stay and play a while. I like lap games."

"No, thanks." He was surprised at the strength of her grip. He had to yank his hand free, and in the process he bumped the table, which made the plates and glasses jump.

Kurt looked irritated as he glanced at Tanya. "Have we got an earthquake going on or what?"

Tanya smiled at Mitch. "Not yet. Tune in tomorrow."

Kurt drained the last of his Scotch. "Well, it's been a long day and that zither music is giving me a headache."

Mitch wouldn't be sorry to see the meal end. "Then you'd better get out of here before Clyde starts tap-dancing on the bar."

"Good Lord." Kurt pushed back his chair. "Think I'll mosey on down to my fifth wheel and turn in. Thanks for the dinner, Ally."

"You're welcome." She stood and gave him a hug goodbye.

Mitch got to his feet, too, and damned if Tanya didn't pop up right along with him. He was hoping she'd decided to stay for the tap dancing and maybe find another victim.

"Think about that book project some more," Kurt said to Ally. "It could really start you off with a bang."

Tanya leaned over toward Mitch. "How about starting me off with a bang?"

"Sorry."

"You will be sorry," she murmured. "You have no idea what you're missing. I know just what to do with stuffy nerd-boys like you. You've never had it like I can give it to you."

Sick of listening to this drivel, Mitch turned and pinned her with a glare. "Look, Tanya, I respect your work and I'm glad you're willing to help Ally. But I'm not interested."

Her blue eyes gleamed. "Oo. Manly indignation. I like that." She winked at him. "I'll bet you're a tiger when you're aroused."

"I think I'll go find our coats." He stepped away from the table.

Tanya clutched his arm. "I'll let you get away this time, but you'll come around. Goody Two-Shoes over there isn't woman enough for you. And don't forget, I'm the one with the mirror over my bed."

Mitch said nothing. Maybe he couldn't keep his private time with Ally a secret in a town like Porcupine, but he didn't have to confirm or deny when it came to this creepy woman. He hoped she'd teach Ally a lot of good photography stuff in a short time and leave.

Maybe he was beginning to understand her connection with Kurt, after all. One might be a loser and the other a world-famous figure, but they both had a corner on the sleaze market. Ally saw that, too, and he was sorry that her uncle and her idol couldn't be everything she'd hoped.

Unfortunately, she didn't know the half of it where Kurt was concerned. Mitch wished Madeline had filled Ally in before she died, but instead she'd left him to deal with this mess. In every other way Madeline had tied up her affairs neatly, but Kurt Jarrett was the huge, glaring exception and there was no easy fix.

For the moment, Mitch had to trust Ally not to let her strong need for a warm family connection screw with her judgment. At least she hadn't turned away from him. But if he maligned her dear uncle Kurt, she just might. He'd have to be careful.

Chapter Nineteen

Ally wasn't sure what Mitchell had said to Tanya, but the woman had switched her attentions to Dave. Serena didn't look happy about that, but Ally decided Serena would have to figure out her own answer to the problem. For the time being, Ally's problem was solved and she and Mitchell were heading out the door of the Top Hat, bound for the Loose Moose.

She realized she was walking right into temptation by going over to the Loose Moose with Mitchell, but she couldn't take any more of Tanya right now. If she expected to be able to work with her tomorrow, she had to get away from her tonight.

When Mitchell had suggested a game of cards, she'd accepted the invitation gratefully. She knew the dangers, and she was flying in the face of them. At the moment, she just— *Omigod*. Coming to an abrupt halt, she gazed up at the night sky.

Next to her, Mitchell caught his breath. "What's *that*?"

"Nature's laser show," Ally murmured. "The northern lights." She was dazzled by the irregular plumes of iridescent green and blue fanning out across the starry sky. For years she'd dreamed about seeing this, and now she was here.

"The northern lights. Amazing. For a second I thought it might be an alien invasion. That green is the color of those little Martian guys with the antennae and ray guns."

"Oh, it is not." She had to smile, though. What a typical nerd comment. "I'd go for my camera, but I don't think I have the right equipment to do that justice."

"You'd want to take pictures of this?" He stood staring up at the sky, his hands in his pockets.

"Of course. It's spectacular." She noticed he was being the perfect gentleman, not trying to touch her at all. That's what she wanted. Sure she did. "Why are you so surprised?"

He waved a gloved hand at the glowing sky. "No fangs, no claws. No real risk involved."

She laughed, sending a cloud of vapor into the air. "I won't always be taking pictures of carnivores, Mitchell. I'll take pictures of other wildlife that's not scary at all. Tanya might have me start off with ptarmigans tomorrow. I saw a flock of them when we went out snowmobiling today."

He glanced at her. "Tar-whatzit?"

"Ptarmigan. With a *p*. It's mostly a ground bird. I guess you didn't hear Clyde say that's what you were eating tonight."

"Nope. Once he said it hadn't been run over, I ordered

it. Tasted strong, though, whenever I dared take a bite. I had to stay alert."

"I know. It's embarrassing that she acts that way." Ally watched his mouth, watched the little puffs of condensed moisture that punctuated his words, remembered how that mouth had felt. Her heart beat faster, thinking of his kiss. "I thought she was gay."

"Gay?" Mitchell laughed. "If she's gay, I'll eat roadkill for the rest of my life. That woman may be a lot of things, but gay isn't one of them."

Ally tipped her head back, letting her hood fall away as she drank in the incredible light show dancing above them. At least the northern lights hadn't disappointed her. "You know, Mitchell, life's such a crapshoot. I finally get the mentor of my dreams, and she's a nympho."

"Stalking wild animals could have brought out her inner wild animal. Maybe after a while you'll get like that, making suggestive remarks, grabbing guys by the *cojones*."

She turned her head to look at him. "I think not."

He smiled. "Those lights . . . turn your face kind of green."

"Like a Martian?"

"Yeah." He moved closer, still smiling. "Except you don't have the antennae. Otherwise, the resemblance is uncanny."

"How romantic." Kidding around like this helped take the sting out of her disappointment. He probably knew that. Besides being sexy, he was also sweet.

"Actually, it is romantic. I loved those movies." He

reached up, took off his glasses and pressed them into her gloved hand. "Hold these for me."

"Why?" She thought she knew why. He was about to plant one on her. And she was about to let him.

He cupped her face in both hands and leaned closer. "I'm not putting any pressure on you. This doesn't mean I expect you to go to bed with me. But I really want to kiss you in the glow from the northern lights."

She was way too eager for this and felt sort of vulnerable as a result. She tried to make light of his offer. "So it turns out you have an alien fetish. Who knew?"

"There are lots of things you don't know about me." And his lips touched hers.

She hadn't thought he could improve on that first kiss, but she'd been wrong. This time his mouth was warmer . . . well, no, *hot* would be the operative word. She tasted the nutty flavor of the beer he'd been drinking, but the overriding flavor was lust, and she couldn't get enough of it.

Oh, how she loved the way this man kissed, without hesitation, as if he knew exactly what he intended and would let nothing stand in his way. She didn't know how he communicated so much with the simple movement of his lips and tongue, but he left no doubt as to what he wanted from her.

And she wanted to give him everything he was asking for . . . and then give some more. Vaguely she remembered that this was supposed to be a no-pressure kiss. Fat chance. Seconds into the kiss, she could think of nothing better than getting naked and attending to unfinished business. She and Mitchell might have little in common, but they had one particular matter they completely agreed on, and he was reminding her of it.

He lifted his mouth a fraction and his breath warmed her cheeks. "I like this."

She had to be honest. "Me, too." And she pulled him back for more. Their mouths fit together as if made exclusively for this. The rest of their parts might go together just as well. Probably would. And thanks to this kissing business, she wanted to find out. She was sure that had been his intention all along.

Kurt had parked his truck and fifth wheel beside David Beedleman's small house on the edge of town, but in a burg the size of Porcupine, one edge of town was only a block from the other edge. He'd angled the fifth wheel so that he had a view out the side window that included the entire street. He'd done that to try and keep an eye on Vivian. The woman was out of control.

She might have her gun, but he had something she didn't know about, a pair of night-vision binoculars. He'd thought they might come in handy, and sure enough, he was already doing some useful surveillance. He'd caught Mitchell and Ally playing kissy-face.

Vivian had said something might be going on between those two. Kurt didn't like the idea of Vivian getting it on with Mitchell, but he didn't want Mitchell involved with Ally, either. Maybe Viv was on to something with her plan to get into Mitchell's pants. And it wasn't like he'd ever expected her to be faithful to him, anyway.

Yeah, he needed to promote that plan of Viv's. He'd thought she was off on another tangent, but maybe she knew exactly what she was doing. She'd said that

Mitchell didn't like Kurt, and the feeling was mutual. That geek had wormed his way into Madeline's good graces and was probably siphoning money like a gas thief at a car dealership.

If anybody was going to siphon from Madeline's accounts it would be Kurt, not that pencil-pusher. So whatever Viv needed to engineer her seduction of Mitchell J. Carruthers, Jr., Kurt would provide. Mitchell was definitely in the way.

Kissing Ally made Mitch forget about everything, even the temperature, which had probably dipped close to zero by this time of night. He should probably cease and desist before their lips froze together, but she tasted so damned good. Ally's kiss was premium-grade, blue-ribbon gourmet fare. He didn't think that had anything to do with her net worth in dollars, but it had a lot to do with her net worth as a person.

Ally had principles, and now he wanted to get past at least one of them, the one that kept her from going to bed with him. He'd lied when he'd said he had no ulterior motives for kissing her. His kiss was loaded with ulterior motives.

She backed off a smidgen, and he came after her, not willing to let up when he could tell she was losing ground to her lust.

"Wait." She slid her fingers over his mouth as she gasped for breath. "I thought . . . you weren't putting pressure . . . on me."

"That's what guys always say." He ran his tongue

along the groove between her fingers. "They're always putting pressure on you. That's what guys do."

"Mitch, I don't feel right about this."

"I do." He tried to get a good hold on her, but between her parka and his, they were chastely separated by a good four inches of down and weatherproof nylon. She kept slip-sliding away. "I have an idea," he said. "I'll bet we could unzip these things and then zip them together, like a double sleeping bag."

"Mitchell, we're in the middle of the street."

"We're in the middle of the street in Porcupine, Alaska, which is not the same as being in the middle of the street in Los Angeles, California." He reached for her zipper.

She brushed his hand away. "Stop it, you crazy man. We're leaving our coats on."

"Okay, but I hope you realize that if everybody had to wear these coats all the time, the human race would die out completely."

That made her smile.

"Your teeth are greenish, too."

"You say the sweetest things. No wonder I crave your body."

"You do?" He grabbed her hand and nibbled on her fingers.

"That's not saying I'll give in to that craving."

"Give in, Ally. Let's indulge in some cheap, tawdry, meaningless sex."

"I couldn't do that to you, Mitchell. I—"

He groaned. "I know. You respect me too much."

"It's true! You got me through the bad time after

Grammy died, so how can I repay you by having sex and then tossing you aside like a used condom?"

"At least that condom had its moment of glory."

"You do realize that you're thinking with your—"

"Probably, and I never realized before how smart my buddy is. He's a Zen kind of guy, wants to live for the moment."

Ally shook her head. "You'd hate me later. And we have to maintain a working relationship, don't forget."

"Okay, I'll draw up a binding contract that absolves you of all responsibility for my state of mind during the act itself and for months afterward. How's that?"

"Mitchell, be serious."

"I'm as serious as a heart attack. Tell me what it would take for you to feel guilt-free about this."

"Nothing." She wiggled out of his arms. "I'd be worried about it forever."

"That's a long time." He wondered if she was strong enough to take a pass. Maybe. "Okay, what are the alternatives to having sex, now that we've made our escape from the Top Hat and Tanya, who seems obsessed with my crotch?"

"Understandable obsession."

"Now you're teasing me."

She sighed. "I am, and I apologize."

"Don't apologize. Go to bed with me, Ally."

She gazed at him for a long time, obviously still struggling with her decision. "I thought we were going to play cards."

"I never intended for us to play cards, and you know it."

"Well, I did intend for us to play cards."

He decided the skirmish could continue more

productively inside than out here. "Okay. How about your place? Mine's a mess." He didn't want her in there prowling around and finding things like a tracking system for the microtransmitter he'd put in her backpack. And there was the little matter of his gun. That might freak her out a bit.

"It's a date. My place." She started down the sidewalk toward the Loose Moose.

"You're on." He glanced back at the northern lights, which were still waving and dancing in the night sky. He would never choose Alaska as his favorite spot in the world, but snowmobiling had been excellent, and the northern lights were cool. Oh, yeah, and the nights were long in Alaska. If he could spend them fooling around with Ally, Alaska would be tolerable.

He followed her to the Loose Moose. So they'd play cards. Maybe the card game would lead to something else. Maybe not. But he needed to remember, regardless of where the card game led, that Ally was rich and he was not rich. She would most likely spend her life in Alaska building a reputation as a wildlife photographer, and he would return to tend the books in Bel Air.

But first he had to make sure she didn't fall prey to Kurt Jarrett, although she seemed pretty savvy about the guy already. Mitch felt the need to stick around, though. And while he was sticking around watching out for Ally's interests, he might get lucky. And he wasn't talking about the poker game.

Ally breezed into the lobby, shrugged out of her coat, and sat down on the bench to take off her boots. "I think we should get some beer out of the refrigerator and take it upstairs," she said. "You always have beer at poker parties, right?"

"Sure."

She was feeling a little reckless, and that probably wasn't a good thing, considering the fact that she was about to spend time in a room that contained both Mitchell and a bed. But strange as it seemed, she felt safer with Mitchell than she had with Uncle Kurt and Tanya.

She knew instinctively that Mitchell wouldn't hurt her, but she couldn't be sure about Uncle Kurt or Tanya. She'd had such high hopes, and yet now it seemed she'd have to learn her craft from a woman she respected professionally but couldn't stand personally. That sucked.

"I'll get the beer." She tucked her boots under the bench and walked toward the kitchen in her socks. "Meet me in my room with the cards."

"Okay."

She glanced at him sitting on the bench, one boot off and one still on. He might be a dork, but he was a really cute dork, and at least he was the person he claimed to be. "I need to say one thing, and I never thought I'd say this. But I'm glad you came to Alaska."

"It was my job."

"No it wasn't. Nobody could interpret your job as needing to run up here and check on me. But I know that's what you decided to do, and I appreciate it."

He looked uncomfortable with the praise. "Listen, it was no big deal. I know I've complained a few times, but I—"

"Mitchell, accept that you did a good thing by

coming up here. You didn't know there would be this major attraction between us. That was totally unforeseen."

"Not exactly." He'd put his glasses back on and now he was regarding her with touching sincerity. "I've felt that tug-of-war from the first time I met you. I've been fighting it, but I knew it was there."

She flushed with pleasure. It was shallow of her, but she couldn't help it. He'd been drawn to her all along. "So that's why you flew up here?" Maybe the original story, that he had a crush, was actually the true story.

"No. At least not consciously. I flew up here to make sure you were okay. Madeline . . . would have wanted me to."

"Probably she would have, if she'd known I had such a wild adventure planned." Ally had a sudden thought. "You don't suppose that Grammy meant to throw us together?"

He shook his head. "I'm sure she hoped you'd find somebody in your league. I'm not, Ally. We both know that."

"I don't know that. I don't know anything about leagues." She was impatient with the whole concept. "What am I supposed to do, find some exotic foreign prince?"

"That's the general idea."

"Well, I'm not in the market for a prince, or a husband, for that matter. So if you're hoping to safely marry me off so you don't have to worry about me anymore, forget it."

His eyes flashed with unmistakable anger. "I'm *not* hoping to marry you off."

She couldn't tell if he was angry with her or himself.

"I'm glad we got that straightened out, then. No wedding. I'll get the beer." As she walked into the kitchen and flipped on a light, she remembered the refrigerator raid they'd staged the night before, and getting caught in here while Betsy and Clyde made whoopee in the lobby.

She'd had some great fun with Mitchell in the short time he'd been here. Although she'd worried that he'd become an anchor around her neck, it hadn't worked out that way. She would miss him when he left.

His reaction to the marriage topic was strange, though. Logically, he should be thrilled if she found the right guy, settled down, and started having babies. Then he wouldn't have to worry about her marrying a fortune hunter. He might also believe that a husband and kids would make her think twice before taking risky trips into the wilderness.

Yet he hadn't seemed as overjoyed with the marriage prospect as she would have expected. No matter how she sliced it, she kept coming to the same conclusion—Mitchell had a crush on her. Although he didn't believe she could ever be his, he didn't want to think about her marrying someone else. A crush would explain everything.

Given the probability of that, she had no business having sex with him, not tonight, not ever. He wouldn't be practical about it, as she'd projected earlier today. He would get in deeper and be hurt worse.

Pulling a couple of beers out of the refrigerator, she closed the door with her hip. Sure, Mitchell might be willing to take whatever crumbs she'd toss his way. That's how a guy would react if he had a hopeless case.

But for her to get his hopes up by giving in to her own selfish urges—that would be cruel. So it looked as if she'd be playing poker tonight and then going to bed. Alone. Thinking of that, she went back to the refrigerator and pulled out two more beers.

Mitch discovered that his bathroom door was still MIA, apparently being repaired by Clyde in his spare time. Since the door from the bathroom into Ally's room could only be locked from the bathroom side, Mitch had instant access to her room. He decided to get the bug out from under her bed before she came in.

Scooting under the bed on his back, he took off his glasses and stuck them in his pocket as he peered around, trying to remember exactly where he'd attached the damned thing. Was it on the inside of the left leg at the end of the bed, or the right leg? If he weren't thinking so much about sex right now, he'd be able to remember.

As he was searching for it, the door opened.

"Mitchell?"

Dammit. "Yeah." How in God's name would he explain this? In the process of fumbling to get his glasses back on and wiggling out from under the bed, he banged his head on the support rail.

"Ouch! You hit your head! Are you okay?"

"I'm fine." He rubbed his head and sat up.

Holding a pair of beer bottles in each hand, she regarded him with great suspicion. "Okay, now that I know you're fine, please explain what the hell you were doing under my bed."

Chapter Twenty

Mitchell scrambled for an explanation. "I thought I saw something."

Clearly she didn't believe that for a minute. "Usually when someone sees something under the bed and goes to investigate, they crawl under on their belly. Scooting under on your back makes no sense."

God, he was so screwed. He pushed his glasses more firmly onto the bridge of his nose, buying time.

"Well, Mitchell?"

"Okay, Ally. I wasn't going to let you know about this, because I thought it might freak you out. But I think your bed is bugged."

She stared at him. "What do you mean, my *bed is bugged*? Are we talking creepy crawly things or are we talking little electronic things?"

"Little electronic things."

Now she was looking at him like he was crazy.

"Mitchell, did you see that movie a while back, *A Beautiful Mind*? It's the one where Russell Crowe plays the genius guy who has imaginary friends and thinks there's some sort of conspiracy he has to untangle."

"I saw it, but—"

"Because that's who you're sounding like—that guy. And never mind about the bug situation. *You're* freaking me out."

"Hold on a minute." He slid back under the bed, finally saw the device he'd planted and pulled it loose. This time when he came out from under the bed he was careful not to whack himself on the head. He already had enough problems without adding a concussion to the list.

"What's that?" She crouched down and studied the microtransmitter.

"A bug."

She continued to gaze at it. "Boy, I owe you an apology. It sure looks like one. But why would anyone put a bug under my bed?"

"Well, I have a theory." Which he would pull right out of his ass. "This lodge would have been the perfect out-of-the-way rendezvous for double agents during the Cold War. I mean, think of it. Russia is right across the Bering Strait." If she believed this woolly tale, he should take up fiction writing.

Her eyes got round. "You think double agents stayed here?"

"Could be."

"So this bug isn't here for me. It's been around a while."

"Probably." Was there a chance he'd get away with this?

"Looks pretty new. Not even dusty."

Or maybe he wouldn't get away with shit. "When I was under there, I wiped it off to make sure of what I was looking at."

"Wow." She set down two of the beers on the floor beside her. "Can I see it?"

"Sure." He dropped it into her hand.

"Fascinating." Then she glanced into his eyes. Hers were very green, and very skeptical. "Now tell me how you happened to know that this was an electronic bug instead of some little doodad that helps hold the bed together."

"I've watched tons of spy movies. Tons."

She nodded slowly. "I can believe that. All right, so you can recognize a bug when you see one. That still doesn't explain why you were under the bed in the first place. And don't tell me you had a hunch there was a Cold War bug under there, because if that's the way your mind works, it's frightening and I don't even want to know about it."

Finally he came up with the story he should have gone with in the first place, if he'd been thinking straight. Except then he might not have been able to remove the bug, and he'd really wanted to do that. "I was checking your springs," he said.

"Checking my . . ." Her eyes began to sparkle a couple of seconds before she burst out laughing. "You thought you could stop them from squeaking? Oh, Mitchell, you're hilarious. We don't have to worry about it, because we're not having sex, but that's so you. Checking my springs. Too funny." She stood. "Let's play cards."

He thought about the pricey little gizmo she still

clutched in one hand. "Um, what do you think we ought to do with the bug?"

"I want to show it to Betsy tomorrow. She'd love to have that as another story to tell about the Loose Moose." She glanced at him. "You want it, don't you? I can tell by the way you're looking at it. After watching all those spy movies, you'd think this was cool to have, wouldn't you?"

He shrugged as if he could take it or leave it. "I wouldn't mind."

"Here." She gave it back to him. "Just promise me you'll show it to Betsy tomorrow. She'll want to keep it, but if you tell her about being hooked on spy movies she'll probably let you have it, instead."

He hoped so. Yes, he could buy a replacement, but he hated wasting something that was perfectly good. Maybe he'd conveniently forget to show it to Betsy. This story of his was pretty lightweight, and the more times he had to tell it, the less likely it would hold up.

"Did you bring your cards?"

"Um, I'll go get them."

She shook her head, still smiling. "You were so obsessed with the squeaking bedsprings that you forgot to bring the cards?"

"I guess so."

Her smile faded. "Maybe the card game is a bad idea. I don't want to cause a situation for you."

He almost laughed at that. She had no clue what a situation she'd caused for him, in many ways. "You won't," he lied.

"I hope not, because if we don't play cards, I'll go stir-crazy. With Tanya spreading her bad vibes all over the Top Hat, Uncle Kurt sacked out for the night, and the outdoors cold enough to freeze your nose hairs, as Betsy would say, there's nowhere to go but here."

So he'd won her by default. Not exactly a compliment, but in his nerd disguise he wasn't allowed to pull out all the stops, wasn't supposed to be able to sweep her off her feet and make her yearn to spend every minute with him.

She looked instantly contrite. "I didn't mean that the way it sounded. I really want to be here with you, Mitchell. You're a lot more fun than I—" She clapped her hand to her mouth.

"Than you thought I'd be?"

"I'll just shut up before I make things worse."

"It's okay, Ally. Geeks are used to being underestimated." Then he winked at her before leaving to get the cards. He probably shouldn't have allowed himself the wink, but maybe she hadn't noticed it because of his glasses.

He'd winked at her. And the effects were still evident— squiggles of sexual awareness dancing through her system, making her want what she shouldn't have. She'd have to force herself to concentrate on this card game and forget about that wink. And his mouth. And the cleft in his chin. And his big brown eyes. And the way his pants had molded around his package while he'd been lying there under her bed.

"Got the cards." The owner of that sizable package walked back in. "I think you still have the matches."

She vowed not to look at his package again tonight.

"Let's sit on the rug." She'd already nixed the bed as too dangerous.

"That works." He sat Indian-style across from her and started shuffling the cards.

She hadn't realized how his sitting that way would emphasize the part of Mitchell she'd just promised herself to ignore. Suddenly that part seemed like all she *could* look at. Needing a distraction, she picked up a beer bottle and decided to open it herself by using the hem of her sweater to help her grip the cap.

It wasn't the best solution in the world. She had to keep changing the angle and tipping the bottle this way and that to get enough leverage.

"Want some help?" Mitchell set the shuffled cards down between them.

"I'll get it." And she did. The cap came off suddenly and beer foamed out onto her sweater, her wool pants, and her socks. "Ack!" She quickly drank several swallows to get the beer back under control, but she still had beer all over her. Fortunately she hadn't spilled any on the rug.

"Anything I can do?"

She put down the beer and stood. "Give me a couple of minutes to change clothes, okay?"

"Okay, or we could kill two birds with one stone and play strip poker." He gazed up at her with a half-smile.

Her pulse rate jumped. "Very funny."

"It wasn't a joke." His smile widened. "I'm a good poker player."

Lust fizzed through her veins, making her light-headed. "Sorry. Not doing that." But she thought about it as she walked over to the dresser and pulled a yellow sweatshirt and sweatpants out of the bottom drawer. Strip poker. No guy had ever proposed that to her before. What fuel for the imagination!

In the bathroom, she closed the door and took off her socks, sweater, and slacks, leaving them in a pile in the corner. She'd wash them out tomorrow. Then she glanced down at the simple cotton underwear she had on, the practical stuff she'd bought for Alaska. Anybody playing strip poker would want to have something fancier than that to lose.

Well, she wasn't playing it anyway, so it didn't matter. She pulled on her sweatpants and tugged the cozy sweatshirt over her head. She'd forgotten socks, but she could get them later. Then she glanced in the mirror to see if her hair was sticking out in all directions.

It wasn't, but the woman looking back at her sure did have flushed cheeks. That woman was thinking about strip poker, and where such a game would inevitably lead. But she wouldn't play. No, definitely not.

She opened the bathroom door and walked back into the bedroom.

Mitchell glanced up and his gaze traveled over her. "Better?"

"Better." But that very male once-over of his had gotten to her, making her nipples tighten and her panties grow slightly damp. The flush spreading through her made those socks she'd forgotten totally unnecessary, so she sat down. "What kind of poker are we playing?"

"Stud."

She should have known. She resisted the urge to fan herself. "Five-card or seven-card?"

"Seven. I gave us each a pile of a hundred matches.

We can say they're worth a dollar apiece. The ante's a dollar." He tossed a match into the space between them.

She tossed one in, too.

"Remember how to play?" His fingers flexed as he picked up the cards and dealt them each two cards down and one card up.

"Pretty much. I might need some coaching." She'd never paid much attention to his hands before, except for the time she'd caught him tapping in rhythm with Clyde's performance on the bar. Now she noticed the sprinkle of dark hair and his obvious dexterity. Very sexy. He had capable hands. Capable of doing all sorts of things. To her. *Ally, stop it.*

"Your bet."

She looked at her cards. Not bad. She looked at his card that was face up. In the process she found herself glancing at his crotch again. Then she dropped three matches in the center.

"Stop doing that."

"Doing what?" She consulted her cards, as if she had no idea what he was talking about.

"Checking out the merchandise."

"In your dreams." She still didn't dare look at him.

"Yeah, that, too. I'll call." He dropped three matches in the pile and dealt the next two cards. "Your bet."

She raised again. With an ace-ten in the hole and an ace-ten on the board, she was sitting pretty. All Mitchell had showing was a two and a six, unsuited.

"I'll call." He matched her bet.

The next cards didn't do much for her, and she couldn't see how they'd do much for him, either, although he had a pair of sixes. She checked. He raised.

She couldn't let him get away with bluffing her, so she called his bet. But each time she glanced at his cards on the floor in front of him, her gaze just naturally traveled slightly higher.

"No fair, Ally."

"What?" She managed an innocent expression as she looked up.

He met her gaze. "I think you're deliberately trying to distract me."

"Hey, we're playing on the floor. Your cards are there, and your . . . your other stuff is right in my line of sight."

"Not good enough. You're not just passing through. You're lingering there."

"Am not."

His lips twitched. "Are so." He held the remaining cards in his hand. "Think you're going to win this one?"

"I might."

He dealt the last card down, glanced at it and dropped ten matches into the pile.

"I think you're bluffing." She added ten of her matches. Her last card had given her a full house.

"Maybe, maybe not."

"Ah, you're bluffing, all right."

"Care to make it interesting?" His gaze challenged hers.

A zing of sensation shot straight down between her legs. "Like how?"

"Loser takes something off."

"I said I wouldn't play strip poker."

"Don't you think matches are kind of boring?" he asked softly.

She had to admit it was way too easy to bet matches.

Win or lose, it didn't make much difference. "I suppose."

"Besides, you're so sure you're going to win. I'd be the one who had to take something off, not you."

She debated. It would be sort of fun to make him do that. He'd probably go with a sock. No big deal. "Okay."

"Let's see what you've got."

This was more exciting than matches, she'd have to grant him that. Adrenaline rushed through her as she flipped over her full house.

He whistled. "Impressive."

"Go ahead. Take something off." She liked being the winner. This was power.

"Not so fast." And he turned over four twos.

That was the moment she remembered that she'd never put on those socks. She had four items of clothing on her body. Taking off any one of them would change the whole game.

Mitch knew he'd lured her into this trap, but dammit, she kept checking him out even though she'd declared they wouldn't do anything. A guy could take only so much of that before he was spurred into action. His last two had been pure luck, but he'd always had luck with cards. He'd been banking on that.

"Time to settle up," he said.

"I had you until that last card!"

"Yep." He could see the wheels going around as she tried to decide how to handle this. He would have felt sorry for her except that he knew what she really wanted to do. She thought he couldn't take the fallout if she fol- lowed her impulses. The only way to convince her was to trick her into giving in and then she'd eventually see he was tough enough.

It wasn't like he'd never had sex with a woman and then walked away, or had her walk away. A guy didn't get to be thirty-two without that happening a few times. But Ally saw him as a delicate nerd who would get his little heart broken. She needed to be disabused of that notion.

"I'm waiting," he said.

"I should have put on clean socks," she mumbled.

He'd noticed she hadn't bothered with another pair of socks. That had clinched his decision to talk her into this, especially after she'd looked so confident about her cards. He'd pretty much known what she had from the expression on her face. She was no card shark.

"All right, here goes." She pulled her arms out of the sleeves of her sweatshirt.

He'd seen this maneuver once in an old movie—*Flashdance.* He'd thought it was sexy then, and it drove him wild now, when the woman in question was Ally and she was sitting three feet away.

"I suppose you think this is funny."

"No, I wouldn't say that." *How about arousing beyond belief?* "But it does look like a couple of midgets are wrestling under there."

"Almost got it. There!" She stuck her arms back through the sweatshirt sleeves, pulled her bra out from under the bottom hem and threw it at him. "Debt paid!"

He caught the soft cotton bra, which came over to him on a wave of delicate flowery scent that made his blood pound. "Thanks. Ready to play again?"

She gazed at him, obviously thinking it over. Her

color was high, and she looked as if the game had really stirred her up.

"Or do you want to quit while I'm ahead?" He was banking on the fact that she wasn't a quitter and wouldn't like losing.

"We need some extra rules," she said.

He kept himself from smiling in triumph. She was in. "Like what?" He loved knowing she was naked under that sweatshirt.

"Like if either of us folds, that hand doesn't count. Otherwise there's no judgment involved, no reason to keep the cards facedown."

"Okay, if one of us folds, that's just a matchstick hand." And he would never fold. Because losing meant winning. For what he had in mind, they both had to be naked.

"And either one of us can stop the game if we get uncomfortable."

"You mean like too cold? Because we can turn up those baseboard heaters." He didn't need any more heat so long as he had her to look at. One glance and he was hot, hot, hot.

"I mean like too embarrassed."

"Are you embarrassed now?" She sure didn't look embarrassed. She looked turned on. Her nipples were making nice little outsies in her yellow sweatshirt.

"No, I'm not embarrassed now. But I reserve the right to stop the game at any time."

"Okay." He was a gambling man.

She took a long swallow of her beer. Then she scooped up the cards. "My deal."

Chapter Twenty-one

Ally won the next hand and Mitchell gave up a sock, as she'd predicted he would. She won the hand after that, too, which took care of his other sock. Now this was more like it. And he'd bragged about his card-playing ability. She could take him.

Next hand he lost his belt. "I thought you said you weren't very good at this," he said as he slid his belt from the loops and handed it over.

"I thought you said you were." Smiling in triumph, she laid the belt on top of the socks lying beside her.

"I usually am pretty good. I don't seem to be getting cards, for some reason. You are, though." He dealt the next hand. And lost his flannel shirt.

Ally made a big production of shuffling the cards while he unbuttoned his shirt, but she was watching. Oh, yes, she was watching. Underneath he wore a white cotton T-shirt and she was extremely interested in the fit of that T-shirt. She'd begun to suspect that Mitchell J. Carruthers, Jr., might be hiding a babe-magnet body underneath his nerd clothes.

When he took off the flannel shirt and muscles galore bunched under the T-shirt, her shuffling misfired, sending cards everywhere. "Whoops." She began gathering them up, meanwhile sneaking peeks at those pecs. She had way underestimated the possibilities.

Mitchell passed her the flannel shirt. "Well played."

"Thanks. My shuffling leaves a little to be desired. I never was great at that." She didn't want him to know how much he'd rattled her with that manly display of muscle. She'd rather have him think she was clumsy.

But, oh, sweet heaven. She was sitting across from a Fruit of the Loom poster boy. If the T-shirt looked this good, she could imagine how he filled out a pair of briefs. She could imagine it way too well. She almost misdealt the cards.

Her luck was still running, though. A pair of aces. Then she got another ace, and bet like crazy. She wanted that T-shirt gone. Yes, the temptation would be intense, but she'd worry about that after she'd forced him to strip away the white cotton that fit him like shrink-wrap.

At the end of the hand, she stared in disbelief as he turned over a flush. She'd never seen it coming.

"Guess my luck changed a little," he said.

She gulped. "Guess so." Well, she could end the game, but then she wouldn't have a chance to get rid of his T-shirt. She'd come this far. Scooting back from the playing area, she wiggled out of her sweatpants. After all, her panties weren't much different from bikini bottoms.

When she gave him her sweatpants, he took them with

great nonchalance. "Thanks." Then he glanced over at her bare legs. "Are you cold? I can turn up the heat."

She thought he already had. His casual attitude toward her increasing nakedness was affecting her more than if he'd openly leered. Then she had the unwelcome thought that he wasn't as impressed with her body as she was with his.

Yet she had reason to believe her body could turn a guy on. She wasn't some inexperienced virgin, after all. She'd had boyfriends. She'd incited lust on more than one occasion by stripping down to her panties.

Then again, maybe he was used to seeing her bare legs. Shorts had been a mainstay of her wardrobe back in Bel Air, and his office looked out on the swimming pool where she'd spent lots of hours in a bathing suit. So seeing her legs was nothing new for him.

Well, that sucked. If she was going to be in a sweat over his body, he should at least have some reaction to hers. She stroked her thigh absently, as if rubbing a spot that itched a little bit. From under her lashes she watched for a reaction.

His expression stayed the same as he dealt the cards. But his breathing didn't. Then he coughed, as if to cover up his reaction.

Feeling a whole lot better, she drained the last of her beer and looked at her new hand to see if this would be the time she'd make the T-shirt disappear. She had to be careful, because she had only two items to get rid of and he had three.

She won. This time she didn't make the mistake of shuffling while he pulled the T-shirt over his head. Good thing. The hem of the shirt was like a curtain going up

on the feature show. What fabulous abs. What a nice soft
mat of dark hair. What pecs. What shoulders.

She glanced away at the last moment, right before he
pulled the shirt over his head and was able to see again.
Then she started shuffling the cards.

"Guess your luck's back."

"Guess so." She took the shirt, which still felt warm.
She wanted to hold it up to her cheek, like Linus with
his blankie, while she gawked at Mitchell in all his
glory. But then she wouldn't look cool. "Need the heat
turned up?" she asked.

"Nope. I'm good."

She thought he probably was. And she, silly girl, had
told him that having sex was a bad idea. Right now it
seemed like the best idea in the world. An outstanding
idea, come to think of it.

She dealt the cards.

"Now the game gets interesting." Mitchell looked at
his cards, smiled, and made a bet.

She had squat. She should fold, and move on to the
next game. She should, but she wasn't going to. Picking
up five matches, she called his bet.

The blood rushed in her ears as the game progressed.
She was going to lose. On purpose. She wanted to find
out what he'd do when she took off her sweatshirt. She
wanted to know if he'd maintain his control in the face
of her going topless.

At the end of the game, she turned over her puny
cards. Her fingers trembled a little, but her voice stayed
calm. "So much for luck."

"Uh, yeah." He sounded hoarse and he paused to
clear his throat again. "I win that one."

She looked into his eyes. Her heart was beating so fast she could barely breathe, but he didn't seem all that cool and collected, either. He hadn't even bothered to pick up the cards and start shuffling for the next hand. She wondered if he'd be able to play cards at all, once she took off her sweatshirt.

Time to find out. Grabbing the hem, she whipped the shirt off. Then she checked his eyes for signs of booby shock.

He looked as if someone had flashed a strobe light in his face. His throat moved in a quick swallow, but otherwise he was perfectly motionless.

Immensely gratified, she decided to rub it in. She waved her hand in front of his eyes. "Earth to Mitchell. Come in, Mitchell."

He blinked and shook his head as if awakening from a trance. "Uh, right."

"Too distracting for you?" She propped her hands behind her and leaned back. "Ready to concede the game?"

"No." His expression evolved from awestruck to intense. He gathered the cards without looking down. "I'm ready to win another hand."

She is so beautiful. Mitch didn't know how he'd be able to tell clubs from spades when all he could do was stare at her. She wanted him to ogle her, too. She flaunted those high, raspberry-tipped breasts, making sure that she didn't block his view as she concentrated on her hand.

Meanwhile, his concentration was shot to hell. Much as he wanted to win the hand and see if she'd peel off those panties, he couldn't seem to get it together. She won easily.

"So?" She gazed at him with interest.

If he took off his pants, she'd find out that he was like a totem pole underneath the restriction of the heavy material. He wasn't ready to announce his condition yet. So he took off his glasses and handed them to her.

"Hey, what's that all about? You can't play without your glasses."

"Sure I can, if I get close enough to the cards."

"Glasses don't count. They aren't clothes."

"I was wearing them. I say they count."

"So I'm fuzzy to you now, right?"

"Uh-huh." Fuzzy might help him out with his control, but he could see her perfectly with his contacts.

"I get it. If I'm fuzzy, you'll be able to pay more attention to the game."

"I'm paying attention."

"No you're not." She smiled. "I can tell. Haven't you ever played poker with an almost naked woman before, Mitchell?"

"Sure." He'd told her so many fibs, what was one more?

"I don't believe you. I think this is your first-ever strip-poker game. And you are so going to lose." She shuffled the cards.

Oh, Lord. He hadn't considered what her shuffling technique could mean under these circumstances. Instead of dividing the deck in half and shuffling the ends of the cards together, she held the entire deck loosely in one hand while she pulled out sections and fed them back in with a chopping motion. Consequently her breasts shimmied in the most tantalizing display he'd ever seen, even counting the strip joint he'd gone to for his twenty-first birthday bash. His mouth watered. His hands clenched. He was over the edge.

"Ally."

"What?" She kept shuffling as she glanced up. Her lips parted as she gazed at him.

What little blood had been left in his brain drained south. He needed to tell her to stop shuffling the damned cards, but his tongue wouldn't cooperate.

"Mitchell, are you all right?"

He shook his head. He was in the grip of a need so fierce it was flooding him with hormones, marinating him in testosterone. He'd never wanted a woman this much in his life.

She stopped shuffling and put down the cards. "You look feverish."

Which he probably was. He was afraid to speak, afraid all that would come out would be earthy, four-letter words describing what he wanted to do to her.

"Mitchell, say something. You look like you're having a heart attack." She rose to her knees and reached across the playing area to put a hand on his knee.

That did it. The minute she touched him, he went up in flames. Adrenaline mixed with desire was a potent cocktail, and he was drunk with it. Grabbing her waist in both hands, he stood in one smooth movement, amazing even himself as he managed to get them both upright without staggering.

She shrieked as he plopped her onto the bed, shoved pillows out of the way, and followed her down.

"Mitchell!" She grasped his head in both hands. "What are you doing?"

Holding her gaze, he ripped off her panties, which were sufficiently wet to make him even wilder. Then he plunged his fingers deep into her hot, wet vagina. Right before he kissed her, the gift of speech returned. "If you don't know, then you're not as smart as I thought you were." Then he kissed her hard while he made her come.

Ally had never climaxed so fast, ever. From the moment Mitchell had grabbed her and flung her to the bed, she'd been halfway there, and when he'd ripped off her panties, tearing the cotton right in two, that had nearly done the trick. A few rapid thrusts from his fingers and she was airborne, flying high on a powerful orgasm.

Wrenching her mouth away from the force of his kiss, she gasped for breath and mentally thanked whoever had invented poker. "Mitch . . ." It was all she had the energy to say. And it did sound right. One syllable fit this unbelievable rush of lust much better than two.

From the time she'd decided to lose a game and take off her sweatshirt, she'd known this would be the probable outcome. She hadn't known when or how, but she'd surrendered to the inevitability. Given Mitchell's personality, she'd expected something less . . . explosive. But she wasn't complaining.

His breath feathered her ear. "That's one."

"What . . . what do you mean?" She quickly found out. While she was still quivering from that first wild ride, he slid down between her thighs and began paving the way for another one.

He didn't waste any time about it, either. No coy little nibbles and licks for this man. He moved right in and proceeded to show how much he knew about this particular activity. And he knew a lot. If anyone awarded a Ph.D. in oral sex, Mitch deserved one.

The moon, sun, stars, and planets flashed behind her eyelids at the intense pleasure. He used exactly the right pressure, exactly the right suction, exactly the right stroke of his tongue to make her writhe in his arms and, finally, arch off the bed. As the waves of another climax crashed over her shuddering body, she clutched handfuls of the blanket and cried out her joy.

His warm breath tickled her damp thigh. "That's two," he murmured.

While she continued to float on a sea of utter satisfaction, the bedsprings creaked as he left her. From the rustling noises she had a good idea what he might be doing. Opening her eyes, she turned her head to look, and was oh, so glad she did. A girl didn't want to miss seeing her gift package being unwrapped.

He shoved down his briefs. Oh, my. To think she'd almost denied herself something that amazing. Anyone groping Mitch under the table would get a handful and then some. Ally hated to see the latex being rolled over all that natural beauty, but maybe she'd get a chance to explore the territory later on.

Climbing back onto the bed, he moved over her. Brazen hussy that she was, she spread her legs and bent her knees, making things easy for him. She'd hate for him to lose his way.

Not much chance of that with a man as focused as Mitch seemed to be. With the smile of a man who

knows his business and is damned proud of it, he sent
that heat-seeking missile straight to its target.

"Mm." Her little expression of delight didn't even
begin to tell the story. If she'd thought she was in para-
dise before, she'd only been cruising down the street in
that direction. This was the place.

Mitch looked into her eyes. "Not bad."

She gripped his hips and wiggled in tighter. "Not bad
at all. Am I fuzzy?"

"You're hot and wet." He withdrew and pushed in
again. "Not fuzzy. Unless you mean here." He reached
down and stroked her curls, rubbing his knuckle against
her clit. "That part's sorta fuzzy."

Instantly she felt the tightening begin again. "I didn't
mean that. I meant can you see me, or am I blurry?"

"You're beautiful."

"You didn't answer . . . the question." But she completely lost track of the question as he continued to rub
his knuckle right there, right where all sorts of happi-
ness lived.

Then he began moving his hips in a slow, easy
rhythm while he kept his knuckle moving, moving,
bringing her closer. The bedsprings kept time with his
movements, and he smiled. "Didn't fix 'em."

"No." She began to pant. "But you're . . . fixing . . .
me."

"Good." He gazed down at her, his eyes hot as they
traveled over her face, her breasts, and down to the spot
where he was giving her a double dose of all things
wonderful. Then glanced into her eyes again. "Want
to watch?"

Her breath caught.

"Yeah, you do. I can see it in your eyes." He paused long enough to snag both pillows and prop them under her head. "Enjoy."

She looked down the length of her body as he settled in again. Wild. Watching him thrust while feeling the friction deep inside threw her into a whole other category of pleasure. And when he slipped his hand between her legs and started in on her clit again, she felt control sliding rapidly away.

The bedsprings squeaked a little faster. Oh, yeah. She kept watching that magic wand of his disappearing inside, returning and disappearing again. He was casting a spell, all right. This was good. This was very . . . good.

As she hovered on the brink of an orgasm, he pumped faster, and she came in a rush, gasping and laughing all at the same time. What a trip!

Slowing down, he kissed her gently on the mouth. "That's three."

And finally she knew what was going on with this counting business, and she got the giggles. "It's not a contest between you and Poopsie, you know."

"I know." He nibbled on her lower lip.

"So why are you counting?"

"Because I wanted to make you laugh besides making you come."

"You did. Both things."

"Anyway, I feel like I could do this all night."

She'd never felt more ready for a long night of sex. "I know what you mean." But then she remembered the jammed machine in the men's room at the Top Hat. "Are you wearing the only condom?" Maybe that's why he was making this episode last.

"That would be a sad state of affairs, now wouldn't it, with me ready to come any second?"

She cupped his face in both hands. "Go ahead and come, Mitch."

"You called me Mitch."

"It works in bed."

He laughed. "Okay. I can live with that."

"So, Mitch, if you come now, and later on, you feel the urge again, I'll take care of you. There are alternatives, you know."

"Oh, yeah?" His dark eyes sparkled. "Like what?"

She ran her tongue over her lips. "Use your imagination."

"My imagination is making me want to come right now."

"So do it."

"I just might." He started moving again. This time he went even deeper, stroking her with long, deliberate thrusts. "And for your information," he murmured, his mouth curving in a soft smile. "The machine in the men's room is fixed."

Considering the way he'd felt when he'd first grabbed Ally and tossed her on the bed, Mitch could barely believe that he'd held off his own climax through three of hers. But it wasn't only Clyde's performance that had inspired him. Ally inspired him.

When he'd felt her body humming beneath his on the bed, when he'd felt how sopping wet her panties were and realized she was ready for action, he'd wanted to make it happen right that second, right when she needed it. And she'd come so gloriously that he'd gotten hooked on the idea of getting her to do it again. The second time had been beyond great, so he'd clamped down on his own response in order to give her number three.

He'd thought he'd had a reasonably good sex life up to now. Nope. Blahsville. He'd never felt this white-hot urgency before, never dreamed of doing it all night, doing it constantly until neither of them could move. Wearing each other out.

And now he was looking into her eyes and watching the tension build there, wanting to know that she was close before he let go. She was getting close. This was the woman of his dreams, someone who matched him urge for urge.

In the back of his mind he'd known it all along. He'd denied the truth because he couldn't see it working out for them. There was the chemistry between them, which meant they were perfect for each other. Then there was the harsh reality of all that money. The idea of her marrying some rich idiot because at least they'd have financial parity sickened him, but it would make more sense than Ally hooking up with a guy like Mitchell J. Carruthers, Jr.

For now, though, he was in her bed and she was welcoming him in wonderful ways, tightening around him and meeting each thrust with a lift of her hips. They didn't have a future, but they had one hell of a present. Gazing down at her flushed face, he watched her build to a climax.

The bed squeaked frantically as he tipped her over

the edge. Then the squeaking became a constant din as he rode hard to his own nirvana. All the way there he watched her face, and knew this was how it was supposed to be between a man and a woman. Then he came, and as glory rained down around him, he refused to think of anything but the wonder of this moment.

Chapter Twenty-two

"Is the poker game over, then?" Ally had propped herself against the headboard with a pillow and was sipping her second beer while Mitch fiddled with the baseboard heater, trying to turn it down. Despite the coating of frost on the window, they'd both worked up a sweat.

He glanced over his shoulder and grinned at her. "Want to get dressed and try it all over again?"

She waved her beer bottle in the air. "Way too much trouble. Hey, forget that thing and come on back to bed."

"Yeah, I can't figure it out." He stood and walked toward her. "Maybe it's broken." He picked up his second beer from the floor and twisted off the cap. "We'll have to stay naked, I guess."

"Now that's a darned shame." She looked him over for about the tenth time, still not believing that such a body had been parading around the mansion for months and she'd never noticed. Clothes really could make the man, or not, as in Mitchell's case.

Not Mitchell. Mitch. The shortened version fit a guy who could play such fabulous bedroom games. "I'm going to take Rudy's suggestion and start calling you Mitch all the time," she said.

"Not just in bed?" He climbed in beside her and put a pillow behind his back so he could lean against the headboard.

"I think I want to use it all the time."

He laid a hand on her thigh. "But if you only used it when you were feeling like making the bedsprings creak, it could be a signal. You could call me Mitchell most of the time, and Mitch when you were ready to get naked."

His hand on her thigh was starting her engines again. But this time it was a lazy, no-pressure kind of arousal, the kind she was content to let build for a while. "In that case, I might as well stick with Mitch."

He stroked her thigh. "That's nice to hear."

"For you it might be nice." She gave in to her impulse and ran her finger along the length of his penis. It twitched in response. "For me it's a problem. I'm supposed to be spending all my spare time with Tanya, not whisking up to my bedroom to have sex with you." She stroked him again, and noticed a definite change in composition. She had a new toy.

He cleared his throat. "Are you saying that sex with me outranks taking pictures of those partridge things?"

"Ptarmigan. I'm afraid so. I've never had an orgasm while snapping a photo." She circled his penis with her fingers and squeezed gently. It began to swell in her hand. It was an interesting sensation, having a cold bottle of beer in one hand and a warm penis in the other.

"You should have told me you wanted to take pictures."

She glanced at him, lying there looking like a Greek statue come to life. Except Greek statues never had an erection and she was giving him a dandy one. "You'd look beautiful on film."

"Um, I was kidding. If you hauled out your camera you'd have to have very fast film to catch me. I'd be out the door before your finger found the shutter."

"Don't worry." She caressed the head of his penis and watched a drop of moisture gather there. "I would never do that."

"No? Why not?"

She glanced into his eyes as she continued to play with his package. "It would destroy the sense of intimacy."

"What you're doing right now is pretty darned intimate."

"It's about to get even more intimate." Scooting down, she turned over onto her stomach so she had the angle she wanted. Then she kissed that warm, velvety tip.

He groaned. "Warning. Contents under pressure."

"I know. Fire at will." She began to lick him.

His breathing changed quickly. "I mean it. Having you do that in the dark is one thing. Watching you do it is . . ." He sucked in air through his teeth. "Ally . . . hold up a minute. Let me get back in . . . control."

"It's a losing battle." But she eased away from him and realized she was still clutching her beer in her other hand. She could ask him to hold it, or she could experiment.

Taking a mouthful of beer, she swished it around,

making the foam tickle her tongue. Because she wasn't a guy, she had no idea how he'd like it, but she'd transformed into a bold chick tonight. Bold chicks took action and asked questions later.

She swallowed the beer and glanced at him. "Ready?"

"For what?" He was still breathing fast.

"Fun with beer."

"I have no idea what you're talking about."

She grinned. "Neither do I, but I want to try something."

"Is this like a party trick?"

"Maybe a private party trick. Here goes." She took another sip of beer and held it in her mouth. Then she pressed her mouth against the tip of his penis and tried to take him in without losing all the beer. Some dribbled out, but most of it stayed.

Mitch gasped. "Oh . . . man. That tickles. Ally, tickling might mean that I'll lose . . . I hope you know what you're . . . doing."

She didn't, exactly, but she had hopes for the outcome. She puffed out her cheeks and got that foam swirling.

"Omigod . . . Ally, that's . . . amaz—" With a moan wrenched from deep in his chest, he came.

Mission accomplished.

Mitch would never look at a bottle of beer the same way again. He'd never be able to play poker without thinking of this night, either. So there were two things in his life forever linked to sex with Ally. Oh, and matchsticks.

Matchsticks would now remind him of the poker game, which had turned into a strip poker game, which had led to incredible sex, which eventually had ended up giving him adventures with beer.

"That was fun." Ally wiggled up next to him still holding her beer.

He couldn't imagine why he hadn't dumped his own bottle all over the bed. Fortunately he'd kept it in a death grip all during the climax and hadn't spilled a drop. "That was more than plain old fun for me," he said. "I'd say from my perspective that falls into the category of extreme fun."

She tapped her beer bottle against his. "Here's to extreme fun."

"Right." He was beginning to realize that he might have miscalculated. Yes, having sex with Ally was a good way to keep track of her. And yes, by doing that he was shutting out the unacceptable types hanging around hoping for some attention.

But it was supposed to be a stopgap measure, and at the moment there was nothing stopgap about it. He had the urge to employ this strategy for quite a while. Like for the next fifty years.

He'd really underestimated how great sex with Ally would be, or how great Ally would be, aside from the sex. He really liked her. Come to think of it, he'd been underestimating all kinds of things lately, starting with the difficulty of the job Madeline had hired him for.

One thing he hadn't underestimated, or at least he hoped not, was Kurt Jarrett's desire to get his hands on Ally's money. The guy was fairly transparent to Mitch.

Ally wasn't willing to see that, yet, but she was a smart woman. Mitch had to stay around long enough for her to wise up. Then he could leave.

Yeah, leave. If the concept didn't thrill him, too bad. He'd known from the beginning that would be the story. If he happened to be falling for the woman lying beside him in this creaky bed in Porcupine, Alaska, that was the breaks. He'd get over it. Maybe.

"Mitch, I need to ask you something."

He took a swig of his beer and hoped it was a question he could answer. "If you want to know if I lost some of those hands on purpose, the answer is yes."

"That's okay. So did I."

He glanced over at her. "All of them?"

"No, just the one where I had to take off my sweatshirt."

That bit of information gladdened his heart. "So what happened after that wasn't a complete surprise to you."

"No. I was wondering if you'd crack." Her smile had definite overtones of smugness.

He didn't care. She deserved to feel smug. "I cracked. I cracked right down the middle. And it was the shuffling that did it."

She laughed. "The shuffling? I thought it was my boobs."

"It was. The shuffling made your boobs dance. If you shuffled like I do, none of this would have happened."

"None of it?" She looked skeptical.

"Okay, it would have happened, but later. That shuffle of yours put me over the top."

"I'm glad."

He met her gaze. "Me, too." And he was glad, no matter what.

"What did Grammy tell you about Uncle Kurt?"

Wham. After a bunch of easy pitches, she hit him with the fast ball. He considered how much he should say.

"Please tell me. Grammy would never talk about him. Uncle Kurt says she hated him because he was living proof that Grandpa Clayton was married before, and she didn't want to think about that. If that's true, it's so unfair, because Grammy was married before, too, and she had my dad when they met. Both she and Grandpa were in the same boat, with kids from a first marriage."

No matter what, he had to make sure he didn't come across as interrogating her. But he had some questions of his own. "So you've been in touch with your uncle Kurt?"

She nodded. "He came down to see me when I was in college. I'd always been curious about him, so I was glad when he showed up. I mean, we may not be directly related, but he's still family."

Mitch had the urge to shake Kurt until his balls rattled. Ally needed an uncle who was a decent human being. Instead she got Kurt. But he wished Madeline had found it within herself to tell Ally the truth about him.

"I knew Grammy would have had a fit if she'd known I was communicating with him, so we e-mailed through my roommate's e-mail address. We used forwarded jokes, with short messages at the bottom. We even devised a loose code, in case anyone should ever read the e-mails."

He *had* read some of the e-mails, and he'd fallen for the whole scheme. Some PI he was. After reading a few, he'd dismissed them as being exactly what they seemed to be. So Kurt had been wooing Ally for a long time. And she was desperate for a sense of family. Once again, Mitch had underestimated the difficulty of the situation.

"So I need to know what Grammy said to you about him. I can tell you don't like him, so I want to know why."

He sure didn't want to be the one to deliver this information. He took a deep breath. "You won't like it."

"I don't expect to like it."

"According to your grandmother, she tried to make one happy blended family out of the situation. Your dad was ten and Kurt was eighteen when she married Clayton, so there was a fairly large age difference, but she hoped they'd be friends. Kurt was invited to spend the summer at the mansion."

"And?" Her gaze was totally focused on him.

He put down his beer and cupped her face in both hands. "Ally, I wish your grandmother had talked to you about this. Long ago. But she was a very modest woman, and I'm sure she couldn't bring herself to say it."

Apprehension flashed in her eyes. "Say what?"

"Kurt sexually assaulted her."

"No!" She pulled away from him.

He'd guessed it might happen. Kill the messenger.

"I don't believe it!" Ally scrambled out of bed, her beer bottle still clutched in her hand. "She must have misunderstood. Misinterpreted something."

"I don't think so. He would have raped her, except a maid heard her screaming and ran to the rescue. Kurt nearly knocked the maid over as he barreled out the door. He hitched a ride back to his mother's house."

Ally continued to shake her head. "It's impossible. He wouldn't do something like that."

"When the maid showed up, he had your grandmother down on the floor. Her clothes were ripped." He hated the look of betrayal in Ally's eyes. "I'm sorry. I know it's tough to hear, but it's true. I checked the story. The maid's name is Suzanne."

"Suzanne." Ally swallowed. "She still works there. I've known her all my life."

"Your grandmother made her promise never to say a word to anyone. She was petrified to talk to me, but finally she did. She's been carrying that image around for more than forty years."

"So nobody knew? Not my dad, or Grandpa Clayton?"

"Your grandmother was humiliated. You have to remember her personality, and the fact that in those days, women were often blamed when something like that happened. Kurt had picked his time well, when her son was off taking tennis lessons and your grandpa was doing business down in L.A."

"I don't get how she could have banned him from the house without Grandpa being told why." Ally put down her beer on the dresser.

"She told your grandfather that Kurt had threatened her and she didn't feel safe in the house with him. From what I can gather, Clayton doted on your grandmother. He almost disowned Kurt, but she convinced him to continue paying him his trust fund allowance."

"Uncle Kurt told me he wasn't allowed at Grandpa's funeral. I thought he hadn't bothered to come, but he said Grammy forbid him to show up."

Mitch nodded. "Not her, personally, but her lawyers warned Kurt that if he wanted to continue getting his monthly allowance, he'd be wise to stay away from Clayton's funeral, so he did."

She picked up her sweatpants from the floor and pulled them on.

He thought that was a bad sign. When she put on her sweatshirt, he knew the party was over.

She faced him. "You're not here because you have a crush on me, are you?"

"No." But he had one now. And watching her shut down after what they'd shared was killing him.

"And it's not paperwork to do with the estate, either, is it?"

"No."

"You're here because of Kurt, aren't you?"

"Mostly, yes."

"He's not going to try and rape me or anything, Mitch. I can guarantee it."

"That's not my big concern, either. I think he wanted revenge against your grandmother for what he perceived was her part in ruining his life. That's how an eighteen-year-old hothead might react. But he may feel he deserves some of your inheritance. Your grandmother told me to stay close."

"I see." She gazed at him. "So was that the reason for all this?" She swept her hand over the scene, from the cards on the floor to Mitch on the bed.

"What do you mean?" He decided to be deliberately obtuse, because in a way she was right. It was technically part of the reason. Not a big part, but it had contributed to his decision. He didn't think that would play well.

"I'm wondering if you thought having sex with me would make your job easier, that's all. You know, bond with me so I'd want to hang around you more, stuff like that."

"Ally, that wasn't it. I told you, I've wanted you from the start. I stopped fighting it, that's all."

Her eyes narrowed. "Damned convenient time to stop fighting it, I'd say. And to think I was afraid to get sexually involved for fear I might hurt your feelings when it was over. You're simply doing what Grammy hired you to do, and sex is turning out to be one of the perks!"

"It wasn't a perk!"

She braced her hands on her hips. "Oh, so you forced yourself to go through with it? You gave a real convincing performance for a guy who wasn't enjoying himself!"

"That's not what I meant." He should probably quit before he ended up any further in the hole. "I meant that I'd never intended for this to happen. Then this morning I kissed you, and you kissed me back, and—"

"My mistake. I thought you were this sweet and dopey guy with a crush. I thought that was cute. I was touched that you'd fly all the way up here." Her expression softened. "And . . . and you're a good kisser. Dammit."

"Sorry about that."

"You should be sorry! You're supposed to be a nerdy guy who's great at details and paperwork. You're not supposed to have a body like *that*." She blew out a breath and glanced away.

Maybe all was not lost. She still wanted him, or she wouldn't have made those last comments about his body and his kissing ability. She was upset and taking it out on him. He could understand that.

"What do you want to do, Ally?"

"I don't know." Hands still on her hips, she stared up at the ceiling. "I mean, I had this great plan to come up to Alaska and learn wildlife photography. Uncle Kurt promised to help. Now you've told me something about him that's very disturbing."

"You asked."

"I know! And I don't want to believe you, but at dinner he was trying to talk me into shortcuts that don't feel right, so maybe he isn't so wonderful. And he brought Tanya Mandell, which sounds perfect on the surface, but she's turning out to be a sex maniac. Then you and I have some fun, and I discover it's only part of your job."

"No, not part of my job. I couldn't resist you."

She sniffed and swiped a hand over her eyes. "And I couldn't seem to resist you, either. That's the hell of it."

"Oh, Ally." He was off the bed and pulling her into his arms before he could consider whether she might deck him for trying it.

She struggled a little, but eventually she collapsed against him and buried her face against his shoulder. "I don't want you to comfort me!" she wailed, even as she wrapped her arms around him and held on tight.

"I know, but I'm handy." He rubbed her back and stroked her hair while she cried. He remembered wanting to do this a couple of times before—at the funeral, and again when he'd come upon her weeping while sitting in her grandmother's bedroom a week later. But they hadn't had that kind of relationship then, so he'd held himself in check.

Finally she stopped crying and lifted her head from his shoulder. "This is no good."

"Why?"

"Because you're naked. I can't have a decent cry against a naked man's shoulder. There's nothing to soak up the tears. You're getting all slippery." She stepped back, picked up the hem of her sweatshirt and pulled it up to mop her face. She flashed him in the process.

He wondered if she knew. He decided to test the waters. "Come back to bed," he murmured.

With the bottom of her sweatshirt still pulled up to show her breasts, she peered at him. "You're just saying that because you got another look at my boobs, and that makes you crazy."

"True."

She sighed and pulled off her sweatshirt. "Who am I kidding? I could get all indignant and send you back to your own room, but I'd only be cutting off my nose to spite my face."

He wished she sounded a little happier about wanting him.

She tossed the sweatshirt at him. "Better wipe off your shoulder." Then she shoved her sweatpants down over her hips and stepped out of them.

She was obviously still mad, and she hadn't performed the most graceful striptease he'd ever seen, but his penis didn't seem to care. It reacted as if she'd put on one helluva show.

She zeroed right in on that reaction, giving him a saucy once-over. "So in addition to handling Grammy's estate, you're supposed to keep me safe and happy. Is that what you're saying?"

He figured that was a fair evaluation. "I guess you could put it that way."

She walked over to the bed and hopped in. "Then come on over here, Mitch. Time to earn your keep."

Yeah, she was furious, both with him and maybe with herself for still being susceptible. But he'd take her any way he could get her.

"I guess I could get all indignant and refuse," he said, crossing to the bed. She was so angry and yet so beautiful, lying stretched out on the sheets, her nipples hard and her body rosy and ready for him. "But that would be cutting off my nose to spite my face." He climbed into bed with her. It was a tough job, but somebody had to do it.

Chapter Twenty-three

Some time later, as Ally was lying in Mitch's arms try-ing to sort out her jumbled thoughts, she heard the lodge's front door open and close. She'd thought Mitch was sleeping, but he roused himself instantly.

"Must be Tanya," he muttered.

"Must be. Let's hope she didn't bring someone home with her. Listening to Kitty-cat and Poopsie would be one thing, but . . ."

Mitch gave her an understanding squeeze. "I know. It has to be tough to find out she has feet of clay."

"Her feet aren't the part that concerns me. I— Oh, no. Is she coming up the stairs?" Ally listened to the unmis-takable sound of someone climbing the wooden steps.

"I think so."

"This has a definite Stephen King feel to it. Did you lock your door?"

"Yeah. Did you?"

Ally tried to think. "God, I don't know. I walked in, and you were under the bed. I was so startled I might have forgotten."

He turned her loose and sat up. "I'll check."

"Don't make noise doing it," she murmured.

The bed squeaked as he swung his legs over the side. "Too late."

"M-i-i-itchell, where are you?" Tanya's voice echoed in the hallway.

Ally shivered. This was one scary woman. Ally had never known anyone who would prowl the corridors calling out for a man. Tanya might be in serious need of medication.

She watched as Mitch crept toward the door. A floorboard squeaked and he froze.

"Are we playing hide-and-seek?" Tanya laughed. "Don't be shy, Mitchell. Come on out. We'll go play in that Murphy bed. You know you want to."

Ally began to wonder if learning valuable tricks of the trade was worth it if she had to work with such a creepy mentor. The entire plan was turning into a fiasco. Well, not counting the sex with Mitch. She'd have to put that in the plus column, no matter what his motives. The guy had moves.

She admired his tight butt as he crept stealthily toward the door.

"Aha!" Tanya's voice was much closer, now. "I see a light coming from under that door. Is that you, Mitchell, you cute nerd? You probably fell asleep reading and left the light on. I can be more fun than any book in the world."

Mitch had almost reached the door when the knob turned. As the door started to open, he threw himself against it and twisted the lock.

"Mitchell, was that you?" She rattled the knob. "Mitchell, open up, baby. Let Tanya make you feel good." Her voice dropped to a sultry murmur. "I have toys. Toys for big boys and girls."

Ally turned on her stomach and put a pillow over her head. Yuck and double yuck. She wondered if Uncle Kurt knew what Tanya was like. Well, of course he must. He seemed to be friends with her, and they'd driven all the way from Anchorage together.

The mattress sagged, and Mitch tugged at the pillow. "It's okay, she's gone."

Ally flopped to her back and stared up at him. "But not forgotten. She could give a person nightmares."

"I was hoping she'd latch on to one of those Paul Bunyan types over at the Top Hat."

"Maybe she did. Maybe you're next on her schedule."

Mitch shuddered. "If I have to share another meal with her I'm wearing my cup."

She gazed at him in amusement. "Your cup? I thought only jocks had those. You know, to protect themselves during a contact sport."

"Eating at the same table with Tanya is a contact sport."

"That wasn't my point."

He shrugged. "So I bought myself one to make myself feel like a jock. Is that a crime?"

She reached out and felt his biceps. "Naked, you look a lot more like a jock than a nerd."

"I work out a little. It's good for your heart, you know. Everyone should have an exercise program. You'll live longer. And besides that—"

"Shh!"

"What?"

"I heard something from downstairs. Like a buzzing noise."

Mitch stayed still and listened. Then he looked at Ally. "Do you know what that is?"

"I'm guessing it's not an electric toothbrush."

"I'm guessing it's not, either."

She sighed. "Well, I, for one, don't want to hear the results produced by that buzzing noise."

"Neither do I, but I don't know how we can avoid it."

"I do." Ally leaped from the bed. "Let's take a shower!"

"Works for me."

"Bring one of the condoms."

"Even better."

The hot water didn't last long enough, so Mitch suggested leaving the water running for the soundproof factor. Once they were out of the shower and reasonably dry, he closed the toilet lid, sat down and invited Ally to climb aboard. Necessity really was the mother of invention. Not that he *needed* to have sex with Ally. Well, okay, a little bit. Okay, a lot. Okay, he was in very big trouble.

By the time they finished getting their goodies in the bathroom, all was quiet downstairs. Mitch crawled into bed with Ally, gathered her close and went right to sleep.

He woke up before dawn, but that wasn't saying

much in the winter in Alaska. Ally was still asleep, and he needed to send an e-mail to Pete. Not much more could be learned about Kurt, but Mitch wanted some info on Tanya Mandell. Anybody this whacked had to have made an impression on somebody.

Easing out of bed, he avoided the creaking board as he walked across her bedroom, through the bathroom, and into his bedroom. If she woke up and asked him what he was doing, he had an excuse all ready. He was checking on the whereabouts of Lurleen. He would actually do that, once he'd e-mailed Pete.

Before he turned on the computer, he pulled on his sweats and tucked his spy equipment in a dresser drawer. Now that she knew he was officially supposed to watch out for her, he wondered how soon she'd revisit the concept of the bug under her bed.

She'd bought his story before, but she might not now. In any event, he might not need the bugs, after all. He planned to stick close to her, even if that meant dealing with Tanya on a regular basis.

Settling down on his still-made bed, he opened his laptop and turned it on. He didn't waste any time on the e-mail to Pete. *"Require any and all info on Tanya Mandell, including personal behavior patterns."*

Right after he'd pushed the send button, Ally appeared in his doorway, looking rumpled and sleepy. She'd pulled on his T-shirt, which hung to the top of her thighs. Once he glanced up, he couldn't seem to look away.

He'd been through more than a few morning-after scenes. Never once had he looked at the woman he'd had sex with the night before and thought, *Bingo, this is it, end of search.* He thought it now.

At this point his brain should be flashing *System Error,* because no matter what mushy thoughts he was having about Ally, the concept had fatal flaws. Not the least of them was her obsession with all things Alaskan. She might heat up his bed, but she couldn't heat up the whole damned state.

"What are you doing?" She yawned and stretched.

Like a man whose brain has been sucked from his skull, he was completely absorbed by the way her breasts lifted under his T-shirt as she stretched her arms over her head. Where Ally was concerned, it took so little to completely mesmerize him. He could put that movement on a continuous loop and watch it for hours.

"I'm . . . ah . . . looking for Lurleen."

"Oh, yeah?" She brightened and crossed to the bed. "Find anything?"

"I just got started." He clicked on one of his favorite sites for tracking people down. These days he didn't see how anyone could disappear. The Internet had changed everything.

He typed in *"Lurleen Engledorfer"* and narrowed the search to Alaska. If she'd left the state, Rudy might be out of luck. But if she was still here, then Mitch gave him a fighting chance. He couldn't picture Rudy having the resources to chase Lurleen all over the lower forty-eight.

"I hope you can find her." Ally sat down next to him and peered over his shoulder. "And I also think you need to give Rudy some . . . tips."

"Tips?" He waited as the program loaded. "About what?"

"You know." Her breath was warm against his neck.

He didn't know much except that he was already feeling peppy, and he'd had his quota the night before. Getting it up four times in one night was not bad for an old guy of thirty-two, but he hadn't expected to be ready again at seven in the morning. Yet here he was, tenting the material of his sweats. That was one rapid recovery. It made him sort of proud.

"About multis," she added. "I think Rudy needs some guidance."

"Oh." Concentrating on the screen became nearly impossible. "Multis." A vivid memory of sliding down between her thighs blocked out everything. He'd never lost himself so completely as he had at that moment. Life had been all about that glorious triangle. He'd become one with her vagina.

"Rudy's sweet, but I'm not sure he understands the finer points."

Mitch didn't think there were finer points. You had to go for the gusto, immerse yourself in the wonderful world of women's orgasms. A guy had to accept that men were simple, one-shot deals and women were complicated and multi-orgasmic. Mitch thought that was amazing, and he liked to make it happen.

"So will you talk to him?"

He could feel the brush of her nipples through the cotton T-shirt. "I thought you believed that an orgasm was a woman's responsibility." He pretended to study the screen, although his hands were trembling so much he wouldn't have been able to double-click on an icon if his life depended on it.

"I thought I did, too. But last night I wasn't making anything happen. You were in charge, and I surrendered to that. It was . . ." She paused as if to catch her breath.

His ego wanted to hear the end of the sentence. "It was what?"

"Um, probably the kind of experience Lurleen was looking for." She still sounded breathless.

He thought she might be as turned on as he was. "Just out of curiosity, did you happen to bring a condom with you?"

"No." Her nipples quivered against his back.

He gripped the computer so he wouldn't accidentally hit the wrong button and destroy every file he had. "Would you consider going in the other room and getting one?"

There was a smile in her voice. "Did I turn you on?"

"Looks like. Did you turn yourself on?"

"I'll be right back."

Breathing hard, he managed to point his mouse at the only Lurleen Engledorfer listed as living in Alaska. One click, and he had her address in Fairbanks. He would have written it down, except that Ally came back right at that moment and tossed a condom onto his lap.

It was a tribute to his self-control that he didn't throw the computer on the floor. Instead he set it on the pine floorboards with a commendable amount of care. But saving the information and shutting the computer down properly didn't interest him.

What did interest him a great deal was the woman who'd stripped off the T-shirt she'd been wearing and had crawled onto his bed with a come-hither smile. He'd thrown off his sweats and rolled on a condom faster than a DSL connection.

And then, because they hadn't done it that way before, and because he needed to shave before he kissed her again, he coaxed her to her hands and knees and tried it doggie style. It was, to put it mildly, stupendous. She came first, muffling her cries against the pillow, and he came second, clenching his teeth and longing for a soundproof room where they could yell all they wanted.

Later, after they'd listed to one side and finally collapsed onto the blanket, she spoke. "Did you find Lurleen?"

Cupping her sweet breasts, he nuzzled her neck, careful not to scrape her with his beard. "Yeah, I found her."

"Good. Now talk to Rudy so he won't go making the same mistakes if they get back together."

"Men don't give other men sexual advice. It isn't done."

She was silent for a minute. "Then you'll have to tell me how you do it, and I'll talk to Rudy."

"I don't *think* so. I'm not about to have you describing in detail to Rudy what we've been doing." He couldn't forget that Rudy had dibs on Ally if Mitch bombed out. Sexual advice from her was not an option.

"I'd talk in general terms."

"Nope. Let Rudy figure it out for himself. I'll help him locate Lurleen. The multis are up to him."

"I most certainly am not going to let Rudy figure it out for himself! He'll mess it up again, like he did the last time. Mitch, he needs direction. We can't let him flounder."

Mitch groaned. "So if I don't talk to him, you will?"

"That's what I'm saying."

"Then I'll talk to him."

She snuggled closer. "Thank you, Mitch."

"But I'm not taking responsibility. If I talk to him, and he still screws it up, it's not my fault."

"Of course not." She took a deep breath, which made her breasts swell in his hands. "I smell coffee."

How he loved touching her this way. "I can't picture Tanya as a domestic goddess, so I'm guessing Betsy's come back to make breakfast. I suppose we should go down." He didn't want to move, but the longer they stayed here, the more likely someone would figure out they were sharing rooms.

She didn't respond right away. "Can I tell you something?"

It didn't take a genius to figure out the problem. "You don't want to go down and face Tanya."

"That's right. I hate the way she acts, especially around you. I would love to call off this mentoring deal."

"Then call it off." Although if Kurt and Tanya left town, he wouldn't have much of an excuse to stay, either.

"She's so well known in the field. What if I ticked her off? She might be powerful enough to have me blacklisted or something."

"Judging from her personality, I can't believe she's very popular. If she tried to badmouth you, people would consider the source. I wouldn't worry about it."

"Damn. I wish I knew what to do. She's a great photographer, and maybe once we're out in nature, she'll get down to business. She has to be serious about her work. Her pictures are too good for her to be a flake all the time."

Mitch gave the best advice he could come up with.

"So you should probably spend some time with her today and find out if she's going to be a valuable teacher or not."

"Alone."

Mitch hated that idea. "I think it would be better if I went along."

"No it wouldn't. She'd spend all her time coming on to you instead of teaching me. So the whole thing would be a waste of time."

Ally was probably right about how Tanya would react if he went, but he still didn't like the idea of her going off alone with that creepy woman. "Okay, then maybe you shouldn't go out with her, at least not yet. Give it another day or so."

"And how would I stall her? This is what she came to do. Listen, why don't you spend the time here getting to know Uncle Kurt? I know you have a poor opinion of him, and so did Grammy, but he might be sincere. Maybe he wants to cash in a little bit, but that's only human, right?"

"It's not 'a little bit' that concerns me."

"He brought Tanya. He knew I thought she was wonderful, and he probably didn't realize what kind of person she was. He was trying to help. I think he should get points for that."

Mitch wasn't ready to give Kurt any points yet. There was something suspicious about this arrangement with Tanya Mandell, and once he heard from Pete, he might figure out what that was. "I think tomorrow's soon enough to go out with Tanya."

"I don't. I'd like to test the waters today and get it

over with. If she's a lousy teacher, I'll thank her for her help and release her from her obligation. Then all of us will be free of her."

"Maybe she won't feel up to it." He could only hope.

"That's possible. And we won't know unless we go down there." She sat up. "Let's get dressed and have some breakfast."

He gazed up at her. "Just so you know, if Tanya's at the breakfast table, I'm eating my food standing up."

Chapter Twenty-four

When Ally and Mitch walked into the kitchen, Tanya was already at the breakfast table along with Clyde. Instead of flirting with Clyde, Tanya was consulting a catalog of camera equipment, a pen in her hand. Ally wondered if Betsy had staked her claim to Clyde with such force that Tanya had decided against poaching.

Ally thought that was a wise choice on Tanya's part. Betsy could probably knock the stuffing out of Tanya and wouldn't hesitate if Tanya came after her man. But Ally was at a disadvantage if Tanya came after Mitch. Ally wasn't much of a fighter, and she couldn't very well stake a claim where she had none.

What she did have was a bought-and-paid-for babysitter. Apparently her grandmother hadn't been too worried about her physical safety, though, which was some comfort. Instead, Grammy had believed Uncle Kurt would try to swindle Ally out of her money.

So Grammy had hired a nerd for the job. True, he had a gorgeous body, but he was still a nerd. No macho alpha male needed for this assignment. Grammy wouldn't have trusted that type, anyway.

At least now everything made sense. Ally didn't have to wonder about Mitch's motives anymore. Knowing he was here on assignment, she could have sex with him with a free conscience.

He had an agenda, to keep close track of her, and she had an agenda, to take advantage of the situation and enjoy some of the best sex of her life. *The* best sex, actually. Nothing else she'd experienced had been remotely close.

She wasn't quite sure what she'd do about that when it came time for Mitch to go back to Bel Air. She could get used to having multiple orgasms at the drop of a hat, or, more accurately, at the drop of a pair of panties. To be brutally honest, she could get used to Mitch in general. Once she'd worked past his nerdy exterior, he'd turned out to be a lot of fun.

"Here they are!" Betsy said. "Sit, sit. I'll bring you coffee. And I'm making oatmeal this morning."

"Sounds great," Ally said. She was starving.

"I'll come over and get my own," Mitch said. "I'm not all that hungry, this morning, Betsy. Toast will be fine."

Tanya glanced up. She sent a perfunctory smile in Ally's direction before focusing on Mitch. "Sorry I didn't see you again last night, Mitchell." She took a top-to-bottom inventory, but lingered at crotch level. "You missed a good time."

"That's the truth," Betsy said. "Poopsie tap-danced on the bar for a solid hour. What a showman." She gazed fondly at her main squeeze.

Clyde blushed. "Thanks, Kitty-cat."

Tanya wrinkled her nose and went back to her catalog.

"Sorry I missed your performance, Clyde." Mitch walked over to the coffeepot, giving Tanya a wide berth.

Ally sat down next to Tanya. Meanwhile she was thinking that Mitch needed more than toast and coffee after all their activity last night. And there she went, worrying like a girlfriend. She wasn't a girlfriend. She was his job. Big difference.

"Hi, Ally." Clyde glanced at her over the rim of his coffee mug. "Sleep well?"

"Great, thanks."

"Ally." Tanya shoved the catalog over toward her. "I've picked out a few pieces of equipment I'd recommend that you buy. See what you think."

"Okay." Ally was relieved that Tanya was focusing mostly on photography this morning. That was an improvement. She looked at the things Tanya had circled— several different kinds of cameras, a tripod, extra lenses and a carrying case.

All together, they'd add up to a nice piece of change. But Ally knew she needed equipment. "Looks like great stuff," she said.

"It is. I've dealt with these people for years, so it'll be easier if I put in the order and have everything delivered to me. You'll get better service that way, and I can make sure the gear works the way it should. You can write me a check today and I'll get the process started."

Ally didn't want to do that. Unless the teaching session went well, she'd be canceling this mentor arrangement. Having Tanya buy equipment would be another link binding them together.

To stall for time, Ally made a big production of thanking Betsy for the coffee she brought over. Finally she turned to her problematic mentor. "Before I go ahead with that, I'd like to spend a little more time working with the camera I have. I'm sure you can show me how to get the most out of it, and then I can move on to bigger and better."

"Good plan," Clyde said.

But Tanya looked annoyed. "I don't know how much we can accomplish until you have the right equipment."

"Maybe not a lot, but I'd still like to wait until you and I have gone out in the field to make those decisions. There are so many techniques I need to master and I want to take it slow, one step at a time. I'd rather buy the cameras one at a time, too, so that I can get used to each one before I move on to the next."

Tanya gazed at her. "You are seriously committed to this career, right?"

"As serious as I can be without any experience or training." Ally decided this was a good time to hedge her bets. "And remember that the pictures I took before were of animals used to being photographed. There's the possibility that I have no talent for the real thing. You might be able to tell that right away, and that would save everyone time, trouble, and money."

"Sounds reasonable," Betsy said. She put steaming bowls of oatmeal in front of Clyde and Ally. Then she paused behind Tanya's chair. "Tanya, you said no oatmeal, right?"

"Right. I'm not a big oatmeal fan."

Out of Tanya's view, Betsy silently mimicked her words. Then she rolled her eyes. "Okey-dokey."

Ally was flabbergasted. Yesterday Betsy had been thrilled to give up her parlor to the great Tanya Mandell. Today she was making fun of her behind her back. She didn't like Tanya much anymore, it seemed. That made a huge impression on Ally. Betsy wouldn't do such an abrupt about-face without good reason.

"So you want to wait on the equipment?" Tanya closed the catalog with an impatient slap of pages.

"Yes, I do. For all I know, I won't be any good at this, and I'd hate to waste the money."

Clyde nodded. "And you might be able to get some of that stuff used, Ally. Lots of folks get into photography and then give it up. Or maybe a photographer dies and all her equipment gets sold." He said that almost cheerfully, as if looking forward to the time that would happen with Tanya's equipment.

"I can't believe you want to nickel-and-dime your future that way." There was a hard edge to Tanya's blue-eyed stare.

"Just being cautious, is all." Ally looked away, uncomfortable with Tanya's obvious hostility. She'd always imagined a woman like Tanya would have an open, curious expression, as if waiting for the natural world to amaze her. Not so in this case, or not this morning, at any rate.

But Tanya had come up here to help, or so she'd said. Ally was determined to be polite. "Here's what I'd like to do. I'd like to go out with you today and observe your technique. Then I can try a few shots. Because my camera's digital, you could critique the pictures right away. How does that sound?"

"I'll bet Tanya needs another day to recover from her

trip up here," Mitch said. "I'm sure the weather will be nicer tomorrow."

"Might as well do it today." Tanya pushed back her chair and glanced at Ally. "Just the two of us, then? Not your uncle?"

"That was my idea."

She stood. "Then I'll walk down to the fifth wheel and let your uncle Kurt know the plan. And we'll need a snowmobile."

"Couldn't we just walk into the woods?" Ally didn't want to make a huge production out of this outing. "I saw some wolves there yesterday."

Tanya shook her head. "We need to get farther away from town if we expect to find anything interesting."

"Maybe you should take two snowmobiles," Mitch said. "I'll drive one and Ally can ride with me, and you can drive the other one."

Ally sighed. She'd thought Mitch understood why he shouldn't go along. "I think it'd be better if you—"

"You're not invited, Mitchell," Tanya said briskly. "This is work. One snowmobile will be fine. Where can we get one?"

Ally was amazed. Maybe now she'd see Tanya's professional side. "Rudy has two," she said. "Maybe he'd be willing to rent one to us." She glanced at Betsy. "Does he have a phone?"

"Be a lot easier to walk down and ask him," Betsy said. "He'll probably let you borrow it for free. That way you can get the snowmobile yourself instead of making him bring it to you."

"I'll go and get it for you," Mitch said, "but how about waiting until this afternoon? It'll be warmer then."

"I see no reason to wait," Tanya said. "My time is valuable. I don't intend to sit around the kitchen making small talk until the weather warms up."

Ally exchanged a look with Mitch. "I'm sure we'll be back by lunchtime." She hoped he'd figure out that right after lunch, Tanya would be leaving Porcupine. Ally couldn't imagine working long-term with such an unpleasant person.

Mitch set down his coffee mug with an air of resignation. "I'll go get the snowmobile, then."

"You can't miss Rudy's place," Betsy said. "It's the little yellow house on the left on the road out of town. He has a sign out front that says THE EGGMAN. He'll love showing off his chickens."

"And you can tell him about locating Lurleen." Ally didn't want Mitch to waste this trip down to Rudy's. It would be the perfect time for a little man-to-man chat.

Betsy turned to Mitch in surprise. "You found Lurleen? Where is that girl?"

Tanya gave everyone a little wave. "Since I don't know Lurleen, whoever she is, I'll leave you all to sort this out." She walked out of the kitchen.

Everyone fell silent for a couple of minutes, as if they were all waiting for Tanya to put on her boots and coat and leave. Finally the front door of the lodge opened and closed.

Betsy sighed. "Her pictures are so wonderful. And she's such a snot."

"Maybe she's under a strain," Clyde said. "She could be having family problems we don't know about."

"Ha." Betsy snorted. "If she has family problems, she's at the bottom of it. I may like sex, but that woman is out of control. I told her in no uncertain terms that Poopsie was off-limits, but poor Serena isn't that forceful, and she doesn't have a real firm grip on Dave, either."

"It was kinda embarrassing, how Tanya went after him." Clyde took a sip of coffee. "Extremely embarrassing, in fact. At first he seemed flattered, but then he started acting scared, like he wasn't sure what wild thing she might do."

"Like grab his privates," Mitch said darkly.

"I wondered!" Clyde shook his head. "I saw you leap out of your seat like your tail was on fire, and you bought another beer when you hadn't finished your first one."

"I agree, she's a disaster," Ally said. "And I feel terrible that you're all having to put up with her."

"Aw, it's not your fault," Clyde said. "I know how it is when you're trying to learn something. I had to put up with some weird folks in New York City while I was trying to make it. 'Course, I finally got sick of having to do that and came home."

"I'm already sick of Tanya," Ally said. "That's why I didn't get involved in buying equipment through her. Unless this morning goes really well, which I doubt, I'll find some way to tell her thanks, but no thanks."

Betsy patted her on the shoulder. "Don't worry about us. We can handle her. If she can show you how to take pictures like she does, then you're way ahead of the game. I was just blowing off steam."

"That's right," Clyde said. "Porcupinians can watch out for themselves. If she can help you up the ladder, you need to go for it."

"I still think you should wait until this afternoon," Mitch said.

"I want to get it over with. In fact, we need to get going. I'm sure she'll be back before long, wondering where the snowmobile is."

"That's right!" Betsy snapped her fingers and turned to Mitch. "You said you found Lurleen! How did you do that?"

"Internet," Mitch said.

"Really?" Betsy looked impressed. "Maybe it's good for something, after all. Poor Rudy nearly died of loneliness when that girl left. Between you and me, I think they had sexual problems. Rudy has a big heart, and probably some other things that are big, but he's short on technique. Just my opinion."

"You could be right." Ally kept her expression bland.

"I thought about discussing it with him," Betsy said. "But I was afraid how he'd take it. I didn't want him to think I was hitting on him, bringing up subjects like that. Or worse yet, offering to tutor him. Those days are gone."

"Yeah, you never know what Rudy might think if you start trying to educate him about sex." Mitch shot Ally a look. "Listen, before I go, is there any oatmeal left?"

Betsy beamed at him. "That's my boy. I knew you were all right, Mitchell, from the minute I laid eyes on you. I've almost forgiven you for breaking down my historic door. Not quite, but almost."

"It'll be good as new in another day or so," Clyde said. "I'm letting the glue dry."

"I haven't heard any complaints about the missing door." Betsy glanced from Mitch to Ally. "I suppose you've made do."

Ally knew she was blushing and couldn't do a thing about it. "We've made do," she said.

Betsy nodded. "In that case, it might be worth a broken door."

Vivian stormed into the fifth wheel, tracking dirt and snow all over the carpet. She unzipped her coat and plopped down on Kurt's unmade bed. "She's hopeless."

Kurt put aside his bowl of instant oatmeal. "You mean she doesn't know how to take pictures?"

"Oh, for God's sake! You think I care about that? Let's not get too deep into this cover story, Kurt baby. Next thing you'll be expecting *me* to know how to take pictures."

"I thought you'd been practicing."

She glanced away. "Well, yeah, I've practiced."

Which meant she'd done zip. Probably the only picture she'd taken had been of his willy. "Viv! You're supposed to know how to work all those cameras you bought. She'll expect that."

She shrugged. "I can fake it."

"I sure hope to hell you can." Kurt had a sinking sensation that all was not going according to plan. At least Vivian had come out of the Top Hat alone last night. He'd been worried she'd get distracted by the waiter and forget she was supposed to seduce Mitchell, instead.

"Don't worry about whether I'll use the cameras right, okay, Kurt? It can't be that hard. What I'm trying to explain to you is that this isn't working because she's totally uncooperative."

"Like how?"

"She doesn't want to buy the camera equipment yet!"

"I guess there's no rush. Once she sees you with yours, she'll want the same thing."

"You don't get it, do you?" Vivian popped up and started pacing around, which wasn't easy in the cramped quarters. She kept bumping into things. "She's not going along with anything. Not the coffee-table book, not the expensive cameras. She wants success the old-fashioned way. She wants to *earn* it. What a ridiculous attitude that is!"

Kurt decided to steer Vivian onto a different subject. This one was going nowhere, and she was getting more furious by the second. "Did you seduce Mitchell last night?"

"No, I did not! He's playing footsie with your Little Miss Perfect, and I was stuck with my vibrator all night long!" She rounded on him and waggled her finger in his face. "I'm warning you, I'm not doing that again tonight. I can't be expected to live that way. A vibrator should be reserved for emergencies only!"

"You're absolutely right, Viv." He spoke soothingly. "We'll work that out. Don't worry." God, how was he going to keep her on task? She'd come up with the idea in no time, but coaxing her to follow through was turning into a nightmare.

"I have to leave." She headed for the door.

"Where are you going?" He wasn't crazy about having her on the loose when she was in this kind of mood. Anything could happen.

"She wants us to go out and take pictures. So that's what we're going to do."

"Out where?"

"Just out, Kurt! Into the wilderness!"

"Wasn't that what you expected?"

She glared at him. "I expected this to move a whole lot faster, is what I expected."

They'd been in Porcupine less than twenty-four hours. He decided it wouldn't be prudent to say that and enrage her even more. "It'll work out, Viv. Once she sees all the cool equipment you have, she'll want the same thing, and then we'll talk her into the coffee table book, and more equipment. I was thinking we could get her to buy into a gallery, and—"

"Peanuts!" Vivian zipped up her coat in one angry movement. "It's all peanuts!" Then she went out the door, slamming it behind her.

Kurt would have followed, except he was still in his underwear. Vivian hadn't even noticed. She hadn't tried any of her usual tricks, like making him eat all his oatmeal by promising him a blow job if he licked the bowl clean. Sometimes he got the blow job and sometimes not. That was the fun of it. He never knew.

Granted, when Vivian was totally focused on sex, she was unpredictable, but at least he was familiar with that behavior. He'd never known her to lose all interest in sex. It made him very uneasy.

Mitch climbed onto a snowy porch and knocked on the door of Rudy's egg-yolk-yellow house. When Rudy opened the door, the stench of chicken poop made Mitch back up a step. What a hellacious odor! He didn't think all the orgasms in the world would make a woman agree to live with that. He smiled weakly. "Hi, Rudy."

"Hey, glad to see you, Mitch! Come in, come in!"

"Actually, I have a favor to ask." He tried breathing through his mouth, which helped some. "Ally and Tanya would like to rent one of your snowmobiles."

"They don't have to pay me. They can just use it." The sound of squawking and rustling of feathers came from inside the house. "Hang on a sec, and I'll get the keys. You sure you don't want to come in?"

"That's okay. No point in getting warm and then cold again. Thanks, Rudy."

"Be right back." Rudy closed the door.

Mitch hung around on the porch and tried to think how to handle this. Maybe it was the chickens *and* bad sex. Rudy was a sweetheart, but he'd never get a woman with this setup.

The door opened and Rudy came out, zipping his parka. "Be right back, girls!" he called over his shoulder before closing the door. "We have to go around behind the house. I keep them in the shed."

"Nice place, Rudy." Or at least it could be, without chickens living in the house.

"I like it." He led the way down the porch steps and along a shoveled path to the back of the property. "I'm glad to have someone make use of the snowmobiles, to be honest. Will you be needing one?"

"No, but thanks. Just the one for Ally and Tanya."

"She's something else, that Tanya. I'm looking for a woman, but I wouldn't want to get tangled up with one like that. She's crazy."

"She's different, all right. Listen, I have some news. I found out where Lurleen's living."

Rudy turned around with surprising speed for a guy of his size. "No kidding? Where?"

"In Fairbanks. Here's the address." He pulled out the slip of paper where he'd written it down.

"Wow, thanks, Mitch!" Rudy stared at the address with great eagerness. "I need to go down there and see her, find out if she's still with that guy."

"Uh, Rudy, before you do, can I make a suggestion?"

"Sure." Rudy kept studying the address. "I know right where this is, too. It's not too far from the airport. We went right by it when I picked you up the other day."

"Rudy, the chickens . . . they smell pretty bad."

"Yeah, they do at first." He put the piece of paper in his pocket and started toward the shed again. "But you get used to it real fast. Sometimes, if I've been out all day I'll come home and go, Whoa, this place stinks! But after about ten minutes, I don't notice it."

Mitch trudged along behind him. "But if Lurleen couldn't get used to it, would you want to change things, so she'd be happy here?"

"I really don't think it was the chickens, man. It was the sex problem. But now that I know that's up to Lurleen, I want to see if she'll come back. If she just needs to be in the right frame of mind, we could rent us some porno movies."

Mitch decided he'd better be more direct. "You can rent all the porno movies you want, but I don't see how she can be in the right frame of mind when she's up to her ass in chicken shit."

Rudy reached the shed and turned back to Mitch. "So

you think it's a combination of things? That the chickens keep her from being in the right frame of mind?"

"I wouldn't be surprised. She might even get used to the smell, like you say, but it would still be hanging in the back of her mind."

"And keeping her from having those multis." Rudy nodded. "You could be on to something. Well, I didn't want to go to the trouble and expense, but I might have to heat the henhouse, after all. This other seemed like the perfect solution, but if it ruins the mood, I have to take a look at that aspect."

"I would."

"But Mitch, I gotta ask you something, man-to-man."

"Shoot." Mitch shifted his weight and hoped the question wouldn't be too embarrassing.

"Do you ever have trouble . . . you know . . . lasting long enough? I mean, to get to the multis, you got to keep going. Sometimes I can't."

Mitch put his hand on Rudy's shoulder. "I have two words for you. Oral sex."

"Yeah? They like that, too? I thought it was just guys who liked that!"

"Girls like it, too." Mitch couldn't believe he was having this conversation, but Ally would be proud.

"Well, damn, I could do that, 'specially if Lurleen gave me a few pointers. I mean, they're built different, but I'm sure I could figure it out. So that's the secret, huh?"

It was as much of the secret as Mitch was willing to discuss. "It should help."

"So I'll go down to Fairbanks and tell Lurleen I've put a heater in the henhouse and I'm up on this oral sex business. That should do the trick, huh?"

"If nothing else, it'll make for an interesting conversation."

"I think it'll work. Thanks, man!" Rudy clapped Mitch on the back so hard he nearly tipped him over into the snow. "I'll let you know how it turns out!"

That was exactly what Mitch was afraid of.

Chapter Twenty-five

When Tanya came back from talking to Uncle Kurt, Ally was waiting in the lobby with her camera in her backpack. "I'm ready," she said. "Mitch is getting the snowmobile. He should be here any minute."

"Fine." Tanya seemed more excited about the idea than she had earlier. "That's great. Give me a minute to organize my equipment, and I'll be right out."

"How's Uncle Kurt?"

"You know, it's a good thing we're not taking him with us. I think he's come down with the flu."

"Really?" Ally reached for her coat hanging on the wall. "Maybe I should go check on him, see if he needs anything."

"I wouldn't. He said he wanted to be left alone so he could sleep. But he was happy that you and I were going out today. That was his dream, that I'd be available to give you some instruction."

"And I do appreciate it." Ally felt a pang of regret that she wasn't able to be more enthusiastic about this gesture Uncle Kurt had made. But the poor guy hadn't known what he was getting into with Tanya the Sexpot, and now for all his troubles he'd ended up getting sick. "When we come back, I'll go see him."

"Good plan. I'll be right out." Tanya went into the parlor and closed the door.

"What's this about your uncle?" Betsy came out of the kitchen. "I caught the tail end of the conversation."

"Tanya says he's come down with the flu."

"Well, it happens. He looked a little rundown last night over at the Top Hat. Does he need some soup? I have some ptarmigan soup in the freezer."

"Maybe later, after Tanya and I get back. She said he just wants to sleep."

Betsy nodded. "That's how I am when I get sick. I want to crawl in a cave until I'm fit for human company again."

Ally lowered her voice. "I hate to say this, but Tanya seems to be acting more normal. Like she wants to take me out and show me the ropes."

"I hope it works out for you, then," Betsy said. "When she came, I was so excited for you. Maybe last night was only a passing phase."

"Maybe." But Ally would always wonder when that phase might repeat itself. Her respect for Tanya would never be the same.

Mitch came through the door, stomping his feet on the mat by the door. "The snowmobile's out there." He glanced hopefully at Ally. "Where's Tanya? Did you two decide to wait, after all?"

"No, we're going. She's doing some last-minute things."

Mitch gazed at her. "I can get the other snowmobile in no time. I think I should go with you."

"I don't." Ally felt a little weird taking off alone with Tanya, but she couldn't picture hauling Mitch along for no particular reason.

"I'm sure Ally can handle it," Betsy said.

Mitch frowned. "I'm sure she can, too. It's just—"

"Relax," Ally said. "It's only a couple of hours."

"Yeah, I know." But he didn't look at all relaxed. He looked extremely tense. "I left the helmets and goggles hanging on the handlebars. As you predicted, Betsy, Rudy wouldn't take any money."

"Then I'll have to think of something nice to do for him," Ally said.

"You might want to contribute toward a heater for his henhouse."

"Rudy's going to heat his henhouse?" Betsy's eyes widened. "He told me that was never gonna happen, that it was dumb to heat a henhouse when he had plenty of room for the chickens in his kitchen."

Mitch took off his coat and hung it by the door. "Have you been in his house when the chickens are in residence?"

"Well, no. I haven't had a reason to go down there. Does it really smell bad?"

"Betsy, you have no idea." Mitch pulled off his boots. "If he wants anybody to live with him, Lurleen or any other prospect, the chickens need to go."

Ally was dying to know what had been said. "So you convinced him to move the chickens. That's a good first step. Anything else?"

"That's most of it."

Betsy started to laugh. "And the rest had to do with sex. Am I right? Was he clueless?"

"He, um, had a few misconceptions." Mitch glanced at Ally. "He's a little clearer about things now."

She smiled at him. "Thanks, Mitch."

"Yeah, thanks." Betsy chuckled again. "Somebody needed to talk to him. I'm glad it was you. Well, I left a pot simmering on the stove. And there's coffee left, Mitchell, if you want some." She paused. "Or is it Mitch now?"

"Rudy thought he should be called Mitch." Ally could feel her cheeks getting warm, but then Betsy suspected something was going on. "So I decided to call him that, too."

Betsy gave him the once-over. "Yeah. Mitch looks better on you. Anyway, gotta go. Good luck out there, Ally."

"Thanks." The minute Betsy disappeared inside her kitchen, Ally sidled over to Mitch. "You really gave him some advice?"

"A little. Listen, Ally, postpone this trip, at least until this afternoon."

"Why?"

"Because . . . because afternoon's a great time to be out there. That's when we went with Rudy, and it was perfect, remember?"

She put her hand on his arm. "Postponing the session isn't going to help anything. Now tell me what happened with Rudy."

Mitch sighed. "He didn't know girls liked oral sex. He thought it was just a guy thing."

"Omigod." Ally clapped a hand to her mouth to hold back a whoop of laughter. "You should get a medal."

"I should."

"Are you saying he'd never . . . ?"

"Never. But he will, now."

"You should get a really big medal, and a parade with confetti, and maybe even a big brass—"

"My, isn't this cozy?" Tanya walked through the door of the parlor carrying her camera bag.

Ally started to move away from Mitch, but then decided not to. Maybe she had no real claim, but it wouldn't hurt to let Tanya know they were together. "I'm off, then," she said, and kissed him on the cheek. "I'll see you when we get back."

"Right." With obvious reluctance, he fished some keys out of his pocket. "Tanya, I assumed you'd be driving. Ally's only been snowmobiling once, and she was a passenger."

"I'll be driving. I've been driving snowmobiles for years."

"I figured as much, in your line of work." He tossed her the keys. "I assume you also know about the avalanche danger this time of year."

"Of course. I'm always careful."

"I think I'll take Betsy up on that coffee. See you two later." With one last glance at Ally, he walked into the kitchen.

"Let's get going," Tanya said.

"Yes, let's." Now that they were on their way out the door, she had the urge to call Mitch back and ask him to go, after all. But that would be silly.

• • •

Mitch went upstairs to check his e-mail, but there was no response from Pete, so he came back down to have a cup of coffee with Betsy. While talking with her, he found out that Ally was feeling a little better about Tanya, and that Kurt had the flu and didn't want to be disturbed. Mitch didn't like the sound of that, but it wasn't as if Kurt could sneak out and join up with Tanya for some funny business without taking Rudy's other snowmobile.

Just to be on the safe side, Mitch got Rudy's phone number from Betsy and called him. Rudy promised not to loan out his other snowmobile to Kurt. Then Mitch put on his boots and coat and walked over to the Top Hat. No one was there at this time of the morning except Clyde, who was checking his liquor supply in preparation for the lunch crowd.

"What's up?" he asked when Mitch walked in.

"I just wondered if Ally's uncle had come in."

"Haven't seen him. You want to talk to him?"

Mitch didn't want to talk to him so much as keep track of him. "Yeah. If he comes in, would you call Betsy and let her know?"

"Sure thing. You want your nude?"

Mitch had forgotten all about Quillamina Sharp. "Sure, why not?"

While Clyde went upstairs to get her, Mitch leaned against the bar and thought about the moment he'd walked in and caught Ally dancing on it. He'd probably known right then that he had a problem with his libido, but he hadn't wanted to admit it.

And now he knew exactly how it felt to lie with her,

skin-to-skin, and enjoy everything that was Ally. He'd never regret having that chance, even if he never got to do it again. For all his complaining about her decision to travel to Alaska, he had to admit that he was glad she'd done it. Last night never would have happened if they'd both stayed at the mansion.

"Here you are." Clyde came back holding Quillamina like a baby doll. "I have to say, this is one ugly broad."

Mitch took her from Clyde and got a whiff of cedar. "But she smells nice." He'd decided to ship Quillamina home as a souvenir. "And the price was right. I wonder if Dave will ever—"

The front door opened, and both of them turned to see who had come in. Damned if it wasn't Kurt, the man who was supposed to have the flu.

"What the hell do you have there?" Kurt asked, looking at Quillamina.

"One of Dave's nude sculptures," Mitch said.

Kurt snorted. "I hope you didn't pay a lot for it."

"Nope." He didn't think Kurt looked the least bit sick. "I heard you were under the weather."

"Who told you that?"

"Betsy, who heard it from Tanya."

Kurt blinked. "Oh. Yeah. Well, when she came down to tell me about the photo trip, I was feeling a little punk. But I'm better now. Came in to see if there was anything to eat."

"I can get you something," Clyde said. "Lunch doesn't officially start for another thirty minutes, but I can make you a sandwich."

"Good. And a beer."

"Coming up." Clyde went into the kitchen.

Kurt walked over and climbed up on a bar stool as if he planned to ignore Mitch completely.

Mitch set Quillamina down on a table and took the bar stool next to Kurt. "Just so you know, Madeline filled me in on the family history."

Kurt stared straight ahead. "Her version."

"It coincides with Suzanne's version."

"I don't know anybody named Suzanne."

"She's the maid you nearly knocked over when you ran out of Madeline's room."

Kurt scowled and turned to him. "Look, whatever Madeline told you, it's a damned lie. I never—"

"It doesn't matter. It's not my place to judge you for something that happened forty years ago. I'm here to make sure Ally gets a fair shake."

"Oh, I'm so sure. You're here because if you get in her pants, then you might talk her into marrying you and you can get your hands on all that money."

Mitch fought for control. He'd never wanted to hit a guy as much as he wanted to hit Kurt. He actually reached for his glasses, planning to take them off before he challenged Kurt to duke it out.

Then he got a grip. "And why are you here?" he asked quietly.

"That is none of your goddamn business." Kurt turned away from him again.

"That's where you're wrong. If you're planning to take advantage of Ally, you'll have to get past me first."

"Yeah, like I'm shaking in my boots, geek."

Clyde came in from the kitchen, a sandwich on a plate. "Here you go." He grabbed a glass and drew a beer from the tap before setting that in front of Kurt, too. "Mitch, can I get you anything?"

"Nothing, thanks. Listen, do you have something to wrap around my sculpture? I'm planning to ship it back home."

"Let me look in the back." Clyde went into the kitchen again.

"I think you and that ugly nude might want to get out of town," Kurt said. "Accidents happen in Alaska, accidents that never get explained."

"I guess you're not completely stupid. You didn't say that in front of a witness." If Mitch had ever doubted that Kurt was a threat to Ally, he didn't doubt it now.

"Get out of town, nerd," Kurt said, still with his back to him. "While you still can."

"You must steal your dialogue from B Westerns, Kurt. That old 'Get out of town while you still can' line has moss growing on it."

"You think you're a smart kid, don't you? You're not as smart as you think you are."

But I'm smarter than you. At least he hoped so.

Clyde came out of the back room with some bubble wrap and tape. "How's this?"

"Perfect. Could you give me a hand for a minute?"

"Sure thing. It tickles me to think of one of Dave's nudes going down to L.A. I never figured any of them would leave Porcupine." Clyde carried the bubble wrap over to the table where Mitch had set down the nude.

Once they began wrapping Quillamina, Mitch lowered his voice and covered it with the crinkle of the bubble wrap. "Give me a call at Betsy's if and when he leaves here, okay?"

Clyde nodded.

Moments later, Mitch carried his nude back over to the Loose Moose. The wind gusting down the street pulled at Clyde's tape job. Glancing toward the end of town, Mitch noticed the wind was blowing the top layer of powdery snow around. Sparkling in the sunlight, it was kind of pretty. Not that he'd ever choose to watch snow sparkle, but he might as well appreciate it while he was here.

Inside the warmth of the Loose Moose lobby, he shucked his boots and coat before picking up his sculpture and climbing the stairs to his room. Quillamina was heavy. It would cost him a small fortune to ship her, but he didn't care. He was growing fonder of her every day.

He unlocked his door and carried Quillamina into his room. Betsy had been in to make his bed. No more rumpled blankets where he'd romped with Ally this morning. He thought about Ally out on the snowmobile with Tanya.

The idea of her being someplace where he couldn't see her really bothered him, but he hadn't been able to come up with a way to stall her. Setting the sculpture on the floor, he turned on his laptop again to see if Pete had found any information on Tanya Mandell.

Ally had thought that Mitch drove the snowmobile like a maniac, but he was a little old lady compared to Tanya. They made an obscene amount of noise as they raced over the landscape, leaping small drifts and sending snow flying in their wake. The helmet and goggles helped cut the wind, but she'd pulled the collar of her coat up over her chin at the beginning of the ride, and it had slipped.

She was afraid to let go of Tanya long enough to pull it back over her mouth, and her lips were like ice cubes. Worse yet, her doubts about Tanya had returned. Surely you couldn't take pictures of wildlife if you charged into their environment like this.

Through the tinted goggles Rudy had loaned her, Ally saw a flock of ptarmigans up ahead. She thought Tanya might slow down so they could try a few shots, but instead Tanya gunned the engine and the flock scattered. Ally wished she'd asked more questions about this trip, so that she'd have some idea of Tanya's plans.

So far the concept seemed to entail barreling through the snow, giving no thought to what creatures might be over the next hill or hiding among the trees. Ally saw no point in trying to spot anything. Any thicket or grove of evergreens they passed was only a blur of trunks, branches, and snow.

Finally Tanya slowed the pace a little. She even seemed to be looking for something. That was encouraging. After all the time she'd spent out in the wilderness searching for animals, she must have a sixth sense about where to find them. Maybe Ally wasn't giving her enough credit.

"That looks like a good spot!" Tanya called over her shoulder.

Ally wasn't sure what it might be a good spot for. A few windswept evergreens clung to the edge of what looked like a sharp drop-off. But Tanya must know what she was doing. She hadn't taken all those amazing pictures by accident.

Tanya stopped the snowmobile about twenty yards from the place where the snow seemed to fall away. "We'll see how this works."

Ally climbed off, glad for the sudden silence. Once the roar of the snowmobile was gone, she could listen for any creatures who might be nearby. But she heard nothing except the wind, saw nothing but the tracks of their snowmobile stretching out in the distance. The wind had really picked up in the last hour. Strong gusts hurled loose snow around, and soon those tracks would be obliterated.

Turning back to the trees, Ally thought she saw movement in one of the branches. Maybe the wind. No! She looked closer and spotted a ptarmigan sitting there, white feathers fluffed out against the cold. Feathers even covered the feet of these hardy birds.

And there was another one, its feathers so white that it was well camouflaged by the snow-covered branches. She was good at spotting things, always had been. It seemed like a valuable skill for this career.

Pleased with herself, she turned back toward the snowmobile, where Tanya was pulling her camera bag from one of the leather pouches strapped to the back. "Ptarmigan," she said. "In the trees."

"Good." Tanya gestured toward the other saddlebag. "Get your camera."

"Right." Excitement made her forget her misgivings about Tanya. Now she'd have a chance to take pictures under the watchful eye of a pro, exactly as she'd longed to do. She unbuckled the leather pouch and took out her backpack. "Do you use a digital camera at all?"

"Sometimes." Tanya hooked her camera bag over her shoulder and started toward the trees, walking cautiously through the crunchy snow. "When it feels right."

Someday Ally would have that kind of instinct, knowing which camera suited the occasion. For now, she had only one, but she would learn. She pulled off her gloves and stuck them in her pocket. Then she grabbed her camera from her backpack and shoved the pack back into the saddlebag.

"I was thinking," she said as she followed Tanya, "that with the right angle, I could shoot them on the branch, with the blue sky as a backdrop. I'm sure you have hundreds of ptarmigan shots, but I'd love to try and get this."

"Be my guest." Tanya paused and set her camera bag in the snow. "I'll let you go ahead. You can have first shot."

Ally's pulse quickened. "I'm so nervous, taking pictures in front of the great Tanya Mandell. Promise not to laugh if I do something stupid."

"Trust me, I won't laugh."

"Thanks." Ally smiled at her. "I guess everyone's a beginner once."

"Some people never get beyond that stage."

"But I'm going to." Ally was filled with new determination now that she was actually on an official shoot with someone who knew what to do. "How close do I try to get?"

"As close as you can."

"Without stepping too near the edge or setting off an avalanche," Ally said, laughing as she kept her eye on the two birds in the tree. "That would end my fledgling career in no time, wouldn't it?"

"It sure would."

"Well, don't worry. I'll be careful." She crept up very close, close enough that she could see the birds looking down at her with their jet-black eyes. "You're lucky I have a camera and not a gun, little guys, or you'd be somebody's dinner tonight."

She had to kneel in the snow to get the angle she wanted. There, that was good. She squeezed off a shot and the birds didn't move. Maybe the nearly perfect camouflage made them feel safe, but she'd eliminated that protective coloring with her angle. They stood out in stark relief against the blue sky.

As she was about to take another shot she heard Tanya's boots crunching on the snow. "Change your mind?" she said, keeping her voice down so she wouldn't startle the birds.

"No, this was always my plan."

"Your plan?" Ally clicked the shutter. "I don't understand." She turned slightly, glancing over her shoulder. What she saw made no sense to her. And then it did, and her veins turned to ice.

Chapter Twenty-six

Mitch stared at Pete's message on the screen. *Finally tracked down news on Tanya Mandell. She's on safari in Africa. Home today, late.*

With a pungent swear word, Mitch yanked open his dresser drawer. Moments later he was outside, headed for the Top Hat. When he'd charged downstairs, Betsy had been nowhere around, so he'd used her phone to call Rudy and tell him to show up at the Top Hat with the other snowmobile. He'd also activated the little transmitter in Ally's backpack.

His nerd disguise was history because he was going after her, but first Kurt would by God tell him who the hell was out there with her. That would determine whether Mitch would need the gun strapped to his ankle. He prayed he wouldn't, but he had a bad feeling he might.

Kurt was starting on his second beer. He'd raised the

glass to his lips, so both beer and the glass went flying when Mitch spun him around, slammed him against the edge of the bar, and squeezed his windpipe with his hand. "Who's with Ally?"

Kurt's eyes bulged. "T-Tanya!" he choked out.

"Wrong answer." He shoved the flat of his hand harder against Kurt's windpipe. "Who is it?"

Betsy and Clyde came out of the kitchen, both wide-eyed.

"Mitch!" Betsy cried. "What on earth is going on? And where are your glasses?"

"That woman with Ally isn't Tanya Mandell," Mitch said. "And Kurt's about to tell me who she is. Right, Kurt?"

"Damn straight he is," said Clyde. He reached under the bar, pulled out a .45 Magnum, and stuck the barrel against the back of Kurt's skull. "This is not a toy, and it's loaded."

"Clyde!" Betsy said. "I didn't know you had a gun! That's so sexy!"

"Her n-name's Vivian Altman," Kurt said. "She's m-my girlfriend."

"I *knew* it couldn't be Tanya Mandell," Betsy said. "That just didn't seem right."

"Your girlfriend." That still didn't tell Mitch what he wanted to know. "And what's she up to, going out there with Ally today, since she's not a world-famous photographer?"

Rudy charged into the Top Hat, his big hands flexing. "Let me at him. Let me at that lying son of a moose!"

"That's okay, Rudy." Betsy moved to intercept him. "I think Mitch and Clyde are handling it."

"We may need Rudy to rearrange his body parts if he doesn't answer the question," Mitch said.

"Glad to!" Rudy gently set Betsy aside and came to tower over Kurt. "Where do you want me to start? Let's start with his privates."

Kurt's wild gaze darted from Mitch to Rudy. "I—I don't know the answer! I wanted to stick with Plan A! But now she's getting all crazy, and talking about Plan B! How was I to know she had a gun?"

Mitch's stress level spiked about a thousand percent. He released his hold on Kurt. "Rudy, let's go. Betsy, call the cops. Clyde, hang on to this pile of crap until we come back."

"He won't be going anywhere," Clyde said. "But I think you'd better take my gun, Mitch."

"Got one," Mitch said. "But thanks."

"*You* have a gun, *too*?" Betsy seemed beside herself with excitement.

"I don't got one!" Rudy came over to the bar. "I'll take it. But bash him over the head with it first, so he won't cause any trouble."

"What's up?" Dave came into the bar. "Damn, Clyde, what are you doing with that gun? I never knew you had a gun."

"Kept it for emergencies, under a stack of towels. Now I'm giving it to Rudy. You got one I can borrow to keep this guy under control? Otherwise I gotta bash him, like Rudy said."

"Don't hit me over the head," Kurt said. "Anybody got a whip? A whip would be good."

"No whip," Dave said, "but I got a chain saw. Be right back."

Mitch couldn't wait around for this nonsense. "No, Dave, forget it!" he shouted after him. "We'll just go with mine!"

But Dave was gone, tearing out of the Top Hat to get his weapon.

Mitch headed for the door. "Come on, Rudy. Forget the gun. One's fine."

"Okay, if you say so." Rudy followed him. "But I really wanted to have a gun, too."

They had their helmets on and were mounting up when Dave came running, carrying the chain saw.

"Man, that looks dangerous, running with a chain saw," Rudy said. "He could fall and damage somethin' important."

"I've got it!" Dave yelled. "Wait! I'll get you that gun, Rudy!"

"Yeah, let's wait," Rudy said, his voice eager. "It's only a couple of seconds."

Rudy had control of the snowmobile, so Mitch gave in. He hoped a couple of seconds wouldn't make a critical difference. He refused to think about the possibility that they might already be too late.

"So where are your glasses, Mitch?" Rudy asked.

"I wear contacts. Listen, if Dave doesn't come right back, can we—"

"He'll be right back. And you got a gun. I thought you were a nerd, but you're not acting like a nerd."

"I'm a private investigator."

"Whew, that's a relief! I was afraid I would have to handle this myself."

Dave tore through the door again, Clyde's gun in his hand. "Betsy's called for backup."

"The cops?" Mitch asked.

"Yeah, she's called them, too, but Ernie's coming with his sled dogs and his shotgun. I'll ride with him."

Mitch wasn't about to hang around until the Porcupine Posse was formed. "Sorry, we can't wait."

"No, no, don't wait! We'll catch up. Go!"

Rudy put the snowmobile in gear. "Dave, do you even know what's going on?"

"Nope." Dave flashed his brilliant smile. "Don't care. I'm in."

"That's what I thought. See ya." Rudy took off down the street. "The thing is, Porcupinians need somethin' to do!" he yelled over the roar of the motor, as if Mitch had asked a question.

Mitch wasn't interested in asking any questions at the moment. All he wanted was to find Ally. To think he'd stood by and let her go out there. He should have come up with an excuse to keep her from leaving. Maybe he should have disabled the snowmobiles somehow. If anything happened . . .

He pulled his hand-held tracking device out of his coat pocket and switched it on. He'd bought it on a hunch right before he'd left L.A and had never tested it. He hoped to hell the thing worked the way it was supposed to.

Staring at the small screen, he located the little blip that was Ally. Or rather, the little blip that was the microchip in her backpack. Now if Ally was close to that blip, and safe, all would be right with his world.

Rudy reached the end of town and stopped, letting the engine idle. "Hey, Mitch! What do we do now? The wind's blown the tracks away. I don't know which way they went."

"Don't worry." Mitch concentrated on that little blip. Dear God, she had to be okay. "I have something here that will tell us. Go northeast."

Rudy hesitated. "What you got, some kinda radar?"

"Something like that. Keep your eye out for tracks, anyway. But if the tracks are gone, I can still aim us in the right direction."

"I have to say, Mitch, you are nothing like I thought you were. You know about guns, and electronic stuff, even sex! You rock, man!" And Rudy tromped on the gas.

Ally had expected that sometime during her stay in Alaska, she might come face-to-face with an angry grizzly. She'd fully expected to deal with a testy bull moose at one time or another, and she knew people had been trampled if they weren't careful. She'd figured on dangerous weather conditions, ice that gave way under her feet, and the possibility of getting lost in an unforgiving wilderness.

She'd never counted on looking down the barrel of a gun. Fear made her heart race. Not surprising. Nobody had ever tried to kill her before. "You're not Tanya Mandell."

"Correct!" The woman, whoever she was, smiled as if Ally had just won the jackpot on *Jeopardy.*

"I can't believe that didn't occur to me." Ally struggled to breathe. In, out; in, out. Her brain needed oxygen to think her way out of this fix. And she would get out of it. She'd come to Alaska to start living, not to die. A gun pointed in her face was a serious obstacle to her plans.

"I'll tell you why it didn't occur to you." The woman looked happier than she had since she'd arrived in Porcupine. "Because you wanted so much to believe that I was Tanya. You wanted to think your dear uncle Kurt had given you this wonderful gift of a fabulous mentor."

She was right about that. Even now, Ally clung to the hope that Uncle Kurt hadn't known this woman was an imposter. If only Mitch had been a trained bodyguard instead of a nerd, he might have found out about this before it was too late. Grammy might have miscalculated by hiring Mitch.

"It was my idea, pretending to be the photographer you idolized. Brilliant, if I do say so."

Even when Ally had thought this woman was Tanya, she'd realized she was a mental case. Now it became obvious. The woman was crackers. Ally didn't know all the psychobabble to describe it, but one thing she did understand with complete clarity. For this chick, pulling the trigger would be no problemo.

"What's your real name?" Ally asked. In order to buy some time until she figured out a way to get out of this gun situation, she needed a name.

"I guess it doesn't matter if I tell you. It's Vivian."

"Well, Vivian, how would you like to spend the rest of your life on the beach in the Caribbean, all expenses paid? I could arrange for that." Ally took stock of her options. Her only immediate weapon, other than her hands and feet, was her camera.

"That's funny." Vivian giggled, which sounded very strange coming from a woman holding a gun. "You're trying to buy me off."

"Think about it. If you kill me, you'll get caught. But

if we strike a bargain, you'll be set for life, without having to watch your back all the time." Ally wondered if she could somehow make use of the trees behind her, or even the birds in them, to create a distraction so she could make a grab for the gun.

"I won't get caught. After I kill you, I'll shove you over the edge. The snow's deep down there. That should be enough, but this is avalanche season. I ought to be able to start a little one, just enough to cover you really good."

Pretty scary stuff, having her own death described. Ally thought she'd take a pass on going out that way. Dying in her rocker at the age of ninety-eight sounded a whole lot better. "But you'll be the last one to see me alive. You'll be a prime suspect."

"Ah, but I'll disappear, too. Neither of us will come back. I'll use the snowmobile to get within hiking distance of the main road and catch a ride out of here. I'll be on a plane out of the country before we're reported missing."

Ally thought she'd have a better position back by the trees, even though that was closer to the drop-off. "I don't get it. How can you profit from killing me if you disappear?" She edged back a step.

"Go ahead and try to get away. You're backing toward the cliff and you'll go over it eventually, anyway."

"I'm just naturally accommodating." Ally took another step back. "So you didn't answer my question. What's in this for you?"

"A fortune. Kurt will be the last living Jarrett, and he'll get it all. What's Kurt's will be mine. Blackmail's such a useful tool, don't you think?" Vivian giggled again.

"So he knows." The last shred of hope died. She had no family. The grief when Grammy died had been terrible, but this was worse. She'd believed in Uncle Kurt, believed he cared about her. And she was nothing to him except a way to get rich.

"Oh, he's in this up to his eyeballs. He'll pay to keep me quiet. He'll pay, and pay, and pay. Your Caribbean retirement plan is peanuts compared to what I'll get. I like peanuts, but I prefer caviar."

As Ally thought about the faith she'd put in Uncle Kurt, how she'd dreamed of a life full of adventure with him as a big part of it, as the father she'd never had, she felt the pain of losing that dream. The pain was quickly followed by a white-hot anger. How dare he? How dare he take her dream and smash it into a million jagged pieces?

Without thinking, she yelled in rage and brought her camera up sharply, knocking the gun away from her face. It fired over her shoulder, the noise a loud, deafening roar in her ears as she tackled Vivian, landing on top of her in the snow. They rolled over and over as she tried to grab the gun, tried to knock it away.

But Vivian held on. With one wild swing of the gun, she managed to whack Ally in the head. Dazed, she lost focus for a second, and that was all it took for Vivian to straddle her and point the gun in her face again.

Panting, Vivian stared down at her, her blue eyes filled with rage. "You are *not* going to stop me."

Ally struggled to get her breath. She figured the only reason Vivian hadn't pulled the trigger was her love of power. That's what the sexual aggression had been all about, and now she wanted to flaunt her power over Ally for as long as possible. Once she killed her prey, the fun would be over.

"You're strong," Ally said. "Stronger than I thought you'd be."

Vivian smiled in satisfaction. "That's more like it. Why don't you try begging for your life? Who knows, I might reconsider."

Oh, sure she would. Ally wasn't into begging, but she was into stalling. The longer she stayed alive, the more likely she could figure out a way to overcome Vivian. "It's a good thing you didn't hook up with Mitch. You're way too much woman for him."

"I knew that." Her lip curled. "Wimpy little nerdling. He missed out. I could have taught him a few things. I'm sure he's boring in bed."

"Oh, yeah, totally." If Vivian didn't kill her, she might be struck dead for telling such a whopper of a lie.

Vivian sighed. "I could have whipped him into shape. He has nice buns."

"I suppose." It was as if they were two girlfriends dishing about a guy they both knew. If the situation hadn't been potentially lethal, Ally might have laughed.

"I insist on nice buns. That's a number one prior—" She paused. "What's that noise?"

Ally couldn't hear much with the wind blowing and her head pressed into the snow.

"Maybe it's hunters." Still holding the gun on Ally, Vivian climbed off her. "Get up, but don't try anything."

Getting slowly to her feet as she kept her eye on Vivian's trigger finger, she brushed off some of the snow. And now she heard the noise. A snowmobile.

She cautioned herself not to get too excited. Sound

carried out here, and the snowmobile could be quite a distance away. It might not be headed in this direction at all. Except that the noise got louder. And louder. Soon she could see it, coming across the open area toward them. Coming fast.

"Get back toward the trees!" Vivian grabbed Ally's camera out of the snowbank where it had fallen during their wrestling match. "If anybody asks, you and I are taking pictures. Got it?"

"Got it." As if Ally planned to let these snowmobilers have a chat with them and leave. Uh-huh. And if Vivian thought Ally wouldn't make use of this heaven-sent arrival, she was completely crazy. Which, of course, she was.

Nevertheless, Ally went back to the trees at gunpoint and brushed the snow off her camera, as if she'd go along with the story like a good girl. But no matter what she tried, she had to be careful not to put an innocent person in the line of fire. Vivian would shoot any witnesses in a heartbeat.

"I'll stand behind you, so they won't see the gun."

"Yeah, they might get suspicious if they see the gun."

"Shut up." Vivian jammed the barrel right under Ally's left shoulder blade.

As the snowmobile came nearer, Ally began to suspect who was driving it. Only one person in the area had both a snowmobile and a bushy red beard. And when she realized who was riding behind Rudy, she got really scared. She felt like yelling for them to go back. Mitch was not up to this.

But if he caught on to the situation, he would try to save her, bless his heart. And Vivian would get great pleasure out of shooting him, after he'd turned down her sexual advances. If she had the chance, she might even torture him first.

And Rudy was big and brawny, but he was also an old-fashioned kind of guy. He would probably hesitate to tackle a woman, so he could be a sitting duck for someone as deadly as Vivian. He'd never expect her to be serious about shooting someone with a gun. He might even assume it wasn't loaded.

They'd probably come out here to see how the photo shoot was going. Mitch had been worried about Ally, so he'd probably talked Rudy into coming out here with him to check on them. Ally's job was to tell them everything was fine and they could go back home now. She wasn't about to let either of them get shot.

As they pulled up and climbed off the snowmobile, she smiled and waved. "Hi, guys! You just missed a pair of ptarmigan! I got a couple of really good shots."

"Is that right?" Mitch was on the far side of the snowmobile and leaned down, doing something with his boot. Probably hadn't zipped it up tight. Then he took off his goggles.

Ally expected him to put on his glasses after that, but he didn't. That was strange. Maybe he'd left them back at the Loose Moose. Good God, now she'd have to worry about him even more if he was blind as a bat.

"So everything's going good?" Rudy stood by the snowmobile, his hands in his pockets. He seemed to be waiting for Mitch.

"Yeah, Tanya and I are making terrific progress. So if that's all you wanted to know, you can head on back. I'm sure Mitch was glad to get a ride, though. He loves these machines."

Mitch came around from the snowmobile, his hands in his pockets, too. "Actually, we had a reason for coming out here besides that."

Vivian laughed. "If you brought wine and cheese, that's very sweet, but we're working. This isn't a picnic."

Mitch drew closer, his boots crunching in the snow. He glanced around, as if taking note of the area where Vivian and Ally had rolled. Then he surveyed the two of them and their parkas, which still had plenty of snow clinging to them.

He didn't seem to be squinting at all. In fact, he acted as if he could see perfectly well. "Oh, I'm sure it's not a picnic, Vivian."

It took a beat before Ally realized that Mitch had called Vivian by her real name. Her gaze locked with his. At that moment she knew he could see just fine without his glasses.

She didn't have time to wonder about that now. Silently she mouthed the words *I know*. His eyesight had to be excellent, because he got the message. His nod was slight, but she saw it.

But Vivian wasn't giving up. "Who are you referring to, Mitchell? There's no one named Vivian here."

"You mean there's no one named Tanya Mandell here," Rudy said. "You're a fake. Tanya Mandell's on one of them safaris in Africa."

Vivian laughed. "I canceled that trip so I could come here! I guess I didn't notify everyone. Where did you hear that, Mitchell?"

"Give it up, Vivian," Mitch said. "Kurt told us who you are. So let's all go back to Porcupine now, shall we?"

"No, I'm afraid I can't do that," Vivian said.

"Yes, you will." Mitch pulled a gun out of his pocket. "Now."

Ally stared at it. Two guns in one day was two more than she'd ever seen in her life, except in the movies or on TV. So Mitch could see without his glasses and he had a gun. It was slightly possible Grammy had hired a bodyguard, after all.

"Why, Mitchell, you little sneak, you." Vivian sounded more excited than worried by this turn of events. "You're not a geeky boy after all, are you?"

"Oh, yeah, I still am. But now I'm a geeky boy with a gun. And we're all going back to Porcupine. The police should be there by now. They might even be headed out this way."

"Nicely finessed, Mitchell." Vivian pulled the gun from behind Ally's back and placed the muzzle up against her temple. "But I hate it when someone gives me orders. Really hate it. And you see, I still have the winning hand. Can you spell the word *ransom*, Mitchell?"

"Don't try it, Vivian." Mitch's gun hand didn't waver.

"Oh, I'll do more than try it. I'll do it. Either you head on back to Porcupine and call off the cops, or your rich little girlfriend's brains will be splattered all over this clean, white snow. And I know how you'd hate to see that happen."

Mitch paled and his throat moved in a swallow. But his voice remained steady. "You wouldn't follow through," he said. "You pull the trigger and you're a dead woman."

"I go back with you and I'm a dead woman. I crave freedom. I crave men. Lock me up in a cage with nothing but women around and no vibrator in sight? It would be a hundred times worse than dying! Don't make the mistake of calling my bluff. I'm not bluffing."

Chapter Twenty-seven

Mitch had played a lot of poker in his life, and most of the time he'd won, not counting when he'd wanted to lose, like last night with Ally. He could usually spot a bluffer. Unfortunately, Vivian didn't show any of the signs.

"You had your little fun giving orders, Mitchell. Now it's my turn. Toss your gun into that snowbank over there." She tilted her head to Mitch's right.

"Don't do it, Mitch," Ally said. "She'll kill us all. That gun is your only insurance that she won't."

"How sweet. Your girlfriend's worried about you, even if she puts herself at risk. It looks like true love. Too bad it's doomed. I'll count to three. On three, unless your gun's in the snow, I'll pull the trigger. One, t—"

Mitch tossed his gun away. He wondered what was going through Rudy's mind right now. Damn, he didn't even know if Rudy had ever shot a gun in his life. But at least they still had something going for them. Then he heard the sound of dogs barking, and wondered what in hell that was.

"That would be Ernie coming with his dogsled," Rudy said. "And Dave."

Oh, yeah. And Ernie might or might not be sober. And he had a shotgun. Mitch would have welcomed a sharp-shooter with a rifle, but a drunk guy with a shotgun—not so much. Mitch noticed that Rudy didn't mention the shotgun, though. Maybe Rudy was playing it cool, wait-ing to see what developed. Mitch wished he'd asked Rudy if he'd ever shot a gun before.

"My, my," Vivian said. "Quite a little gathering we'll have out here. Now you can all go back together. I'll contact you and let you know where to send the check."

The dogsled pulled up alongside the two snowmo-biles and Dave hopped out first. "So what's going on? Ernie said he wasn't sure. He'd had a couple of drinks, and the phone connection wasn't so good when Clyde called, but he got the idea that he should come on out here and see what was happening."

"Hold it, everybody!" Ernie reached into the dogsled and pulled out a shotgun. "There's a couple of ptarmi-gan in that tree about ten feet above where you're stand-ing. Them's real good eatin' and I just ran out of the ones I had stashed in the freezer. Just let me get a shot off, and then we can see what's what."

"Ernie, wait!" Mitch trembled to think what might happen if Ernie started shooting in Ally's direction.

"Don't do that, Ernie," Dave said, starting back to-ward him.

"They taste great, I'm tellin' ya. Now hold still, everybody!"

"No!" Vivian yelled. "Do not—"

The shotgun roared. A snow-covered branch cracked and fell right on top of Ally and Vivian. As they went down, another shot rang out.

Mitch leaped forward and pulled away the branch. "Ally! My God, Ally!"

She lay there motionless.

Vivian, however, staggered to her feet and started searching the snow for her gun.

"No you don't!" Rudy was on her immediately. He pulled out Clyde's gun and shoved the barrel under her chin. "Don't try anything or I'll drill ya! Don't worry, Mitch, I got her. You see to Ally."

Mitch dropped to his knees and took Ally by the shoulders. Slowly he turned her over, his heart pounding with fear at what he might find.

Her eyes opened. "Mitch? What happened?"

His breath came out in a rush. She was alive. But she might be shot and not realize it. "A branch fell," he said, his voice thick with worry. "Where does it hurt, Ally?"

"The back of my head."

He slid his hand gently under her head and groaned in relief when he didn't feel any blood. "That's it? Nowhere else?"

"I have another bump on the side of my head, where she hit me with the gun. And probably some bruises from wrestling in the snow."

He looked her over from head to toe. "But no bullet holes."

"No, no bullet holes. Mitch, you're grinning like you just won the lottery."

"Yeah. I know." He couldn't stop looking at her. She was alive. She was *alive*.

Ernie came wandering over carrying his shotgun in the crook of his arm. "Everybody all right? Sorry about that."

Dave grabbed him. "Ernie, you shouldn't have fired that gun. What if your aim had been off?"

"Looks like it was off! I missed those danged birds and hit the branch by mistake! Didn't mean to have the branch collapse on those ladies."

"This one I got ahold of is no lady," Rudy said. "You got any rope in your sled, Ernie?"

"I reckon."

"Then how about getting it so we can tie her up good and tight?"

Vivian glanced up at Rudy. "Say, handsome, have you ever let a woman tie you up before you have sex?"

Rudy cleared his throat. "Can't say as I have."

"Believe me, you'd love it, and I know exactly how it's done. How about you and me go back to town right now, and I'll give you a personal demonstration?"

"Sorry," Rudy said. "I got me a girlfriend. Besides, next on my list is oral sex. If that goes okay, I'll ask Lurleen about this tying-up stuff."

"Here's your rope." Ernie returned carrying a coil over his shoulder. He still had his shotgun, as if hoping the ptarmigan would show up again.

"I'll help tie," Dave said. "I was a Boy Scout. I know my knots."

"I could give all three of you some experience with

bondage," Vivian said. "We can start right now. How about it?"

"Bondage?" Ernie said. "No, thanks. I don't go for fancy investments. I got everything in CDs. Listen, Dave, how about you ride back on one of them snowmobiles? Once she's trussed up, she won't be able to ride, so I'll carry her back to town on the sled."

"I can do that," Dave said.

"That would be great, Ernie," Mitch added. And then maybe Dave would go with Rudy, and Mitch could take Ally. Right now he didn't feel like trusting her to anyone else.

"Then I'll go rearrange things in there so it's all ready." Ernie walked off, shotgun still cradled in one arm.

Mitch gazed after him. "What he did worked out great and maybe saved your life, but he could have gotten you killed. I don't know whether to hit him or kiss him."

Ally brushed some of the snow out of her hair. "You know, Mitch, all things considered, that's exactly how I feel about you."

Ally rode back with Mitch because Rudy and Dave obviously thought it was the right thing to do. But she had some very mixed feelings about him. Yes, he'd come to her rescue, but that didn't completely erase the fact that he'd been dishonest with her from the beginning. He'd had sex with her under false pretenses. She didn't like that.

Well, she'd liked the sex, but she didn't like the false

pretenses. He'd planted that bug under her bed, no question. Double agents, indeed. He was the double agent, masquerading as a nerd when in fact he was a . . . what? Not a nerd, that was certain. No wonder he had that killer body.

Maybe he drove a snowmobile well because he was used to a motorcycle. Maybe all along he'd been toying with her, laughing at how naïve she was to believe he was a nerd with a crush. Instead he was a professional hired to guard her with his gun, his surveillance equipment, and his body.

She kept returning to the subject of his body, probably because she had to wrap her arms around that body while they whizzed back to town. Yesterday, although she hadn't loved the loud machine, she'd loved riding it with Mitch. Anticipating his movements and matching his rhythm had felt sexual.

It still did. And that was a problem, because she didn't know where she and Mitch stood right now. He'd finished his job here in Alaska. He'd probably finished finalizing all the details of the estate. He'd lied to her, but he'd given her great orgasms. She was in lust, maybe even a little in love. How was she supposed to process all that?

When they arrived in town, Uncle Kurt's fifth wheel was still there, as if nothing had changed. But two official-looking SUVs were parked in front of the Top Hat. Things had changed.

Mitch eased back on the gas. "They'll want to talk to you. But I can take you to the lodge first, if you want some time."

She hadn't known exactly what she wanted until

she'd seen that fifth wheel. Now she did. "Please stop at the Top Hat. I want to talk to Uncle Kurt."

"You've got it." He pulled in next to one of the state trooper vehicles.

"And after that, I want to talk to you."

"Whenever you say."

She couldn't resist a dig. "Because you work for me? Is that why you're being so cooperative?"

He shut off the motor and took off his helmet. "No." He stared straight ahead. "In fact, I've decided to quit."

Panic set in. "You promised you wouldn't! I remember that distinctly." Among other things. She also distinctly remembered the look in his eyes when she'd whipped off her sweatshirt, and the way he'd torn her panties off, and the way he'd loved her better than any man, ever.

"That was when I thought you still needed me," he said. "Aside from the fact that I bungled this assignment, I don't think you—"

"I'm here, aren't I? If you hadn't come out there when you did, I would be dead right now."

He sighed. "I should have figured it out sooner. All the evidence was there."

"I should have figured it out sooner, too." She took off her helmet and goggles before climbing off the snowmobile. Then she looked into his eyes, so vulnerable without the glasses. Her heart ached for him. He thought he'd failed her. That, more than anything, made her ready to forgive. "Neither of us saw this coming, Mitch."

"But I was paid to see it coming."

She gazed at him. "Do you allow yourself to make mistakes?"

"Not when someone could die."

"But I didn't." She hung the helmet and goggles on the handlebars. "I'm going in. I'd really appreciate it if you'd go with me."

"Of course."

As she walked into the Top Hat, she wondered if that was how it would be with Mitch from now on—polite agreement, knocking himself out to do whatever she asked. She wanted the other Mitch back, the one who kicked down doors and raided refrigerators and ripped panties.

But first she had to deal with Uncle Kurt. He was sitting at a table with four officers in uniform. The dashing figure of her fantasies had been reduced to a man who slumped in his chair and looked twenty years older than he had yesterday.

When she walked in, he leaped up, but one of the officers put a hand on his arm, and he sank back to his seat. "Ally! Thank God." His eyes glistened.

One of the officers left his chair and came over to talk to Mitch. Then he and another officer took off and a vehicle started up outside. Apparently they were going to intercept Ernie and the dogsled to take charge of the other prisoner.

Betsy rushed over to give Ally a hug, and Clyde came from behind the bar to do the same. "Anything you want, Ally. It's on the house."

"Thanks, Clyde. Maybe later. I need to talk to my uncle."

"Sure, sure, Ally. You do that." He patted her on the back and led her over to one of the empty chairs at the table. Ally took the one opposite Uncle Kurt.

He started talking immediately. "Ally, so help me, I

didn't know what she was up to. I thought it would be little things we'd do to get some money. Sure, she talked about Plan B, but I never thought—"

Plan B. The plan to kill me. "Uncle Kurt, maybe you shouldn't be saying anything. You really need a lawyer."

"It's okay." He waved a hand. "They read me my rights. I don't care. They can write down anything they want. I deserve whatever happens to me." He glanced around. "Where is she?"

"She'll be along." Mitch came up to the table but didn't sit down.

"Is she . . . okay?"

The concern in her uncle's eyes revealed so much. Poor slob, he really did care about Vivian, who was such a demented creature that she didn't care about anyone but herself. Kurt had been a means to an end. Maybe he even knew that, and yet he wanted to know she was okay.

"She's fine, Uncle Kurt," Ally said gently. "But she'll be going to jail." She thought he would be, too, but no sense in pointing that out. He probably had guessed.

"She'll hate that," he said.

"So she said. Uncle Kurt, I have to know, did you . . . did you go along with . . . with Plan B?" She felt Mitch's hand on her shoulder and was grateful for that warm, reassuring pressure.

"I didn't go along with it, Ally."

Relief flooded through her. She hadn't totally misjudged him.

"But I didn't stop her, either, did I? When she left the fifth wheel today, she was in a strange mood. I knew she had a gun in her suitcase. I should have stopped her. I should have warned you. I should have done something."

Ally had nothing to say. Yes, he should have. He was a weak man and he would pay for that. But at least he hadn't wanted her dead. "You'll probably think this is stupid," she said, "but I want to thank you."

"Thank me?" His eyes widened. "For almost getting you killed?"

"No, for helping me keep my dream alive. I know you did it all for yourself, but you gave me a reason to plan and scheme. I came up here because of your encouragement. I may not make it as a wildlife photographer, but—"

"Sure you will." He reached across the table, as if to squeeze her hand, but one of the officers restrained him. "You will," he said, his voice cracking. "You're a winner, Ally. You'll make it."

"Thanks." She couldn't sit here any longer or she was liable to start bawling, which was not something she wanted to do in front of these officers of the law. "I have to leave."

"We'll need a statement," one of the men said.

"Sure." She swallowed, not daring to look at Uncle Kurt. What she said could land him behind bars for quite a while. "Could we . . . do it at the lodge?"

The officer nodded and got out of his chair. "We can do that."

Mitch squeezed her shoulder. "I'll go with you."

"Thank you, Mitch." She gave him a watery smile. "I'll take all the help I can get."

What a class act. If Mitch hadn't been hooked on Ally before, he was after watching her deal with her uncle and then, without flinching, sit at Betsy's kitchen table and tell the trooper everything he needed to know to build a case against Kurt. She'd played it straight, something Kurt hadn't done.

And neither had Mitch. Oh, he'd told her some of it, but not the whole story. He could hide behind her grandmother's skirts and say that was the way Madeline had asked him to handle the assignment. That much was true, but Madeline wasn't around and she'd told him to use his best judgment. He'd decided to keep up the masquerade as long as possible.

His reasons weren't all that honorable. He'd been afraid if he told Ally the truth, she wouldn't have anything to do with him. Sure, that would have impacted how well he could do his job, but that hadn't been his major concern. Staying close for personal reasons—sexual reasons—had been his primary motivation, no matter how he'd tried to rationalize otherwise.

Maybe if he'd come totally clean about his purpose in following her to Alaska, he might have done a better job of protecting her. Maybe if he hadn't spent so much time dreaming about her body, he might have considered that Tanya Mandell was an imposter in league with Kurt Jarrett. Maybe he would have done his damned job instead of spending most of his energy enjoying the perks, as Ally had phrased it.

All in all, he was very impressed with Ally's behavior and pretty much disgusted with his own. He had an idea of what he might do to make it up to her, but that, too, he would have to keep secret, because he might fail. If he failed, he didn't want her to know. She'd suffered enough.

Finally the officer finished with his questioning and left. Ally sat in the kitchen chair, staring at her hands.

"You did the right thing." Mitch was afraid to touch her, afraid his touch wouldn't be welcome. If someone had treated him the way he'd treated Ally, he wouldn't be all that friendly.

She looked up, her expression bleak. "I think he regrets what he's done, but I'm beginning to realize that he could turn around and do the same thing again, if somebody stronger comes along and talks him into it."

"Unfortunately, I think that's true."

"It's really the pits when your last remaining relative has no moral fiber, you know?"

"Yeah."

She glanced at him. "I don't think you can relate. I'm guessing your family members aren't likely to get involved with a crazy person who might decide to kill you."

"No, I suppose not."

"Some people get all the money, and some people get all the luck."

"Ally, for what it's worth, I don't think you need a cheerleader. Kurt was right about one thing. You're going to make it, and make it on your own. You're a winner."

She gazed at him for several seconds, not commenting one way or the other. "So what are you, really? What's your bio say about Mitchell J. Carruthers, Jr.?"

"I'm embarrassed to tell you, considering how I fouled this up."

"You found out who she was within twenty-four hours. That's quick. The only bad part is that she was quicker. She moved to Plan B in less than twelve hours. Even Uncle Kurt didn't know that would happen, and he was in on the whole scam. So what's your job description, Mitch?"

"I'm a combination PI and bodyguard." And didn't he feel stupid telling her that. She might have been impressed before today.

She leaned her chin on her hand. "Not a geek."

"Yeah, I'm obviously still a geek, too, in spite of how I've tried to outlive that label."

"So you're a reformed geek."

"Right. That's why I was so perfect for what your grandmother wanted. The geeky side of me could handle the details of the estate. The PI and bodyguard persona could look out for your safety. At least that was the idea."

She slapped her hand down on the table. "Will you stop? I don't know how you found out that Vivian was a fake, but you did find out, and then you came to the rescue."

"I was almost too late." The scene would figure in his nightmares for many months to come. "And if Ernie hadn't decided to shoot himself something for dinner—"

"If you hadn't organized the troops, Ernie wouldn't have been there. Nobody would have been there. I'd be underneath ten feet of snow, and Vivian would be on her way to South America, or wherever she planned to hide out until Kurt got his mitts on the Jarrett fortune." She put her hand over his. "I owe you, Mitch. And although I wish you hadn't lied like a rug, I—"

"About that." Since she'd started the touching stuff, he decided he was safe to hold her hand in both of his. "I should have told you everything from the very first."

"No, not from the first." She looked into his eyes. "I

would have thrown a fit. But you should have told me before we had sex."

"Yes."

"But then we might not have had sex."

He sighed. "And that's why I didn't tell you. You complain about lack of moral fiber in your one remaining relative. If I'd had any moral fiber, I would have told you why I was in Alaska that night, before the poker game."

"Do you regret not telling me?"

He gazed at her and remembered the way she'd shuffled those cards, how her breasts had danced with each movement, how wet she'd been when he'd ripped away her panties. He'd promised himself there would be no more lies between them. "No," he said. "God help me, I don't regret it."

She stood and held out her hand. "Then how about once more for old times' sake?"

Chapter Twenty-eight

*S*o their brief affair was about to end. Mitch had said he was leaving the job—essentially leaving Ally. She accepted that, but she knew this had been more than just a job to him, and she wanted to give him a going-away present. Besides, after nearly dying today, she needed some solid evidence that she was still very much alive.

Once they were in her room, she didn't play games. She was more than ready for hot, glorious sex with a guy who knew his way around that subject. She started stripping off her clothes when she noticed that he was standing there, watching her.

Maybe he was thinking that this would be their last roll in the hay. She'd thought that, too, but she didn't care to dwell on it, and didn't want him to, either. No point in getting morose. It might dampen the mood, and she wanted the mood to be sizzling.

"Hey, Carruthers, last one in bed's a rotten egg."

"I was just thinking . . ."

"Uh-huh. Exactly what I was afraid of. No thinking. Action."

"Ally—"

"We'll talk about our goodbyes later," she said gently. "Afterward. Right now I need to live in the moment."

He nodded and started taking off his clothes. He even managed to find a condom he'd thrown on top of her dresser the night before. Seeing Mitch naked, aroused, and in possession of a condom was enough to make Ally's day.

"You left that out for Betsy to see when she cleaned the room?" Ally glanced at the foil envelope he tossed onto the pillow before climbing in next to her. Betsy must have loved finding that piece of evidence.

"Your room," he said, gathering her into his arms with a smile. "Your responsibility. I had enough troubles hiding all my James Bond stuff."

"Speaking of James Bond stuff." She cupped his face in both hands. "You put a bug under my bed."

"Yes, ma'am, but I took it out again before anything interesting happened on that bed." He stroked her hip.

"Something interesting could have happened before you showed up, mister."

"Oh, yeah?"

The more she thought about it, the more the concept of him bugging her bed turned her on. "Yeah. What if I'd decided to masturbate that first night? Would you have listened?"

"I had to keep track of your actions, didn't I?"

"So you would have listened." She was on fire for him, and yet all he'd done was lazily stroke her hip while they talked about his surveillance equipment. His other piece of equipment, the deep probe attached to his body, pressed against her thigh. He might find the topic of masturbation of interest, too, judging from the condition of that piece of equipment.

"Of course I would have listened." He slowly dipped his head and teased her nipple with his tongue.

Such a whisper of stimulation, and yet she'd begun to tremble in anticipation of a climax. "And then what?" She arched her back, lifting her breasts higher, inviting more. He continued with soft licks, applying no real pressure. He was driving her nuts. "Would listening have aroused you?"

"Yes." His breath was hot against her breast.

"What would you have done?"

He licked a circle around her nipple. "Ally, are you getting kinky on me?"

"Who's kinky? You were planning to listen to me masturbate."

"Only if you actually did it. There was no reason to think you would."

"But did it cross your mind?"

"Maybe." He nipped her lightly.

"It did!" Her breathing grew shallow as she quivered in his arms. "Sex was on your mind, even then, wasn't it?"

"Guess so." He took her nipple into his mouth and played with it a while.

"What would you have done if I had? Tell me."

"Oh, I dunno. Turned up the volume on my recorder?"

She groaned, moving her hips restlessly, wanting him to place his hand, the one stroking her hip, several inches to the left.

"Do you want to know if I would have masturbated, too?" he asked softly.

Thinking of that nearly gave her a climax on the spot. "Uh-huh."

"The answer is yes." He lifted his head from her breast and feathered a kiss over her lips. "Yes, I would have masturbated, and wished I could walk through the door between us and replace your hand with mine, like this." At long last, he touched her.

And she exploded with embarrassing speed, crying out wildly, her hips thrashing as he stroked her with his knowing fingers.

"I love how you come apart so fast."

She gasped and trembled in his arms. "You . . . talked me . . . into coming."

"You talked yourself into it. You're the most exciting woman I've ever known." His kiss was deep and thorough, submerging her once again in lush sensuality.

She loved hearing that she was a standout in his experience with women. Maybe he wouldn't forget her right away. Maybe she'd stay on his mind for weeks or months. She wouldn't mind being a permanent memory, but that might be too much to ask. Now that she realized who he really was, she could imagine him with plenty of affairs.

But she wouldn't think about that now. This was her time. As she opened her mouth to receive his tongue, she drew it in, letting him know what she needed more than anything else, even more than another orgasm.

He pulled back and looked into her eyes. "Yeah, me, too." He picked up the foil packet from the pillow, tore it open and took out the condom. "Last one of the vending-machine variety."

"Uh-oh. And us with a long Alaskan night ahead of us." She was prepared to raid Betsy's medicine cabinet. Betsy knew what was going on, anyway.

He put on the condom. "Notice I didn't say we were out."

"We're not?"

"There's a little pile on the dresser, right next to where I found this one."

"Oh." Heat rushed through her as she imagined using that little pile all through the night. "Compliments of the management?"

"Looks like." He moved between her thighs.

"Any objection to using that supply?" If he had any, she'd find a way to overrule him.

"No objection." He angled his hips and thrust deep. "A guy can only stand on principle for so long before he cracks."

"Glad to hear it." She cupped his firm butt and looked up into his eyes. They'd turned that warm, liquid brown again. Lust was there, certainly, but she glimpsed something more, something he might not want to admit.

She wouldn't push him. He wouldn't want to get tangled up with a woman who planned to make her mark in the wilds of Alaska. She'd settle for this and be grateful for one more night of Mitch's brand of outstanding sex.

He eased back and thrust forward again. "At least this time I didn't have to beat you at poker to get you naked."

"You didn't beat me." She lifted her hips and matched his rhythm. "I lost on purpose."

"Mm." He picked up the pace, making the bedsprings squeak in a steady tempo. "I'll bet you shuffled that way on purpose, too."

"Nope." The squeaking grew louder as they bounced against the mattress. "That move was unplanned."

"I like this game the best." His breathing changed, becoming rough.

She gripped him tighter and gulped in air. Oh, this was going to be very good. "What . . . game is it?"

"It's called 'making Ally come.' "

"Then deal me in."

And he did. She went off like a rocket, and he followed right after, shuddering and moaning in her arms.

In the end, they used most of the condoms and staged another refrigerator raid so they wouldn't have to leave the lodge for food. Betsy didn't come home at all during the night. Ally suspected she'd decided to leave the lodge to the two of them, which was fine with Ally.

Eventually, toward dawn, they slept. As light filtered through the frosty window the next morning, Ally woke up with a start to find Mitch no longer in bed with her. But she heard him moving around in his room.

Pulling the sheet off the bed, she wrapped it around herself and went over to see what he was up to. She found him completely dressed in his nerd clothes. His suitcase was packed.

She'd expected this moment, although she hadn't thought he'd leave quite so abruptly. Maybe abrupt was better, but it sure was hitting her hard. "Are you going somewhere?"

"Um, yeah. I need to visit my contact in Anchorage, Pete Showalter. I went downstairs a few minutes ago and called Rudy to give me a ride to the Fairbanks airport."

"I must have been out. I didn't even hear you get up."

"You had a rough time yesterday."

"So . . . this is it?"

"No, no. I'm planning to stop by tomorrow. Rudy's going to drive me to the airport and check on Lurleen. He called her and the boyfriend's gone. If all works out well, he'll stay overnight and pick me up again tomorrow, so I can come back and tell everybody a proper goodbye. So this isn't goodbye for us, either."

"It feels like it."

His gaze was troubled. "I know. Ally, I can't figure out how to make this easier on us. Would you rather I didn't come back tomorrow? I could fly out of Anchorage."

"No! Please come back again before you leave for good. Please."

"Okay, if you're sure."

"I'm sure. That will give me twenty-four hours to get used to the idea that you'll be gone."

He sighed and rubbed the back of his neck. "It won't be easy for either of us. I suppose last night didn't help."

"I suppose it didn't, but I don't care. I wouldn't trade last night for anything."

"Me, either." He crossed to her and cradled her in his arms. "You have big things ahead of you, Ally. You have plenty of good people around to help, too. The lawyers and tax people your grandmother hired are excellent. And Porcupine is the right spot to launch your career. You chose well."

She tried to imagine Porcupine without Mitch. As much as he'd complained about being here, he'd become an integral part of her image of the town. But he didn't want to stay, and she wouldn't try to keep him.

"And you'll go on to bigger and better things in L.A."

She rubbed her hands along the arms of his ugly jacket. "Any more nerd assignments?"

"Nope. I'll burn this jacket when I get back. For now, it's all I have to wear. Pete should get a kick out of it."

Outside the window, a horn beeped.

"That's Rudy and Slewfoot Sue." Mitch gazed into her eyes. "Remember, I'm coming back."

"I know." She blinked, determined not to cry. He was coming back, but not to stay. He wouldn't be spending the night. They wouldn't make love. For the first time she admitted they'd been making love, not just having sex.

"See you." He kissed her.

She wrapped her arms around him and hung on, and dammit, the tears managed to sneak out and dribble down to her mouth. He'd be able to taste them. He'd know she was losing it.

The horn beeped again, and he released her.

She stepped back, wanting to give him the space he needed to leave.

He gave her a lopsided smile. "It'll be okay."

"Sure."

He gestured toward a bubble-wrapped object standing over in the corner. "Take care of Quillamina. I'll get her when I come back." Then he went out the door, closing it quietly behind him.

She used the sheet to mop her face. She would make it through this. After all, yesterday she'd almost died. So why did this feel so much worse?

Tanya Mandell hadn't wanted to see Mitch, but he'd persisted, desperate to give Ally something to feel joyful about after all her disappointments. Tanya had started out the dinner jet-lagged and grouchy, but once Mitch had begun telling the story of someone impersonating her in order to kill an heiress and gain a fortune, Tanya had hung on his words until he'd finished.

"Amazing." She sipped her wine. The real Tanya Mandell was in her mid-fifties and a blonde like Vivian, but much stockier in build. She wore soft earth tones and native jewelry. But the biggest contrast was Tanya's manner. She was quiet and dignified, with a very perceptive gaze that seemed to miss nothing.

"Ally's uncle chose to have his girlfriend impersonate you because he knew Ally thinks you hung the moon," Mitch said.

Tanya smiled. "Nope, not me. She'll have to blame that moon placement on someone else."

"She was so excited when she thought that you would be her mentor."

"Mm." Tanya's expression grew cautious.

"So I was hoping—"

"Mitch, you've told a fascinating story. And I'm glad to hear it from you first, because once it hits the papers, I'll have reporters at my door wanting a reaction. Thanks for the heads-up, so I know it's time to leave town again. I'm not a publicity hound, as you may have heard."

"You could hide out in Porcupine."

"With the woman whom my double almost wasted? Not a good strategy. Look, I know what you're about to ask, and I just can't. I realize she can pay, but I don't need the money. What I need is time to relax and rejuvenate after my last trip."

•

Mitch refused to give up that fast. "I brought some of her work."

"I'm sure it's good. And I can tell you care very deeply about her. But I just can't—" She paused as Mitch laid out the pictures Ally had brought from L.A.

Then he added the wolf shot and the ptarmigan pictures he'd had printed late this afternoon. He was counting on Ally not missing her photos. While she'd slept, he'd changed the memory card in her camera and hoped she would think all the abuse it had taken yesterday had somehow erased her shots.

Tanya leaned forward and spent a fair amount of time looking at the pictures. "Good eye."

"She has an incredible eye. She did all that with her digital. If she could get a little bit of instruction, she'd be fantastic. And she's easy to get along with. I know you may worry that she's a spoiled rich brat, but she's the exact opposite. She's warm, and funny and full of life."

Tanya glanced up. "You're in love with her."

He was shocked into silence. Of course he was. He just hadn't had the guts to say it, even silently in his mind. This woman had blurted it right out, as if those words didn't have the power to make his life miserable forever. "That's not important."

"I'm sorry you don't think so. I happen to think it's the most important thing in the world."

This was not the direction Mitch wanted the conversation to take. "What I meant was, I'm not prejudiced. Anyone can see she has talent."

"Oh, you're prejudiced, all right, but she has talent. I wish her well."

"Tanya, please. Please consider going up there, even if it's only for a few days. Porcupine's a great place. The people are terrific. There are wolves in the woods. You'd love it. Besides, you can show them what the real Tanya Mandell is like. They have a pretty skewed picture right now."

"Does Ally know you're in love with her?"

He paused. "I don't know. Maybe. It doesn't matter. What matters is that she get the best start she can, and—"

"I'll do it."

"You will?" He felt like leaping across the table and kissing her. But she probably wouldn't care for that. And they were in one of the finest restaurants in Anchorage, so the management probably wouldn't care for that, either. "Thank you. I appreciate this more than I can say."

"You're welcome. Did you see our waiter anywhere?"

"No, but if you're ready to go, I'll get him. I'm sure you're tired."

"*Tired* doesn't even begin to describe how I feel. But I want to finish my wine before we leave. Oh, there he is." Tanya waved and the waiter hurried over. "Can you scare up a piece of paper and an envelope for me?" she asked.

Moments later the waiter returned with some restaurant stationery.

"Excellent. Thank you." Tanya pulled a pen out of her satchel and began to write. "Just finish your meal, Mitch. I need to write a note to Ally." Then she blocked what she was writing with her arm.

Okay, so she didn't want him to see what she was

saying to Ally. That made him a little nervous, but the main thing was that she'd agreed to go up there. Ally would have her mentor, the very same one she'd dreamed of. This time it would be real.

Tanya finished writing, folded the paper, and tucked it in the envelope. Then she sealed it and wrote Ally's name on the outside. "Give this to her when you go back tomorrow. I'll be up this weekend. I'll plan to stay for a week. Then we'll reevaluate. I assume you'll be there?"

"Uh, no. I'm heading back to L.A."

"Mm." Tanya picked up her wine glass. "To dreams."

Mitch toasted Ally's dream. He didn't really have a dream, just a fantasy. Dreams were based in reality, but fantasies were wisps of smoke, imaginary visions, impossible ideas. He'd work on getting rid of his once he was back in L.A. Maybe it would dry up and blow away in the Southern California sun.

Ally spent her first day without Mitch trying to ignore the huge gap he'd left. She wandered through Serena's store and ended up buying herself some jewelry made from porcupine quills. Then she finally broke down and bought one of Dave's chain-saw nudes and carried it over to the Top Hat.

After ten minutes in the rowdy bar, her nude was christened Porcupiana Sharp, Quillamina's twin sister. But when some of the lumberjacks wanted to dress her up, Ally refused to let them, in case Dave came in later. She hung out at the Top Hat with Betsy and Clyde and retold the story of yesterday's drama whenever anyone asked, which was often.

Word seemed to have leaked out that Ally was worth a lot of money. To her surprise, nobody seemed to care. Everyone treated her the same as they had before. But she was still glad that they'd come to know her before the information became public.

When people asked about Mitch, and most did, she told them he'd had to fly to Anchorage on business. She didn't tell them that he'd only be dropping by tomorrow for a couple of hours, and then he'd be off to L.A. That would raise too many questions, now that the town saw her and Mitch as a couple. Only Betsy and Clyde knew that Mitch wouldn't be staying.

Finally, after an early dinner, she announced that she was exhausted and walked back to the lodge. She and Mitch had missed the northern lights the night before because they'd been so eager to hop into bed. She'd miss them again tonight because she couldn't bear to see them without Mitch.

She'd have to get over that kind of thing. And she would. But not tonight. Tonight she would crawl into bed, pull the covers over her head and hope that she could sleep, and if she slept, that she could handle her dreams.

Fortunately, she really was exhausted. And she didn't dream. But she woke up the next morning with a feeling of excitement. Mitch would be coming back. She tried to tamp down her feeling of anticipation. Getting high now would only mean sinking lower after he left.

But logical as that sounded, she couldn't control the bubble of joy that she carried around with her all morning. He was due back sometime during the lunch hour. Logically, he and Rudy would show up at the Top Hat.

Betsy had speculated whether they might be bringing Lurleen with them.

Ally sat at a table where she could see the door and tried to eat her ptarmigan sandwich and drink her coffee. Betsy sat with her and made small talk that didn't seem to require much in the way of answers, as if she knew that Ally was on edge. Every time the door opened, Ally's heart started to pound.

After the third time the door opened and somebody other than Mitch came through, Betsy pushed back her chair. "I'm getting you a beer."

"Thanks, but I already have coffee."

"You're jumpy enough without drinking more of that stuff. You need to wind down. I'm getting you a beer. And one for me, too. I'm getting nervous just watching you."

Ally glanced up at her. "Is it that obvious?"

"Girl, every time the door opens, you act like your butt's on a hot burner. I want you to be cool when that boy comes through the door. Make him think you're doing just fine without him."

"But I'm not."

"I know that, and you know that, but he doesn't have to know that." Then she patted Ally's shoulder. "Love's hard. I'm the one who can tell you that." Then she walked over to the bar and ordered two beers.

Love. Ally hadn't want to say the word out loud, hadn't even wanted to think it. But if love didn't describe this incredible ache she was battling, nothing else did. Well, sometimes love didn't work out. This looked to be one of those times.

Then the door opened, and Mitch walked in. Ally

tried to follow Betsy's advice and block her feelings, but once his gaze locked with hers, she knew that yearning was written all over her face.

Betsy set the beer down in front of her with a sigh. "I can see I'm about thirty seconds too late with this beer."

Chapter Twenty-nine

All the way back to Porcupine, Mitch fought the idea that he was coming home. Yet one look at Ally sitting there having her lunch, and he felt more at home than he ever had in his life. The airplane ticket in his pocket taunted him, letting him know that home was hundreds of miles away. He had to use that ticket. He would only be an anchor around her neck if he stayed.

Behind him, Rudy came in with Lurleen, and suddenly the place was buzzing. Betsy hurried over to hug Lurleen, and even Clyde came out from behind the bar to shake her hand. Several others got up to welcome her, too. Apparently Rudy hadn't been the only person in town who'd missed Lurleen.

Mitch was happy for Rudy. Lurleen was perfect for him, a big girl with red hair almost the same color as his. She had a hearty laugh and a no-nonsense attitude. After they'd picked Mitch up at the airport, she'd taken him aside and thanked him for teaching Rudy the facts of life, both concerning chickens and women's sexual needs.

But Lurleen and Rudy's future wasn't the main item on his mind at the moment. As Mitch gazed at Ally, the hubbub in the tavern faded into background noise. He walked over and sat down across from her, a goofy smile on his face. He was so glad to see her it was ridiculous. And he'd only been gone for a day.

"Hey, Mitch." She looked just as happy to see him. "Did you take care of your business?"

"Yes, I did." He took off his nerdy orange parka. Betsy had tried to get him to take the other, nicer one, but he'd thought it was a complete waste, so he'd worn the godawful orange coat, much to Pete's amusement.

After hanging the parka over the back of his chair, he reached into the inside vest pocket for the envelope he'd carefully tucked there. He handed it to Ally. "I brought you this."

She took the envelope with a puzzled frown and looked at her name written on it. "That's not your handwriting."

"No."

She opened the letter and glanced at the signature at the bottom. Then she laughed. "Tell me this isn't from Vivian."

"It isn't from Vivian."

Ally looked at the signature again. Then she lifted her head and stared at him, her eyes wide.

"Yeah, it's from the real Tanya Mandell." He was so excited he could barely sit still. "Read it. Read it out loud." He wanted to hear her saying the words Tanya had written, confirming that she was coming to Porcupine.

"'Dear Ally, Thanks to your friend Mitch, I've decided to come to Porcupine this weekend and meet you.'" Ally met his gaze again. "Mitch? Is this for real?"

He nodded, too pleased with himself for words.

"Omigod!" She leaped up and came around the table to hug him. Then she stood there staring at the letter and quivering. "How did you do this? What did you say? What did she say? Is she really coming?"

"She's really coming." Mitch had never been this thrilled about any present he'd given.

"I have to sit down." She put a hand to her chest and fumbled her way back to her seat, still staring at the letter. Then she began to smile. "Mitch, did you see this letter?"

"Uh, no. She didn't show it to me, although I watched her write it." His elation faded some as he wondered what else Tanya had said. He hoped she hadn't gotten him into hot water.

Ally kept reading, and her smile wobbled and disappeared. Then she sniffed and wiped her eyes.

This wasn't the reaction Mitch was looking for. "What's wrong? She didn't say it was all a joke or anything, did she? She promised me she would come. She said this weekend, and she'd plan to stay a week and then see how it went. Ally? God, Ally, what's wrong?"

She looked up at him, her eyes swimming. "Nothing." She sniffed again. "Mitch, will you marry me?"

He nearly fell off his chair. "M-marry you?"

"Yeah." She took a long, shaky breath. "Because I love you, too. And I don't know what to do about the fact you hate Alaska, but you seem to like it a little better than when you arrived, so maybe—"

"Ally." His brain was spinning. "What's in that letter?"
She shoved it across the table.

He skipped over the first part, which she'd already read aloud. The next sentence was about the week Tanya planned to stay in Porcupine. Then she'd started a whole new paragraph.

> *I don't know how you feel about Mitch, but he's madly in love with you. He admitted it, but said it wasn't important. I disagree. Any man who would track me down and recruit me with the enthusiasm Mitch has shown is worth taking a look at, Ally. I know he dresses kind of like a nerd, but you could fix that. If I were you, I wouldn't let this one get away.*
>
> *Sincerely,*
> *Tanya Mandell*

Mitch felt as if he'd been hit over the head with a brick. He opened his mouth and tried to speak, but nothing came out. Finally he cleared his throat a couple of times and managed one sentence. "Ally, I didn't tell her to write this."

Her smile was watery. "I'm sure not."

"You don't want to marry me. I don't have any money and I'm out of a job."

"But is it true? Are you madly in love with me?"

"That's not the point." He was drowning.

"It's the only point. Do you love me or not?"

He looked into her eyes. He'd promised himself no more lies. "Yeah. Yeah, I do."

Her eyes shone. "Then it's settled. We'll get married."

"No, it's not settled! Ally, think of what you're saying! You're on the brink of a new career. You need to be free to go where you want, do what you want. You don't need a husband, and you sure don't need me, a guy with nothing to offer you."

She snatched up the letter. "Are you kidding? You have this to offer!" She shook it in his face. "No one, *no one* has ever done something like this for me. And you don't even really want me to be a wildlife photographer!"

Mitch became aware that everyone in the Top Hat was staring at them. He lowered his voice. "I do, Ally. I want whatever makes you happy."

"And that's why we should get married!" She glared at him as if daring him to contradict her.

He ran a finger under his collar. "Maybe . . . maybe we should go somewhere else to discuss this."

Betsy walked into his line of sight. "Don't you even *think* about sneaking away to settle this. We've been watching things develop ever since you two got here. We've been a part of it so far, and we deserve to see how it's going to come out." She crossed her arms over her sizable chest as if that settled the matter.

Leaning forward, Ally smiled at Mitch. "It will all come out okay, right? You wouldn't turn down my proposal and embarrass me in front of all these fine people, would you?"

"He'd better not," Rudy said. "I like you, Mitch, but if you don't do right by this lady, you'll answer to me."

Mitch found himself weakening fast. It seemed as if

everyone in the room wanted the same thing, including him. But he still worried about the huge gap between his puny financial resources and her tremendous inheritance.

Her gaze searched his. "If it's Alaska that bothers you, Mitch, just remember that warm weather is coming. And we'll have to take trips back to Bel Air to check on the place. You won't lose the sun and heat permanently."

Clyde hooked an arm around Betsy's waist. "And long nights have certain advantages."

"Alaska's not the problem," Mitch said.

"You don't love me?" Her composure began to crumble.

"No, no! I love you!" Boy, that really seemed to echo through the room.

Her smile returned. "Then it must be my freaking fortune."

"That would be it."

"You're worried 'cause she's rich?" Rudy shook his head. "And I thought I was messed up, putting chickens ahead of Lurleen, but you're worse. A rich woman falls in love with you and wants to get married, and you're *worried*? You should be thanking your lucky stars!"

"Yeah," Clyde said. "It's not every day you get to marry for love *and* money. And Ally's not the type to lord it over you. We can all see that."

"I've heard enough." Dave walked over to the table. "I came in on the last part of this, but I get the drift. Mitch, if you're too chickenshit to marry this woman, then stand back, because there's plenty of men in Porcupine who would love the chance."

Suddenly Mitch got a picture he didn't like at all. "Such as you?" he asked, remembering Dave's maneuvers not so long ago.

"Well, no. Serena and I have come to an understanding, so I'm off the market. But that leaves plenty of others, guys who wouldn't let their egos get in the way of a good thing."

And that, Mitch realized, summed it up nicely. Dave might not be so good with a chain saw, but he'd certainly nailed this situation. Mitch stood and held out his hand. "Thank you, Dave, for pointing out that I'm a total geek."

"You're welcome." Dave flashed his gleaming choppers. "Least I could do for the first person who bought one of my sculptures."

"Mitch," Ally protested. "You're not a total geek."

"Yeah, I am. I'm also crazy about you." He dropped to one knee in front of her and took her hand in his. "Ally, will you marry me?"

Her grip tightened, and her green eyes glowed like the northern lights as she met his gaze. She took a deep breath. "Yes."

And the crowd went wild.

A beauty looking for her inner nerd.
A nerd looking for his inner beast.
Their sparks are igniting more than heat!

VICKI LEWIS THOMPSON
New York Times Bestselling Author of *Nerd Gone Wild*

Gone With the Nerd

ON SALE AUGUST 2005!

Movie star Zoe Tarleton is determined to snag the coveted role of a plain-Jane chemist. All she needs is for her decidedly uncool attorney, Flynn Granger, to teach her the Oscar-winning subtleties of geekdom. California's "Bigfoot Country" is the ideal secret hideaway for coaching. That means rehearsing the steamy scenes too. Who'd have guessed that Zoe and Flynn's performances would be so convincing? Unfortunately something is turning their hot love story into a hair-raising thriller. The killer bees, a broken stairway, and a hot tub hot-wired for deep fry are no accidents. Someone's out to get them. It's just Zoe's luck. She's finally found the man of her dreams and the role of a lifetime—and both of them could be her last.

"Smart, spunky, and delightfully over the top—
provides constant entertainment. Thompson's newest
Nerd romance possesses all the sparkle and vibrancy of a
Vegas show, and it's just as sexy."
—*Publishers Weekly* on *The Nerd Who Loved Me*

"A sharp, sassy, sexy read. Stranded on a desert island?
I hope you've got this book in your beach bag."
—Jayne Anne Krentz on *Nerd in Shining Armor*

Visit www.vickilewisthompson.com